# Beneath the Destiny Stone

## SARAH CHARLES

Beneath the Destiny Stone

Cover Art by Sevannah Storm

*To Phillip Bossie.*
*Never forgotten.*
*Eternally loved.*
*(1982 – 2019)*
*—Thanks for reading my book, long*
*before it was a book worth reading*

# Chapter One

My granda once met the devil himself.

At least, that was the story he was telling his friends. They sat at their usual corner table of the Caledonia Club—Old John, William, Robert, and Granda. Above them, an olive-green lamp illuminated a haze of cigar smoke and dust motes. A Scottish flag hung behind their heads, and on a pedestal in the corner sat a bust of Robert Burns, there to remind them what becomes of *the best laid schemes o' mice an' men*.

His voice carried across the club to my spot behind the bar, and I smiled to myself. Of all Granda's stories, I loved this one most.

"There I was, storming the shores of Normandy, gunfire blazing on all sides." He paused for dramatic effect. "But it wasna the bullets I feared. Nay. It was the man standing before me with fire in his eyes." He stared each of his friends in the eye. "Auld Clootie."

Jones, the Caledonia Club's shift manager and sometimes cook, laughed beside me as he counted out cash for the till. "What the fuck is a clootie?"

I gave the bar a final wipe and tossed the rag into sanitizing solution. "It's a Scottish thing. They don't like to say devil, so they've got a bunch of nicknames for him."

Jones smirked. "You sure they're not talking about their Depends? I bet John's wearing an old clootie right now."

I laughed despite myself. "Don't start. It's already bad enough I have to deal with that lot."

As if to punctuate my point, William knocked over his drink, and the rest of the table hooted and hollered.

Jones jotted down the register balance in an old-fashioned paper ledger and bumped the drawer closed with his hip. He raised an eyebrow. "You sure you want to do this now?"

I glanced at the old men and sighed. "Better now than after they've cashed that bottle of Glenlivet."

He put a hand to my shoulder. "I have complete and utter faith in you. You've got this!" He yanked his phone from his pocket. "Now if you'll excuse me, I'm just going to check out some job sites for completely unrelated reasons..."

I flicked him in the forehead and snickered. "Dick." He handed me the ledger, and I headed from the bar to join the old men.

"...so, I shot off his horns and shamed him back to hell," Granda finished with a grin. The old men laughed and nodded in approval.

"It takes bigger stones than Auld Clootie's to take on a Highlander," said Old John.

"Aye. Aye. True enough." William nodded.

I pulled a chair from a neighboring table and squeezed in next to Granda. He flashed me a wide grin. "Ah, Fiona, love. I was just tellin' the lads about the time—"

I gave him a quick peck on the forehead. "I heard you, Granda."

He patted my cheek. "Such a bonnie lass." He beamed at his friends. "Isna my granddaughter the bonniest lass ye've ever seen?"

Robert raised his glass in salute. "Stunning."

William winked. "Like a young Audrey Hepburn."

I rolled my eyes. Sure, I looked exactly like Audrey Hepburn, except for my face full of freckles and head full of curls. I supposed we were both brunettes, though, so there was that.

"Oi, Poof." Old John waved an empty whisky bottle at Jones. "We need another."

I grimaced at John's words and snatched the bottle from his hand. "What did I tell you?"

His brows crinkled. "What? I just said—"

2

I glared down the bridge of my nose at him. "Do I have to call your wife and make her come get your old homophobic ass?"

Jones sauntered to the table with a fresh bottle. "It's all right. We all know why he likes to suck on them cigars all day." He winked at Old John and set the bottle in front of him.

Everybody burst out laughing, except for Old John who flushed purple. I slid the ledger in front of Granda.

He held it at arm's length and squinted at the numbers. "What am I lookin' at?"

I gnawed on my cheek. "We didn't break even this month."

He gave a half-hearted shrug. "Aye, well...business'll pick up."

I took a deep breath. "No, it won't. We have three customers, and they're all at this table."

William lit a cigar. "Aye, but Robert drinks as much as five men."

"Used to say the same o' your mum," Robert shot back, and the old men cackled.

I looked Granda in the eye. "We need to bring in a younger crowd."

"How should we do that? Turn the place into a disco?" Granda gestured around the empty bar. "Bring in a few go-go dancers?" The old men laughed.

I narrowed my eyes. "Be serious."

"All right, all right." He patted my hand. "What is it you're wantin' to do?"

"A lot of bars sell craft beer now." I licked my lips. "Stuff that's locally produced. I've been researching it and—"

"Christ Almighty." Granda put a hand to his heart. "Yeh want to sell bathtub ale?"

William raised his pint. "Why should ye when the good Lord's seen fit to bless us with Guinness?"

Lord, there were more beers in the world. "Not everyone likes Guinness. We should have a variety."

Robert's mouth fell open. "Who doesna like Guinness?"

Granda's lip curled. "Tories and communists, that's who."

"Ye didna find all these namby-pamby drinks in Scotland." Old John waggled his pointer finger toward me. "Guinness and whisky, that's all we needed."

"First off," I scoffed, "Guinness isn't even Scottish. It's Irish. And second, how do you know what they drink? You haven't been there since 1945." Granda and his friends immigrated to our little town south of Detroit right after the war, but the way they talked, you'd have thought they were here on holiday and fought in the Battle of Culloden themselves.

Old John swayed, whisky in hand. "Aye, but my soul will return to the mountains and glens once I'm good and dead,"

"Aye. Aye," they agreed.

I turned my attention back to Granda. "Hear me out."

"By yon bonnie banks, and by yon bonnie braes," Old John sang.

"Where the sun shines bright on Loch Lomond," the rest joined in.

My lips tightened into a grimace. "Really? We're doing this now?"

"Where me and my true love will never meet again."

"Christ." I snatched the whisky bottle off the table and chugged.

"On the bonnie, bonnie banks of Loch Lomond."

I returned to the bar, head hung in defeat. Jones disappeared into the kitchen, and with no customers to serve, I kept myself occupied scrubbing the already spotless countertops and dusting the already dustless shelves. I was in such a mindless daze that when my phone rang, it startled the shit out of me, and my duster knocked into Granda's prized possession—an old message in a bottle he kept next to the top-shelf liquor. I had to sacrifice my phone to save it.

"Shit. Fuck. Dammit." I righted the bottle and swooped the phone off the floor. "Hello."

"Did I catch ye at a bad moment?" came my best friend Sean's amused voice.

"No. Yes. I don't know." I laughed. "I'm sorry. What's up?"

He took an audible breath. "Oh...nothin' much."

4

I snorted. "And by nothing, I assume you mean lots of cool stuff you refuse to tell me about."

Sean worked in some kind of Special Forces unit for the British military, so he was always tight-lipped about his job. Which I understood...theoretically. But in my opinion, there should be a best-friend loophole for super awesome, secretive government stuff. It seemed only fair.

He gave an awkward chuckle. "Never mind all that, how's it going with *you*?"

I scanned the nearly empty bar. "Great...Your great granda's being a homophobe, my granda won't listen, and I'm pretty sure I'll need to sell a kidney to pay the next electric bill."

He laughed. "Anything else? Your granda didna mention...uh...something special?"

"No." I narrowed my eyes at Granda's table. "Why? What are you two up to?"

Anticipation-laced silence radiated from his end of the line. "I shouldna say. It'll ruin the surprise."

I let out a bark of laughter. "They're two bottles in. I doubt he remembers the surprise."

"You're coming to Scotland!" he blurted as if he couldn't contain it any longer.

"What?" I squealed. "When?"

"Tomorrow." His voice rose an octave in his excitement.

My stomach twisted. "Tomorrow? I can't leave tomorrow. What the hell, Sean? Why would you wait until the day before to tell me?"

He huffed. "And give ye time to find an excuse not to come?"

"No," I said with forced patience, "but you could have given me enough time to, I don't know, make sure the Club doesn't tank."

He heaved a weary sigh. "For Christ's sake, Fi. It's a pub, not a hospital. Nobody's going to die if you're gone for a week."

I gritted my teeth. "So you say."

"Look, we've got it all planned." The sound of a running faucet and clanking dishes muffled in the background. "Your granda has your shifts covered. Plane tickets already bought. And I'm on leave. All ye have to do is pack and get on the plane."

I pinched the bridge of my nose. "It's not that simple. We can't afford for people to cover my shifts. I'm salary. Everyone else is hourly."

"Please. If your granda doesna have ten grand stuffed in that ol' mattress of his, I'll eat my bonnet." When I didn't respond, his voice softened. "It'll be fine, Fi. I swear. Ye worry too much."

"I'm the *only* one who worries around here."

"Fine." His voice turned petulant. "Dinna come and see me. It's only been two years..."

I groaned. "Christ. You're as bad as the old men. Is that a Scottish thing, or do I just invite emotional blackmail?"

The worst part was his guilt trip was working. I missed the hell out of Sean. Every summer growing up his mom used to ship him across the pond to stay with Old John, and the two of us raised all sorts of hell together. On one memorable occasion, we nearly burned down the Caledonia Club after an incident with Barbie and the deep fryer. In our defense, it was really Captain Hook's fault. He's the one who made her walk the plank into the French Fry Sea, not us.

"So ye'll come?" Hope colored his voice.

I bit my lip. "If I can get everything arranged in time."

"Come on, donkey..." Fondness filled his voice, and my heart swelled at the old school nickname.

Growing up during the height of the Shrek era with a Scottish best friend and the name Fiona, we had heard nonstop Shrek jokes for most of our youth. When I threatened to beat Ashley Wilson's ass after she called me an ogre, Sean teased it was stupid to get mad, because, really, I was much more like Donkey than the Princess. The nickname had stuck ever since.

I sighed. "I'll try."

"Ye'll come." He sounded certain now. "We'll have a grand time, ye'll see. The adventure of a lifetime."

I hit end call and joined Granda, his eyes sparkling as he told another story. "...and when she told me she'd stick the needle straight in my eye if I didna sit still and let her stitch me, well, I kent—"

"You knew she was the woman you were meant to marry." I slid into the seat next to him.

He raised an eyebrow. "Have ye heard that one then?"

I grinned. "Just a time or ten."

"Ah, well, good." He polished off the last of his whisky and raked a sleeve across his mouth. "Ye could stand to learn a thing or two from your ol' granda's tales."

I flashed him my cheekiest grin. "Like what? If I ever meet the man I want to marry, I should threaten to poke out his eye?"

"Now you listen to me, girl." He picked up his cigar, ready for a lecture. "To be with your gran, I crossed an ocean. I gave up kin and country and all I held dear. And I never once regretted it. Not for one second." He stared at me, unblinking, as if determined I absorb his message. "If you're ever lucky enough to find a love like that, let nothin' stand in your way. Nothin'."

The old men raised their glasses. "Slàinte."

Granda's gaze fell to the ring on my hand—Gran's wedding ring. She had given it to me not long before the cancer took her.

I kissed his cheek. "I miss her too." He squeezed my hand. "So..." I licked my lips. "I just got off the phone with Sean..."

Old John made a disgusted noise. "But the lad canna be bothered to call his great grandfaither, now can he?"

"I'll have him call you tomorrow. Apparently, I'll be able to relay the message in person." I shot Granda a glare. "How could you not tell me?"

He raised an eyebrow. "Seems an odd way to thank your ol' granda."

"I'm grateful. I am so grateful. You know I've always wanted to go. It's just—" I scanned the Club and bit my lip. "Granda, there's so much to take care of. I've got to make arrangements before I go somewhere."

"Like what? Tell your ol' Granda, and I'll fix it for ye."

"How will you get around? And what about your pills?" I met his gaze and held it, so he knew how serious I took his health. "You always forget if someone doesn't remind you."

His eyes narrowed. "What do ye take me for? Some bairn just weaned from his mither's teat?"

I swallowed. "No, I—"

"You listen to me, girl." He smacked his hand on the table. "I've looked Auld Clootie in the eye and lived to tell the tale. I brought down a hundred Nazis with my bare hands. And I survived sixty years o' marriage to your grandmither. I think I can manage just fine without your hen-pecking."

William leaned forward. "My daughter'll drive him to the Club."

Old John tilted his head toward Jones in the kitchen. "Put the poof in charge o' his pills."

"The boy wants to see ye, lass." Robert sniffed. "Ye'll break his heart if ye dinna go."

"Oi, John, maybe she'll come home with a great-great-grandson for ye." William snickered.

I wrinkled my nose in disgust. "I'm not going to sleep with Sean, you old pervert!"

But it was too late. The table devolved into bickering, with Granda defending my virtue, and Old John arguing that any lass would be lucky to have his great grandson. I just shook my head and extricated myself from the table.

Back behind the bar, I glanced at the clock. Two hours left to figure out which bills weren't getting paid, and how to keep Granda alive while I traveled.

"Jones," I yelled into the kitchen. "I need you to dose Granda's whisky while I'm gone."

"Roofies or dick pills?" he called back.

"Heart pills." I let the door swing closed, then thought better and stuck my head back in. "How do you feel about switching to salary?"

Jones put his hands on his hips. "With all this overtime coming up? Hell no."

"Please," I whined. "I'll cover ten of your shifts. Whichever ones you want. You'll make more in the long run, I promise!"

He threw a handful of fries at me.

"So that's a yes?"

He threw another handful and turned his back on me—a yes.

# Chapter Two

"Holy shit, Sean!" I said after a mammoth, rib-cracking hug at the baggage claim.

I gestured from his chin-length hair to his ridiculously muscled arms and chest. "When did *this* happen? You look like if Kurt Cobain ate Arnold Schwarzenegger."

He gave a wry smile and slung an arm around my shoulder. "Ye'd be amazed what a diet o' nineties action stars can do for the physique." He hoisted my suitcase. "Shall we go?"

"I don't know, man. I'm not about to find Sylvester Stallone all tied up in your fridge, am I?"

He sucked air between his teeth. "About that..."

I laughed and knocked into him with my shoulder. God, I missed this. We hadn't seen each other in two years, not since he got his super-secret, mystery job. We still talked on the phone all the time, but it wasn't the same.

We left the airport, and rolling, green pastures turned to pine thickets, then sprawling, suburban houses. I hoped this meant we were close, because I hadn't eaten since I'd picked over my airline meal of gray meat in red sauce.

As if on cue, my stomach growled. "What about food? Can we stop somewhere?"

"My flat's above a chippy. We'll grab a pizza on the way up."

I wrinkled my nose. "Pizza from a fish shop?"

He scoffed. "Says the lass who buys her knickers at the grocery store."

"Oh my god." I huffed an audible breath. "It's *not* that weird." Sean had never gotten over his first introduction to

Walmart. He couldn't wrap his head around being able to buy a bicycle and a piece of fruit at the same place. "Besides, I don't normally get my underwear there. It was an emergency."

"Emergency?" He scoffed. "It was bloody two in the morn'."

"Yeah." I shrugged. "And I didn't feel like doing laundry. So...emergency."

He snorted, and the two of us fell into a comfortable silence. After a time, he turned down a brick road lined with shops.

"Now *this* feels different!" I couldn't get over how close together the buildings were.

If the shops didn't have different colored facades, I wouldn't have been able to tell where one building ended and the next began. I supposed bigger cities in the US might be equally cramped, maybe New York or Boston. But I was used to the Midwestern sprawl, where buildings came with attached parking lots and enough space between them nobody dreamed of walking from store to store.

Sean led me to his flat, the smell of fried foods wafting from the chippy below. He tossed my suitcase on the floor. "Make yourself at home. I'll be right back." He disappeared out the door, and I walked about, inspecting his apartment.

It was strange. I had known Sean as long as I could remember, but this was the first time I'd seen how he lived. His decorating style fell somewhere between rich executive and twelve-year-old boy. A black leather couch and two matching chairs framed a stone fireplace with a television above the mantel. An upscale rug in shades of gray, white, and black covered a spotless wooden floor. In the corner, a bookcase boasted hardback books, mostly biographies and boring-looking history tomes.

But then there was his artwork. Framed and matted pictures of superheroes ran along the walls, a few of which I recognized from years ago when we'd gone to the Motor City Comic Con. I paused in front of a picture of Spider-Man. I ran my fingers over Stan Lee's signature and smiled. Sean might have an important job and expensive taste in furniture, but he was still the same old dork he had always been.

The door creaked open, and Sean entered, a tied plastic bag and a six pack in his arms.

"You know," I said, "I think I've got it figured out."

He set his bags on the marble-topped coffee table. "Oh, aye? What's that?"

"Your super-secret military job." I nodded at a picture of the Avengers. "They've given you some kind of Hulk juice. That's why you're all big and muscly now. They've turned you into a super soldier."

"Hulk juice?" he said with mock affront. "First off, Bruce Banner became the Hulk because of *Gamma radiation*." He cracked open a beer and handed it to me. "Second off, if you're going to guess super soldier, the obvious comp is Captain America. Have I taught ye nothing?"

I took a sip of beer. "Well, if you'd just tell me what you do, my guesses wouldn't be riddled with terrible analogies, now would they?"

He didn't laugh like I expected. His face twisted into a strangely nervous expression, and I stilled, surveying him. His eyes were red-rimmed and bagged, and his skin looked pale even for him. I was about to ask what was wrong, but my phone rang.

I put it to my ear. "What's up?"

"Jukebox died." Desperation laced Jones's voice. "The old men are about to riot."

"Christ." I put a hand to my temple. "Can't you stream them something?"

He moaned. "And eat up all my data?"

"Whatever." I laughed. "Tell you what, you go over, and I'll pay your bill." Jones huffed, which I took for assent. "Love you." I made kissy noises into the phone. He grumbled something about not being paid enough for this shit and hung up.

Sean raised an eyebrow. "New beau?"

"No, just Jonesy from the bar." I raised an eyebrow. "Why'd you say it like that, though?" He sounded almost irritated.

12

His jaw clenched. "Because ye have terrible taste in men."

I scoffed. "Please. It's the men who are terrible, not my taste." In fact, most people thought I was *too* picky.

Jones gave me shit for months when I broke up with my last boyfriend. Apparently not knowing how to change a tire wasn't a good enough excuse to end a relationship. But the way I saw it, a girl had to have standards, and I just couldn't respect a man who lacked basic life skills I'd managed to master at the age of eight.

Sean snorted, and I tossed a pillow at him. "Whatever. Don't act like you're any better. Remember Vanessa?" One summer a few years back, Sean had a fling with this girl Vanessa. Apparently, she hadn't appreciated Sean meeting me at the bar after one of their dates, and she wound up slashing my tires.

"Aye, well, she wasna my finest conquest..." His eyes narrowed as his gaze fell to the phone in my hand. "Let me see that contraption."

I snickered and handed it over. "Okay, old man."

Sean hated technology. He absolutely refused to use social media, still read a print newspaper, and, for all I knew, probably had an abacus tucked away in the closet. He stuck my phone into his pocket.

"Hey!" I snatched a toss pillow from the couch and wielded it like a weapon. "Give back the phone, Sean. Don't make me hurt you."

He tossed his hair over his shoulder. "You're on vacation. No more calls from work."

I lowered the pillow. "All right. I hear you." I held out a hand. "Now give it back."

He nodded toward the bagged food. "After ye eat."

My stomach growled, and I acquiesced, even though my fingers itched to text Jones for an update. Instead, I peeked inside one of the Styrofoam boxes. "What the hell is this?" It wasn't pizza, and it wasn't fish, but it was deep-fried and vaguely resembled a giant empanada.

He opened his own box and inhaled the smell of cheese. "Pizza crunch."

My jaw dropped in reverence. "Do you mean to tell me this is a deep-fried pizza!" I took a bite and moaned with pleasure. "That's it. I'm staying here forever."

"Aye?" His eyes lit with hope.

"No." I sighed. "But it's tempting."

Sean plucked the remote off the coffee table and clicked through channels until he landed on a show about a book club. We ate our pizza crunch and drank our beer in silence until I realized something about the main character.

"Holy shit! That's The Hound!" My head nearly exploded at the realization my favorite Game of Thrones character had once been sexy as hell.

I turned to Sean to commiserate, but he was staring off into space, looking all broody and pensive. I nudged him with my foot. "Hey, what's your deal?"

"Huh?" He blinked and gave a forced smile. "Nothin'. Uh, yeah, it's The Hound."

I narrowed my eyes. "Sean..."

He ran a hand through his too long hair and averted his gaze.

I kicked him again. "Out with it."

He took a deep, audible breath. "I don't know." His shoulders slumped. "Ye ever look back at your life and realize ye made all the wrong decisions?"

I pulled my legs onto the couch and twisted toward him. "Like what?"

He shrugged and didn't seem inclined to say more.

Concern tightened my chest. He clearly needed to talk about whatever was bothering him. Maybe if I got the ball rolling, he would open up.

"Sometimes I wish I skipped college and put that money into the bar instead." I bit my lip. "I mean, what's the point of a business degree if the place fails before I get started?"

His eyes softened. "Maybe it's a sign ye were meant for somethin' else..."

"Like what?" I stared at him, puzzled. Taking over the Caledonia Club was the only thing I had ever wanted to do. My dreams centered around bustling crowds and house bands and newly felted pool tables, stuff that might seem silly to others, but meant the world to me. And one day, I'd make it happen. At least, I would if it didn't tank before Granda retired.

Pink tinged Sean's cheeks, and he waved the question off. "Sorry. Here I am getting all philosophical, when I'm supposed to be showin' ye a good time."

I grinned. "Does that good time involve a bottle of single malt and me cruising for dudes in kilts?"

"Even better." Sean disappeared into a bedroom and returned a few minutes later wearing a pair of hunter green, skin-tight leggings and a burnt orange, belted tunic, which altogether gave him the look of a medieval pimento olive.

I burst into giggles. "Hey, Robin Hood, you know, your shirt's supposed to cover your ass if you wear leggings."

"They're not leggings," he said primly. "They're hose."

This made me laugh even harder. He tossed me a shopping bag, and I rummaged through, pulling out a white linen dress, a green, wool sort of over-dress thing, and a pair of odd leather shoes.

"Oh my God." I paused between each syllable. "You're taking me to a ren-fair, aren't you?"

He grinned. "To a castle."

My eyes went wide. "A ren-fair at a castle!"

He shrugged. "In a manner o' speaking." His eyes lit with mischief. "That's not all."

I cocked my head. "What?"

He leaned in. "Tonight, I'm going to tell ye all my secrets."

Eyes wide, mouth open, I froze. "Don't you fuck with me." His grin broadened. "Don't you fuck with me!" He nodded, and I flung my arms around him. "You're really going to tell me what you do?"

"Aye." His grip tightened. "It's time ye kent everything."

# Chapter Three

"Are you sure we didn't miss it?" I asked, as we neared the bridge to Edinburgh Castle. The esplanade we had just crossed had been conspicuously empty, and the sun already neared the horizon. "I don't think most ren faires go this late."

"About that..." Sean's voice turned sheepish. "It's not *exactly* a ren faire."

"It's not?" I stared up at his face. "Okay...What is it?"

He adjusted the belt around his tunic. "A surprise."

I laughed. "Now you've got me really curious. Is it a private tour?" He shook his head. "A themed ball?"

His eyes sparkled with mirth. "Ye'll have to wait and see."

I tugged at his shirt sleeve. "Well, come on then. You know I can't stand a mystery."

"Hold on, there's just one thing." His gaze fell to his feet. "I ken it sounds strange, but I need ye to not talk when other people are around."

Tilting my head, I studied him. "Are you serious?" He nodded. My brow furrowed. "Okay. Why?"

"Trust me, it'll be easier if ye don't." He put a hand on my back. "It'll all make sense soon enough, just bear with me until then." He gave me a gentle shove toward the bridge. "Come on. Our castle awaits."

Two guards manned the gate on the opposite side of the bridge. They wore bright red uniforms and tall fuzzy bear hats like the ones you see in pictures of Buckingham Palace.

"Are they for real?" I couldn't decide if they were guards or elaborately costumed ticket takers. Either way, I found them adorable as fuck.

At least, I did until they raised their guns. We froze. One of the guards crept forward.

"What the fuck, Sean?" My voice came out waspish with fear.

"Shut up." He kept his eyes trained forward.

"That you, Cameron?" called the guard.

"Aye, mate." Sean strode forward. "Stand down will ye? You're scarin' the new recruit."

The guard lowered his gun. "Apologies. Wasna expectin' anybody 'til shift change."

Sean inclined his head in my direction. "Seems they've decided *her* training is more important than *my* vacation."

The guard winced. "Called ye in on holiday and e'rything? That Eugene's a right bastard."

"Aye, he is that." Sean handed over a piece of paper and a pair of IDs, which the guard scanned.

"First trip is it?"

It took a second for me to realize he was talking to me. I bit my bottom lip and gave a nervous shake of the head. I didn't know what was going on, but Sean's advice about remaining silent seemed pretty fucking apt right about now.

The guard's features softened in sympathy. "Dinna be so nervous, love. It's not as bad as ye think. Ye ask me, worst part is the clothes. All that wool'll have ye walking about like ye've got a case o' the jock itch."

Even if I could speak, I wouldn't have known how to respond. And not just because I had no "jock" to itch. What the hell was he talking about? What trip? And what did Sean mean when he said he was here for my training?

Sean took an innocuous step between us. "She's posing as a nun who's taken a vow o' silence." "They want her to get used to not speaking."

"That's a good role." The guard sounded impressed. "Hard to mess things up when ye canna speak."

I didn't know about the nun part, but I hoped the rest was true, because I couldn't seem to settle on a facial expression that didn't scream liar-liar-pants-on-fire. Fortunately, he wasn't paying attention to me anymore. He had his eyes glued to the slip of paper Sean had given him.

"All right, then. Everything seems in order." He called over his shoulder to the other guard. "Open up."

He returned our paperwork, and Sean and I walked unimpeded through the gatehouse door.

Once the lock clicked behind us, I tugged on Sean's sleeve. He bent, and I whispered in his ear, "Can I talk now?"

He nodded. "Aye, but keep your voice low, just in case."

"All right." I slapped him upside the head.

"Ow." He rubbed his temple. "What was that for?"

I ground my teeth together. "Are you kidding me? What the hell, Sean? How did we start the evening going to a ren faire and wind up breaking into a national monument instead?"

He snorted. "We dinna *break in*. I got permission from the colonel himself to bring ye." He patted his pocket. "How do ye think I got the paperwork?"

I glowered. "If I'm allowed to be here, why do I have to pretend to be a...a—" I gestured at his costume, "whatever the hell you are. And why can't I talk?" I narrowed my eyes. "Just be straight with me."

"I will—I am." A blush tinged his cheeks, and he dropped his gaze. "We've a bit of an arrangement, me and the colonel. Bringing ye was part o' the deal."

My fists clenched. "What does that even mean? Sean, I swear to God, if you can't do better than that, I'm out of here."

"Ye canna go!" His gaze darted about. "Listen, it's taken a lot of work to arrange this. Can't ye just trust me?"

His eyes pleaded with me to comply, and I softened. Whatever this was, he had obviously gone to a lot of trouble to make it happen. And honestly, how bad could it be? We were dressed like extras in a Monty Python sketch, for Christ's sake.

"All right." I poked him in the ribs. "But if I wind up in a Scottish prison dressed like Maid Marian, I'm whooping your ass."

He ruffled my hair. "Fair enough."

I always thought of a castle as one big building, like an oversized stone mansion, but this was more like a miniature city. Buildings loomed in every direction—a cafe, a hospital, the governor's house. Sights I might have found interesting if Sean weren't hustling me forward like we were late for a court appearance. We looped past cannons and museums and a little pet cemetery until we came to a stop in front of the Royal Palace.

"There'll be armed soldiers once we get inside." He put a hand on my shoulder. "Dinna freak out. It'll be fine, so long as ye stay quiet."

"Umm...you telling me not to freak out, just makes me want to freak out even more." I clutched his arm. "Why can't I talk? At least tell me that."

As if considering his words with care, he tilted his face toward the sky. "I told ye I had a deal with the colonel." I nodded. "Well, no one else kens about it, and it's just easier if they dinna realize you're an American."

"Uh, yeah, that sounds shady as fuck." I put my hands on my hips. "Are you blackmailing him or something? Why would this colonel help you trick a bunch of soldiers?"

He shot an anxious look toward the palace door. "I'll explain later. It's nothing like you're thinking, but it's too complicated to go into now." I didn't budge. "Dammit, Fi. The soldiers dinna matter. The colonel is the highest-ranking man in there, and he's given ye his permission. Now will ye quit bein' a pain in my arse and do as I ask?"

I stared at him, shocked. Sean never snapped at me. I mean, *never*. It was so out of character, it made me question whether *I* was the one being the asshole. Hell, maybe I was. I kept jumping to every worst possible conclusion when Sean was trying his damnedest to do something special for me.

I licked my lips. "All right, fine, but you have to promise you'll explain later."

His head bobbed in agreement. "I will. I swear. It'll all make sense soon, I promise."

Reluctantly, I followed him into the palace. Half a dozen armed guards stood stationed inside. I didn't panic since Sean prepared me this time, but I still felt uneasy.

A man, who I assumed must be the colonel, marched forward. He was a severe looking man with sharp eyes and a trenched brow. He wore full fatigues with insignia around the collar and an emerald green beret.

"Stand down." When he spoke, everyone in the room stood taller. The soldiers lowered their guns. "Johnson, man the door. Cameron, bring the recruit and come with me."

He strode into the adjacent room, and we followed into an enormous chamber with oak-paneled walls and a painted mural border. Geometric, plaster designs covered the ceiling, and a large, stone fireplace filled most of one wall.

"The king's dining room," Sean whispered in my ear. Impressive as the room was, I didn't understand why he had brought me here. Then the colonel stepped into the fireplace, and I really didn't know what was going on. What the actual fuck. I hadn't been in Scotland long, but that didn't seem normal.

His head disappeared behind the stonework, and he pushed onto his tiptoes.

I raised my eyebrows at Sean in silent question. *Just wait* he mouthed. Keys jangled from the vicinity of the fireplace, and a few seconds later, the back wall of the hearth swung open.

My mouth fell open. Sean tugged me close. "There are secret passageways all over the castle." His voice was little more than a breath, but the excitement in his words rang clear. "There's a whole network of underground vaults and tunnels."

Part of me wanted to throw on a fedora, grab a whip, and barrel into the vaults like Indiana Jones hunting for the Ark. But what in the hell? This serious man, an important, respected colonel, agreed to show me whatever lay hidden in those tunnels. Clearly, this wasn't typical tourist fodder. Whatever Sean had on this guy; it must be big. I glanced at Sean. Excitement lit his eyes when he met my gaze, and the knot in my stomach loosened. This was Sean. He'd never put me in danger. I was being ridiculous.

Sean nudged my back, and we followed the colonel through the secret passageway, into a darkened room. The musky air was cool and damp against my skin. Sean closed the hearth door, and as soon as the latch clicked, bright, fluorescent lights hummed to life.

We stood at the top of a set of ancient stone stairs, rough and irregular, as if carved from the earth with a hammer and chisel.

He caught my elbow. "Watch yourself. The steps can be slick."

I managed all right, despite the lack of traction on my weird medieval shoes. The stairs emptied into a small room, empty except for an industrial vault door that formed the back wall. In its center hung a large metal wheel with combination dials on each side. He went to one dial, the colonel to the other, and they each twisted in a combination. It must have been a long string of numbers, because it took a good minute before they finished. After a series of high-pitched beeps, the colonel cranked the wheel, and the vault door opened.

Sean ushered me through, and I about crapped my pants...or hose...whatever.

"The Honors of Scotland." He gestured to a velvet draped display. "The oldest surviving crown jewels in all the British Isles."

Goosebumps erupted on my flesh. Mere feet stood between me and millions of dollars' worth of ancient gold and jewels.

He waved me toward the display. "Go ahead."

I inched forward. A gold crown, rimmed with fur and studded with gems lay next to a silver gilt scepter topped with polished rock and pearls. A silver sword adorned with oak leaves and acorns rounded out the collection. I circled the display to get a better view of the last item—a large, flat, rectangular stone with iron hinges on its side. I stared at it, puzzled. For the life of me, I couldn't figure out why they'd place a dusty old rock next to the finery of ancient kings.

Sean joined me. "Do ye ken what that is?" I shook my head. "The Stone of Destiny." He ran a hand along its surface. "For centuries kings of Scotland were crowned atop this stone. Some claim it's the verra stone Jacob used for a pillow in the book o' Genesis."

"Enough with the history lessons." The colonel's voice cracked like a whip. "Help me send it up."

I jerked at his voice. I'd been so distracted by the jewels, I'd forgotten we weren't alone. The colonel stood in front of a control panel on the far wall, his features carved into an impatient expression. Sean scampered over, and the two punched in more codes.

"Stand back." Sean's warning came moments before the display rose from the ground. He returned to my side and pointed at the ceiling. "See where it looks like elevator doors? It opens to a shaft that leads to the crown room. They keep the jewels there during the day and secure 'em down here at night."

The colonel rapped a key on the control panel, and the display stopped its rise. The platform hovered ten feet in the air.

Sean pointed to a trap door in the floor where the display had just been. "The most important treasure the vault protects lies beneath the Destiny Stone."

Next to the trap door sat twin dials, same as the vault, and again, the two twisted in numbers. I watched in disbelief. What could possibly require more security than the crown jewels?

An office, it turned out. Not even a nice office—just a musty room with a small computer desk and a handful of chairs. A whiteboard, covered in complicated-looking math equations, spanned most of the far wall, and a world map, studded with pushpins hung to the left. The only other objects in the room were a tall, rectangular frame, bolted to the floor, and a couple of leather duffel bags.

The colonel tossed one of the bags at Sean's feet. "Get it booted. I'm going to change." He climbed back through the trap door.

Goosebumps prickled my skin. "What is this?"

"Give me a second, and I'll explain." Sean slid behind the desk and tapped away on the keyboard.

I busied myself studying the map. "Holy Roman Empire?" I chuckled. "I think your map's a little out of date." Red light flashed across the map face, and a strange, humming noise filled the room. It was a low, menacing sound, like a swarm of angry bees. The frame lit up like a Christmas tree, a series of bulbs glowing along the top.

Sean pressed a final key and waved me over. "All right. Ye wanted to ken what I do." He nodded to the frame. "Well, this is it."

The buzzing grew louder, and the lights along the top changed from red to yellow. Sparks shot between the frame.

I swallowed, my lips suddenly dry. "What is it?"

"The British government's most powerful weapon."

The lights turned from yellow to green, and the sparks became full on lightning bolts.

The hairs on my arm stood on end. Nausea churned in my belly. "Sean, I don't like this. Let's get out of here. You can tell me the rest later."

The door swung open, and the colonel returned. He wore a ruffled shirt and doublet with a leather jerkin over top. My mouth fell open. What the fuck?

The colonel looked down the bridge of his nose at Sean. "Ye ready, soldier?"

Sean strapped the leather bag to his back. "Almost, sir. I just need to give her the rundown on entry protocol, and we're set."

The colonel's expression was at once disappointed and piteous. "Ye had to ken I'd never allow this, lad." He gave a clenched, half-smile and pulled a small pistol from his jerkin.

Sean leaped between me and the colonel. "No! Ye canna! Ye promised!"

"I promised to send her through…and I will. Ye can bury her on the other side." The colonel tilted his head. "Now step aside, lad."

Sean remained frozen in place.

Anger flamed in the colonel's eyes. "I don't have time to mollycoddle ye, soldier. Either ye believe Scotland's worth the sacrifice, or you're a liability. Which is it?"

Sean waved his arms. "No, wait—"

The colonel raised his gun. I screamed. Sean dove in front of me, shoved me back, and together we fell, into the crackling frame.

# Chapter Four

There was no time, not to breathe, not even for my heart to beat. It happened in an instant, a flash so fast by the time my brain processed it, it was already over. The pain of it caught up to me in memory—the swelling and stretching of muscle and tendon as my body inflated like a helium-filled balloon. I became formless, just a mass of elastic skin and shapeless bones, oozing and bubbling like boiling pitch. Only my eyes kept their form—solid and immutable. Nothing more than frozen orbs, cryogenized in their sockets.

A loud crack ripped through the air, and with it, my body reformed. I slammed into the ground. The wind knocked from my lungs. The searing pain of it left me momentarily paralyzed. Then it passed, and I rolled onto my stomach and vomited.

Sean patted the length of me. "Are ye okay? You're not hit?"

I raised my head to look at him and toppled into a pile of my own sick.

He scooped me out of the mess. "Oh, Fi, I'm sorry. I'm so sorry. Hold on." He cradled my head as he rummaged through his leather bag. Cool glass prodded my lips, and minty liquid pooled on my tongue. "This'll help. Drink."

I did as he asked, too sick to question or argue. The nausea faded surprisingly fast, but my thoughts still felt muddled. I couldn't make sense of my surroundings. We were in a pine forest. Bright sunlight filtered through the trees, though I could have sworn it was just night. I had the sense days had passed without my knowledge.

I rubbed my eyes, trying to focus on him. "Where are we?"

He didn't meet my gaze. "The Caledonian Forest. Outside Perth."

I knew this was wrong, but my thoughts were too cloudy to figure out why. "No...we weren't here. We were..." I blinked several times, as if that would somehow clear my thoughts. "I think I had a seizure."

"It wasna a seizure." He sounded exhausted and guilt-ridden. "What's the last thing ye remember?"

"I don't—" My gaze fixed on his clothes, and I sucked in a breath. "That man, the colonel, he tried to—" I looked around in a panic. "Where is he? How did we get away? We have to call the police!"

I tried to rise, but Sean clasped my arm. "We're safe." His gaunt skin and shaking hands did nothing to reassure me.

I yanked my arm free. My breath came in a panicked rush. "How do you know? What happened?"

He scrubbed his hands over his face. "If he's not here now, he's not coming. He'll have gone on with his mission."

I ran my fingers through the roots of my hair and tugged. Either he was making absolutely zero sense, or I had blacked out during several very important conversations. "His mission? What mission?"

He gave me this weary, sad-sap stare, and my last thread of patience snapped. Who was he to sit there, looking all tragic, when he was the one responsible for this? "You know what, don't tell me." I pushed to my feet. "I don't want to know. Just take me to the closest embassy. I'm done."

He heaved a weary sigh. "We canna go to the embassy, Fi. It doesna exist."

"What do you mean it doesn't exist?" I paced the leaf-strewn clearing. "Can you please, for the love of Christ, say something that makes sense?"

He directed his gaze to the forest floor. "Sit. There's a lot to tell, and we need to build a fire before nightfall."

"I'm not sleeping in the woods, Sean!" My hands balled into fists. "Just say what you need to say and get me the fuck out of here."

"Sit," he repeated.

The determination on his face told me he had no plans of moving, and since I didn't know where the fuck we were, I pretty much had no choice but to humor him. I shot him a nasty glare before I sat back on the forest floor.

He looked at his hands folded in his lap and took a deep breath. "Six years ago, I joined the service. I told ye I enlisted because I couldna afford university, but that was a lie."

I sucked in a sharp breath. This wasn't how I expected his explanation to begin, but he had my attention. I had never understood why Sean joined the army. He had always been such an activist. Anti-gun. Anti-war. Anti-colonialism. So, when he joined, it made about as much sense as a vegan getting a job at a slaughterhouse.

"Ye remember how into the Scottish independence movement I was back then?" I nodded. "Well, I went to this rally, and that's where I met the colonel. O' course, I didna realize he was a colonel at the time. I just thought he was some bloke who was down for the cause." He paused, closing his eyes as if gathering his thoughts. "Anyway, we formed a sort of friendship, and once he kent he could trust me, he told me who he was and what he intended to do."

A chill ran through me, because I knew the colonel's plans couldn't be good, and because Sean had been dumb enough to get swept up in them.

He studied his hands, flexed his fingers, released. "He explained signs and protests would never be enough. If we wanted real change, we needed to disrupt the power structure from within."

"Oh God, Sean." I moaned. "Please tell me you're not involved in some anarchist shit."

He ran a hand over his smooth chin. "Anarchy wasna the goal. Changin' the world was. And the colonel had the means to do it." His mouth tightened into a grim line. "So I enlisted, and after a time, he recruited me to his unit."

A shudder ran through his body, and he rubbed his arms. "Ye see, the colonel heads a department unlike any other in the

British Military. A special forces team that deals in alternative warfare. In..." He bit his bottom lip. "In time travel."

He stared like he tried to gauge my reaction, but all I managed was a dumb gaze. Had he just said time travel? He had to be fucking with me. Either that, or he was crazy, which was beginning to seem more and more likely, because his expression didn't waver in its sincerity.

After an eternity of me staring with my mouth agape, he continued, "We're not the only country with the technology. Russia and the States have had it longer than us. China's just now catching up. We're basically all just playing this game where we try to stop each other from changing the past, while trying to shift history in our own favor."

Cold sweat broke out on my skin. Memory flashed back from our time in the vault. "So that frame?"

He nodded, lips thin. "It transported us to the year 1396."

I let out a disturbed chuckle. "Of course. That makes perfect sense. We escaped the crazed gunman by jumping into the dark ages."

Sean's face flushed red. "He's not crazed. He's calculating and driven and—"

"A murderer." My voice held no humor.

He winced. "That too."

Wind rustled through the trees, and I shivered. He handed me a cloak from his bag, and I wrapped it around myself without a word.

He sat across from me and continued his story, undeterred, "Ye see, while all those soldiers ye saw tonight have been blindly followin' orders, the colonel and I have been workin' on our own plan—one that'll restore Scotland to the independent nation it was always meant to be."

I steepled my fingers. "Let me get this straight. You and this colonel hatched some kind of time-travel coup. Then for some reason, you brought me along, which the colonel was okay with, until he decided to change his mind last minute and kill me instead?" I leveled a hard stare. "That's the story you're going with?"

28

He huffed. "It is, but it isna as ridiculous as you're makin' it sound."

Pressure built behind my eyes. "Do you hear yourself? It's the epitome of fucking ridiculous. Time travel does not exist, Sean! Something's wrong with you. You're sick in the head."

Shooting to his feet, he put his hands on his hips. "I can prove it."

With a huff, I rose to face him. "Okay, prove it."

Turning toward the edge of the clearing, he motioned for me to follow. "I'll show ye."

He led me through the woods, hacking at branches with his sword to clear the way. I didn't believe for a second he'd show me any proof to verify his story, but if it got me out of these woods, I wasn't going to argue.

After a time, we came to a stop in front of a field of purple flowers. He pointed with his sword. "The main road's across that field. When we get there, we need to stay low and silent. People see us lurkin' off the path, they'll think we're bandits."

Low and silent, my ass. I planned to hitch a ride with the first person I saw and hightail it straight to the airport.

Only, the first person I saw wasn't driving a car. He was riding a horse pulling a cart. Sean glanced at me. The two of us lay on our bellies, peeking through the grass on the edge of a dirt road. I jutted my chin. This didn't mean anything. Sure, the guy on the horse wore a tunic like Sean's, albeit it dingier and patched on one arm. And yes, his cart contained what appeared to be stacks of animal furs. But there could be lots of explanations. Maybe he was some Scottish version of Amish.

A few minutes later, two nuns sauntered by. Each carried a wicker basket filled with bread. The nun nearest us scowled at her companion. "Dinna be giving all your alms away before we reach Horsegate, Margaret."

I heaved a relieved breath and smiled. Nothing strange about nuns.

"I'd rather work a week in yon leper house than spend an hour on the Horsegate." The other nun shuddered.

My smile fell. Admittedly, leper house was harder to explain. But maybe that was just some weird Scottish slang. Like, maybe leper house meant hospital...that was possible...right? But then two guys in full fucking knight's armor came down the road, tossing a medicine ball back and forth, and I couldn't make sense of that even if we had time traveled. Knights were supposed to be on horseback, carrying lances. Not doing old-timey gym exercises down packed dirt roads.

"They train in full armor to increase their strength." He sounded like David Attenborough narrating a particularly fascinating species of bird. "It can weigh up to 50 kilos."

I looked at him, clenching my hands at the light of excitement in his eyes. "Is this fun for you? Really interesting, is it?" The smile fell from his face. I rose to my feet, brushed the bracken from my dress, and walked in the direction from which we'd come.

"Where are ye going?" he called.

"Home." I didn't look back, but the sound of his footsteps crunching on leaves followed behind me.

~ * ~

Back at the clearing, Sean yanked a long piece of jerky from his bag and bit off a mouthful. "So ye believe me now?"

I stared in disbelief. "What the hell do you think you're doing? It's not snack time." I pointed toward the center of the clearing. "You want me to believe you? Fine. Open that fucking portal and take me home."

He swallowed and offered me some jerky. "There's no goin' home. Portal has to open from the other end, and nobody kens we're here."

I snatched the jerky and whipped him across the head with it. It broke, and I chucked the remaining stub at his face. Then I burst into tears. I didn't know what to believe. Time travel couldn't possibly exist. But then, what about those people? No one at the castle so much as blinked at our clothes. How was I standing in the middle of the fucking woods right now? This was all so fucked.

"I'm sorry." Desperation painted his words. "Please, dinna cry. I've mucked the whole thing up. I didna mean for it to be such a shock."

A laugh gurgled from my throat. "You tell me you've brought me hundreds of years back in time, and there's no way home, and it's the shock you feel bad about?"

He put a hand on my shoulder. "I'm sorry."

"You're sorry?" I smacked his hand off my shoulder and jabbed a finger into his chest. "You did this. You brought me here. What were you thinking? Why?"

He didn't meet my gaze. "It was the only way to protect ye."

My eyebrows shot upward. "Protect me. You almost got me shot."

He scrubbed his hands over his face. "I know. I—" He winced. "I got in over my head..." Closing his eyes, he took a deep, audible breath. "About a month ago, I started to get cold feet. Not about the mission. I still believe in what we set out to do, but I couldna stomach the thought o' never seeing ye again."

His gaze met mine, and his voice vibrated with emotion. "I'm in love with ye, Fi, and this isna how I intended to tell ye, but there it is."

My hands turned to ice, and a numb buzzing filled my ears.

He continued his confession, unaware of how close I was to blowing a gasket. "I love ye. More than my country. More than my mission. More than anything."

Any other time, Sean confessing his love for me would have left me devastated. Breaking his heart would have broken me in return. But the fact he did it now, professed his love moments after destroying my life...well, he could just fuck right off for all I cared.

He blinked, and a few tears spilled down his cheeks. "I told the colonel I'd changed my mind. He argued with me. Told me I was bein' selfish. That love o' country required sacrifice, and he couldna let me resign anyway, knowing what I did about him and his plan."

He raked a sleeve across his cheek. His hands shook. "I held firm. Told him I had to at least see if ye felt the same. That's when he suggested I bring ye with me. Said it was the best he could do. Otherwise, he'd have no choice but to kill us both. I swore to him I hadna told ye anything, but he said he couldna take my word for it, seein' as I'd just proven myself disloyal. I kent he meant what he said, so I took the deal. I called your granda, arranged the trip, and..."

My teeth carved into my lip. My body shook with too many emotions, too many thoughts. Part of me still didn't believe this was real. The other part was terrified it was. My brain was fried, and the only clear thought in my head was that Granda was alone, and I had no way to get back to him.

"Fi, please." His hand slid over mine. "I ken this is a lot to take in but talk to me. Tell me what you're thinkin'."

A mad chuckle escaped my lips, and I looked at him. "I'm thinking you're a stupid, selfish son of a bitch. Did you really believe that man was going to let some random girl tag along on your mission?"

"I trusted him." His voice broke. "What choice did I have?"

"You could have told me!" My voice sounded shrill, even to my own ears. "We could have gone to the American authorities. We could have—"

His shout cut through my words. "You wouldn't have believed me! Even now, after what I showed you, you still barely believe me."

"Don't you dare put this on me!" I marched forward, shoved him hard in the chest. "How are you going to fix this? What are we going to do now?"

His hands gripped my wrists, and his jaw set. "We're goin' to carry out our mission."

# Chapter Five

Hours later, Sean and I lay in a tent he had packed in that Mary Poppins bag of his. The inky night sky had taken on a purplish tinge that made me think it must be close to dawn. I hadn't slept a bit. Not that I hadn't tried. Escaping into dreams seemed far preferable to my current waking nightmare, but I couldn't settle my mind enough to make it happen.

"I'm hungry." I gave him a hard kick. He groaned, which made me smirk. The stupid bastard.

"There's jerky and some dried fruit in the bag." He sounded wide awake. Apparently, I wasn't the only one with a case of insomnia. Good. I hoped he'd spent the entire night sick over what he had done to me.

I rifled through the bag and my hand brushed a burlap sack filled with something hard and metallic. Or rather, lots of little somethings. After a bit of groping, I realized they were coins. I pulled one out and squinted in the pale light of the fire outside our tent.

"Is this gold?" I surveyed him. "How did you get this?"

He shifted. "The colonel has his ways. We'll have to use most of it for our mission, but there should be more than enough left to make sure we live a comfortable life."

I gritted my teeth at the casual implication we would be spending our lives together. I barely wanted to share the same tent with him. If I wasn't scared shitless by the thought of being alone in a world I knew nothing about, I'd have already ghosted him. That was, assuming this was real. Despite what I'd seen, I still wasn't convinced we'd time traveled. Maybe I'd had some psychotic break, and any minute now I would wake to find I'd been talking to a potted plant this whole time.

Still, I set all that aside, because the big-ass bag of gold seemed the more pressing issue. Earlier, I had avoided asking questions about Sean's so-called "mission." I didn't have it in me to deal with any more fucked up news, but considering the amount of gold in that bag, I thought maybe I'd better find out what he intended to do with it.

I forced my voice to casual evenness. "What exactly is this mission?"

"To bring an end to the Stewart line." He shifted upright. "Once we do, James VI won't inherit the English throne, and Scotland and England will remain independent nations."

"Oh, is that all?" My voice oozed sarcasm. "How do you plan to do that?"

"By funding a coup." He patted the bag. "Robert III is weak. That's why we picked this time. The Camerons already have a standing army. We just have to convince them to put it to use."

My hand clenched around the coin in my hand. "So murder? That's what you're saying?"

"This is war." His voice hardened. "People die. It canna be helped. Any king worth his salt would happily give his life for the benefit o' his nation."

I almost laughed. Not out of humor, but because of the ridiculousness of his words. "You're so full of shit. You can tell yourself whatever you want, but murder is murder."

"Aye, well, ye want to talk about murder, what about the millions who have died on account o' English tyranny? Do ye have any idea how many Scots have been slaughtered at English hands? How many Irish? How many indigenous populations sacrificed and exploited in the name of imperialism?"

"Who's to say it won't happen anyway? You don't know what killing the king will do. What if someone worse takes his place?"

He took a deep breath as if to force patience. "We might not ken for certain, but we have a fair idea. We've done the research, played with simulations. All the evidence suggests our plan will work."

I shook my head. Never in my life had I been more disgusted, and that was saying something considering where and when I currently found myself. "What happened to you? The Sean I know would never hurt anyone."

"Aye, well, maybe ye dinna ken me as well as ye think."

He went quiet, and I stared at his darkened silhouette, thinking those might be the truest words he'd spoken all night. The arrogance. The unbridled gall of thinking he had the right to snuff out men like pawns on a chessboard. That he even believed he'd get away with it...A thought dawned on me, and for the first time since this mess began, a glimmer of hope cut through the chaos.

"What makes you think the other time soldiers won't come for you? Don't you think it's a little crazy to assume two men can pull one over on the entire British army? They've got to have ways of tracking you."

He shifted, adjusting the blankets beneath him. "No one kens more about the program than the colonel. He made sure we'd be untraceable."

A thrill ran through me, despite his words, because I heard the tremor in his voice. He wasn't nearly so confident as he tried to sound.

"Okay, but say they do come. They'd take us home, right?"

"Fiona..." He heaved a weary sigh. "There's no goin' home. Ye need to get that through your head before ye drive yourself mad."

"Just humor me. What if they come?"

"Then we're both dead. Ye canna truly believe they'd let ye walk free now ye ken about the program. Nay. If they found us, they'd bring us back, torture us for information, and make us disappear."

"But it's not our fault! Well, it's your fault, but you at least tried to back out. That has to count for something." I hated the desperation in my voice, but I needed to cling to some kind of hope.

"Come on, Sean. There has to be a—"

"Shh!" He slapped a hand over my mouth. "Something's out there." After pausing for a second to listen, he pressed a knife into my hand. "It's probably just a wolf, but, just in case, be ready to grab the gold and run. We'll meet in the heather field if we're parted."

He didn't wait for a response, just filled the pouch on his belt with gold, drew his sword, and disappeared into the night. Meanwhile, I was still hung up on the *just* part of "just a wolf." Like was that really the best-case scenario? I palmed the knife. My heart raced. Christ, I could barely chop an onion. How was I supposed to stab some wild animal to death?

I strained to hear what was happening outside. At first, I detected nothing, though I couldn't decide if that was good news or bad. Sean's voice broke the silence. "Easy, lads."

I clamped a hand over my lips so my heart didn't fly out of my mouth. Who the fuck was he talking to? Had the time soldiers come? Would they really kill us?

I heard the jangle of coins, followed by a thud. "I want no trouble."

Bandits, I realized. My hands grew clammy, and my body trembled. A wolf would have been so much better.

"That's a hefty bit," said a gruff voice.

"Ask me," said another, more nasal voice. "Anyone what's got this much coin on his belt, got himself a whole lot more stashed away somewhere."

"Take off your boots," ordered the first voice.

"I'll check the tent," said the other.

Sean's voice rang loud and wild with terror. "Run!"

I sprang like a sprinter at a gunshot. I didn't know how I remembered to grab the gold, but I did. Just as I lifted the tent to dip out the back, some big dude crashed through the front. I screamed. The tent collapsed on top of him, and I bolted.

I hit the tree line and glanced back. Sean fought some guy with a sword, and the man from the tent ran straight toward me. I dipped and darted through the trees. My vision sharpened with adrenaline. Branches clawed at my skin. An arrow whizzed past my head and landed in a tree in front of me.

"Stop!" the bandit shouted. "Hand o'er the gold, and I'll let ye live."

Then a distant scream, feral and agonized. It radiated deep in my belly. Raw pain and unbridled fear. And when the scream grew silent, I knew, Sean was dead. He was dead, and if I didn't hurry, I would be too.

I tossed the bag to the ground. "Take it!"

Another arrow sailed past me; this one grazed my arm. I put on speed and dipped right. The sun peeked over the horizon, but the footsteps kept coming. I darted through a cluster of pines that spit me onto a road. A yelp of joy escaped my lips. People! A giant group of them, all bunched up with carts and animals and wheelbarrows in front of a gated wall.

"Help!"

Heads turned. Confused, suspicious faces peered in my direction.

"Please!" I rushed into the crowd and pleaded with the man closest to me. "He's after me. I'm being chased! He killed my friend. Please!"

The man narrowed his eyes and ambled back.

The sun cleared the horizon. Somewhere in the distance, a rooster crowed. Guards opened the gates, and people filtered into the walled city. A few lingerers stared with confused interest. Tears welled in my eyes. "Please!" What was wrong with these people? How could they not care?

"What'd she say, Devin?" a woman asked the man next to her.

An old man glared like I had done him personal harm. "English."

I searched the crowd, desperate for a single, friendly face. My eyes filled with tears. I ran toward the guards. They had to help.

"Stop her!" The bandit burst through the trees onto the road. "That's my goodwife. She's run off with my gold!"

A few stragglers crowded toward me.

"Whore!" someone shouted.

"Thief!" shouted another.

I didn't wait to hear more. I bolted through the gate. Dipped and darted around animals and carts. People gasped and shouted in surprise as I passed. Though I feared it might slow me, I risked a glance back. The bandit was caught in the crowd, but it wouldn't keep him tangled long. Cutting onto a side-street, I wound left and right. Around houses. Behind trees. My lungs screamed. My heart hammered. No way I could keep this up much longer.

Another quick glance, I didn't see him, but I couldn't get complacent. I turned onto a winding, narrow road and tensed. The area was too exposed. Just a few houses on vast sprawls of open land. I should turn back. Heavy thumps sounded behind me. Footsteps. He was coming. Had to hide. I spotted a chicken coop next to a giant stone house and dashed toward it. After hopping a fence, I darted across a sweeping yard. So close. Pecking chickens squawked and scrambled. Then I dropped, face first into the dirt.

I hadn't tripped. My leg gave out. It took a second for me to understand why—An arrow stuck out of my thigh. A vague sense of surprise coursed through me at the sight because I suffered no pain. Then there he was. The bandit. He stared at me through beady, watery eyes. An evil grin spread across blackened teeth, and my legs grew warm with piss.

He yanked my hair and pulled me to my knees. At first, he didn't speak, clearly exhausted by the chase. "The gold—" he panted, "—whore."

"I don't have it." A whimper escaped my throat. "I threw it in the woods. Didn't you hear me?"

He growled in frustration and dragged me by the hair toward the road. "Where?"

"I don't know." Tears streamed down my cheeks.

I tried to pull my hair free of his grip, but my fingers were clutched around something smooth and hard. Sean's knife, I realized. I hesitated, not sure what to do. Between my leg and the way he dragged me, there'd be no way I would be able to land more than a flesh wound. And that would probably just piss him off.

Then again, this bastard would probably kill me anyway. Might as well give him a few scars to remember me by.

I squeezed the knife's handle. Mustered all my rage and pain and fear. "Fuck you, motherfucker!" I slashed and stabbed at any body part within reach.

He shouted in pain. Warm blood splattered across my cheek. He reeled back and punched me in the face. My brain sloshed against my skull, and my vision went to static. It cleared in a burst of pain as he threw me to the ground. The impact pounded the arrow deeper into my thigh. Nerves screamed. Every ounce of pain my brain had been protecting me from ignited at once, and my body went cold.

He hit me again and again. "Sardin' cunt whore." He seized my throat and squeezed.

I strained against him. Kicked with my good leg while my injured leg burned and tore.

"Whore." Spittle flew from his mouth. "Shrew. Ruttin' sow."

The arrow shredded muscle. My lungs were bricks in my chest. I couldn't do anything but take the beating and pray for the end to come fast.

And eventually, it did come…in a way. Pain gave way to the peace of suffocation. His smothering hand became a blessing. Serenity and warmth suffused my body. My soul detached and began to float away.

Then a jerk. A sudden influx of air. Pain. Crushing. Dead weight. He had collapsed on top of me. I didn't understand. I wanted to push him off, but I was too hurt, too weak.

"Get her to Mairi," a voice shouted.

The weight lifted from me. My body writhed and arched with pain. I caught sight of a dark-haired man, walking away with the bandit slung over his shoulder. Arms lifted me. A boy. Black spots clouded my vision. He carried me into the stone house. The air was smoky and dark.

"By the fire," an old woman commanded. "Blankets. Get a move on, ye wee fool."

# Then the world went black.

# Chapter Six

I woke with a scream.

I lay atop a quilt on a packed dirt floor. Next to me, an open fire crackled and spit sparks. My injured leg lay propped on a stack of pillows. And a little old lady with a snow-white braid stared at me through steely eyes.

She clucked in disapproval. "Lord's seen fit to test ye today. Donald," she shouted over her shoulder, "get the strap."

"No!" I howled in a fit of panic. I didn't know if she meant to tie me or whip me, but after what I had been through, I couldn't stomach either. I tried to get up, but only managed to knock over the pillows. A bolt of pain through my thigh, and I cried out in agony.

A young man with a head full of frizzy, dishwater blond hair arrived with a leather strap. I wailed and flung my arms in front of my face.

"Nay! Nay!" he pleaded, his voice horrified. "I mean ye no harm." He raised his palms to the old woman. "Mairi, I didna mean to—"

"Never ye mind." She waved him off. "The lass's mind's been fear-addled. She canna tell friend from foe." She tugged my hands away from my face.

I whimpered and cowered.

"Look at me, lass." She didn't raise her voice, but there was such an air of authority in the command, I obeyed as if compelled. "The arrow has to come out. I hoped ye'd stay asleep for it, but the Good Lord's seen fit to make ye feel this pain." Her grip tightened, and her iron eyes bored into mine. "Ye'll endure it, and when it's done, ye'll take that pain and make it your strength. Do ye understand?"

I burst into tears. How was this real? Why was this happening to me? I was a good person. I didn't deserve this. I shook my head. "I can't."

"Ye canna?" She dropped my wrists and rose. "I suppose that's best. I've too much to do to be wastin' my time on a whore who got what's comin' to her."

Disbelief and rage flared inside me. If she knew what I'd been through, if she felt one second of this pain, she wouldn't dare say those words to me.

Donald gasped. "Mairi!"

"A man's dead on her account." She glared. "Thought ye could tempt him and nothin' would come o' your sin?"

"No!" My teeth clenched so hard I thought they would break.

"Course ye did." She gestured toward the door. "Now look what ye've done. A man's dead on account o' ye."

"Fuck you, you old bitch," I growled through halting gasps of pain. I gritted my teeth. My fists were knots. "He deserved to die."

An approving grin spread across her face. "That's right, lass. *He* deserved to die. Do *ye*?"

I groaned as a fresh wave of pain lanced through me.

She grasped my hand and squeezed. "Choose."

That single word hit me with the impact of a thousand arrows. I didn't choose to come here, or to be chased, or shot, but what came next was up to me. And when it came to a fight, Buchanan's never backed down. That is what Granda taught me, and I would do him proud.

I inhaled a ragged breath. "Do it."

Mairi nodded. "On your side."

Screaming at the agony of movement, I rolled.

The boy, Donald, crouched next to me and handed me the strap. "To bite down on."

I shoved it in my mouth. It tasted of sweat and leather and made me gag.

42

Lips compressed into a thin line, Mairi peered down her sharp nose at me. "I'll be swift as I can."

The boy gripped my shoulder and hip. Even though I knew he was trying to help, I flinched at his touch.

Mairi dropped to her knees and examined my leg from back to front. "Good. Good," she muttered. "I should be able to avoid the bone." From a neat stack of utensils piled on the ground beside her, she selected a pair of shears. "Tighten your hold."

Donald's fingers hardened against my flesh. Mairi cut the arrow below the fletching where a thin strip of wood still held it loosely attached. The arrow vibrated as the feathered end snapped free. The leather strip muffled my moan. She didn't pause to let me recover. Wrenching the arrow stub to the right, she snagged a hammer, and pounded the shaft like a stubborn bit of nail on a plaster wall.

Sparks popped in front of my eyes. Despite the roaring fire, my skin chilled, cold as a corpse. Every hammer blow sent waves of nausea, as my flesh parted, and nerves burned in white hot agony. The arrow tip poked through the front of my thigh, and I spit out the leather strap and vomited.

Tears and snot smothered my face. She paused long enough for me to empty my stomach. Then she shoved the strap back in my mouth and gave a final tap.

Bile scorched my raw throat. Wails turned to whimpers.

"Ye've done well." Mairi brushed sweat dampened hair off my forehead. "It's almost over." She wrapped her old, gnarled fingers around the protruding arrow tip and yanked.

It slid through my leg with excruciating ease. I bore down on a final moan. My muscles contracted and blinding pain arched my back. Then my body went flaccid as the pain reduced by half in a rush of blood.

I teetered on the edge of consciousness. The pull of black oblivion nearly stole me into sleep, but a new burst of pain brought me back from the edge. Blinking, I focused on Mairi, who filled my wound with some sort of goopy paste. She wound my leg with a strip of bandage and secured it with a tight knot.

She put a hand on my forehead. "Rest, lass. The bigger fight's yet to come."

~ * ~

"Look who decided to come home." Mairi's acerbic voice snapped me from sleep.

The room was dark, the fire reduced to a few glowing embers. I couldn't make out faces, just shadowy outlines.

"Lad, get me my besom. I'm about to beat your master bloody."

"Glad to see ye too, Aunty," an unfamiliar voice replied.

A thrill of fear ran through me at the deepness of his voice. He didn't sound angry or aggressive, but he was a man, and that was enough. My heart raced. I wanted to run and hide, but all I could do was lay there and breathe through the pain and fear.

"Hal, wait 'til ye hear—" Donald's voice squeaked with excitement.

Mairi cut him off. "Where've ye been? Ye left in the wee hour o' the morn' havin' murdered a man and didna see fit to return until the black o' night?"

"I told ye, I had business at the guild." Irritation tinged the man's voice, as if this were an old argument he desperately didn't want to have once more.

"Dinna lie to me, laddie!" Her voice turned waspish. "Ye went to defile that shrew. Meanwhile, I'm left to wonder if ye've been hanged for murder."

*Murder.* Sean had been murdered. He was dead, and I was alone, and oh god, I hurt so bad.

The unfamiliar voice laughed. "If I had been arrested for murder, ye'd have heard about it within the hour, and ye ken it well. Those hens ye cluck about with spread gossip faster than plague on a ship." Mairi grumbled something indiscernible, but the man spoke over her. "And Coira's not a shrew; she's shrewd. There's a difference."

Mairi scoffed. "Aye, the letter d."

The man sighed. "Let it be, will ye? She leaves for Paris on the morrow. Give my ears a rest until she returns, aye?" He yawned. "How fares the lass?"

Me? Did he mean me? My heart pounded even harder. What would he do with me now he had returned?

"Heart's still beating." Her voice softened, and a note of pride tinged her tone. "She's a fighter, that one."

"Ye should have heard her, Hal!" Donald chimed in. "Cursed like a tanner's bastard! Never heard a woman talk like that. Had an odd way a speakin' too. Bet she's one o' them cave people from the isles."

"Hold your wheesht, fool. She wasna in her right mind." Mairi's voice brooked no argument, and the boy silenced.

"What of her people?" Concern filled the man's voice. "Did she say where we can find her kin?"

*Kin.* Oh god, Granda. How long had it been? He was probably halfway to Edinburgh by now, prepared to scour every inch of the city for me. I knew Granda. He wouldn't give up on finding me, not until his dying breath. I had to get back to him. I had to find a way.

"We'll have to ask her in the morn', assumin' she lives 'til then." Mairi yawned. "But enough o' that. Tell me what happened with the constable."

"Well—" Amusement tinged his voice. "—as ye can see, he didna see fit to hang me."

She sniffed. "And why not?"

"Are ye disappointed, Auntie?" His chuckle held only love for the old woman.

"I'm going to string ye up myself if ye dinna get on with it."

"I had naught to worry about, my dear aunt"—his voice vibrated with excitement—" seein' as yon defiler was a known outlaw."

She gasped. "An outlaw! Wait 'til I tell Winnie MacSheah! She willna believe it. Ooh, I canna wait to see her face when she hears my nephew brought down an outlaw. Oughta shut her up about her godson rescuin' that baby from a pig."

"Cluck. Cluck. Cluck," the man said, though there was humor in his voice.

"Oh hush," Mairi chided.

His tone grew earnest. "Ye think she'll live?"

"What am I? The Good Lord reignin' on high? How should I ken?" Mairi's chair squeaked as she rose to her feet. "But what'd 'ye say we give the lass your room for the night? If she is to expire, let it be in a bed, not the cold, hard floor."

Her words pierced through my thoughts, and I vaguely registered how strange it was to hear people talk so casually about my death. Even stranger was the fact it didn't scare me. If I died, at least the pain would end, and I wouldn't be alone...

The dark-haired man scooped me off the ground and carried me to an upstairs room. Though my initial reaction to his arrival had been fear, calm settled over me at the feel of his warm, strong arms. He placed me in a bed and covered me with a rosemary scented blanket.

"Good luck." He put a calloused hand to my cheek. "I hope ye live. I've never met a lass who curses like a tanner's bastard."

Then he disappeared, and I drifted back to sleep.

# Chapter Seven

Late. I was so late! This city had a real pine tree problem. Why did I even pay taxes if they were going to let pine trees tear through the roads? Now Granda was going to be late for his leeching. He never remembered to put them on himself.

A pine tree burst through the road. It split the concrete and grew in an instant to its full height. I swerved to avoid it. Bumped along a road made of tree roots. Then I came to a stop in the parking lot of the Caledonia Club. Finally!

I ran inside. "Granda, I'm sorry I'm late!"

Jones glared from behind the bar. He yanked a fistful of gold from his pocket. "You really fucked up." He thrust his hand in front of my face. "Look at this!" The gold turned to sand and slipped through his fingers into a pile on the bar. He brushed it onto the floor, which was now covered in sand dunes.

He thrust a pine branch at me. "I'm not cleaning that shit up."

"Of course not." I took the branch from him and swept. Only, every time I cleared a bit, new sand filtered in.

"Fiona." Granda's voice snapped my gaze up from the desert beneath my feet.

"Oh, Granda, I forgot." I flicked my gaze to Jones. "I need a double of leeches, on the rocks."

Granda held up a hand. "Before ye do that, I could use a bit o' help." He thrust his hand into his chest and tore out his heart. He held it before me, all shiny and red like a pair of wax lips and gave it a little shake. "It doesna seem to be workin'. Can ye fix it for me?"

With a plop, he dropped it into my hands. I shook my head in exasperation. How many times had I told him? He just had to pump it. Oh well. I'd have to do it myself. I pressed the heart between my palms, squeezed and released, squeezed and released. Granda sighed with relief. "That's better, lass. What would I do without ye?"

With a glare, Jones pointed an accusing finger at the floor. "What about that sand?"

The sand had risen to my knees. "It's okay. I've got this." I shifted Granda's heart to one hand and held the pine branch with the other, squeezing and sweeping, squeezing and sweeping.

"Faster." A moan poured from Granda's lips. He clutched his chest. The sand rose to my thighs. I pumped harder. Swept faster.

"I need that gold." Spittle flew from Jones's mouth. "You promised me overtime."

"Lass!" Granda dropped to his knees.

"Granda!" I pumped faster, but his heart was turning to sand.

"The gold, whore." Jones morphed into the bandit. The club fell away, and we were in the woods. I bolted through pines. Granda disappeared from my view, but his cries continued to fill my ears. "My heart! My heart!"

"I'll save you, Granda!" I searched for him in a desperate haze, pumping and running, pumping and running. Grains of sand slipped through my fingers. The bandit drew closer. His hand grasped my shoulder...

"Lass. Lass! You're screamin' again."

I opened my eyes. Mairi hovered over me. She slid an arm beneath my shoulders and helped me sit. "Drink this." She put a wooden cup to my lips. A noxious, bitter, herb-laced concoction slipped down my throat. She put a hand to my forehead and pursed her lips. "Fever's still blazin'. I'll get some leeches, aye." She disappeared out the door, and I fell back asleep.

~ * ~

Sweat coated my skin. A sour, herby taste clung to my tongue, and crust coated my eyelashes. Gross. I needed a shower, and a toothbrush, and...clothes? What the hell? I never slept naked. And this wasn't my bed. What bar-rando had I gone home with last night? I grimaced. Well, I hoped I had fun, because I couldn't remember any of it.

I scanned for my clothes, but I didn't see them crumpled anywhere. Maybe he'd hung them in the...non-existent closet. I looked around. No dresser either. Just a trunk next to a small table with a pitcher and basin. What kind of weird ass room was this? Whatever. It didn't matter. I needed to get the hell out of here. I had this creeping sensation something wasn't right.

A shadow of a nightmare niggled at my memory. A man. And pain. And—no, this was stupid. It was a dream. I drank too much and had a one-night stand. That was all. And to prove it, I pushed off the quilt and looked at my leg.

A whimper escaped my throat.

No. No. No. No. No.

A scab-crusted scar ran across the front of my thigh, puffy and red and about an inch long. My fingers darted to the back of my leg and grazed down a matching line of raised tissue. I collapsed into a heap. I hoisted the blanket back over me and curled into a ball. I tried to breathe, but everything was coming back to me now—Sean and the bandit and the little old lady.

I didn't know what to do. My chest hurt. My hands tingled. My breath came shallow as if I breathed through a straw. Had to calm. Had to breathe. My sight fell upon the trunk across the room. It was solid and sturdy, everything I wasn't. I focused on it, forced my eyes to follow the pattern of the grain, the swirls and knots and uneven stain. Eventually, my heart slowed. My breathing evened. And the tears began.

They came hard and ugly, choked and snotty. Great gulping sobs that wracked my body and drenched my pillow. I cried so long my tongue went dry, and my eyes swelled like I had been in a brawl. I cried until my stomach muscles ached, and my throat turned raw. I cried until I hollowed to an empty shell, until emotions lacked all meaning, and I no longer had the strength to care. And when the tears finally ran out, I laid there and stared at a bit of chipped green wall paint.

Time passed. Hours, days, minutes, I didn't know. Eventually, the sludge in my brain loosened enough for me to realize lying in bed wasn't a permanent solution. I had to think. I had to plan. I had to worry about what came next, but the thought of facing my new reality overwhelmed me.

I wished Gran were here. She always knew what to do. World turned into a dumpster fire. No problem, Gran would just hand me a fire extinguisher and tell me to get to work. But this...I didn't even know where to begin. Of course, Gran would have had an answer for that too. *Can't begin anywhere but the beginning.* Only, I didn't know where the beginning was. Not that she'd have accepted that excuse. She'd have looked at me with a knowing smile and said *it's wherever you choose.*

Then Mairi's voice rang in my head, also telling me to choose, to take control of my own fate, and that seemed to matter. What could I control? Not in the grand scheme of my fucked-up situation, but right now, here, in this room. I looked around. My gaze landed on the pitcher and basin. I could clean myself. *That* I could do. I dangled my legs off the side of the bed, took a deep breath, and rose. Balancing most of my weight on my good leg, I tested the injured one with gentle pressure. It held. I tried a step. The muscles were stiff and inflexible. They fought against even the slightest bend at the knee. No matter. The other leg could compensate.

I hobbled across the cold, wood floor, braced my weight against the table, and peered in the pitcher. Water! Tears burst from my eyes at the sight of it. It was a small win, the tiniest possible thing that could go right, but a win, nonetheless. I poured the water into the basin, splashed my face, and scrubbed. It dawned on me I should be much dirtier. Somebody had bathed me, cared for me. That Mairi woman. More tears fell, this time for her, out of gratitude, out of the realization that kindness still existed.

Wind gusted through the open, glassless window. It chilled my wet skin and covered me in goosebumps. Shivering, I hobbled to the trunk, slow and stiff, but determined to solve at least one more problem. I finagled open the lid while balanced

50

on one foot and scooped out an armful of clothes. I sorted through until I found a shirt and pair of pants, like the ones Sean had worn, only black.

The pants, hose as Sean had called them, were way too long, loose in the thighs, but snug in the ass. The tunic fell to my knees. The arms dangled inches past my fingertips, and the chest stretched so wide, it was like wearing a sleeping bag. I rolled the arms and legs to keep from tripping and made my way back to the bed.

Now what? I tried to think of something productive, but my thoughts kept creeping to the bad place—to Granda alone and worried, to Sean and his death, to me and my uncertain future. A fresh set of tears filled my eyes.

The door swung open. Sadness turned to instant fear. I screamed bloody murder. And so did the boy...

Boots pounded outside the door. "Donald!" a voice shouted. Two more people burst into the room—Mairi and the dark-haired man. They stopped short at the sight of me, and my scream choked off at the sight of them, as did Donald's. We stared at each other in a stunned silence.

"It's a miracle!" Mairi made the sign of the cross.

The dark-haired man's brow furrowed. "You're wearin' my clothes."

And I burst into tears. Again.

Never in my life had I been such a weepy thing, but my emotions were so beyond my control at this point, I didn't try to fight them.

This, apparently, made the man extremely uncomfortable. He shifted from foot to foot, and his voice came out stiff. "It's fine. The clothes arenae a problem. Ye can have 'em. Just—just stop."

Mairi shot him a scathing look and put her arms around me. "Hush, lass. You're safe now." With a gnarled thumb, she brushed my cheek dry of tears. "Where can we find your kin? We'll bring 'em to ye right off. They must be fuddled with worry."

She waited for my answer, but my jaw just sort of fell open and out came an anguished creak.

"It's fine." She gave an empathetic nod. "I understand."

"Understand what?" Donald looked back and forth between Mairi and the dark-haired man.

"She's no kin to speak of." The dark-haired man spoke in a hushed tone, but it carried, nonetheless. His face went taut, and he lumbered closer. "Listen." He directed his gaze toward the vicinity of my feet. Silky, black hair fell past his shoulders onto his chest. "We'll, uh, see ye safe, aye. Mairi'll get ye to a nunnery or a—"

"Rest!" Mairi shoved the dark-haired man toward the door. "The lass needs rest. Out with ye. Out."

The man's brow knit in suspicion, but he didn't argue. Following him out the door, Donald flashed me a final grin.

She turned to me. "I'll bring ye food, aye?"

I nodded, no longer crying, but still unable to speak.

She slipped out the door. Shaking and confused and relieved all at once, I clutched the quilt to my chest. A few minutes later, voices carried to my room from downstairs, muffled at first, but growing louder and clearer with every passing second—Mairi and the dark-haired man.

"Now listen to me, laddie." Her voice ricocheted through the floorboards.

"She's not stayin'." The man's bark matched Mairi's in its ferocity.

I squeezed my eyes closed, not sure what scared me more—the thought of being put out on the street or the violence that could come of living with an angry man.

# Chapter Eight

I lay on my belly, ear to a gap in the floorboards, as I listened to two strangers fight over the fate of my future.

"God's delivered us a gift in that girl." Mairi's conviction was absolute.

"He's delivered us a pain in the arse." By the sound of footsteps, the man began to pace. "All that cryin' and moanin' and screamin' all the night. I canna take it, Mairi. She has to go."

Oh, *he* couldn't take it? My hands clenched into fists, and it took all my self-control to not pound them against the floor. Fuck him. Maybe he should try getting shot with an arrow and brutally attacked. I'm sure he'd be perfectly fucking stoic.

Crack. The unmistakable sound of a heavy-handed smack. "That's for bein' uncharitable." Another smack. "And that's for your blasphemy."

Oh, shit! Take that, asshole! There was a moment's pause, in which I imagined him rubbing his face and holding back tears, but that was pure fantasy on my end.

"Have ye lost your ever-lovin' mind?" Disbelief peppered his words.

She remained undeterred. "God's answered my prayers, boy. I'll not have ye—"

"Your prayers?" Incredulity sharpened his tone. "What've ye been prayin' for? Another mouth to feed?"

"I've been prayin' for help! Look at these hands. Ye think it's easy for me, liftin' and shovelin' and sewin' all the day? I'm old, Henry." Her voice softened. "I'm not goin' to be around forever."

The silence that followed was thick with emotion, and when he spoke once more, his tone was gentle. "Listen, if ye need a servin' girl, I'll get ye one. Just not—"

"So we're in agreement." Her voice snapped back to its business-like tone. "I'm thinkin' two pence a week and a new shift if she makes it to year's end. Or mayhap she should have the shift right off—"

A deep growl rumbled from the man's throat. "Mairi..."

"She'll be needin' clothes, lad." A smile tinged her voice. "Unless ye like seein' her walk about in your hose."

He scoffed. "I dinna *like* seein' her walk about at all. Ye want a servin' girl, fine, but it'll be a lass o' my choosin', not yours.

"I'll take the lass God sent me, thank ye verra much." Her words came clipped with an air of finality to them.

"God didna send her to ye, and ye dinna want a servin' girl any more than ye did when I offered two years ago." An intense pause followed his words. "I ken what you're up to, Mairi, and I'll not be a party to your schemin'."

"Why, lad," she said in a silky voice, "if I didna ken any better, I'd say the lass has ye afeard."

"Aye, afeard for my sanity, ye meddlesome ol' fussbudget. Ye canna keep throwin' lassies in front o' me and think I'll change my mind. It didna work when ye invited the cobbler's daughter for supper eight Sundays straight. Nor when ye had the priest threatin' me with hellfire. And it willna work now. I'm happy with Coira, and no amount o' your connivin' will change that."

Oh, hell. This was all some elaborate matchmaking scheme? No wonder he was pissed. What if I explained I had no intention of marrying him or anybody else? Would he listen? Would I even get the chance?

"You're right, lad." Mairi's voice deflated.

No! Fuck. She couldn't give up. He might be a dick, and I might not want to be used like some pawn in the medieval dating game, but, dammit, I needed a place to live.

The beginning of some retort worked its way out of his throat. Then her words seemed to register, and he faltered, recovering with a sputtered, "Damn right, I am."

"What happens betwixt ye and Coira isna for me to judge." My heart raced at her sudden contrition.

"Nay. It isna." The man's wary tone suggested he was equally disconcerted, though I doubted for the same reason.

Mairi didn't miss a beat. "And your love for her is so strong, no amount o' temptation could lead ye astray."

"Aye...uh...well, that's not precisely what I..." He trailed off, seemingly unsure how to finish.

"Nay, nay, I see it now. I've been a fool." The sound of spoon scraping against a kettle punctuated her words. "Ye have an iron will, and this girl, nor any other, will soften it."

"Aye." His voice sounded so wary, it almost came out a question.

"Good. Then ye've naught to fear by extendin' a Christian hand to a lass in need. I'm sure ye'll barely notice her presence, focused as ye are on Coira."

Oh, she was good. Like Johnnie Cochran with the glove good. Thank God she was on my side.

"You're twistin' my words, old woman. I've already told ye—"

"It's a good thing too, lad. Imagine what Coira might hear if I told Winnie MacSheah ye forced me to send perfectly good help away because ye couldna control the lust in your heart. Ye ken how ol' Winnie likes to talk."

"Ye wouldna..." His voice tinged with horror.

"I would."

Forget Johnnie Cochran, she was John fucking Gotti. Christ, she must really hate this Coira chick if she was willing to blackmail her own nephew.

"But...but—we dinna even ken if she's qualified." His voice rose an octave. "She's got no references. She's—"

"She'll be fine, lad. You're gettin' yourself all flummoxed o'er what-ifs and mayhaps."

He didn't respond.

"Look, if she canna handle the work, I'll send her off myself. Ye have my word."

He grumbled something, and a few seconds later, the door slammed closed. Unless I was mistaken, that door slam meant he had gone off to sulk...which meant Mairi had won...which meant I had a home. So why did that thought fill me with dread?

~ * ~

A half hour or so later, Donald entered my room with a food tray. "Mairi says to tell ye she's sorry about the delay. Somethin' about it takin' awhile for the ass to take the bit." His nose wrinkled. "Whatever that means. We dinna even have a donkey." He placed the tray on a bedside table.

I gave him a weak smile, the most I could manage after spending the last half hour imagining worst-case scenarios about what life here would be like. The most insane of which involved Henry murdering me in my sleep and telling Mairi I had run off to join the circus. Granted, this didn't seem particularly likely, but I didn't know. He didn't have any problem killing the bandit, maybe he considered unwanted squatters' fair game.

Still, this kid had nothing to do with my anxiety, and he deserved to be treated with respect. So, I followed the smile with a satisfactorily polite, "Thank you."

I expected a nod or maybe a "you're welcome." Instead, he burst into giggles and plopped down next to me. A giant grin spread across his face. "Say it again."

"Thanks?"

He laughed and clapped his hands. "Ye've a braw way o' speakin', ye ken that! From where do ye hail? The Isles? Castile? It canna be France. They all sound like they've got sawdust up their noses."

"I uh..." Fuck. I wasn't prepared for this. What the hell was I supposed to tell people? Some place across the ocean none of you realize exists? "Um...y-you know...here and there." My voice came out all stiff and stuttering.

His eyes went wide. "Are ye a gypsy then?"

"What? No." I shook my head. "And you shouldn't call them gypsies. They're Romani."

His lips pursed in a quizzical expression. "I dinna think they're like the fair folk. Ye can call 'em by name."

"No, that is their..." I squeezed my eyes closed. "Never mind." Priorities, Fiona. Christ.

I took a deep breath, not sure what I should say next. There was a lot I needed to know, but I wasn't sure what half of it was. I finally settled on, "You're Donald, right?"

He nodded.

"I'm Fiona."

His grin widened, and the slight vibration of his chest told me he was stifling the urge to laugh. From anyone else, this would have irritated the hell out of me, but there was something soothing about this kid with his big, old, puppy dog grin. He seemed so genuinely happy, being around him made it easy to forget how very unhappy I currently was.

"So, you're Donald. The old lady is Mairi." I ticked off each name with a finger. "And the dark-haired man...?"

His forehead wrinkled. "Who? Hal?"

I damn near laughed. "Hal?" Hal sounded like the name of some guy who worked at a bowling alley and thought Applebee's was fine dining. Not a medieval archer with ten yards of chest and a dysfunctional relationship with his overbearing aunt.

"Well, Henry to most." He grinned in a proud sort of way. "I'm the only one who gets to call him Hal."

"And he's good to you?" It dawned on me that I didn't have the slightest clue what counted as "good" here. "I mean he doesn't beat you or—"

He laughed. "Hal? Nay. I've been his apprentice two years now, and he's never raised a hand to me. Now Mairi on the other hand..."

As if he had summoned her by name, she swung open the door. Her eyes narrowed. "What in the name of St. Lawrence do ye think you're doin'?"

Donald's face blanched. "Mairi, I was just—"

She put a hand to her hip. "Thought ye'd hide in here while there's work to be done?"

"Nay. I—"

She pointed a gnarled finger toward the door. "Out!"

Donald rushed toward the exit, looking awkward as hell because he kept trying to cover his ass like he feared he might get a swat. Mairi shut the door behind him, and for a second, I could have sworn an amused smirk crossed her face. When she turned back to me, though, her expression was all business.

She held a basket in her arms, filled to the brim with cloth and spools of thread, which she carried over to me. Her gaze drifted to the tray of uneaten food. "Canna get it down?"

"No," I said. "I haven't tried yet."

"Well, get on with it, lass. We've not much time." She shoved the basket into my arms. "Ye need to mend these by supper time."

I goggled. I'd never so much as sewn a button but admitting that felt dangerous. Mairi was all that stood between me and the streets, and if I couldn't prove myself useful, she might not think I was worth the fight.

"Ye'll be eatin' supper downstairs with the rest of us tonight." Her eyes raked over the four-poster bed. "And ye'll have to sleep with me and Donald from now on."

I nodded, even though I'd rather peel off my own skin than leave the safety of this room.

She studied my face. "Ye heard me and Henry row earlier."

It wasn't a question, and I didn't deny it.

A withering sigh escaped her lips. "Dinna let what ye heard sour your opinion o' the lad. He's a good man, but he'd rather walk barefoot through a patch o' brambles than risk his soles gettin' soft in a pair o' shoes, if ye ken what I'm sayin'."

I didn't have the slightest clue what she was saying, but I nodded, nonetheless.

"Anyhow, ye'll be fine so long as ye put in the work and save the tears for your bed. Too much emotion, and he gets..." Tapping her lip, she paused as if searching for the right word. "...uncomfortable."

I snorted. "Yeah, I gathered."

For some reason, that made her smile. She patted my hand. "Well then, I'll leave ye to it." She headed toward the door and paused just long enough to look back. "Make me proud, lass."

I eyed the basket of mending. So much for having a roof over my head, because "proud" wasn't going to happen. It'd be a miracle if I could manage "satisfactory." Sighing, I pulled the tray of food into my lap. Might as well eat while I could. It might just be my last meal.

# Chapter Nine

I looked from the needle in my left hand to the thread in my right. "All right, you little bitch. This time you're going through."

I narrowed my eyes, licked my lips, and aimed for the eye of the needle.

Motherfucker.

Why? Why wouldn't the stupid fucking thread go through the stupid fucking hole? Twenty times I had attempted to thread the fucker, and every single time it bounced right off. Was this some kind of trick needle? Like those birthday candles that never go out? Maybe Mairi was downstairs, laughing her ass off, and any minute now she'd come explain this was all some elaborate joke.

Or maybe I was just an idiot.

That was me. Fiona Buchanan—idiot extraordinaire. Too stupid to realize her best friend was lying to her, too stupid to avoid getting thrown in a time portal, too stupid to hide from a bandit, and too stupid to thread a stupid fucking needle. Fuck.

I stabbed the needle with the thread. God, what I wouldn't give to stab that bandit instead. I'd push it through, nice and slow. Death had been too good for him. If there were any justice in this world, he'd be tied to a chair, and I'd be using this needle to— Holy shit! The needle! The thread had gone through!

This was very exciting, for all of five seconds. Then I remembered I had to actually do the sewing, and that sobered me right up. Dammit. What I wouldn't give for five minutes' access to YouTube. One video tutorial, and this wouldn't be a problem. It was galling. How did these people live without instant access to information?

I snatched a pair of hose off the stack and held them before me. A large gash ran across the left knee, but the rip was fairly straight and only a little frayed. Okay, that didn't seem so bad. I could probably do this. I just had to stick the needle through and pull, right?

I gave it a go, and yeah, the needle went through, and after a while, the rip closed, but it didn't look right. The stitches were all over the place. Some were large, others small. Some were so close the thread got all bunched and thick, others so far apart I wasn't sure if it would hold. And for some reason, I could see the stitches. When Gran hemmed my jeans, the thread never stood out all obvious. It just sort of disappeared into the fabric, but mine were front and center. Maybe because she had a sewing machine, and I stitched by hand. I was going to go ahead and go with that, because otherwise I was totally screwed, and I didn't have it in me to cope with that at the moment.

I moved on to the next item—a large tunic with a small burn on the right arm. Judging by its size, it had to be Henry's. I scowled at it. Just thinking about that asshole made my teeth grind. I didn't know what his deal was. Maybe he was one of those guys who got off on being a jerk. Mairi said he wasn't that bad, and Donald seemed to like him, but after what I'd heard today, I couldn't see why.

I finished Henry's tunic and retrieved the next shirt.

I mean, okay, I guess he wasn't *all* bad. He had saved me, and he hadn't kicked me out...yet. He sure was a surly son of a bitch, though. All that whining and moaning because I dared to cry. If it made him uncomfortable, he should have turned his ass around and walked out the door. Nobody asked him to stand there and gawk. In fact, I would have preferred it if he'd left. The thought of that irritable bastard watching me break down during the worst moment of my life made me want to gouge out my own eyeballs.

I tied off a knot and moved on to the last item, a white shift that probably belonged to Mairi.

Then again, could I blame him for what he thought? He didn't know me. He had only ever seen me at my worst. Between that and the fact he probably figured I'd try to seduce him the first chance I got, I could hardly blame him for not wanting me here. Hell, *I* didn't want me here. I just didn't have any better options.

I put the finished shift back in the basket. Maybe I should give him a chance. If I didn't want him to judge me for my ten minutes of tears, I shouldn't judge him for the ten minutes of conversation I overheard. We could make this work. We could—

The door creaked open. "Mairi, I'm finished," I called, "but I'm not sure I did the stitch..." My voice trailed off as Henry, not Mairi, entered the room.

It was the first time I had seen him while fully awake and without tears clouding my eyes. How had I not noticed how massive he was? He had biceps like boulders, and a chest that nearly spanned the width of the door. Nervous energy ran through me. This was my chance to make peace. I could thank him for saving me. I could explain I had no intentions of colluding with Mairi. I could...smack that grimace off his face.

What the hell? Why was he glowering? He was looking at me the way I looked at a sink full of dirty dishes, and I was just not here for that nonsense, no matter what I'd just resolved.

His jaw clenched, emphasizing the squareness of it and the light dusting of his five o'clock shadow. If his lips weren't squashed into such an ugly scowl, I might have found him attractive.

"I'm to help ye down the stairs." A muscle in his jaw ticked.

I raised an eyebrow. "What?"

I had heard him. I just wasn't used to offers of help being spit out like curse words.

He took a deep breath as if hunting for some inner reserve of patience. "Ye have an injured leg. I'm the only one with the strength to carry ye. So the chore has fallen to me."

The *chore*? This asshole. I gritted my teeth. "I don't need your help."

62

This was, of course, bullshit. My leg still didn't bend right, and I struggled just walking across the room, but I'd rather scooch down the steps on my ass than give him the satisfaction of complaining.

His eyes widened in surprise, before they narrowed, and scowl lines formed trenches around his mouth. Apparently, he hadn't expected me to deny his help. But a few seconds later, his face softened, and his eyes lit with what I thought might be pleasure. A vindictive smile spread across his face. I gulped.

He leaned against the wall and crossed his arms. "Go on then. Do it yourself."

This was probably the moment where I should have sucked up my pride and admitted I needed help. But if I had done that, well, I just wouldn't be a Buchanan, would I? With a force of will that would have made Granda proud, I rose from the bed, kept my head held high, and hobbled toward the door.

"Forgettin' something, aren't ye?" He nodded toward the basket on the bed.

I gritted my teeth. Such a dick, this guy, but I'd be damned if I let him see even an ounce of irritation. I flashed a brilliant smile and limped back to the bed. Nope, not bothered at all. Never mind the ache in my leg had worked its way to my hip. Or that carrying the basket would make it harder to balance. I was going to keep this fucking smile on my face if it killed me.

After a long and tedious back and forth, I finally made it to the doorway, basket in hand. I paused at the top step. The stairs were steep and narrow with one side butted against the wall and the other open without so much as a rail or rope to keep me from plummeting to my death. This was dumb. This was really dumb.

"Somethin' amiss?" I had never heard his voice so bubbly.

I forced a grin. "Not at all." Shifting my weight to my good leg, I took a deep breath, and swung my bad leg forward.

"You're not seriously goin' to—" He didn't get the chance to finish.

My bad leg landed on the step beneath me. I shifted my weight, and down I went. My stomach did a flip. The stairs rushed toward me. "Motherfucker!"

Before my face smashed into the stairs, a hand plucked me from midair. A second later, I was stable and back on the landing.

"Are ye mad?" His voice boomed with such fury, it sent a rat scurrying with fear across the rafters. Heart racing, my hands quivered around the basket I still somehow held. I had almost died...again. And he had saved me...again. It took all my effort not to toss the basket down the stairs, fling my arms around him, and throw myself into those life-saving arms.

"Thank you." My breathing was still hard and shallow, but I managed the words.

He cocked his head. "What was that ye said?"

"Thank you," I repeated.

A slow grin spread across his face. "Nay, afore that."

"Huh? I didn't—" I groaned. I had just shouted "motherfucker" at the top of my lungs. Great. That was probably enough to get a bitch stoned to death in this backwater. I groped for some sort of explanation. "Um, mother lover." I stared at my feet. "I was...uh...calling out for the Virgin Mary."

I glanced at his face to see if he was buying any of it. Oh hell, he looked just like Granda whenever his horse won at the track. This wasn't good.

Cheering with glee, he swooped me into his arms, and ran me down the stairs, dropping me off at the dinner table next to a grinning Donald. "Mairi, did ye hear what your gift from God just shouted?"

"I heard her!" Donald giggled. His eyes sparkled. "Where'd ye learn to curse like—"

Mairi put a hand on Donald's shoulder, and his words choked off. His face twisted in pain as her talon-like nails dug into his shoulder. "Be a good lad and go wash up." He yelped and scrambled across the room to where a pitcher and basin sat on a shelf.

She turned to Henry, her face blank and voice innocent. "I didna hear a thing." She tapped her left ear. "One o' the failings o' old age. My ears arena what they once were."

His smile flattened to a thin line. "Ye didna hear her shoutin' from thirty paces away, but the sound o' my footsteps wakes ye from a dead sleep?"

She shrugged. "The body is a mystery." She shot me a dangerous look that said in no uncertain terms she had heard exactly what I said, and I'd be dealt with later.

I flushed. I had been reckless, careless, and proud. My worst traits on full display at a time when I needed to be more careful than ever. And after all Mairi had done for me...I was an asshole. I needed to do better.

She ladled stew onto pieces of dark brown bread, and when Donald returned from his wash, he passed them out. They didn't bother with plates, and it took all my self-control not to grimace when he set the food directly on the table. The old, weathered tabletop had to be teeming with bacteria. Wouldn't that be my luck—I survive an arrow wound, only to die from salmonella.

Foodborne illness potential aside, the food looked pretty good. It reminded me of this open-faced sandwich I used to get at Lou's Diner, this great little Elvis-themed restaurant down the road from the Club. And it smelled good—like garlic and onion and something unidentifiable, but comfortingly savory.

"Oh, ye've finished already!" Mairi eyed the mending basket I had set on the floor. "Such swift work!" She said this in a voice of perfect surprise, as if she hadn't just ordered me to have it finished by dinner. "It would have taken me two days to mend all that." She narrowed her gaze on Henry. "Ye'll be pleased to ken with the lass helpin', I was able to stop by the market and get a bit o' pork for the stew, just like ye like."

He grunted. Apparently, no amount of pork would make up for Mairi ignoring my cursing.

Donald, however, seemed more than pleased. A lopsided grin spread across his face. "Smells good, Mairi!" The basket between us caught his attention, and he swiped a pair of hose off the top. "I've been lookin' for those!" Giving them a shake, he held them out to examine. Air hissed audibly on a sucked in breath, and his smile morphed into slack-jawed shock. "Oh..." He dropped the hose into his lap. "Aye, uh, well...thank ye."

Henry snatched the pants from Donald and inspected them with a grin. "She sewed 'em on the outside!" Bursting into peals of laughter, he held them up for everyone to see. "Even *I* ken ye have to flip the fabric. And look!" He tugged the pants on either side of the patched hole, causing the stitches to gape. His laughter turned into a full out chortle. "Such a help, indeed, aye, Mairi?"

Face hot, I stared at my food as the sound of his laughter echoed in my ears. My hands shook. A knot formed in my stomach. Tears welled in my eyes. My nails dug into my palms. I would not cry. I would not cry. Fuck this asshole. I would not cry.

A peek at Mairi revealed she, at least, found no humor in the situation. Her lips were pressed so tight, they threatened to disappear. "Never mind that. Ye can hardly blame the lass for a bit o' befuddlement after what she's been through."

The challenge in her glare seemed to dare him to say another unkind word. To his credit, he was smart enough to keep his mouth closed, but the smug, self-satisfied look on his face said plenty.

A few moments of uncomfortable silence passed, and she cleared her throat. "Let's say grace."

She led us through a prayer I didn't recognize, and despite the fact I damn near vibrated with embarrassment-induced rage, I managed to force a choked amen out.

When the prayer ended, I didn't look up. I couldn't bear to meet anyone's eyes. One glance at Mairi, and I'd slip into a shame spiral. One glance at Henry, and I'd explode into a rage typhoon. So I stared at the table and tried to force deep breaths through my clenched teeth, hoping to God nobody spoke for the rest of the meal.

Determined to hold myself together, I picked up my sandwich. I bit off a big chunk and chewed. The meat was overcooked and the vegetables limp, but that didn't bother me. It was the bread I couldn't seem to choke down. It was like gnawing on cement. It took a full minute before it finally softened, and, even then, it just morphed into a paste-like substance that could have been used to mortar siege walls.

"Lass," she said in a tentative voice, "what are ye doing?"

I forced the paste down in a painful gulp and raised my eyes. All three of them stared at me with expressions of amazed horror. Donald held a piece of meat between his fingers, frozen halfway to his mouth. I looked from his hand to the half-empty piece of bread in front of him, and I realized my mistake. They hadn't forgotten plates; I'd just eaten the plate.

"I ken ye must be hungry." Her voice warbled with more concern than when I had an arrow sticking out of my leg. "But if ye must eat the trencher, at least give it time to soak up the gravy."

I wanted to dig a hole, crawl into it, and die. This was fucking mortifying. Worse, somehow, than the sewing debacle, because at least, I could sort of explain that. But what excuse could I give for basically munching on flatware?

Henry laughed, that same condescending, triumphant laugh. "When ye did all that prayin', Mairi, did ye ask God to send ye a jester? Cause if ye did—"

The hold on my self-control began to slip, my hands trembling under the table.

"Hold. Your. Tongue." Her words came clipped and furious. "You're flirtin' with blasphemy, and I'll not have it."

"Look at her." He sneered. "She doesna even ken how to eat, let alone stitch a simple hole. Give it up, Mairi. She's soft in the head. Take her to the nuns. They're the ones who deal in charity, not us."

Rising to her feet, she opened her mouth to shout, but the last thread tying my tongue to sanity snapped, and I beat her to it.

"I am not stupid!" I glared at Henry, my nails digging into my palms. "So what if I can't sew? Can you?" He fumbled for an answer but seemed too taken aback by my reaction to come up with one. "That's what I thought. I guess that makes you an idiot too."

He bristled. "Sewin' is women's work."

"What about non-women's work?" My teeth ground together. "Can you read? 'Cause guess what, I can."

He let out a barking laugh. "Please. Ye canna read."

Slamming a palm on the table, I leaned forward. "Yes, I can." A growl roughened my voice. "And I can write. And I can do math you've probably never seen. So, between the two of us, you tell me which one is soft in the head."

Donald's gaze bounced between us, and Mairi bit her lip.

Henry continued to laugh. "Do ye hear? The lies this lass—"

"H-e-n-r-y."

His words cut off, and the way his jaw flapped open was almost comical.

I flashed him my cockiest grin. "Well, I guess you know how to spell your own name, at least."

Silence fell over the table. Then Donald, damn near buzzing with anticipation, leaned at the edge of his seat. "Is that how ye spell it?"

Henry grimaced. He squeezed his eyes closed and dropped his head into his palms. His voice came out pained and disbelieving. "Aye. 'Tis."

Donald looked from Henry to me, then back at Henry, and he burst out laughing. Mairi turned her sharp eyes on Donald, and for a second, I thought she might scold him, but she chuckled too. The sound of their hilarity sucked the tension from the room, and, after a few seconds, I couldn't help but join in.

To my surprise, Henry laughed too, and for a moment, we were like a table of old friends instead of reluctant housemates who had just been moments away from murdering each other. It was a surreal moment, and when it came to an end, we all just sort of stared, unsure what came next.

Taking a deep breath, I raised my eyes to Henry's, and forced myself to say the two hardest words in the English language. "I'm sorry."

His lips turned up at the corners, and a blush crept over his cheeks. "I suppose I wasna bein' particularly kind myself..."

"I get it," I said. "Look, I know you didn't ask for me to be here, and I'm sorry for the trouble it's caused you. But I want you to know I'm not looking for a permanent home, or a husband, or anything. I just need a place to stay until I figure out my next steps." I fought to keep my voice even. "If you could please help me for a little while, I promise I'll make myself useful. I'm a hard worker, and I learn fast. I promise I'll do better than..." I glanced at the basket. "Than that."

He smirked, but this time it lacked his previous derision. I waited for his answer, not sure if I had said enough, but also not sure what else to say.

"Come on, Hal, let her stay," said Donald.

Mairi raised her hand in pledge. "I promise I willna meddle."

Henry rolled his eyes and chuckled. "Two months. It's the best I can do. Any longer and..." He grimaced. "Well, things'll get...problematic."

I nodded. "Understood."

He gave the tiniest of nods back, and after that, we ate our food in contemplative silence.

Two months. Could I do it? Could I figure out how to survive by then? I looked at my empty trencher. Well, I had already learned lesson number one—don't eat the plate. I smiled to myself. How hard could the rest be?

# Chapter Ten

I lurked in the shadows, broom in hand, ready to strike. My prey—a fat, gray, sociopathic rat—stood just feet away, gnawing on a bit of bread. The cocky bastard. Well, I hoped he enjoyed those crumbs, because they were about to cost him his life.

For weeks, that furry little fucker had been messing with me. Twice now he had skittered across my feet in the dead of night. The second time, he had paused and stared me dead in the eye, just to let me know he was doing it on purpose. Even when he was out of sight, he made sure I knew he wasn't gone, chittering from the rafters, threatening to dive-bomb my head the moment I fell asleep. Well, no more. Tonight, I would sleep without fear.

Tightening my grip, I took a deep breath, and slammed the broom down. "Got ya!" I shouted.

I lifted the bristles, and the rat stared at me, dazed. Giving itself a shake, it scampered off, which, for some reason, startled the shit out of me. I screamed and slammed the broom down again and again until the broom snapped, and the rat lay dead.

Mairi hustled over at the commotion. "What's all that shriekin' about?" Her eyes landed on the broom, and her face contorted with fury. "What have ye done to my besom?"

"It's not my fault!" I pointed at the bread next to the dead rat. "Blame whoever keeps leaving food all over the house."

She bristled. "So ye think to blame *me*?"

I gaped. "*You're* doing this...? On purpose?"

She put her hands on her hips, and her nostrils flared. "In this house we respect the Fair Folk."

70

My mouth fell open. Fairies. We were living with vermin because she wanted to feed the fucking fairies. I took a deep breath and forced down my irritation. "It's attracting rats."

Mairi scowled. "Better than invitin' the ire o' malevolent sprites."

I couldn't believe this. In every other regard, she was even more of a neat freak than me. "They spread plague, Mairi! You can't think this is—"

Before I got the chance to say more, she popped me in the mouth. "Dinna be reducin' God's holy wrath to the likes o' rats." She turned on her heels and huffed out the door.

I rubbed my cheek. Great. That had gone just about as well as the time I tried to convince her not to store food in a lead-glazed urn she kept prized on a shelf. This morning's sewing lesson was about to be *real* fun.

I glared at the rat. "This is all your fault."

I snagged a couple ales and followed Mairi out the door. We sat in our usual spot on the grass, halfway between the house and the smithy. The clang of hammers on steel punctuated the chatter of clucking hens, and the wind swirled about, carrying with it the mingled scents of herbs, cow shit, and garden roses.

Mairi thrust my practice cloth and a threaded needle at me. "Ye ken what to do."

Sure, I *knew* what to do. That didn't change the fact I had the fine-motor skills of a crayon-clutching toddler. Still, I had no choice but to try, so I set to work. This time I thought I was doing pretty good. I made it three whole stitches before I earned my first hand smack.

"Too big."

I undid the offending stitch and tried again.

Smack. "Not straight."

I rubbed my hand. That one stung. Two more stitches. Two more smacks. I gritted my teeth. The skin on my hand flamed red. Any more of this, and I'd end up with a bruise. I barely had the needle in position for the next attempt when her hand came flying.

This time, though, I caught it. "That isn't helping."

She pursed her lips. "Tell me, then, shall I smother your fingers in kisses? Will they awe me with unforeseen nimbleness and fortitude?"

"I don't know, but *this* isn't working." I shook my throbbing hand.

This sewing shit was going to kill me. Possibly, literally. Mairi'd promised to help me find work as a servant once my time here ended, but who would want me if I couldn't handle even the most basic tasks?

I stared at the measly three stitches she hadn't smacked out of existence. If I was going to learn, I needed to do it without her hovering over me. "What if I helped with a different chore now and practiced sewing on my own at night? I'm not much help to you doing this."

She tapped her lip with a bony finger. A doubtful line furrowed her brow.

"What about ale?" I raised my cup. "I know a little about brewing—beer, not ale, but I could—" I bit off my words. "What?"

She scowled. "First off, I dinna ken what foreign nonsense this beer o' yours is, but I'm not about to risk my grains for it. And second, if I canna trust ye with a bit o' thread, I certainly canna trust ye with the family's ale."

"Fine." I scanned the yard. "How about gardening? Or cleaning?"

Mairi looked down her nose at me. "With that leg o' yours?"

"It's getting better." Which was true, even if I still walked with a limp. I had taken to doing stretches and strength training any time I found a spare minute or two, and I was proud of the progress I'd made. Although, if I were being honest, manual labor might still be a little more than I could handle.

"What about Henry?" Desperation tightened my throat. "Does he have account books that need updated? Receipts that need filed? Inventory that needs tallied?"

72

Mairi paused to consider. The creases on her forehead softened, and she tilted her head. Without a word, she rose and headed toward the smithy.

I also got to my feet, but not to follow. I just wanted to get a few minutes exercise in before she returned. Ten seconds into a deep squat, my muscles vibrated with fatigue.

I was doing my damnedest not to lose form when Henry's scandalized voice rang out behind me. "What do ye think you're doin'?"

Mairi pinched the bridge of her nose and raised her eyes to the heavens. "St. Bonaventure, help me. If ye must relieve yourself, go behind the tree."

"What! I wasn't going to the bath—" Nope. No bathrooms here. I readjusted. "I wasn't relieving myself. I was exercising." Blank stares. "Um...training my leg to be stronger."

Neither appeared convinced, so I hopped aside and pointed to the turd-free plot of grass. Relief washed over both their faces, and I stifled the urge to laugh.

I nodded to the basket in Henry's hand. "What's that?" Two pairs of pliers, not all that different from Granda's, sat atop thousands of metal rings.

Mairi grinned. "The lad's goin' to teach ye to chain mail."

I wrinkled my nose. "That doesn't seem like a—" She flounced off, not bothering to let me finish. "—good use of time."

I eyed him and grimaced at the muscle ticking in his jaw. I had no doubt he'd rather chew those rings than teach me to make mail from them. Mairi must've coerced him into this. But why? It made no sense. Unless... Son of a bitch. This was all part of her crazy matchmaking scheme. No wonder he was grinding his teeth so hard, I could hear them squeak.

I stared at my feet. "Sorry about this."

He scowled. "Aye, I'm sure ye are."

I bit the inside of my cheek. Between getting no sleep because of the rat, and Mairi being pissed at me, I was in no mood for his shit. "What's that supposed to mean?"

"Forget it." He sat in the grass next to the basket. "Let's get on with it so ye can quit wastin' my time."

I dropped to my knees next to him. "How is me learning to do *your* work wasting time?"

"Because I'll have to sit here for the next hour tryin' to teach ye somethin' ye'll not be able to do." His words came sharp and overly enunciated, as if he were speaking to a child.

I huffed. "You don't know that."

He rolled his eyes. "I'd say I have a fair idea."

Snatching one of the pliers, I met his eyes. One of these days this dude was going to stop underestimating me. "Show me."

"Fine." He held up one of the rings in demonstration. "Ye see the gap at the top? All ye have to do is close it." Placing the pliers on either side of the ring, he squeezed until the gap closed.

"That's it?" He had to be joking. "*That's* the impossible task I'll never be able to figure out?"

Smirking, he tossed me a ring. "See for yourself."

I tried to mimic him, but the wire was thick and didn't want to budge. I bore down on it with all my force, and the ends shot past each other, so it looked like a stubby wreath with a bow.

I refused to meet his eyes, knowing the smug look I'd find on his face. Instead, I picked up another ring and tried again. This time, I focused my attention and increased the pressure gradually until the wire just started to budge. Holding it at that force, the pieces came together in a gentle kiss of ends. It was perfect! I held it up, cocky as all hell. "Don't tell me that was the hard part."

His brow furrowed, and he gawked at me like he had just figured out I was really Kaiser Soze. "Who are ye?"

"Umm, I have no idea how to answer that."

He cocked his head. "Ye've clearly ne'er worked a day in your life, seein' as ye dinna ken how to do the simplest tasks. Ye must've had tutors to ken your letters and numbers so well. So how in the bloody hell does a pampered princess like ye have the hand strength to close thick gauge wire?"

I wrung my hands, not sure what to say. I had never thought of them as particularly strong, but I supposed years of twisting off bottle caps and pitching softballs had built up the muscles. Of course, I couldn't tell him that. So I did the only thing I could do—avoided the question.

I nabbed another ring. "This is it? I just need to close all the rings?"

"Nay." He scooped up four already closed rings and slid them onto an open ring like keys on a chain. After closing the final ring, he tossed the grouping into a pile. "Ye'll do that with e'ry five."

"Got it."

He stared.

I made a shooing motion. "You can go now. No need to waste any more of your time."

He didn't budge. "Answer my question. Who are ye? What of your people?"

My people... Grief swirled instantly at his words. I'd done my damnedest over the last week not to think of Granda. I couldn't cope with the idea of him all alone, worried, with no one to take care of him, and here this dude was poking my wounds with a stick.

I dropped my gaze. "I don't want to talk about it."

"Why not?" Challenge tinged his voice.

"Because it's none of your business!" Christ, take the hint, asshole.

He sucked in a deep breath, his ribcage expanding to make his already substantial chest appear even bigger. "You're livin' at my house. I'd say I have a right to—"

"What do you want to hear?" My voice cracked like a snapping belt. "That my family's as good as dead? That my best friend betrayed me? That I have no chance of ever going home?"

Tears welled, and I dug my nails into my palms to keep them from falling.

Henry took an audible breath. "I'm sorry," he said, his voice soft and earnest. "I shouldna have pried." He put a hand on mine. "If it helps any, I do understand."

I raised my eyes to his. Remembered pain shone in his gaze, and I swallowed. Maybe he did understand. Some of it, at least. Hell, even *I* didn't understand all of it. Every time I thought about what happened, my thoughts got all jumbled and grief took hold. Especially when it came to Sean.

I didn't know who he was anymore. I could not wrap my head around the kind, faithful best friend I had known my entire life also being the guy who was okay with murder and lied without compunction. Every moment between us was suspect now, and I wondered what else he had lied about. Like the portal. Did it not work both ways, or had he just told me that to keep me from leaving?

Hope and desperation hit me so hard at the thought, every muscle in my core contracted. The portal might be out there. There was a real possibility Sean had lied about time travel being a one-way trip. For all I knew, it was just waiting to return me to my world of hot showers and electric lights. To Granda. My throat tightened. I had to find out, had to...go back to the woods.

A nauseous wave of terror worked through my belly as I remembered my flight through the trees, the sheer panic of knowing any second, I might die, the pain of what followed. How could I face that again? It was no good telling myself the chances of getting assaulted twice in the same place were small, because that other bandit, the one who had killed Sean, was still out there. I clutched a link of chain in my hand, shaking and nauseated.

"Fiona..." I started at Henry's voice. When I met his eyes, his expression was so full of pity, I knew he had read the emotions right off my face.

He cast his hazel eyes downward. "I want ye to ken, ye dinna have to be afeard. So long as you're here, you're under my protection. So ye can...rest easy."

I blinked. Under his protection? The protection of the guy who looked like he could wrestle a full-sized grizzly with his ripped ass blacksmith's arms and wide barrel chest. The protection of the guy who had already taken down a bandit. The protection of the guy who was so damn irritated by me being here going home would be the kindest repayment I could give him. Maybe I didn't have to be brave all by myself. Fondness

76

replaced the enduring annoyance I typically held for Henry, and I promised myself I'd find a way to pay back his descendants if I made it back home.

I raised my eyes to his and held his gaze. "If you really mean that, help me."

He licked his lips and averted his gaze, instantly regretful.

"Please." I laced the word with every ounce of my desperation and need, and it drew his eyes to mine. "I need you to take me into the woods. There's a chance I might find a clue there that will lead to my family."

His forehead wrinkled. "I thought ye said—"

I cut him off. "It's a small chance, but I have to try. Will you help me?"

He seemed to think for a moment, opening his mouth like he meant to ask questions and closing it again without speaking a word. Finally, his jaw set. "Aye, I'll help ye, lass."

# Chapter Eleven

Mairi draped a cloak around my shoulders. "Have your wits about ye. I ken ye like to blather, but the forest is a place for vigilance." Yanking my cloak strings taut, she tied them in front of me. "And dinna let the lad stop by the tavern on the way back. He'll try to convince ye, but I want ye both straight home."

I tried to give her a reassuring smile, but it felt plastic. I was about to leave this place and maybe never come back, and I had no way to warn her. She was going to flip when she found out I disappeared. When she found out *how* I disappeared. She'd be convinced she'd shared her home with a witch for the last month. Or a demon. Or maybe a fairy. Oh God, let it be fairy. At least she had a healthy respect for them.

Henry sidled over from the ale barrels, carrying two water skins. He handed one to me and tied the other to his belt. "Ye ready?"

"Ready as I'll ever—" I paused and looked him over. "Where's your bow?"

His eyebrow arched. "In my room, last I checked."

I stared. He stared back. I damn near started tapping my foot out of impatience. "Well, are you going to go get it...?"

He laughed. I continued to stare. His eyes rounded. "You're serious?" Slack jawed, he gaped at me. "Look, lass, I dinna mind helpin' ye, but if ye think I'm about to risk gettin' sewn into a hide and havin' the hounds released on me..."

I put a hand to my chest. "Is that some kind of joke?"

His eyebrows shot up. "It's the king's woods! O' course it's not a jest."

I rubbed my temples. Of all the asinine bullshit. This dude went to the tavern every night strapped to the nines, and nobody so much as blinked. But the forest, a place full of wild animals and outlaws and who knew what else, was off limits?

I put my hands on my hips. "How are we supposed to protect ourselves?"

He waved off my concerns with a meaty hand. "Dinna fash about bandits. They're night creatures. Dinna like to strike in the daylight."

I wasn't at all convinced that was accurate. Last I'd checked, the sunrise hadn't stopped my attacker.

"As for wild beasts..." He shrugged. "Well, most of 'em'll sooner avoid ye than try and eat ye."

"Most?" My gaze fell to his sword. I had no doubt he could handle himself in a sword fight, but how much damage would a sword do against a pack of wolves or a big ass bear?

The skepticism must have been plain on my face because he half-laughed, half-scoffed. "I'll at least be able to buy ye enough time to flee, lass. Have some faith."

I nodded because what else could I do? Even if he were armed with nothing more than a slingshot, it wouldn't change anything. Granda was waiting for me, and if I had to face a horde of angry grizzlies to get to him, I would.

Taking a deep breath, I regarded Mairi. This was it. Perhaps the final goodbye. There were a thousand things I wanted to say to her, but few I could. So I just hugged her. "Thank you."

When I pulled away, her eyes raked over me. She put a hand to my cheek. "Be careful, lass."

Henry and I headed off, and as we walked through the town, an odd sense of detachment washed over me. No fear or hope or sadness. Just the distant thought I'd better take note of everything I saw along the way. Snapshots of this strange world to carry with me into my own, or into the beyond.

Some sights were familiar. Dirt roads and tall grass fields. The diminutive stone church we attended on Sundays with its cozy, attached cemetery. But as we continued, new sights appeared. Fields gave way to wattle and daub houses. Roads widened and grew congested. Rogue pigs and stray dogs barreled through groups of travelers who wore surprisingly vibrant and patterned clothes. We passed tipsy high-rise apartments with clothes lines strung between buildings, and filthy, polluted creeks littered with rotten food, entrails, and chamber pot leavings.

The only thing that stirred any emotion in me was the city wall. I froze at the sight of it. Heads on spikes peered down at us, blackened and rotting. Birds feasted on bits of flesh and pecked out eyeballs. I stared, entranced. Had they been there when I first passed through the gate? Would that be me in a few days, rotting away, dead in the woods while animals gnawed on my remains?

Henry pointed to one of the heads. "That one. Third post from the left."

I raised a questioning eyebrow.

"The bandit," he said. "That's who you're lookin' for isna it?"

My mouth parted, but no words came out. I studied the head. His face was unrecognizable. Birds and flies had made quick work of his eyes and nose and most of the flesh on one cheek. Only his ratty black hair and foul yellow teeth remained.

Seeing him there, reduced to a wig and a grin should have soothed me. Evidence he had gotten what he deserved. But the sight of so much death in the moments before we crossed into the woods seemed too much like foreshadowing.

Henry put a hand on my back and nudged me gently forward. "Come on."

My feet obeyed, but my mind fought me with every step. Vigilant. I had to be vigilant, just like Mairi'd said. I kept my hand on my knife, and my gaze darted from side to side as we walked. The brush to our right rustled, and I jumped back, pulling my knife.

"It's a wee hare, lass. Relax." Henry's voice filled with laughter.

"I know." I scowled at the rabbit as it darted into the trees. This was all Mairi's fault. If I was any more vigilant, I'd give myself a heart attack.

I told myself I had to chill and just keep pressing forward, but it wasn't long before something else darted across the path, and I screamed. Dropping to the ground, I threw my arms in front of my face, and waited for a blow that never came.

Gentle hands tugged my arms away from my face. Henry crouched before me. "It was just a deer." This time, there was no laughter in his voice.

I wished there had been, because then I could get mad. Instead, my eyes welled with tears as heat crept up my neck to my cheeks. Staring as though he thought he should say something, he helped me to my feet.

I held up a hand. "Don't. I know I'm being ridiculous. I just—"

He put a hand on my shoulder. "Nay. You're right to be afeard."

I knew he was trying to help, but that was probably the worst thing he could have said. I gulped, and my voice came out in a pathetic squeak. "I am?"

"Aye." He pointed to the left. "About a thousand paces that way, ye'll find some o' the most dangerous creatures on all the isle."

My voice cracked. "Bears?"

He shook his head. "Worse."

"Wolves?"

Again he shook his head. "Geese."

I stared. His face was dead serious, and despite my frazzled nerves, I couldn't help but laugh. "Did you just say geese?"

"Aye." He continued along the path. "They're the cleverest o' all the woodland creatures, and that makes them the most dangerous."

Sniffling, I dried my eyes. "Oh yeah?"

"Aye. Cleverer than the owl and the wolf and even the fox..." He paused for dramatic effect.

Having grown up with a master storyteller, I knew my cue. "How do you know?"

He pointed into the thicket. "That way lies a small loch where the geese like to swim. And that loch is the verra spot where a goose once outfoxed a fox."

Just like that, thoughts of bandits and bears disappeared, as I settled into the familiar comfort of stories.

Henry gestured toward the cloudless sky. "It was a braw day, same as today, and a fine, fat gander was sunning himself on the shore, when along came a fox. Well, as ye can imagine, the fox couldna believe his luck. Sunday dinner just sittin' there, waitin' to be eaten."

He skipped over a pile of horse dung. "So the fox crept over to the goose and pinned his wing to the earth. The gander awoke, scared for his verra life. He honked and hissed and tried to fly away, but the fox held fast. Resigned to his fate, the goose stopped fighting. 'Go ahead,' he said, 'do what ye will with me.'" Henry laughed. "The fox snickered. 'Tell me, goose, what would ye do right now if ye were me?' 'That's easy,' the gander replied. 'I'd fold my wings, shut my eyes, say grace, and eat ye.'"

His hands became animated as he told the story. "'Then that's what I'll do.' True to his word, the fox folded his paws, closed his eyes, and prayed. With the fox's hands clasped in prayer, the gander's wing came free. He flew off, honking with laughter all the way, and the poor wee fox was left with naught but prayers for his supper."

I chuckled. "Pretty good, but I've got you beat. My granda used to tell a story about a goose who—" My lungs deflated. A cold sweat broke out on my forehead, and my legs went numb. Ahead and to the left stood a field of purple flowers. I pointed across the field. "It's through there."

Memories crashed like breaking waves. Sean's voice sounded in my head, that monstrous scream as I ran in fear.

"How did ye get a wagon through—" He stopped and stared at me. "What is it?"

"His body! Oh god. Those heads. He'll be—No. No. I can't." I knew I wasn't making any sense, but I couldn't think straight.

For the first time, it dawned on me Sean's body would still be there, black and rotting, just like those heads. I couldn't do it. No matter what mistakes he'd made, he'd been my best friend, and the sight of him in a state of decomposition would fuck me up for life.

"He probably willna be there. Animals have likely—" I turned my wide, horrified eyes on him. He clamped his mouth closed. "I'll, uh, just go on ahead and check, aye."

A few minutes later Henry called my name.

A cold weight settled in my belly. Sean's body must be gone. Henry wouldn't call me otherwise. Animals must have—I leaned over and vomited.

"Fiona!" he shouted again.

I choked down the bile still rising in my throat. "I'm coming."

He waited at the edge of the field. "Look." He shuffled aside, and I gasped. Running forward, I dropped to my knees.

A rectangular mound of dirt surrounded by stones lay at the center of the clearing. A crude stick cross lashed together with twine jutted from one end. A grave. How? Why? I ran my hand over the loose dirt, overcome by the complexity of my emotions.

He suddenly became very interested in the field of purple flowers—an attempt to give me what privacy he could within the small clearing.

I leaned down. "I miss you," I whispered to the dirt. I squeezed my eyes closed. "And I'm so fucking mad at you. Do you know what happened to me? Do you know what you've done?" With a deep breath, I steadied myself. "I'm so confused, Sean. I don't know if I'm supposed to hate you or cry for you or piss on your grave. You were—" My voice cracked. "You were my best friend."

I burst into tears. All the hurt and betrayal and loss I had tried to ignore came bubbling out at once. Facing my emotions was excruciating, but also healing in a way I never would have expected. After a good, long cry and a fair bit of cussing, I felt a little bit lighter and a lot more ready to face what came next.

Wiping my face clean, I heaved a giant breath. I ran my hand over the grave dirt one last time. "If you're up there watching over me, now's your chance to make things right. Help me find the portal."

I rose, and Henry brought me a bouquet of heather from the field, which I placed on the grave.

"I'm sorry about your godbrother," he said, which was how I had described Sean to him when I'd given him my altered version of the events that led me here. "Some good's come from it, though, aye? If he's buried, some o' your kin must live!"

"Uh, yeah." I forced a smile, despite the nausea roiling in my belly at his words. Who had buried Sean? Surely not the bandit. Maybe some random passersby? I tried to shake off the niggling suspicion something wasn't right. What did it matter? He was buried, and I had a portal to find.

I drew my eyes from the grave. "They would have left something...my kin. Something to let me know where to find them. Will you help me search?"

"What am I lookin' for?"

I paused. Hell if I knew. The portal would probably be underground somewhere, but where? How would I find the entrance...if it even existed? Maybe I'd have to press a knot on a tree like in the *Princess Bride*. My very own Pit of Despair. Unfortunately, *despair* was the operative word. The more I thought about it, the more impossible it seemed I'd find anything. Even if they somehow managed to build an underground lair without the use of modern tools or anyone noticing, how would they power it? They would need lights and computers, not to mention the massive amount of current it would take to fuel that frame. Not easy in a time before the grid.

"I'm not sure. Look for something strange, something that doesn't belong in the woods. Probably on the ground or in a tree." I hooked a thumb toward the opposite side of the clearing. "You start over there. I'll start here."

I ran my hands along the trunk of the nearest birch. I tugged on branches, rattled leaves. Aside from a beetle and some peeling bark, I found nothing of interest, on that, or any of the next dozen trees.

"Fiona, come here!"

My heart did a rat-a-tat-tat. "You found something?" I dropped the pine branch in my hand and ran to Henry, who stood in the middle of the clearing near Sean's grave.

His gaze fell toward the ground. "Tracks."

Instantly, I deflated. Thousands of tracks probably ran through these woods. Hell, half of them were probably from us.

"I ken they canna be your kin's. Too much time has passed, but ye told me to look for somethin' unusual, and I've never seen tracks like this before." He pointed to the nearest set of prints. "They start here." He drew his finger along an imaginary line to the field. "And head straight that way."

"Probably just some hunters." I tried to keep the impatience out of my voice, but I couldn't care less about tracks right now. Still, he had been kind enough to distract me with a story when I was scared. The least I could do was be polite enough to listen.

"How did they get here?" He gestured toward the opposite end of the clearing. "There's tracks headin' out, but none comin' in."

I frowned. He was right, the prints began in the center of the clearing and only went in one direction.

Tilting back his head, he took in the clouds. "It's like they fell from the sky."

Fell from the sky... My stomach roiled. Like *I* had fallen from the sky. I flashed back to that moment, me lost, somewhere between there and here, my body pulling and morphing and melting as time tore at muscle and bone. Then I'd landed, fell right out of the sky onto the very spot where those footprints started.

I knew then, knew with a marrow-deep certainty, the time soldiers had come.

I glanced at Sean's grave that should not exist. I remembered his words—*if they come, we're both dead.* I recalled the look on his face, the genuine fear in his eyes. *That*, at least, hadn't been a lie.

For a moment, I froze, as cold and motionless as if I were encased in ice. Then the icy shell shattered in an explosion of panic, and I dove into the trees. I groped and tugged and assaulted every bit of nature within reach. Where was it? Goddammit, where? If I didn't find the portal, I had a lot more to worry about than plague and starvation. Fuck. It might not even be safe at home. What was to stop them from tracking me to Detroit? We'd have to leave. Go into hiding.

Discontinuing my search of the trees, I stomped around the clearing, hoping for the hollow sound of a trap door beneath dirt.

Witness protection. That's what we would need. I'd have to go to the FBI or CIA or whoever the fuck dealt with foreign governments. I'd tell them what I knew. They'd protect me, right?

"Lass," Henry said. "What are ye doin'?"

"Looking." Abandoning my stomping, I dropped to my knees at the edge of the field. I pulled reeds out by the roots, slapped the ground, and tossed dirt. Tears surged, hot and desperate.

"Lass!"

I ripped stalks of heather by the fistful.

"Enough!" His voice boomed like a drum. "There's nothin' here."

I shoveled dirt around. Banged the earth with my fist.

"Fiona!" His footsteps pounded behind me.

Continuing my frantic search, I didn't bother to look at him. "Leave me alone."

"Move!" He wrenched me to my feet and drew his sword. "Stay back."

I looked around in a panic, my heart racing with fear, even though I wasn't sure what I was supposed to be scared of. A rustle sounded in the brush near the trees. I screamed, and three piglets burst into the clearing.

Once I realized what they were, I sagged with relief. How many cute woodland creatures were going to send me into fits of PTSD by the end of this trip?

"I need ye to back up, verra slowly. We're going to climb that tree." Henry took a giant step backward, his eyes trained on the tiny piglets.

I tilted my head, confused. "They're just baby pigs."

"Now!" He gritted his teeth. "Unless ye want to meet their mother." Taking another step back, his foot landed on fist-sized stone. His ankle rolled, and he dropped to his knee with a muffled *umph*.

For a second, the forest seemed to pause. The piglets quieted. The birds stopped their chatter. Even the wind held its breath. Then chaos.

A giant boar pounded through the trees, grunting and snorting and brandishing its tusks. Henry shot to his feet. "Go!"

We ran to the edge of the clearing, and he boosted me onto a tree branch. Bark bit into my thighs as I looped around the limb and pulled myself upright. The grunts were louder now, angrier, more like a dog's bark than a pig's squeal.

"Shite!" he shouted, followed by a loud bestial shriek.

I shifted to a better vantage point. His back bit into the tree trunk. His sword was plunged into the boar's chest, but that didn't stop it. The pig thrust forward. It snorted and snarled, intent on protecting its babies, even at the cost of its own life. The sword dug deeper; its tusks grew closer to his leg.

Son of a bitch. I had to do something. I pulled my knife from the hidden pocket in my dress. The blade wasn't big, or particularly sharp, just an everyday utility knife Mairi'd given me, but it would have to do.

I jumped from the tree and circled round.

"What are ye don', ye wee fool?" His voice strained against the force of the pig.

"I don't know!" I threw myself on the boar's back. It bucked and kicked and gnashed its teeth, but I clung to its coarse fur and stabbed. It had hide like granite. My blade went in maybe a quarter inch. The pig bucked harder, and I went flying, along with the knife.

I landed a few feet away. Piglets squealed behind me. I raised my head, stars clouding my vision. It took a second for my eyes to focus, and when they did, I realized I had only managed to piss the pig off. It charged at Henry with even more ferocity. Scant inches remained between him and the boar's tusks. In a last-ditch effort, I crawled forward and hooked its hind leg. I didn't have the strength to drag the pig off him, but the distraction was all he needed. Quick as an asp, he wrenched his blade free and brought it down on the pig's head.

The boar collapsed in an explosion of blood. The piglets squealed. I screamed. He slid down the trunk to the ground, and I crawled over to him. "Are you all right? Did it get you?"

Blood soaked his tunic, but I couldn't tell if it belonged to him or the boar. I yanked up the hem of his shirt and searched for a wound.

His fingers clamped around my wrist like a vice. "I'm fine."

"All right..." The anger in his voice took me aback.

A vein in his forehead bulged. "I told ye to stay in that tree. What in the bloody hell were ye thinkin'!"

My hackles raised. He had to be fucking kidding me. "I just saved your life, asshole."

He scowled. "I had it under control."

Making a garbled, disgusted noise, I threw up my hands. "You know what, I'm not doing this with you." I stowed my knife. "Let's go."

Glowering, he tried to stand, only to fall back to the ground.

"You *are* hurt!" I crouched beside him.

"I'm fine." Air hissed between his teeth as he adjusted his position. "My ankle's a bit tender is all."

His ankle? I had forgotten he tumbled over that rock. I took hold of his leg, swatting his hand when he tried to stop me.

"Quit being a brat. I just want to look." I rolled his pant leg and gasped. His ankle was fat as a melon and bruised purple. "You fought on this?" Admiration took away my breath. This dude was a badass. Even Granda would have been impressed. He began to push himself back up, but I held his arm. "Don't be an idiot. You'll never be able to walk on that ankle."

Sweat beaded on his skin. "Well, we canna sit here all the day, now can we?"

Tugging the hose away from his skin, I used my knife to cut the fabric below the knee.

"St—Stop that." He stumbled over his speech in his shock. "It's the only pair I have after ye ruined my last ones."

I cut the cloth into strips, which I tied around his ankle like an Ace bandage. "There." I was pleased with my handiwork. I helped him to his feet, but he still struggled to put weight on his foot. Wrapping his arm around my shoulder, I propped him against me. "Here, lean on me."

"I'm fine." His jaw jutted. "I dinna need your—"

"Yeah, yeah, I know. You're a big tough man, and you don't need anybody's help." I slid my arm around his middle and braced his weight. "Now shut up and walk."

We traipsed through the field of purple flowers toward the road, Henry limping beside me as I did my best to prop him up. Instead of a hindrance, the weight of his massive bulk leaning against me set me at ease. Even with that twisted ankle, I knew he'd do anything he could to keep me safe.

"Hey." His voice brightened. "What'd'ye say we stop at the tavern on the way back. I could use summit to drink."

I nearly agreed, but then I stared down at my filthy tunic. "We're covered in blood."

He shrugged, and I paused to consider. A nice, stiff drink sounded pretty good after fighting a wild boar, discovering there was no way home, and learning time-soldiers were here and probably after me. "Do they serve whisky at this tavern of yours?"

"Whisky?" He frowned. "What's that?"

I sighed. "The only thing that would make me risk Mairi's wrath."

"Aww, c'mon." He squeezed my shoulder as we limped forward. "She willna ken."

"No." I lifted my chin.

He stuck out his bottom lip. "I fought off a boar for ye."

I pretended to consider. "No."

And so it went, the rest of the way home. Maybe not as pleasant a distraction as the story he had told me earlier, but a distraction nonetheless, and one I desperately needed. A thousand different problems crashed down on me, but right now, this ornery bastard was the only one I could handle. I'd just have to save the rest for morning.

# Chapter Twelve

"Mairi, come here." I waved her to my spot by the window.

She peeked over my shoulder. "What is it, lass?"

I pointed to a blond man cutting through our yard on his way to the smithy. "Do you know him?"

Squinting, she leaned forward. "Oh aye. That's the peacock knight. Must be comin' for his armor fitting."

My shoulders relaxed. Not a time soldier then. It'd been a while since I'd gotten freaked out by a new face, but then, it'd been a while since I'd seen a person I didn't recognize. A month had passed since Henry's and my trip into the woods, and, by now, I knew more or less all the people within a five-mile radius, by sight if not in person. Every now and then, though, on Henry's shop days, or like now, someone new would appear, and I'd get the complacency shaken right out of me.

It was a good thing, I supposed. Not that I liked being scared, but I needed the periodic reminder that just because everything seemed normal, it didn't mean I was safe. The time soldiers were out there...probably. I was like eighty percent sure. Only, I didn't know what they were waiting for.

Closing the shutters, I sagged in my seat. There went my quota of excitement for the week. Back to the tedium that had become my life. Every day played out the same. Wake up. Yard work. Cooking. Cleaning. Rinse. Repeat. I didn't even get to have fun in the evenings. As soon we finished supper, Henry and Donald abandoned me for the taverns, and I was stuck listening to Mairi's latest gossip about so-and-so's daughter and you'll-never-guess-whose husband. At this point, if the time-soldiers didn't kill me, I was pretty sure boredom would.

I hoisted the besom. "Do you want me to sweep first or shell the peas?"

"Nay, I— Well..." She clenched and released her fists. "I wanted to have a word with ye..."

"All right..." I studied her face with considerable concern. She never hedged, and her obvious reticence made me more nervous than that stranger in the yard just had.

I joined her at the table, and, after a pause, she cleared her throat. "It's time we talked about your future."

A cold knot formed in my belly, and it took all my self-control to keep my voice from wavering. "Did you find a new job for me?" This was good news. At least, that's what I kept telling myself. A permanent position meant security, guaranteed meals, and a place to lay my head when Henry finally kicked me out, but deep down I knew it really meant losing everything all over again.

"Not precisely..." Mairi placed an arthritic hand on mine. "You're a hard worker, lass, and ye've learned a great deal in the time I've had ye, but it's not enough..."

My throat went tight, and I couldn't bring myself to respond.

She steepled her fingers and peered down her sharp nose at me. "Ye'll never make it as a servant. When they see ye canna sew, and the troubles ye have at the market, and—"

"That wasn't my fault!" My voice came out in a squeak. "How was I supposed to know the baker weighted his bread?"

This seemed so unfair. I'd already learned so much. I just needed more time. I'd figure it out.

Sympathy flashed in her eyes. "A good servant kens to anticipate such deceit." She patted my hand. "With time, I'm sure ye could do it, but ye've less than a month left, and we need to be realistic. If I found ye a house to serve in, ye'd be out on the street in less than a fortnight. Then what would ye do?"

I bit my bottom lip and gave a slow nod. My eyes watered, and I refused to blink for fear a few rogue tears might lead to full blown sobs. "So, it's off to the nunnery?"

Mairi's frown deepened. "I'm not sure that would go so well either…"

I swallowed. "Then what?"

"We'll find ye a goodman." She didn't so much as blink as she said it, as if a husband were as transactional as applying for a loan.

I couldn't believe she wanted to marry me off to some stranger. "But…But…isn't that basically the same thing? I mean, I'd still be expected to sew and cook and clean. The only difference is I won't be able to leave if things get bad."

"The only difference"—Mairi leveled her gaze on me— "is a good man canna cast ye out if *you're* bad. We just willna mention your…um…domestic shortcomings until after ye've wed."

I couldn't breathe. Marriage. To a stranger. I'd be some man's property, no better than his slave. I couldn't even argue against it. What choice did I have? I was so fucking useless she didn't even think the nuns would take me.

I rose on wobbly legs. "Can you excuse me? I need some air."

Mairi's features softened. "Sure, lass. Why dinna ye fetch some water for me? Rain barrels are dry, so ye'll have to go to the pump." She brushed a thumb across my cheek. "Give it some thought, aye. I ken it's not what ye expected, but I think ye'll come to see it's what's best."

The sad thing was, as I headed out the door, I realized she was probably right. I just never imagined the best I could hope for would be cleaning up after some man who could legally beat me for undercooking the peas.

Taking a left at the church crossroads, I followed the dirt path to the community pump. Were there really no other options? There had to be something, but what? I wasn't even sure what medieval women were allowed to do—aside from prostitution and servant's work.

Let's see…I could learn to spin. Wouldn't that be the ultimate cliché, a girl who didn't want to get married becoming a literal spinster. I supposed it didn't matter. I didn't have time to learn, and I would drown in the tedium of thread anyway. I needed something active, something social, something unpredictable and chaotic...like the water pump was right now.

Holy crap! Had I just stumbled onto some medieval fight club? Apparently, ours weren't the only barrels that had run dry over the last rainless week. A mob had formed around the old, rusty pump. Men and women shouted at one another. Kids ran and shrieked in giddy zigzags while babies cried, and people shoved and squeezed their way toward the tap.

Two boys about Donald's age knocked into a stringy, mouse of a girl. Her water bucket skidded into the muddy pool beneath the faucet. A woman with a toddler clutched to her leg, somehow managed to kick the fallen bucket out of her way and replace it with her own. An old man with a hunched back and discolored walking stick shouted angry nonsense from the side, shaking a blue-stained fist.

As I approached the outskirts of the crowd, I stared at the old man. Maybe I could be a dyer. I could live with blue hands. It might be kind of fun—like playing with a chemistry set. I headed toward him, prepared to assault him with a list of dying questions, but was forced back when I caught a whiff of him. He smelled like a litter box full of month-old piss. The intensity of it made my eyes burn and lungs ache. I didn't know if the smell was a byproduct of the dying process or if he had an unfortunate problem with cats, but either way, I checked dyer off the list.

"Fiona, hello!" came an annoyingly peppy voice. "Bonnie morn', no?" Tiffany, our teenage neighbor from the dairy farm next door, strode over to me.

I didn't know what surprised me more about this girl, that she was a medieval woman with a name I'd assumed had been born in a mall at some point in the 1980s or her ability to speak at twice the rate of normal human beings.

"Hi, Tiffany. How are—"

"I've had a grand day! Ye willna believe who stopped by the farm. The Earl o' Sutherland's Hall boy!" She gave an ear-splitting shriek. "I'm in love! He told me all about the castle..."

94

As she prattled on, my mind drifted to her farm. I liked cows. In fact, cows were the only thing I liked better in this time. They were way tinier than modern cows, more like large dogs, and I found them irresistibly cute. I'd never made cheese before, but I could learn. Maybe I could convince her to teach me if I could just get her to shut up long enough to ask.

"...o' course ye ken what I'm talking about, living with that braw gem o' a man."

"Uh huh," I said, because her intonation seemed to require it, but then her words seeped in, and I laughed. "You mean Henry?"

She fanned her face. "Who else would I mean?"

"Of course," I said with mock earnestness.

"What, ye dinna think so?" Her wide, vacant eyes nearly bugged out of her face.

I mean, okay, he was ripped, and his hair fell so silkily about his shoulders he could have been a Pantene model. But, c'mon, his nose was precisely one size too big for his face. I bit my bottom lip. Okay, I kind of liked his nose. With those dark, long lashes, his face would be too pretty without a hefty schnoz. Besides, it gave him character.

Physical appearance aside, though, the dude needed about five good years of counseling before he'd be marriage material, and somehow, I didn't think medieval Perth had too many therapy clinics. I looked around the crowd and gulped. Then again, at least Henry didn't smell like cat piss and always had a good story ready.

New, louder shouts erupted from the cluster around the pump. The man with the cane hobbled backward. The two boys who had shoved the girl charged at one another, cackling like idiots. The bigger of the two barreled into the smaller one. This knocked him into the woman who had just filled her bucket. Water slopped down the side of her dress and pooled at her feet.

Enraged, she swung the empty bucket at the boy's head. He ducked, and the bucket knocked into the back of a running child. The girl fell to the dirt, scraped her knees, and screamed like she'd broken every bone in her body.

"For fuck's sake." Thrusting my bucket at Tiffany, I marched into the horde. "That's enough!"

My voice wasn't any louder than the rest of the crowd, but there was an intensity behind my words that cut through the masses. The decibel level reduced by half as people stopped their bickering to turn and stare.

I picked up the screaming toddler. "Whose baby is this?"

A woman emerged from the crowd, and I shoved the kid into her arms. I glared at the teenage boys. "If you want to act like children, go home to your mothers. Grown folks are trying to work here."

A scowl formed on the taller of the two's face. He inched forward and towered over me in an attempt to invade my space. "I'm a man grown." He thumped his chest. "I'm not about to let some wee lass talk down to me."

I snorted with laughter. Man grown, my ass. This kid might be tall, but he was skinny as a string bean, and I could have played connect the dots with the acne on his face.

He cocked back his fist. "Do I need to teach ye some manners?"

I snorted. "That's cute." I snatched him by the ear and twisted.

He howled with pain. "Let go!"

"I will. As soon as you apologize to these fine people for disturbing them." A nearby woman cheered at my pronouncement.

"I didna—" He stooped, trying to relieve the pressure on his ear.

I gave it another sharp twist. "Now."

He clutched his ear. "I'm sorry. I'm sorry."

His partner in crime laughed, and I turned on him. "And you, aren't you the tanner's lad?" He stopped laughing, and his face paled. "Do I need to tell your father you've been down here acting the fool?"

He raised his hands in a pleading gesture. "We was jus' gaming with each other. Please, marm. Ye dinna need to bring my da into this."

96

Making a noise of disgust, I released my captive's ear. "Get over to that pump. Both of you. You're going to fill every one of these buckets."

The crowd, which had gone mostly silent, switched on at those words. People shoved and jabbed, trying to be the first to get their buckets to the boys.

"Nope. We're not doing that again. You," I pointed to the woman whose water had spilled, "you go first." I gestured to the old, ammonia-smelling man. "You're next. Come over here. Line starts with you."

One by one I queued them up. I had no idea why they listened to me. Maybe it was the novelty of a woman taking charge. Maybe they feared my cauliflower ear. I didn't know or care. For the first time in a long time, I was running shit, and it was glorious.

As I headed back to the house, water buckets in hand, still running high from bringing order to a mob, I remembered the last time I experienced such a rush. Three years ago, during Lent, the health department had shut down the Elks Lodge, and all their customers showed up to the Caledonia Club's fish fry. We'd been under-staffed and under-prepared, but I stationed Jones at the fryer, put Granda and Old John behind the bar, gave William and Robert two tables a piece, and I took the rest. And we'd handled ourselves like bosses.

That had been the moment I knew for sure I wanted to take over the bar. The club came alive that day, restored for a short time to its former glory, and I vowed to myself when I took over, every day would be like fish fry day.

I bumped the door open with my butt, careful not to spill any of the water I'd collected. "Sorry that took so long. You wouldn't believe how many people..." I paused as the scent of something marvelous filled my nose. "What's that smell?"

There was something familiar about it—sweet and grainy and sticky like brown sugar oatmeal or warm shortbread cookies. I inhaled again. No, neither of those. It smelled like—"Honey Nut Cheerios!"

Mairi raised an eyebrow. "What are ye on about?"

"Can I taste that?" I didn't know what she had brewing in that kettle, but I was sure it would taste like childhood.

She shrugged. "If ye want. It's just malt for the ale."

Then I had one of those moments. One of those stars-colliding, beam-of-light-shining-down-from-the-heavens kind of moments. Ale! I could brew ale! Holy shit, this was huge. Life changing! And, for once, not in a devastating way. I wanted to pump my fist in the air and cartwheel through the living room. Fuck yeah! I didn't have to be some *man's* wife; I could be an alewife! I could get a job at a tavern, work my way up. Hell, maybe one day I could even *own* my own tavern. I could still have my dream, even if it came six hundred years ahead of schedule.

"Lass," Mairi said, a note of concern in her voice. "Ye've a queer look on your face. Are ye well?"

I grinned. "Hold off on the matchmaking, Mairi. I've got a plan!"

# Chapter Thirteen

"All right, be honest." I passed tankards to Mairi, Donald, and Henry. "Don't worry about hurting my feelings. Give it to me straight."

I waited with bated breath as they each took their cups. After a bout of extreme pleading with Mairi to teach me to brew, followed by a week of intensive lessons, Mairi'd finally given me the go-ahead to try my own batch.

My palms itched with sweat and shook with nerves as I waited for their reactions. I wasn't even sure why. I'd done exactly as Mairi'd taught me, and honestly, brewing wasn't all that difficult. You just boiled malt, added some gruit, which was just a fancy name for flavoring, tossed in some yeasty grains from the last batch of ale, and did a lot of waiting and straining.

Unfortunately, brewing was so easy, every goodwife in Scotland could do it. So, if I wanted to sell mine, it would have to be better than fine—it would have to be outstanding. But for my first batch, I'd settle for decent.

Mairi took a sip. God, she had a stony face. Not a hint of reaction, good or bad. And why was she taking so damn long to swallow? She was rolling the ale around her mouth like she moonlighted as a goddamned beer sommelier. After an eternity, which in reality probably amounted to ten seconds, her wrinkled neck quivered, and she swallowed. She gave a clipped nod. "A bit light on the malt, but I've had worse."

I bit my lip to keep from squealing. In Mairi-speak *I've had worse* was basically the equivalent of giving me a high five and bursting into a rendition of "We are the Champions".

Grinning, I looked to Donald, who was chugging his ale like a frat boy. This, of course, didn't mean anything. If I'd served him a cup of dirty bath water, he'd have pounded it just as fast and asked for seconds. I swore the kid was half goat.

After a few more glugs, he set his tankard down and burped. "It's good. Tastes just like Mairi's."

She raised her nose in the air. "Not *just* like mine."

Chuckling, I turned to Henry. His cup sat on the table, barely touched. "Did you try it?"

He gave a curt nod. "Aye."

"And?" I couldn't believe he was making me drag it out of him. What kind of sadist was he?

Huffing, he turned his body away from me. "Why do ye want to work in a tavern anyway?"

"What?" I'd heard him all right, but I didn't know what the hell was up with that petulant tone of his. "I'm sorry, do my career plans offend you?"

"Where's your sense o' decency? Ye'd prefer men pawin' at ye to bein' wed?" His knuckles cracked under the strain of his grip on the table. "What kind o' lass chooses that?"

Donald's mouth fell open.

Delight lit Mairi's eyes. "He's not wrong, lass."

Sitting forward, I leveled Henry with a hard stare. "The kind who's about to be homeless and doesn't like being told what to do."

The table vibrated as he slammed his hand down. "Well, there's the truth if I ever heard it. Ye think ye ken what's best about everything, never mind what your elders say."

"My elders! You're one to talk." I glanced at his ringless finger. "Where's your wife then?"

Doubled over, Donald heaved with silent laughter.

Mairi held up a finger. "She's speaking sense, lad."

Glowering, Henry turned his head, and I did my best not to dump my tankard over his head. Such an asshole. I thought we'd gotten past this him being a dick for no reason thing.

100

"Why do you even care?" My voice shook with rage. "You spend money at the tavern every single night, but I want to go there and *make* money, and it's a problem? That's bullshit."

"Fiona!" Mairi pursed her lips. "Language."

Donald snickered.

A gnarled sound escaped Henry's throat. "Dinna compare yourself to me, lass. *I* can handle myself."

"And I can't?" My fingers curled around the edge of the table.

He gave a derisive snort. "Ye screamed in fright at the sight o' a wee deer in the woods. How do ye expect to handle a pub full o' rowdy lads?"

"The same way I handled that boar." My face grew heated. "Or did you forget about that?"

Scoffing, he turned his head. "Dinna get all high and mighty. Your knife didna even pierce its hide, and I already had it skewered."

"That's not the point." I bit down on my bottom lip to keep it from trembling.

His brow furrowed. "Then what is?"

Me. The point was me. And how I wanted to live my life. I'd realized something these last few days. Bad shit was going to happen. Maybe time soldiers would come, or I'd get eaten by a bear, or maybe I'd get a papercut and die because I didn't have a goddamned tube of Neosporin. I didn't know, but eventually something *would* kill me. I had no control over that. The only choice I had was how to *live* until it did, and I'd be damned if I spent another second wallowing in worry and fear.

"You know what, there's no sense in arguing." Pushing my chair back from the table, I gave him one last glare. "It doesn't concern you anyway."

"Aye." He practically growled the word. "Until you're bangin' on my door askin' for a place to stay because ye canna handle the work at the pub."

"You know what," I rose to my feet, "I wouldn't ask you for help if—"

"All right. That's enough," Mairi cut in. "Your tempers are getting' the better o' ye. I think it's best if we—"

"No." My gaze snapped to her. "If he thinks he's so smart, let him prove it." Smirking, I met his gaze. "Are you willing to put your money where your mouth is?"

He threw up his hands. "What the hell does that mean? Half the words that come out o' your mouth are pure nonsense."

"It means a bet." I turned my chair around and straddled it, leaning over the back. "Take me to the tavern tonight, and we'll see who's right and who's wrong."

He huffed. "Why should I?"

"Because a man should be able to back up his words." *And so should I.* I didn't need to prove anything to Henry, but I did need to prove it to myself. It was all well and good to tell myself I wasn't afraid in the relative safety of this house, but if I was really going to do this tavern thing, I had to know I wouldn't crack the second I set foot in the real world.

Henry froze. Now that I'd brought his manhood into the equation, he couldn't very well say no, but by the way his forehead was all scrunched up, he sure seemed to be hunting for some kind of loophole. After several seconds of narrow-eyed contemplation, the lines on his forehead disappeared, and a slow smile spread across his face. "Ye've offered me a bet, lass, but ye havena given me any stakes."

"What are you talking about? The stakes are bragging rights." I hooked a thumb toward my chest. "Proof I'm right, and you're a big dummy who doesn't know what he's talking about."

Still wearing that smug grin, he leaned forward. "Not good enough."

I shrugged. "I don't have any money, if that's what you're after."

"That's not what I want." His voice came out a soft purr.

I swallowed. He couldn't possibly mean... I fought the urge to fan my face as heat warmed my cheeks. I had to get a grip. That should have pissed me off, not gotten me all hot and bothered.

"Name your terms," I said, managing to maintain some small reserve of dignity in my voice.

Grinning, he leaned forward. "If I see ye so much as flinch at the tavern, ye have to give up this ale-brewing nonsense and find yourself somethin' more suitable."

"Or *someone*." Mairi's voice vibrated with delight, the cogs clearly turning in her devious little matchmaking head.

Raising my chin, I fought to maintain my bravado. "And if I win?"

His gaze drifted to the door and then back at me. He licked his lips. "I'll let ye stay an extra month."

I tensed. An extra month could change everything. If I found a job now, I could use the extra time to save money. I wouldn't have to sleep on the streets until I earned enough coin for rent. It was a hell of a risk, though—my dream for the chance of a few weeks comfort? Then again, maybe it didn't matter. If I couldn't make it through a single night at the bar without getting shell-shocked, owning my own tavern was a fool's dream anyway.

I studied his face. "What about Coira? Isn't she coming back?"

At the mention of his long-absent girlfriend's name, his muscles stiffened, and weirdly, so did mine. I'd gotten used to the dynamics of this house, and the reminder of this extra, unfamiliar player reminded me once more how fleeting my situation here was. Soon I'd be gone, and she'd be back, resuming the space in their lives that I currently held.

"Aye, well... She doesna come by the house often." His eyes flicked to Mairi, seemingly out of reflex. "She might not even ken you're here."

That didn't seem particularly likely. Even if she didn't stop by, I'd met enough people in the neighborhood, somebody was bound to eventually mention me in front of her. "What if she finds out?"

Tipping back his head, he studied the ceiling. "Then she'll be displeased for a time and get over it."

I opened my mouth, then closed it. That sounded... dysfunctional. I had so many questions, but none of them were my business, and it would be rude to pry. I'd just have to handle myself like a mature adult and get the dirt from Mairi in the morning.

Suddenly, my body seemed lighter, as if I'd just removed ten-pound weights from my shoulders. Holding up my ale in toast, I grinned. "All right, I accept your terms." I took my first sip of my own brew. Not half bad. Not great, either, but good enough to work with as a baseline recipe.

That was, assuming I still had need after tonight's trip to the tavern.

# Chapter Fourteen

"Mind your manners while you're out." Mairi's voice was stern. "You're a member o' this household, and I expect ye to represent yourself accordingly."

Snorting, I pulled on my cloak. "So you're saying I *shouldn't* strip nude and dance on the tables?"

She swatted my ass. "Keep talkin', ye wee rascal. I've a mind to stitch your mouth closed and do the whole world a favor."

"Before I've even had the chance to drink?" I gasped. "Now that's just mean."

"Dinna be drinkin' to excess, either." Staring down her nose at me, she jabbed me with a gnarled finger. "I mean it. If I have to hear Winnie MacSheah tell me she heard ye were at the tavern, playin' the fool, I'll murder ye and die o' shame myself."

"Relax." I jostled my change purse, which hung clipped to my belt next to my tankard. "I've only got enough for two pints."

"Aye, well, dinna let the lad get too deep in his cups either. Her eyes zeroed in behind me. "Ye hear that, lad?"

Henry appeared by my side, his face shorn and hair damp like he'd just run a comb through it. "Aye, I heard ye."

His gaze raked up the length of me, pausing at my unbound hair. His eyes darkened, and a flush of heat warmed my cheeks. Typically, when bumming around the house, I wore a head scarf. I didn't technically have to since I wasn't married, but it was just easier than fussing with my hair and helped keep it clean.

But this was the first night I was going out, and I'd taken the time to wash and oil my hair into springy ringlets. I'd even darkened my lashes with a bit of coal and glossed my lips with some berry tinted fat. It was nice to see all the effort being appreciated.

Mairi frowned. "And another thing—"

"Sorry, Aunty. We're late. Got to go." Grabbing my wrist, Henry tore out the door with me, hand in hand, not slowing until we reached the winding, dirt road. We paused to catch our breath.

"That was amazing!" I panted. "I mean, it didn't even make sense—late for the *tavern*—but it worked!"

He grinned. "It's not *what* ye say that matters. It's that ye dinna give her the chance to respond. Your mistake is lettin' her get into her stride."

Giggling, I tugged him forward, fingers curling around his calloused palms. "Fair enough, oh wise one, but I found the fatal flaw in your plan."

"Oh, aye?" He raised a brow. "What's that?" We took a right at the church crossroad.

"We forgot Donald."

A dark chuckle escaped his lips. "Nay, poor lad's stuck with Mairi tonight. Said it wouldna be safe, her alone in the house."

"Oh, please." I snorted. "That woman's not scared of anything. She probably just wants the two of us alone together."

"Aye." Henry's voice trailed off, and this awkward moment occurred, in which we both seemed to realize we were still holding hands.

At once, we dropped each other. Heat scorched my cheeks. The sensation of his hand in mine had been so comfortable, it barely registered. Now its absence left my fingers stiff and cold. God, I must be desperate for human contact. Not good. If I were smart, I'd find some fuckboy at the tavern and take care of things before my libido made me lose my goddamned mind.

Making our way to the High Street, we passed by shop owners giving final sweeps to their stoops and double-checking locked doors before heading home for the evening. The sun still shone high in the sky, and I realized this was probably the earliest I'd ever gone out to a bar outside of work. Back home, the night didn't even get started until after eleven. But time ran differently here, and with the curfew bell set to chime at nine, day-drinking was the only sort of drinking.

Henry turned off the main road and led us down a narrow alley. Cutting through to a winding side-street, he brought us to a stop in front of a stone building shaped like an igloo. "Are ye sure ye want to do this?"

I cracked my knuckles. "I didn't come all this way for nothing."

Music and shouts carried through the tavern windows. Sounds of laughter and banging and some off-key drunkard belting a tune filled my ears. The air smelled sticky-sweet like barley and, at the same time, sour like stale piss, smoke, and too many bodies. I breathed it all in, and to my delight, found I wasn't the slightest bit scared. It just seemed like going home.

He grasped my hand. "Let's go somewhere else."

"What?" I eyed him. "Why?"

His cheeks tinged pink, and he ran a hand through his hair. "I wanted to win the bet, so I brought ye to the unruliest pub I could think of." His gaze fell, and he shifted from side-to-side. "Now that we're here, though, I think maybe that's goin' too far. I'll take ye to a quieter tavern."

Tugging my hand, he turned to leave, but I resisted. It was probably a fool's move. I mean, what easier way to win the bet than spending the night at a nice tame bar? But the sounds from inside kept calling to me—*Fiona, you're a rock star. Come inside and party like one.* And who was I to argue?

"No, this one's good." I opened the door and peered through a haze of hearth smoke. Two men to our left were beating each other bloody. A one-eyed fiddler jammed out atop a table in the back, while patrons danced a reel around him. A group of ladies by the hearth cackled and tossed back drinks, their head coverings piled on the floor. And to the right, men sat at tables, shooting dice and playing cards, coins heaped in piles next to tankards and bread.

More men joined in the fight, and the violence spread. One man threw a chair. Two others tackled him to the ground, and he disappeared in a sea of fists.

"*Now* are ye ready to go?" Henry's voice rumbled smugly in my ear.

I grinned, enjoying the security of his warm hand on mine. "Not even if you paid me." I kicked a bit of broken chair out of the way and dragged him to the bar.

"What'll it be?" a broad-shouldered barmaid asked as we squeezed between a man with blood running down his forehead and a lady with an infant to her breast and a tankard to her lips.

We handed over our cups.

"A strong and a weak." Henry reached into his sporran.

"Yeah, that's not happening." Before he could pull his change, I bumped him out of the way with my hip and slid a farthing across the bar. "Two strong, please."

The barmaid shrugged and took the coin. He frowned in a very Mairi-like way, but I didn't care. Tonight was about moving forward and having fun, and I intended to do both. The woman returned with our drinks a few seconds later.

I scanned the room. "Is this place hiring?"

"What?" Horror filled Henry's voice. "Ye canna mean to work *here*."

"Could be." The barmaid gave me a quick once-over. "I'll ask the mistress when I get a minute." A customer yelled for a drink at the other end of the bar, and she left to take his order.

Hand gripped around his tankard, his knuckles blanched. "Fiona, I mean it. Ye canna—"

"Should we find seats?" I scanned the room. "C'mon. There's an empty table over there." Side-stepping a man who flew across the floor after a particularly brutal punch, I strode toward the table.

Henry closed in behind me. His warm breath on my neck sent shivers down my spine. "If you're goin' to ignore me, fine, but dinna run off like that. You're goin' to get yourself trampled." He slid onto the bench seat of the empty table.

"C'mon, aren't you even a little impressed?" I held up my tankard. "I didn't spill a single drop." His scowl made me laugh, and I gave him a playful shove. "Will you lighten up? I'll be fine."

"Easy for ye to say." His gaze darted about the pub as if searching for threats. "I'm the one what's goin' to have to fight when some sot knocks into ye."

A body squashed behind me, and a hand cupped my ass. "Be a good lass and get me another drink, aye?" said a slurred voice, too loud in my ear.

Fire erupted in Henry's eyes, and he bolted to his feet. But before he had the chance to clear the bench, I had the man's fingers in my grip, and his wrist bent back.

"Oi!" His mouth twisted with pain and befuddlement. "What're ye doin' that for?"

"Touch me again, and next time I break them." Tilting my head toward the bar, I released him. "Now go get your own drink. I don't work here...yet."

Eyes glazed and confused, he swayed.

A booming laugh erupted behind him. "Ye heard the lady, peasant, move. You're taintin' my air." A tall, ridiculously handsome, broad-chested man strode up to the drunkard and face palmed him out of the way.

Not sure what to make of this newcomer, I stared with fascination. Nothing about him made sense. Not his clothes, which were silk when everybody else in the tavern wore wool. Nor his grin, which was full of mischief and overly intimate. Nor the fact he seemed familiar, though, for the life of me, I couldn't figure out why.

Squinting, I searched my memory. "Do I know you?"

"I'm sure ye do." An arrogant grin split his face. "But nay, we havena met." He gave a flourishing bow. "Sir Gavin of Keyth, at your service." Rising, he stared at me, waiting for some response, like he expected me to faint or swoon or maybe shriek and throw my bra at him.

"Oh." Ignorance made my voice come out wholly unimpressed, which made me sound bitchier than I'd intended to be.

Instead of taking offense, his smile widened, revealing a shockingly straight set of white teeth for a time before orthodontists. He looked past me to Henry. "Who *is* this interesting creature?"

Surprised, I glanced at him. I hadn't realized they knew each other. I just figured he was some random dude trying to spit game.

"No one ye need to concern yourself with." A note of warning edged Henry's words.

Gavin studied Henry's face as if he found his reaction even more interesting than my own.

I extended a hand. "Fiona." Grasping my hand in his, he pressed his lips to my flesh. His lips lingered for an obscene amount of time, and he didn't pull away until Henry let out a low growl. "That's enough, Peacock. She's a maidservant, not a courtesan."

Flashing me a sly smile, Gavin raised my hand. His thumb caressed Gran's ring. "Interesting gem for a maidservant..." He shrugged and slid onto the bench opposite Henry. "Not that it makes any difference to me. Round arses dinna discriminate between the classes."

Henry grumbled something as I sat beside him, but I was too focused on his earlier words to pay attention. He'd called Gavin "Peacock."

Smacking the table, I leaned forward. "That's how I know you! You're the Peacock Knight! You came to our house the other day."

Gavin's eyes sparkled. "The one and only."

Unable to help myself, I snickered. "So what's a knight like you doing in a place like this?"

As if to prove exactly how unfit this bar was for a man of noble blood, a guy the table over whipped out his dick and pissed on the tavern floor.

Unfazed, Gavin shrugged. "Clearly, ye havena spent much time with the nobility if you're askin' me that. Tedious, the whole lot of 'em." He glanced at the ring on my finger. "Or perhaps you're already aware..."

"All right, Peacock, enough blatherin'." Henry dropped his coin purse on the table. "We've a score to settle."

110

Tossing his own purse on the table, Gavin removed a leather bag from his shoulder and rummaged through.

I took a sip of my ale. Holy hell was that good—nutty and robust with a hint of fruity aftertaste. It made Mairi's ale taste like piss-water and mine taste like straight up piss. Not only that, that alcohol content had to be twice as high as what we brewed at home. Clearly, I still had a lot to learn.

Gavin retrieved a pair of bone dice and a deck of hand painted cards from his bag. "What'll it be, Gow Chrom? How shall I lighten your purse today?"

Fingers twitching, I stared at the cards. "You don't play poker, do you?" Despite my best attempt at sounding casual, the longing in my voice rang clear.

Gavin raised a brow. "Never heard of it."

Henry glared from beneath thick, dark lashes. "Fiona. You're not gamblin', whatever the game. Can ye please just sit there and act like a lady for once in your life?"

Ignoring him, I directed my full attention on Gavin. "Want to learn?"

He handed over the deck with a grin.

"Ye dinna have enough coin to play." The way the words rushed out of his mouth, Henry sounded almost desperate.

"Sure I do." Nodding at his cup, I flashed him a cocky grin. "I paid for your drink. You owe me a ha'penny."

His nostrils flared. "Fine, but dinna come cryin' to me when ye've lost your last coin, and your cup's run bare."

I chuckled. "What? You think I can't get drinks?" Cashing the last of my ale, I tapped the shoulder of a balding man at the table behind us.

When he turned and saw me, his cheeks flushed red. "Aye?"

Flashing him a pretty smile, I placed my cup in his hands. "Buy me a drink, won't you?"

His eyes widened, and he damn near knocked over his bench in his haste to stand. "O' course!"

"You're so sweet!" I gave him a demure smile. His blush deepened, and he scampered toward the bar.

I raised my voice to be heard over the crowd. "Make it a strong one!" Turning, I faced Henry and grinned. He glowered.

A booming laugh resonated from deep in Gavin's throat. "I like this one, Gow Chrom! Ye should bring her more often."

"Why do you keep calling him Gow Chrom?" I picked up the cards and sorted through them. They were oval, and instead of spades, clubs, and diamonds, leaves, acorns, and wolves decorated the cards' fronts. Hearts were still the same, though.

As if imparting a grave secret, Gavin leaned forward. "Gow Chrom means crooked smith." He inclined his head toward Henry. "And since yon armorer is the shiftiest bastard I ever met, I thought it fitting."

I laughed and raised an eyebrow at him. "What do you say to that, Gow Chrom?"

His answering "hmph" made me giggle. I poked him in the ribs. "Come on, enough with the sour puss. We're supposed to be having fun tonight."

When he still didn't smile, I turned my pokes into tickles, until finally, I broke him, and he cracked a grin. "Enough. Enough!"

When I didn't relent, he caught my arms, and twisted them into a pretzel, restraining me against his chest. Heat shot through me, and for a moment I forgot our play fighting and sunk into him. His arms tightened around me, and every muscle in my core clenched. Holy hell. This was dangerous. I was beginning to like his touch a little too much, and only complication led down that path.

Gavin cleared his throat and nodded behind me. "Lass..." The balding man had returned with my drink.

As if I were suddenly something foul he couldn't bear to touch, Henry shoved me off him.

"Sorry that took so long." The man shifted from foot-to-foot. "Barkeep must've gone to the pot. I was waitin' forever."

"Thank you." Taking the cup from him, I forced a smile, despite the hurt surging through me. Here I was, mentally trying to convince my lady bits that jumping Henry's bones was a bad idea, and here he was looking at me like I was garbage. Stupid lady bits.

"It's nothin', nothin' at all." The man hovered there for a second as if trying to come up with more to say.

Henry's face flushed a furious red. "Leave."

The man jumped and scuttled back at the glare on Henry's face.

Gavin laughed.

Narrowing my eyes, I snarled at the two of them, "Quit being jerks. That was rude."

He raised an eyebrow at Henry. "What's a jerk?"

Still scowling, he shrugged.

Whatever. I collected the cards and sorted out hands, starting with a straight flush and working my way down to a single pair, explaining the rules as I went. "Got it?" I asked when I finished. "Or do you morons need me to explain it again?"

By the glazed looks in their eyes, I could tell they hadn't fully grasped the game or the word 'moron,' but neither were about to admit it. All the better for me.

I tossed my coin on the table. "Ante up."

Three hands later, my single coin had grown to eight. Gavin couldn't seem to grasp the concept of bluffing, and Henry was so damn competitive he matched me every time I raised, regardless of his hand.

As I shuffled for a fourth hand, a serving girl arrived at the table. At first, I was glad, because man, could I use another drink, but then she wedged herself between me and Henry and slipped an arm around his neck, and suddenly my nails were digging into my palms, and I had the irrational desire to throttle this bitch.

She stroked his arm. "It's been awhile."

I downed the last dregs of my tankard. Who did she think she was, knocking me out of the way? I didn't care what he got up to with skanks at the bar, but she should at least show some respect in front of me. For all she knew, I might be his girlfriend. For that matter, what about his girlfriend? I bet she wasn't fine with him getting slobbered on by big-tittied barmaids. At least, I wouldn't be. Not that it was my problem, anyway, even if it somehow felt like it was.

"We could use some drinks." My voice resonated, loud, hard, and irritated.

The girl blinked as if surprised to find me sitting there. "Oh, that's right. I'm supposed to tell ye Brigid'll see ye now."

My brow knit. "Who?"

Her vacant eyes widened in confusion. "Are ye not the one lookin' for work?"

"Oh, yeah." I scowled at Henry. "That's right. I am."

"Are ye?" Gavin's gaze bounced from me to Henry. A canny smirk formed on his face. "Ye could come work for me."

"Maybe I will." I flashed him a smile built of spite, before giving Henry a final icy glare. Then I threw back my shoulders and propelled the slutty waitress forward. "Take me to her."

She led me to a back room where a wrinkly woman with raven hair sat behind a makeshift desk.

"You're the one lookin' for work?" Brigid's gaze raked over me. "Ye'll do. Come to me in six months. One o' my girls is in a family way, and I'll be needin' somebody once she's spawned the welp."

"Six months!" My voice rose an octave. "I need a job now."

Shrugging, she hunched back over her work. "Ye can try the Happy Friar or the Merry Mummer, but from what I hear, they're havin' to let girls go with the price o' barley what it is."

My stomach dropped to somewhere around my knees. So that was it? Dream gone. Forced to marry some strange man or off to Gavin's to be the same cog in a different wheel? No. Fuck that. I wasn't about to give up that easily. "Don't pay me. Just give me food and let me sleep on the floor. I'll help with whatever you want."

"If you're in that much need, try whorin'." She dismissed me with a flick of the hand. "I'm not some monk, dolin' out charity to every beggar what comes to my door."

Despite how insulting I found it to be referred to as a "beggar," pride wasn't going to get me my tavern. I gulped down an angry retort. "All right, forget food. Just let me learn."

Her brows arched. "Learn?"

"I want my own tavern one day. I already know how to brew." This was technically true, even if I couldn't do it all that well yet. "I just need to learn the rest."

She laughed. "There is no rest. Ye want a tavern, buy one. It's simple as that." When I neither moved nor replied, she peered at me from beneath raised brows. "Do ye have coin?" I shook my head. "A home?"

I licked my lips. "For the time."

"Take my advice, lass." Yanking a quill pen from her bottle of ink, she held it hovered over a scroll of paper. "Do enough whorin' to pay your rent. Then do like the other alewives and sell from your home. If the ale's good enough, ye'll earn enough to buy your tavern."

"Wait." I held up a hand, sure I couldn't have possibly heard her right. "You're saying I can sell ale from my house?"

"O' course ye can." She unfurled her paper and scribbled something across the top. "Why couldna ye?"

Honestly, I had no idea, but that just seemed way too easy. "What about permits? Or an inspection? Or—"

Exhaling a heavy sigh, she stowed her quill. "A sign, lass. Put up a sign and be done with it." She waved me out the door. "Now off with ye. I dinna have time to be talkin' all the day with soft-headed lassies."

I left, not sure if my situation had just improved or become infinitely harder. It was like being handed a driver's license without having ever sat behind the wheel, but I'd figure it out. I had to...

I strode past the bar, ducking as somebody's tankard flew across the room. A space cleared as two men tumbled to the floor, and I came to an abrupt stop. Across from their tussle, the serving girl delivered a fistful of tankards to our table. She bent over and took her payment in the form of a kiss.

An unnatural rage flared at the sight of her lips on Henry's. Fuck her and fuck him. How dare he shove me from his arms as if I were something gross and foul, but this random bar wench could stick her tongue in his mouth at will?

My fists balled at my sides as Henry gently disengaged from the kiss, smiled at her, and tapped her chin. My feet carried me toward the table, seemingly of their own accord. I slid onto the bench next to Gavin as the girl flounced off, a horrible, unnatural smile plastered on my face. Henry watched the girl depart and startled when he returned his gaze to Gavin and found me sitting there.

His Adam's apple bobbed, but then Gavin slid closer to me, and his jaw hardened in unspoken challenge, practically daring me to say something.

Too bad for him, that wasn't my style. I'd rather chew glass than admit that kiss bothered me. Strapping on my brightest smile, I stroked Gavin's arm. "Should we play?"

He smirked. "It is a night for games isna it?"

I took a sip from my freshly filled tankard and grimaced. "What's wrong with this ale?"

"That chit of a servin' wench brought us the weak, but dinna fash." Digging through his bag, he retrieved a glass bottle filled with amber liquor. "I'm a bit of a sorcerer, ye see." He poured a dollop into his cup. "I can turn even the weakest of ales strong."

I gasped. "Is that whisky?"

He swirled the liquid in its bottle. "Aqua Vitae."

"Let me see that." I snatched the bottle and put it to my nose. Holy shit! I didn't care what he called it, that was whisky. Gut rot whisky—Granda wouldn't have let me polish our spoons with it—but whisky all the same. "Can I have some?"

He nodded. "O' course!"

"Nay!" Henry's voice drowned out Gavin's.

I ground my teeth. "I didn't ask your permission."

Laugh lines crinkled around Gavin's eyes. "What's the harm, Gow Chrom?"

"She's...she's my servant. I have a right—" Henry's words cut off as Gavin ran a finger along my hand, circling Gran's ring.

"A servant, aye?" He chuckled to himself. "Gow Chrom, I've met blind men who can see more than ye." He raised the bottle to my cup.

116

"Wait!" Tipping my ale back, I chugged until the cup emptied. "Now go ahead. I don't like to mix."

Gavin laughed. "Ye really can drink well, aye?" He poured half a finger into my cup.

"I can." I nudged my tankard closer to him. "So don't be stingy."

"Fiona!" A vein pulsed in Henry's forehead.

"It's potent." Gavin's tone held a hint of caution. "Are ye sure ye can handle it?"

"Please." I gestured around the room. "I could outdrink any man in this pub."

Glancing at Henry, a devilish smile crossed Gavin's face. "Shall we play a different sort o' game, then?" He poured his ale onto the floor and split the whisky between our tankards. "Let's see if you're as good as your word. If ye can finish that," he nudged his coin purse toward me, "this is yours."

Lifting the purse, I tested its weight in my palm. "I can't match that." I dumped my own, much lighter purse on the table. "This is all I have."

He winked. "Then ye'll have to wager yourself instead."

The sound of Henry's fist slamming against the table, cut through the cacophony of tavern noises. Heads spun in our direction. I stared, horrified. Okay, I knew I'd been flirting, but that hardly justified him asking me to put my body up for collateral.

The offense must have been plain on my face, because Gavin waved his arms. "No, no, I meant nothin' sordid. If I win, I'd like ye to attend the merchant's gala with me. If I must go to the infernal thing, I'd rather do it with a lass who kens how to have a bit o' fun."

My shoulders sagged in relief. Even though I wasn't exactly sure what a merchant's gala was, the way I saw it, this bet was all gain and no risk. "Deal."

I reached for my cup, but Henry stayed my arm. "Forget it. We're leaving."

Ripping my arm free, I turned on him. "No, we're not."

"Yes, we are!" His booming voice drew the attention of the patrons at nearby tables. "Now!"

Ire swelled in my gut, and I shot to my feet. "Or what? You going to kick me out on the streets?" I tapped my lip. "Oh, wait, you're already doing that."

The color drained from his face. A thrill of pleasure stabbed at my insides at his response. Teach him to lecture me after slobbering all over that waitress. "I need the money, so I'm going to drink. If you don't like it, go cry to that whore barmaid. I'm sure she'll be happy to console you."

Grabbing Gavin's cup, I poured half of his whisky into my own tankard. "There. Now it's a fair bet."

He clapped his hands in delight. "Ye finish all that, and I'll buy ye an ermine gown."

"I'm warning ye." Henry spoke through clenched teeth. "Do as I say, or I'll leave ye here."

"Then go." Staring him straight in the eye, I took a swig from my cup. It singed my tongue, raw and bitter. Gran's castor oil went down smoother than this swill, but that familiar whisky heat burned in my belly, and I kept drinking.

As if repressing the urge to laugh, Gavin chewed his bottom lip. "If ye want to go, I'll see her safely home."

Henry stared at me with this ugly, furious sneer. Too bad I had zero fucks left to give. I was committed now.

By the time Gavin finished a quarter of his significantly smaller cup, his eyes were glassy, and his cheeks flushed. Not even a contender. I took another big gulp. Good. That money would go a long way toward rent.

"Tell me." He traced a finger down my neck, his voice slurred. "Which duchy was it?"

Furrowing my brow, I cocked my head. "What?"

"That ye fled from. Father wanted ye to marry a man you didna like, aye?" He swayed into me. "What's your rank? Duchess? Princess?"

Nearly choking on my mouthful of whisky, I swallowed it down and giggled. "You think I'm a runaway princess?"

He stroked my finger. "The hands never lie."

Snorting, my head fell to Gavin's shoulder as Henry reached for my cup.

I pulled it back and straightened. "What do you think you're doing?"

"Where's your dignity, woman?" His face flushed nearly as purple as the vein pulsating on his forehead. "You're drunk and makin' a fool o' yourself. It's time to go."

"I am not drunk," I said with all the hauteur I could muster. "I'm buzzed."

Which was true, until I gulped another big sip. That one did me in. Even as the whisky haze settled over me, a shadow of shame at my lack of tolerance grayed my mood. A year ago, I could have drunk twice as much and walked a balance beam. Now my vision was starting to split and couldn't figure out if I was leaning.

Gavin swayed against me and nuzzled my neck. "Ye smell divine."

"You're a nice," I hiccupped. "A nice guy." I tried to pat his head but tapped his face instead. We both burst into peals of laughter. Raising my tankard, I took down the last of the whisky. Warmth crept through my chest. I didn't know why I thought it tasted bad earlier. It was amazing. Best thing I'd ever had.

Struggling, I attempted to set my cup on the table. "Finished." The tankard toppled, and I squinted at it, confused.

"Here, have mine." Gavin nudged his cup toward me.

Before I had the chance to take it, Henry chucked the tankard across the room.

"Dinna be like that, Gow Chrom." Tilting his head toward the smoke hole in the ceiling, Gavin swayed. "Sssun's ssstill up." He put a hand next to Henry's on my arm as if he meant to play a game of tug o' war with my limb. "Plenty o' time 'til curfew."

"Remove your hands, Peacock." Henry's gravelly voice brooked no argument, and Gavin released me. Henry leaned toward me across the table. His teeth bit into his bottom lip. "Have ye no shame?"

"Shame?" The whisky in my belly ignited into flame, and suddenly my mind was as clear-headed as if I hadn't drunk at all.

"*Shame?*" My voice grew louder, shriller. I staggered around the table, and Henry rose to meet me. Tears sprang from my eyes, and I shoved him hard in the chest. "Don't you talk to me about shame, asshole. You're the one kicking me out because of some girl you're not even faithful to." My voice choked. "You can't say anything. If I want to take a hundred men to bed, you don't get to say a goddamned..."

Something hot and furious flamed in Henry's eyes. He seized me around the waist and next thing I knew, he'd hoisted me over his shoulder.

The world turned upside down, and I yelped with surprise. "Let go!" I pounded his back, as he carried me through the tavern. "Put me down you goddamned son of a bitch."

But he didn't put me down, not when we got outside. Not even when I vomited down the back of his shirt. He kept walking, and I kept screaming until at some point between the tavern and home, I blacked out.

# Chapter Fifteen

I wasn't sure of the time. Four, maybe five in the morning? All I knew was the sun hadn't yet risen, my head pounded, and my queasy stomach had nothing left in it to throw up. I stood in the back yard, chilled near frozen after a whore's bath at the rain barrels, but I couldn't bring myself to go back inside. Not when I had a night full of memories to relive in painful, mortifying detail.

Why? Why had I acted like that? I'd been so jealous and vindictive. Like a few lingering touches meant I owned Henry. Like he owed me. Which was crazy. I wasn't his girlfriend, and he'd already done more for me than anyone could expect. I'd been ungrateful, petty, and immature. Not that these were new traits, by any means, but this time seemed different, like maybe I'd finally gone too far.

I needed to apologize and quick, but I had no idea when I'd get the chance. I couldn't do it in front of Mairi. I shuddered to think what she might do if she overheard what happened. I stared out at the smithy. Maybe I could meet him before he started work for the day. Donald would give us a few minutes alone, and—

Holy shit. I squinted at the smithy. Smoke wafted from the roof. Somebody had lit a forge fire, and there was only one person that somebody could be. My stomach gave a queasy flip. I must have pissed Henry off so royally he'd chosen to sleep in the workshop rather than in the same house as me.

I didn't know what to do. Should I go to him? Demand he hear me out? Throw myself on my knees and beg forgiveness? No. That would be foolish. I should give him time. Let him cool off a bit. Besides, he probably wouldn't appreciate being woken before the cock crowed, especially by a girl who'd thrown up on his best tunic and called him a motherfucker for all his troubles.

Only, my feet didn't seem to agree with that logic, because the whole time I'd been debating with myself, I'd also been walking straight toward the smithy. Pausing at the door, I acknowledged this was probably going to make things worse and went in anyway.

He wasn't asleep like I'd imagined. Sitting ramrod straight atop an anvil, he stared into a low-burning forge fire. I knew by the slight raise of his shoulders he heard me come in, but he didn't turn his head or say a word.

I walked over to him, and he slid to the side, making room on the anvil, which was tall and long, like a love seat made for broadswords. A million words rattled in my head, a thousand different versions of the same apology, but for some reason, I couldn't muster the courage to say a single one. So, for the longest time, we just sat together, staring into the forge fire. Lost and silent.

Then, as the peat died to embers, his hand closed around mine. Warmth ran through me at his touch, and strength surged through me, emboldening me to finally speak the words I'd come to say. I twisted toward him. "Henry..."

"I willna see ye homeless." His voice was low and raspy. "I willna see ye put in harm's way for a bit o' bread in your belly and a roof o'er your head. Not when I have those things to freely give."

Closing my eyes, I hung my head. "That's not—" I heaved a great breath. "I can't—" God, why was this so hard? I tucked my legs against my chest. "You don't have to do that."

His lips parted like he meant to protest, but I shook my head. "No, listen. You don't owe me anything." My voice grew thick. "I'm sorry. I'm *so* sorry for ever making you feel like you did."

I blinked back tears, but a few trickled out anyway. "I'm the one who owes you. You saved my life. You gave me a home.

122

Because of you, I have the chance to live a dream I thought I'd lost forever."

Weariness stole over his features. "Ye mean to marry Gavin then..." His head fell in a slow, reluctant nod. "Ye'll be a woman o' wealth. Titled. Free to do as ye please." He smiled, but it looked more like a grimace. "Any woman's dream."

Gaping, I stared in disbelief. "That's not my dream. I want to own a tavern."

His eyes widened in surprise.

"That's what I'm trying to tell you." My bottom lip vibrated with emotion. "You haven't condemned me to some terrible life; you've given me the chance to live the life I've always wanted."

Hope lit his eyes. "Ye dinna plan to marry Gavin?"

I wiped the tears from my cheeks. "I don't plan to marry anyone."

After a relieved breath, he paused and tilted his head. "Never?"

Sniffling, I shrugged. "I don't know. Maybe."

His jaw fell open, incredulous. "You're serious?"

Not sure why he was acting so surprised, I stared at him. I'd said as much to Mairi in front of him at least ten times. "Is it really so strange?"

Gaze bug-eyed, he nodded. "Aye."

I shrugged. "I'm fine with strange. It's happy that matters." My eyes flicked to his, and I studied his face. "What about you? Are you happy?"

A shadow fell over his features. "What do ye mean?"

"This thing between you and Coira." I pursed my lips, searching for the right phrasing. "It's not exactly normal either, is it?"

In fact, if anything, his situation was weirder than mine. I'd met plenty of unmarried women, but in all my time here, I'd never heard of anyone dating. People were either married, or they were single. There was no in-between.

"Well..." He paused to consider. "I'm not unhappy. We understand each other, me and Coira. We—" He ran a hand through his hair. "We dinna expect more from each other than we're able to give."

I didn't know what to make of that, but for some reason it made me sad in a way that had nothing to do with jealousy.

His eyes narrowed as he scrutinized my face. "Tell me, though. What's your reasonin' for not wantin' to wed?"

"I don't know." I shrugged. "It's not like I'm *against* marriage. If I met the right man and fell in love, sure, I'd consider it, but—"

"*Love!*" He spoke the word as if it were the craziest thing he'd ever heard. "You're unbelievable. How do ye expect to fall in love *before* ye marry?"

I understood what he meant. In an era of arranged marriages, love was an after-the-fact bonus, not a prerequisite. But even here, it wasn't unheard of for lovers to run off and elope, so the idea couldn't be that foreign to him.

"Have you honestly never been in love?" I gawked. "Not even as a lad? No neighborhood farm girls who made your heart flutter. Nothing?"

His lip curled. "Love is somethin' bards made up to make lassies swoon. In the real world there's lust, and there's respect. Nothin' more."

I ran my thumb over Gran's ring. "You're wrong."

"Ye think so?" His voice rang with honest curiosity.

"I know so." My stomach tightened with love and longing. "To marry my gran, my granda crossed an ocean. He gave up kin and country and all he held dear. If that's not love, I don't know what is."

His gaze fell to my hand. "That was your grandmither's ring, aye?"

I cocked my head. "How'd you know?"

"Ye always touch it when ye talk about her." He played with the hem of his tunic. "Was she— Is it like Gavin said? Did ye come from wealth?"

Hesitation froze me in place as I considered. In some ways, I'd grown up richer than Gavin. Hell, than the king himself—no amount of jewels and gold could compete with the luxury of indoor plumbing. But compared to the people in my time, we were as blue-collar, lower-middle class as they come.

"We were...ordinary." There, that was a good compromise. It wasn't an outright lie at least.

Henry snorted. "Ordinary? You? Impossible."

His words should have made me nervous. Just another reminder that I stuck out like a puzzle piece in the wrong box. But his tone held only admiration, and his eyes...well, they held something else.

My flesh began to tingle, and I forced myself to break eye contact. Dammit. Had I learned nothing tonight? He wasn't mine. He wasn't for me. I swallowed. "Yup, just regular old people. Granda owned a tavern. Nothing fancy."

He leaned closer. "And your parents?"

God, he smelled good, like cloves and rosemary, and just a hint of smoke. I gulped. "They died in a...*carriage* accident not long after I was born."

His brow furrowed. "You're a mystery, ye ken that?" An amused smirk played on his lips. "I've heard words come out o' your mouth even the meanest street urchin wouldna deign to say. And when I think on that, I can believe ye grew up in a tavern." His ribs rose with a deep inhale. "But sometimes when ye speak, it's with the command o' kings. Like you're used to bein' obeyed without question." He glanced at Gran's ring. "And when I think on that, and the fact ye can read, and that ye wear a gem on your finger no tavern owner could possibly afford... Well, I have to think there's more to your past than you're tellin' me."

Fuck. Fuck. Fuck. My gaze darted around the room. "Maybe so, but, uh...a woman should have a bit of mystery about her, don't you think?" I cringed internally. Did I really just say that?

"Oh, c'mon." A frustrated huff puffed out his chest. "That's all you're goin' to say? At least tell me where the ring came from. Was your grandfaither a bandit? Did he win it in a dice game?"

My shoulders sagged with relief. The story of Gran's ring was one tale I could tell. "You really want to know?" Eyes wide and eager, he nodded. I smirked. "You won't believe me."

His hand slid over mine. "Tell me!"

"A fairy gave it to him." I waited for his groan, and he didn't disappoint. "It's true, I swear!" My knee fell against his as I shifted into a more comfortable position. "It happened when he was a boy, right on the banks of Loch Lomond."

He chuckled. "Now I ken you're lyin'. Ye've already told me ye were born in a distant land."

"*I* was, but not Granda." I sat a little bit taller as Granda's familial pride flowed through me. "He was a Highlander through and through. A Buchanan from a long line of Buchanans who could trace their lineage back to the first clan chief."

"A Buchanan, aye?" Fog glazed his eyes as if he were mentally cross-referencing everything he knew about me with everything he'd ever heard about Buchanan's. "Well, I suppose I shouldna be too shocked. Ye do have the Northern temper."

Choosing to ignore that, I continued with my tale. "Anyway...one day he walked down to the loch to do a bit of fishing, and he found a goose all tangled up in a net. So, like any decent person, he cut the bird free. Only, it turned out not to be a goose at all. It transformed, right there on the shore, into a beautiful fairy woman. She was so grateful for him freeing her, she offered him one free wish."

"So he wished for a ring o' gold and jewels." He nodded in approval. "Verra practical."

"No!" Laughing, I smacked his shoulder. "He wished for a long life full of love and adventure."

A grin split his face.

"The fairy waved her hands," I demonstrated the gesture, "and up from the water rose a blue glass bottle stoppered with wax." Holding up my hand, I brandished Gran's ring. "Inside, he found this ring and a note, telling him what he needed to do to make his wish come true."

"A note?" His nose wrinkled. "I've never heard o' a fairy writin' letters."

Grinning, I met his eyes. "*That's* the part of the story you have a problem with. Not the fairy goose?"

He scoffed. "How's a wee lad supposed to ken how to read?"

126

"I don't know." A snort escaped my nose, and I giggled. "That's just how he told it. But you're taking the story too literally. My guess is someone tossed a message in a bottle into the loch, and Granda just happened to find it."

His eyes twinkled, even as he smirked. "Aye, or the whole story's made up, and your granda made a secret fortune rustlin' cattle."

Memories flitted through my mind of Granda watching his old western flicks, and I smiled to myself. "I'm not saying he wouldn't have stolen a cow or two if he'd had the chance, but the bottle, at least, was real. I've seen it."

Creases formed in Henry's forehead as his eyebrows raised in surprise. "The letter too?"

I nodded. "You could see it through the glass, but he'd sealed it back up, so I never got the chance to read it, and he never would tell me what it said."

My chest tightened at the realization I'd never discover the answer to that particular mystery. There were so many questions I would have asked Granda if I'd known I'd never see him again. So many things I would have said. I stared out the smithy window and sighed. Nothing I could do about it now.

"Fiona?" His voice was soft, full of concern. "Are ye well?"

"Huh?" My gaze refocused back on Henry. "I'm fine. I was just thinking I'd better head in before Mairi wakes and finds me gone." I studied his face one last time, reassuring myself no lingering resentment hid behind his eyes. "So, we're all right now, me and you?"

With his slight bow of the head, the weight that had been sitting on my chest since the tavern lifted, and I rose to leave.

Henry's hand clasped mine. Warmth flowed up my arm. "Ye can still stay, ye ken."

"What?" The heat of his touch traveled to my chest.

His eyes locked on mine. "Build your tavern. Live your dream. I dinna care. Just stay."

"I—"

"Mairi needs ye, and the lad'll be gone for his journeyman travels soon. And..." His words trailed off, but I heard what remained unsaid.

I looked at our intertwined fingers. Thought about how easily they'd come together. About how natural it felt for the two of us to sit here and talk. About how I hadn't been the only one to act jealous last night.

Things were happening between us, whether I wanted them to or not, and if I agreed to stay, it would set things in motion, from which there'd be no turning back. And deep down, I wanted to go down that path with him. I couldn't deny it anymore. Not after what happened tonight. But I knew Henry too well to use him as a fuckboy, and I knew myself too well to ever consider being a sidepiece. My love for people was either whole-hearted or not at all, and somehow he had managed to work his way into the former.

But before I made my decision, there was one thing I had to know. "What about Coira?"

"I'll...Well—" His jaw jutted defensively. "I'm allowed. It's my right to have a maidservant."

Maidservant. He might as well have punched me in the gut. I stiffened and removed my hand from his. "But I wouldn't be your maidservant anymore."

I turned and walked away, feeling his eyes on my back with every step.

# Chapter Sixteen

Mairi ripped the blanket off me. "Up!"

I winced. Going back to sleep had been a bad idea. I'd slipped right into a hangover coma, and now my body was punishing me for coming out too soon. Lightning bolts zipped and zapped inside my skull. My stomach churned with bile.

"Had a good time last night, did ye?" Her voice came clipped and harsh.

I rose from the mattress, as slow and careful as a post-op patient trying not to split stitches. What was with this hangover? A few hours ago, I'd been fine. Just a mild headache and low-grade nausea. Now electric currents shot through my brain like... Fuck. Like I was having a migraine. It had been years since I'd had one, thanks to quarterly injections from my doctor, but the last dose must have finally run out, and I didn't have so much as a Tylenol to help me through it.

Mairi glared, the scowl on her face more severe than I'd ever seen it. I bowed my head and braced for whatever punishment she planned to dole out.

"Ye ought to be ashamed." Her clenched fists vibrated with rage. "Never mind the damage ye've done your own reputation, drinking to excess in public, ye'll be lucky if Henry doesna lose half his customers once word spreads, he's got a wanton drunkard for a maidservant."

Keeping my gaze averted, I refused to argue, no matter how improbable that seemed. I might not give a shit about reputation, but I knew Mairi did, and I also knew she'd have to deal with a shit ton of passive-aggressive comments from the old gossipmongers she hung around with. I'd done wrong, and I'd take my licks.

Her voice rose an octave. "And now, I'm goin' to have to visit every house from here to the Horsegate to try and fight the rumors." She whipped a finger in the direction of the washing barrel. "On a laundry day, nay less."

"I'm sorry." My voice came out hoarse and laced with pain. "I'll do the wash. You don't have to worry."

She narrowed her eyes to dagger points. "That's the least ye'll do."

My eyes welled with tears, partly from an honest sense of shame and partly because my skull threatened to split in half, and I was scared to death I might throw up on Mairi's shoes. Fortunately, she was in too much of a huff to linger. She snatched her cloak, stormed out of the house, and slammed the door behind her.

Crumpling onto the mattress, I pulled my knees to my chest. Never in my life had I been sicker or more wretched. It wasn't even her anger that bothered me so much. I'd pissed her off before, and I was sure I'd do it again, but behind all that rage, she seemed hurt, and that I couldn't abide. Somehow, I had to make it up to her, and I didn't think laundry would be enough. At the same time, for me, it might be *too* much. Laundry was grueling work, and I couldn't see straight with the force of this migraine.

Somehow, though, I found the force of will to drag my ass out of bed and lumber over to the wash tub. Two weeks' worth of dirty clothes swam in a vat of murky, gray lye water. Sprigs of lavender floated in the mix in an attempt to combat the slight ammonia smell of the lye.

I heaved the tub off the floor. The thing had to weigh eighty pounds. Dirty lye water sloshed down my front, as I maneuvered out the door. Outside the sun scorched my eyes. Forge hammers banged in the smithy, and every blow struck like a spike to the brain.

130

I dropped off the tub by the boulder we used for laundry, took a deep breath, and headed back to the house to do it again with the rinse bucket.

By the time I was ready to begin, water soaked my front, my fingers were stiff with cold, and flashing spots sparked in my vision. The clamor from the smithy grew louder. The sun brighter. I vomited a mouthful of stomach acid, spit, and wiped my mouth on my sleeve. Then I pulled a tunic from the tub, draped it over the boulder, and beat it with my laundry bat. The impact of wood against rock jolted through my body. Bones. Stomach. Head. Noise upon noise. My eyes watered. Snot dripped down my face. I rinsed the shirt and spread it on the grass to dry.

I moved onto the second garment. My vision blurred, and I had to squint to focus. I tried to throw up again, but my stomach just cramped, and my mouth filled with phlegmy froth. Still, I kept going. I couldn't let Mairi down.

By the time I got to the third shirt, my body gave out. I collapsed onto the grass and curled into the fetal position. Retching and sobbing, I covered my ears with my arms. I told myself I had to get up, but even my inner voice rang too loud in my head.

The noise from the smithy abruptly stopped, and a few seconds later, Donald's voice ripped through my skull. "Hal, come quick. I think she's died!"

I tried to tell him I was fine, but the second my voice rose above a whisper, my head gave a jolt, and I abandoned the attempt. The ground beneath me vibrated from the stampede of running feet. Then Donald and Henry were hovering over me. I rolled onto my back and stared at them.

"Fiona, what's happened?" Donald knelt beside me. "Are ye ill?"

Groaning, I tried to focus on him. "Give me a few minutes. I'll be all right."

"Go inside and lie down." Concern pulled at the corners of his mouth. "Ye canna work like this."

I shook my head, which was a big mistake. Stomach acid shot up my esophagus and scorched my throat. Swallowing hard, more tears leaked from my eyes. "I can't. She'll kill me." I took a deep breath. Then another. And another, until I was sure my voice would come out steady. "I'll be all right. There's not much left."

"Your face is the color o' mushy peas." Donald's voice gave a puberty-laden crack. "You're not well."

"Dinna bother arguin' with her." Leaning over, Henry peered down his nose at me, jaw clenched. "She thinks she can take the world on by herself."

Donald looked up at Henry. "Hal, she canna—"

"Just go back to," I swallowed a dry heave, "work. I'll be fine"

"Eejit." Shaking, Henry scooped me into his arms and carried me toward the house. "Finish the wash, lad," he called over his shoulder before kicking the door open and ferrying me up the stairs.

My eyes glossed with unshed tears. "Henry...You don't have to—"

A muscle in his jaw ticked. "For once in your life, be silent." He deposited me in his bed and disappeared out the door. A few minutes later, he returned with a Bannock and tankard. "Finish these and go to sleep." Then he left without another word.

The steady crack of Donald beating the laundry carried through the window, though the volume was much milder at this distance. Thankfully, the clang of forge hammers never resumed. I finished my meal and sunk into Henry's pillow. It smelled like him—hints of peat and rosemary. I inhaled deeply and next thing I knew, hours had passed, and Donald was shaking me awake.

"Hurry. Mairi's here." His voice squeaked. "Hal's distractin' her in the yard, but there isna much time."

I rose, headache gone, but stomach still sour, and followed Donald down the stairs. When I saw the room, I gasped. Food simmered in the kettle. Every surface had been dusted and swept. Fresh hay lay strewn across the floor.

Donald grinned. "Hal did it, while I minded the laundry."

My breath hitched, and I thought I might cry all over again, this time out of gratitude. Moments later, Mairi and Henry bustled through the door. Henry paused at the threshold while she strode around the house, assessing every square inch for fault. She couldn't find a thing to complain about, which, for some reason, seemed to piss her off even more.

She marched over to me, her face just as sharp-lined with fury as when she left this morning. "I'll have ye ken, Winnie MacSheah's godson saw ye at the tavern. Gamblin' too, were ye? It's not just unseemly; it's unchristian."

I bowed my head, not foolish enough to defend myself.

Donald stuck his finger into the kettle and tasted its contents. Somehow Mairi sensed this act, even though her back was to him. "Get your fingers out o' the pot afore I cut 'em off. And raise that chain. I've cookin' to do." She tossed a paper wrapped package on the table. "Now out o' my sight, the lot o' ye."

In silence, the three of us filed out of the house. "Thank you," I whispered when the door clicked closed. Henry didn't look at me. He just shouldered past and headed toward the smithy.

Donald put a hand on my shoulder. "We were happy to do it." His gaze flicked toward Henry's retreating back. "The both o' us."

"Has he said anything?" I bit my lip. "I mean, about last night?" For the life of me, I couldn't figure out where we stood. It seemed like he couldn't stand the sight of me right now, yet he'd gone to so much trouble to help me.

Donald grimaced. "He hasna exactly been in a talkin' sort o' mood."

"Oh..." My stomach twisted, guilt riding on a wave of nausea. I forced a smile. "Well, thanks again. You saved me today."

"Fi..." His eyes filled with pity. "About Henry...Just be patient with him, aye."

I nodded. "Sure."

Donald headed to the smithy, and I curled in the grass behind the blackberry bush and took a nap.

Sometime later, Mairi called us in to eat. As soon as Henry's butt hit the chair, he leaned back and closed his eyes. Within moments, his breathing deepened, and I was pretty sure he'd fallen asleep. Considering he'd pulled an all-nighter, I was surprised he'd made it this long.

Carrying a clay bowl, Mairi arrived at the table. "A thank ye for all the embarrassment and trouble ye've caused me." She set the bowl down and flashed a sadistic grin. "Go ahead, then. Eat."

Heat drained from my face. Sheep dick. Mother fucking sheep dick.

A few months back Mairi whipped up this delicacy when a neighbor traded Henry a batch for a length of chain. I threw a fit and flat out refused to eat them, earning myself an empty belly and a slap in the face. Clearly, she hadn't forgotten the incident any more than I had.

"Go on." She shoved the bowl toward me.

I stared at the pile of dicks. Rubbery, curling members, studded with veins. Instead of roasting them like before, she'd boiled them, and they maintained a disturbingly flesh-colored tone. I swallowed. My stomach churned. I couldn't do it. I'd rather spend another day doing laundry with a migraine than go through the psychological trauma of eating a penis.

I put a hand to my stomach. "I'm sorry. I can't."

She leaned forward. "Ye'll not have another meal until ye've eaten what I've given ye."

Taking a deep breath, I forced my voice to calm respectfulness. "There's no point eating food I'm going to throw up. It's wasteful."

"The *point* is atonement." She stared with intense, unblinking eyes. "I love ye, lass, but ye've disobeyed me and shamed every single member of this household with your unladylike behavior. As penance, you're goin' to humble yourself and do as you're told." Her gaze snapped to the bowl. "Now eat."

What could I say? She was absolutely fucking right. Plucking one of the penises from the bowl, I stared at it. I could do this. If I ate fast and barely chewed, it would be over quick. I just had to pretend the dick was something else. A hotdog. A

134

flesh-colored, foreskin-having hotdog... My stomach heaved. Who was I kidding? There was no making this better.

Donald plopped into the seat beside me, his face still wet from a scrub at the rain barrels. "Sheep johnnies!" He snatched one from the bowl and ripped off the head with his teeth. I proceeded to throw up.

"Fiona?" He shifted his chair out of the pile of mess I was creating on the floor.

Mairi huffed. "Quit bein' dramatic."

Henry jolted awake at the ruckus and slammed a hand on the table. "For the love o' Christ!"

It was a mark of how angry he sounded that she didn't mention his blaspheming. I finished vomiting and righted myself. Mairi and Donald sat frozen. Henry's gaze darted from me to the vomit to the bowl full of dicks, and understanding flashed across his face.

He met Mairi's eyes, and his lip curled. "Get Fiona the pottage." He shoved the bowl of dicks at Donald. "Eat those outside. And Fiona," his voice rose an octave, "I swear to God if ye ever drink that much again, I'll not save ye from the consequences." Leaning back in his chair, he crossed his arms. "Now can I please have a goddamned meal so I can get some sleep."

At once, Donald and Mairi jumped to their feet. Donald hustled outside with the sheep dicks. Mairi doled out pottage, and I sat in stunned silence.

Once she passed out fresh trenchers—these ones topped with chunks of pork and thick gravy—we ate. Nobody spoke a word. The air hung thick about us, tense and tenuous as each of us retreated into our own private thoughts. So, when Donald burst back through the door and announced we had a visitor, all three of us jumped in our seats.

He waved in a boy, maybe a year or two his junior. He wore a turquoise tunic—wool, but high quality—and sturdy leather boots. He held a neatly tied package, wrapped in decorative paper with a delicate velvet pouch looped through the bow.

He raised his eyebrows. "Fiona?"

When I nodded, he handed me the package. "Sir Gavin o' Keefe sends his regards."

My mouth flapped open, too stunned to speak.

The boy barreled on as if determined to relay the message before he forgot his script. "Sir Gavin wishes to concede he lost the wager betwixt ye but asks ye do him the honor o' accompanying him to the merchant's gala despite his loss."

"I...uh..." I couldn't seem to form words. I glanced at Henry, who sat pale and rigid as a corpse. Dammit, this was the worst possible timing. Couldn't the kid have shown up while Henry was in the smithy? "Tell Gavin I'm sor—"

"O' course she'll go!" Mairi shot from her chair. Putting an arm around the boy's shoulders, she guided him to the door. "Tell Sir Gavin she'll be delighted to join him! Now there's a good, lad." She shoved him outside and closed the door behind him.

I thought my eyeballs might pop out of my skull. "Mairi, what the hell?"

She strode back to the table. "He's a duke's son. Bastard son, but still..." She shrugged. "Ye'd be a fool not to go."

A crash reverberated through the house as Henry's chair clattered to the floor. A second later, he was halfway across the room, storming toward the door.

"Wait!" I rose to go after him.

Mairi seized my arm. "Let him go." The door slammed closed.

"What's wrong with you? Don't you see he's upset?"

Shifting in her chair to face me fully, she nodded. "Aye, I see it well, but unlike ye, I see a fair bit more."

My lip trembled. "What the hell does—"

"Listen to me." Eyes boring into mine, she squeezed my hands. "The lad needs to feel what he's feelin' right now. Do ye understand?"

I shook my head. I didn't understand. Any of this.

She gave my hands a squeeze. "Then just trust I'm right. We've all got demons; it's time he fought his."

I nodded and blinked back tears. I was so tired of fighting with Henry. No matter the topsy-turvy the state of our tenuous relationship, no matter what happened in the end, I didn't want to see him hurt. And even though I didn't know what demons he was supposed to be fighting, I had to trust that Mairi was right. She wrapped her arms around me, and I laid my head on her shoulder. After a day of everything going wrong, one thing finally felt right.

When I finally straightened, she elbowed me in the arm. "A duke's son...Verra well done!"

A teary chuckle escaped my mouth.

Nudging the package toward me, she grinned. "Well, come on then. Let's see."

I untied the ribbon, pulled off the velvet pouch, and tipped its contents onto the table. Silver coins spilled into a hefty pile. Although I still wasn't good enough with the money to know at a glance how much the coins were worth, judging by the expression on her face, it must have been a substantial amount.

I unfolded the paper on the package, revealing a silk gown—turquoise, of course—trimmed with white, speckled fur. It was the most beautiful dress I'd seen in all my time here.

My jaw fell open, and when I met her eyes, I was struck too dumb to speak. Between the coins and the dress, I'd just gone from a pauper to...well, if not rich, at least financially stable.

Mairi cackled and clapped her hands. "Just wait until I tell Winnie MacSheah about this!"

# Chapter Seventeen

Henry glared at the root cellar door I'd scavenged from the hovel across the street. "Get that filthy rubble out o' here."

I tapped my foot. Any excuse he could find. He'd been picking at me for weeks—I chewed too loud; he didn't like my humming; how dare I take the last Bannock when he'd been saving it for afternoon snack. But he wouldn't get to me this time. No way I'd let him draw me into another fight.

I forced my voice into non-confrontational evenness. "I can't. The rain'll ruin my work." I gestured at the various lists, calculations, and conversion tables I'd scrawled across the wood with a charcoal stick. My best attempt at organizing a business plan without the use of Excel, or, for that matter, paper and pen.

"Look at this place." He made a gesture that encompassed the room. "I can hardly move. Get these barrels out o' here, too, while you're at it."

"Really?" I raised a brow. "You can hardly move?" I had bought four more ale barrels in addition to Mairi's three, but they were tucked against the wall in line with the other casks, not in the way of anything.

"I like my house *tidy*. So, get your mess out o' here."

Setting down my charcoal stick, I turned to fully face him. "No."

"No?" His voice rang with challenge.

I rose from my chair. "I'm not about to ruin my ale because you feel like being a dick."

A bark of indignant laughter rumbled from his throat. "Oh, aye?"

"Aye." I rolled the word in a scathing mock burr. Turning, he marched toward my ale barrels. I darted after him. "Don't you dare!"

Crouching, he circled his arms around the kegs middle.

"Stop it!" I yanked at his arm. "Goddammit, stop!" Grabbing him by the hair, I pulled. He howled with pain as I wrenched and twisted. "Let go!"

"Get off me!" His neck strained back.

"Never!" Digging my heels in for support, I tightened my hold.

"What in the name o' St. Raphael is goin' on here?" A voice cracked through the air, sharp as a bolt of lightning.

We froze. Dropping Henry's hair, I put my feet to the floor. He released my barrel, and we stood before Mairi like a couple of naughty children caught roughhousing next to the good china. Her narrow, assessing eyes raked over us.

Though I expected her to yell, after a moment's pause, she tilted her chin in the direction of the door. "Best get to work, lad."

Eyes on his feet, Henry did as she suggested, and I returned to the table.

She filled a couple tankards and slid one over to me. "What did ye do, force him to drink more o' your ale?"

I gave her the side-eye and glowered.

As if trying to squelch a laugh, she clamped her mouth closed. "No really, what was it about this time?"

Shrugging, I picked up my charcoal. "More nonsense." I crossed out *paper* and *quill* from the list headed, *things I want,* and added it to the list entitled, *things I need.* I hadn't wanted to spend any more of my dwindling coin on non-essentials, but I didn't want to hear another damn word out of Henry's mouth. Let him find a way to complain about paper.

My gaze dropped to the bottom corner where I kept track of cash and expenditures. I couldn't believe how fast I'd blown through Gavin's money. Well, not *blown through.* I'd been very particular in my spending choices, and a good chunk of the cash wasn't gone, just set aside for future rent. Still, after buying four barrels, two bushels of malt, a copper kettle, and a variety of herbs and spices, I had just enough left to buy either a mattress or a blanket, but not both.

I sighed. The first few months in my new place were going to be rough. I supposed I could always sell Gavin's dress if my situation got too bad, but I didn't want to resort to that unless I absolutely had to.

Mairi put a hand on my back. "Oh, come on. Enough with the sour face. I'm sorry I jested about your ale."

I sighed. "It's not that."

Okay, it was a little bit that. After fourteen different brews with fourteen different flavors of gruit, I still hadn't found a recipe good enough to sell. I was on my last batch, and if this one didn't work, I'd either have to give up or get used to sleeping on the floor.

She gave a sympathetic nod. "I ken it's been hard with the lad lately."

"*Hard?*" My charcoal stick snapped in two. "He's been a complete and total ass. For no reason!"

She snorted. "I wish ye'd met my goodman. Ye'd rethink your definition o' arse."

My eyes widened. I hadn't realized she was ever married. "Was he...mean?" I couldn't think of a polite way to ask if he'd been an abusive fucker like so many of the men the women here got strapped with.

A grimace deepened her forehead wrinkles. "Terrible temper, and jealous as a barbary pigeon. Had it in his head the butcher had eyes for me. For years we'd row every time I came home with a cut o' pork." Her voice filled with laughter. "So ye ken what I did?"

I raised an eyebrow. "Stopped buying pork?"

Laughing, she grinned. "I bought a wee pig."

I groaned. "If this story ends with, 'Then we killed it and ate it,' I don't want to hear."

"Well, aye, we did, but that isna the point." Her eyes danced with mirth as she leaned forward. "While he was at the tavern, I wrapped the wee beastie in my nightshift and brought

140

him into the bed with me." Her voice bubbled with laughter. "Well, he's deep in his cups by the time he comes home, and it's late, naught but hearth light to see by, so all he's able to make out is me in bed with my arm around a body..." She giggled. "So he gets to hollerin' and pulls his sword. 'I'll kill ye,' he shouts. 'We duel at dawn.'"

Mairi laughed even harder, and I couldn't help but laugh too.

"Poor pig runs out the bed, squealin' with fright and knocks my goodman straight on his arse." She snorted.

Covering my mouth with my hands, I gulped. "Oh, god, he didn't hurt the pig, did he?"

She waved off my concern. "Nay, he laughed, and after that, I never had any problems buying pork again."

"So he got over his jealousy because of a pig." A chuckle escaped my lips. "That's a new one."

"O' course he didna. Ye think a man can change who he is just like that?" Her eyes twinkled with mirth. "But it didna matter, because from that day on, every time I wanted a bit o' bacon, I'd give him a choice. He could either send me to the butcher or duel the pig."

I smirked. "You realize all I took from that story is that I should knock Henry over with a barn animal, right?"

Winking, she raised her tankard in salute. "If it works, it works."

Bending my head over my work, I chuckled. "Maybe the neighbors will let me borrow one of their cows." I scanned the list of gruit flavors I'd already used.

Mairi gasped.

"What? Cows are off-limits?" Drawing my eyes from the board, I looked at her. She wore this very strange expression, confusion and shock all wrapped up in wrinkles.

"This isna my ale." Her voice came out breathy with astonishment. "It must be yours."

My stomach heaved with dread. "Oh, God, what's wrong with it? Tell me it's not like the time with the rue."

On one of my first attempts developing a new recipe, I accidentally used her rue instead of my rosemary, and long story short, Donald got the shits for a week.

"Nay." She sounded like she could barely believe her own words. "It's good. It's actually good."

My breath hitched. My body buzzed. "Are you serious?"

She nodded, and a few prideful tears slipped down her cheeks. "Ye did it, lass."

I let out an ear-piercing squeal. "Oh my god. Oh my god. Oh my god!" Snatching my cup, I sloshed half the ale on the table in my haste to drink. I took a sip, and holy shit, it was good! Really, really good! Light, yet full-bodied, almost shandy-like.

Unbelievable! Of all the batches I'd brewed, I never expected this would be the one to turn out. I'd flavored it with galangal root, a spice I'd never even heard of, but bought because it had a vaguely citrus-like smell, and nobody at the market seemed to know what a lemon was.

The door creaked open, and Henry came inside. "Oi, lad." Mairi waved him over. "Come and try the lassie's ale. I havena had a cup this good since the fair."

A sneer darkened his face. "Not thirsty." He strode past the table, snagged a stale Bannock from the shelf, and headed back outside.

All the joy inside me burned to ash. He'd been pissing me off all week, but *that* hurt my feelings. This was my biggest accomplishment since the day I'd come here, and he couldn't be bothered to take a sip? Such an ass. I wanted to knock him to the ground and shake him. If only I had a pig...

Mairi put a comforting hand on my back. "Best get started on the pottage. Can ye fetch me a bucket o' water?"

I nodded, mind more on him than her request, but then her words seeped in, and I froze. Bucket! Who needed a pig when I had a bucket! "Mairi, I need your help."

"All right, lass." Puzzlement tinged her voice.

I grinned. "Where can I find some rope?"

~ * ~

A few hours later, thick stew bubbled in the pot, my chores were done, and I'd created two new columns on my board: *marketing* and *distribution*. Under *marketing* I had two items listed—*old biddies* and *town crier.* I figured word of mouth would be the best and cheapest form of advertising, and for that, I planned to enlist the help of the fastest tongues in the west— Mairi and her gossip-loving cronies. After that, a few pennies slipped into the town crier's palm, and I'd have the next best thing to a radio ad.

Distribution, however, was a trickier matter. I didn't want to wait until I had my own place to start selling. The more money I had up front, the better, and if I already had a customer base, life might not be quite so difficult when I moved. I sighed when my eyes fell on the single word beneath the *distribution* header: *Henry.* Three question marks followed his name, because it seemed so damned unlikely I could convince him to let me sell from the house. Not when he'd just spent the morning waging war against my ale barrels.

Mairi came back inside with a bit of rope. "I hope this is long enough, because it's all I could find."

I took it from her and tied the rope to the handle of a water bucket. "Should be plenty."

"Me and Donald willna be gone longer than an hour or two, so dinna dawdle." She glanced at the door. "I mean it. If I walk through that door and water crashes on my head, ye'll be made to suffer."

I held my fingers in a scout's honor gesture. "I promise you won't get wet." I set the bucket on the table. "You don't have to leave, you know. It's a simple prank—it won't take long."

She donned her cloak. "Nay. I've been promisin' Donald I'd take him to see Shona anyway. Might as well do it now. Asides, it'll be easier for the two o' ye to settle things between ye without an old woman hoverin' in the wayside."

I nodded. She was probably right. The prank might lighten the mood, but if things were really going to change, we needed to talk. I hugged Mairi and thanked her, before I leaned back, brow furrowed. "Who's Shona?"

She pushed in her chair. "Donald's intended."

"Intended?" I damn near choked on the word. "What do you mean intended? He can't get married. He's a baby!"

She shrugged. "Lad's sixteen. Asides, it's not like they're weddin' on the morrow. He still has to finish his apprenticeship, doesna he?"

My mouth parted, but I was at a loss for words. I knew this was how things were done here, and that was fine...for other people. Not for the kid I'd come to think of as a little brother. He should be having fun, enjoying life. He wasn't ready to take care of a family. Christ, the kid still laughed at fart jokes.

My mind reeled from this new information as Mairi departed, and I got to work on my prank. I considered filling the bucket with ale instead of water. Dousing Henry with the beverage he'd snubbed held a certain poetic appeal, but I couldn't bring myself to waste it. Instead, I filled the bucket with regular old water, cracked the door, and propped the bucket over the ledge. I tied the rope to the window shutter, backed up, and admired my work.

Everything appeared correct, at least, as far as I knew from what I'd seen on cartoons and sitcoms. I'd never actually done the prank before. Laughing to myself, I wondered if *anybody* had ever done this prank before. Maybe I'd be the first person in history to pull the old water bucket over the door gag. I liked the idea—Fiona Buchanan, pioneer of pranking classics.

With nothing left to do but wait, I returned to my work. I put an asterisk beneath the word *Henry* and considered. What objections could he raise to me selling ale out of the house? His voice sounded in my head: *Ye think I want a bunch o' drunkards in my home, tearin' up the place, stealin' whatever they lay hands on?*

I wrote *Strangers* next to the asterisk.

It was a fair concern, even if he hadn't voiced it yet. Mairi probably wouldn't like strangers in and out of the place all day either. I put a dash beneath the asterisk and wrote: *sell outside.* I added another dash and wrote: *only on shop days.*

I wiped the charcoal from my hands and decided that was a pretty good start. He already opened the smithy twice a week to customers. So, if I only sold on those days, he couldn't complain about people showing up.

People showing up...

Oh my god. He already had a customer base. The realization set off an explosion in my head, a world of infinite business possibilities. My fingers tingled, and goosebumps formed on my skin. We could be partners. Customers who came for ale might pick up a length of chain or a new axe. Those who came for weapons might enjoy a nice pint while they browsed. This could be huge. With our combined efforts, we could make a fortune...that was, assuming he didn't reject the idea purely out of spite.

Pacing the room, my heart rate quickened. I had to be patient and wait to pitch him the idea until I caught him in a good mood. Oh hell, fuck patience. I was too damn excited. Running to the window, I flung open the shutters, and shouted Henry's name over and over until the hammering stopped, and he emerged from the smithy.

A few seconds later, his panicked voice carried through the window. "Fiona! Are ye well?" The door pushed open. "What's happ—"

*Crash.*

Down came the water, followed by the bucket.

And down went Henry.

"Oh shit!" I'd forgotten the stupid bucket and clearly my knot tying skills needed work. I ran to him, and my foot landed on mud-slicked earth. I lost traction. For a second, I was flying, arms outstretched like Superman. I bowled into Henry, landing on top of him in a giant bellyflop.

The air knocked from my lungs, and it took me a second to remember the body beneath me was not just some muscly pillow there to catch my fall. I sucked in a painful breath, and sat back on my knees, straddling his waist.

"Are you all right? Are you hurt?" I clutched his chin and turned his head from side-to-side, scared to death I'd given him brain damage. A giant goose egg already formed on his forehead, and his eyes looked glassy. "I'm so sorry. I didn't mean for it to hit you. How bad is it?" I thrust two fingers in his face. "How many fingers am I holding up?"

He wrapped his hand around my splayed fingers. "Fiona..." His voice creaked with pain.

"Yes?" I hovered over him. "What is it? What do you need?"

He squeezed his eyes closed. "Shut up."

I stared, blinking a few times, my mouth hanging open. I snapped it closed. For a second, neither of us spoke. Then I couldn't hold it in any longer. "But you're all right, aren't you?"

A slow smile spread across his face. He chuckled. "That didna last long, did it?" I laughed, too, and for a moment, the world felt right again.

*Too* right, maybe. I suddenly became very aware I was straddling him and judging by the way his body tensed beneath mine, he had become aware of it too. Our eyes locked. His hand rose to my face, and he tucked a loose piece of hair that had fallen out of my headscarf behind my ear. My body buzzed. My stomach clenched.

Before I had the chance to think what it would mean, or why it was a bad idea, I leaned down to kiss him. His arms slid around me, and he pulled me close. Heat radiated between us as our lips met.

And then Henry's girlfriend walked through the door.

# Chapter Eighteen

We scrambled to our feet.

"Coira..." Henry's voice leaked out on a shocked breath.

Her arctic blue eyes bored into his. She was beautiful, no doubt. White blonde hair, tall and lithe, skin expertly painted to pale, poreless perfection. A veritable medieval Barbie...that was, if Barbie suffered from acute lead poisoning. I wondered how far gone she was. Generally, the more made-up a woman was, the crazier she was—a condition the priests attributed to vanity, but I recognized as a by-product of lead in the cosmetics. Of all the stupid history trivia Sean had rambled on about, I sure was glad my brain had latched onto that bit. I was crazy enough as it was.

"It's one thing to indulge in a moment o' lust." Her voice shook. "A man canna help himself, but this..." Her hands clawed into fists. "To bring a whore into your home... Unforgivable."

A groan lodged in my throat. She meant whore literally, believing I was a prostitute. Probably thought I was one of the girls from the Horned Mare or some streetwalker who'd popped into the neighborhood to make the rounds. The poor woman. She had no idea about me or anything else that happened while she was in France. The full weight of our kiss settled on me, and I thought I might drown in the guilt of it.

Henry took a hesitant step toward her. "Let's go somewhere and talk, aye?" He held out a hand. She stared at it, then raised her eyes to his. "Please." His voice croaked.

She tensed. Something about his voice seemed to strike her wrong. Maybe it was the weariness in his tone. Or she wasn't used to hearing him plead. Whatever the reason, her body trembled. Her mouth parted, and for a second, I could have sworn I saw fear behind her eyes. Then again, maybe that was just my imagination...Coira turned on me. Her pupils dilated to black orbs, and her nostrils flared. And then she lost her ever-loving mind.

"Why is this whore still standin' here?" The way her voice shrieked, I was surprised nearby dogs didn't howl.

His shoulders sagged, and he heaved a weary breath. "Coira, let us talk."

She ignored him, eyes trained on me. Her hand slipped into the purse on her belt. "Is it coin ye want?" Fist full of change, she whipped it at my face. "Take it and see if ye can buy your way out o' hell, ye filthy strumpet."

Coins peppered my skin like shrapnel. I put my hands up to block, but one of them hit me in the eye. "Fuck!" I slapped a hand over the socket. My eye watered and stung.

She reached for more coins, but Henry forced her arm down. "That's enough." His voice was soft and oh so weary. "She's not a whore."

I blinked until my vision cleared. My hands balled into fists, but I made no move toward her. I'd give her that one. A literal eye for a figurative one. It seemed only fair.

"Is that so?" A sneer darkened her delicate features. "Let me guess." Her voice turned high and mocking. "She's just a poor widow, tryin' to earn some coin to feed her starving bairns." She spat on the floor, and her voice deepened. "A whore's a whore."

I gritted my teeth and reassessed my earlier opinion of her sanity. Crazy or not, though, she deserved her chance to rage, even if it went against my every instinct to stand there and take it.

"I'll give you two some privacy." I turned to him. He wouldn't meet my eyes, which for some reason infuriated me more than Coira whipping coins at my face. "I'll be in the smithy."

"Like hell ye will!" She stormed toward me. "You're nothin but a walkin', talkin' cunnie to him. Ye got that?" She shoved me. "He's nothin' left to say to ye." Her hands balled into fists. "Get out! Ye hear me? Now, afore I claw out your eyes!"

I bit my lip and sucked air through my teeth. The pulse in my temple throbbed. Still, I said nothing.

"Coira..." Henry heaved like he might be sick. "Fiona lives here."

She gasped. Silence fell over the room. "She what?"

He licked his lips. "Fiona's my..." He looked at me, eyes pleading. I turned my head away, unable to bear the word *servant* coming out of his mouth.

"...cousin. She's my cousin. Come to stay with us for a time."

*Cousin?* What the fuck? I didn't have time to consider the lie, though, because Coira chucked the water bucket at me.

I ducked and moved. The bucket bounced off the wall and rolled across the floor. She plucked a peat brick from the stack. "Mountain refuse." She whipped it at me. "We've laws here against incest, ye ungodly heathen."

The bucket rolled to a stop near her feet. She swooped it up. Henry lunged for her arm. She cocked back, and the bucket caught him in the face.

"Christ!" His hands flew to his nose. Blood gushed between his fingers.

She stalked toward me. "Too ugly for the sheep? Is that it? Thought ye'd come to the city and see if your cousin would give ye a sympathy rut?"

I dodged another turf brick.

"If ye think I'm going to let ye come to this house," she hurled another brick, "and slink your way into his bed." Coming to a stop in front of me, she jabbed me in the chest with a sharp nailed finger. "Then you're—"

I smacked her hand away, startling her enough that she shut the fuck up for a second.

Eyes hard, I inched close. "That's the last time you touch me." My voice was harsh and raw as nails. I shot Henry a scathing look.

This was all his fault. Lying, cheating, toying with hearts. He could have warned her I was staying here, could have owned up to what happened between us, but he'd made the coward's choice.

"This is between you and Henry." My jaw ached with how hard I gritted my teeth. "Work it out with him."

I headed for the door and made it two steps before she shoved me from behind.

I stumbled, caught my feet. "Bitch, I fucking warned you."

I yanked off my head scarf as she lunged, wild-armed and sloppy, but full of piss. I caught an elbow to the nose, a knee to the hip, but I came in quick with a couple of rib shots. Her fist glanced off my collar bone. I landed a solid right hook and came in for the follow up jab, but he circled his arm around her waist and dragged her back. My fist hit air.

"That's enough. Both o' ye!"

Coira clawed at his arms.

I panted, fists clenched. I looked at him, his face covered in blood, the knot on his head swollen and bruising black. I seethed. "Make your choice."

Coira wailed a feral scream. "Whore!" She lunged for me, but Henry held her back.

"What in the name o' St. Vladimir!" a sharp voice cracked through the room. Mairi entered, followed by Donald. Her gaze jumped from me to Henry's bloody face, to the writhing body in his arms. "Coira." Her tone that made it sound like a swear word.

My nails dug into my skin. Coira had stopped thrashing, so Henry set her down and rubbed his palms on his shirt.

She turned on him. "Outside. Now!"

He met my eyes, and I glared. *Don't you dare walk out that door,* I thought, but couldn't bring myself to say. He hesitated. His mouth worked like he searched for a set of magic words that would turn everything back to rights.

"Four years I've stayed by your side." Her voice came out on a hiss. "Will ye forsake me now? For *her*?"

He blanched. His hands trembled, and he looped them around his belt. When he looked at me, his eyes were full of apology. But that didn't stop him from following her out the door.

150

I slumped into my chair at the table. My body pulsed with leftover adrenaline. Her shouts carried through the window, jabbing at me like the sharp nailed finger she'd poked at my chest.

Donald put a hand to my back. "Can I get ye somethin'? Are ye thirsty? How about some ale?"

"Already got some, lad." Mairi's voice sounded from the barrels. "Why dinna ye go to Henry's room and give us a moment, aye?"

Squeezing my shoulder, Donald nodded then disappeared up the stairs.

She swept into the seat across from me, slid me an ale, and leaned in, all business. "Out with it. Why's the shrew keening like a banshee?"

"She got the wrong idea about me and Henry." My fists clenched in my lap. That was bullshit. This entire afternoon had been nothing but lies and bullshit. Coira hadn't misunderstood. I wanted him, and he had wanted me...at least he had until it cost him something.

I caught the words "whore" and "letters" in a jumbled stream of shrieks from outside. I rubbed my temples.

Mairi raised an eyebrow. "What did Henry have to say about it?"

Biting my lip, I drummed my fingers on the tabletop. "That I was his cousin."

She barked with laughter. "Lad's cleverer than I thought."

"Clever?" I gestured toward the toppled bucket, scattered coins, and peat brick landmines. "That's what he got for being clever."

"Nay." She patted my hand. "He got to keep *ye*."

"What does that even mean?" What did she think that I'd masquerade as his cousin so I could play mistress to a serial cheater? Fuck that.

She gave an exasperated shake of the head. "Think, lass. What would happen if he told Coira ye were his servant?"

I laid my head on the table as the last of the adrenaline drained from my body. "She'd make him get rid of me."

"Aye." She nodded. "But kin canna be so easily dismissed."

Coira shouted something about "cousin" and "spinster," and I wondered how much of what Mairi said was true. Coira had been screaming outside that window for well over five minutes, and I hadn't once heard Henry's voice. Clearly, she had him by the balls, and if she squeezed hard enough, I might find myself on the streets before I secured a place to stay.

"Dinna fash." Mairi patted my hand. "I willna let her take ye from your home."

"It's not my home!" My eyes welled with tears. "I'm leaving, aren't I? That was always the plan. This doesn't change anything."

"When?" Coira's shrill scream grated against my eardrums.

For the first time since they'd gone outside, Henry's voice rang out in answer. "Soon."

I went very still. Mairi leaped from her chair and put her arms around me, but I felt no comfort from her touch. I didn't feel much of anything at all. It was over. My time here had reached its end. I stood in a daze, collected my cloak and coin purse.

"Lass, where are ye goin'?" Concern laced her voice.

"To find a home." I headed out the door, away from Coira's shrieks and Henry's silence.

# Chapter Nineteen

"Fiona, stop!" Mairi caught up to me on the winding dirt road. Putting a hand to her heart, she gasped for breath. "I'm an old woman, dinna make me run."

"Go back inside, Mairi." I stared at my shoes. "I have things to do."

"I'll not stop ye, but you'll listen to what I've come to say before ye go." Her voice brooked no argument.

Closing my eyes, I spewed a great breath. I couldn't deal with this right now. I needed to be alone to cry and rage and scream—I needed to hate Henry. And if she defended him, I didn't trust myself not to take my frustration out on her. But it didn't matter. She would have her say whether I liked it or not.

My shoulders raised on a heavy sigh. "Go on, then."

She met my gaze and held it. "He doesna love her."

I swallowed. Her words went down like broken glass, but I managed to keep my face indifferent. "That's between the two of them. Makes no difference to me. Now if you'll excuse me..."

"It makes *all* the difference." With her gnarled hand, she gripped my shoulder. "You're not a fool. Ye must see how he feels."

"Nope." I shook my head. "Can't see feelings, Mairi. Just choices."

She scoffed. "The lad didna *choose*. He reacted." She tapped her temple. "Men are simple creatures, lass. They dinna think things through."

I scrubbed my hands over my face. "What do you want me to do? Put my life on hold and hope he comes around?"

"Nay, ye wee fool." She raised a fist. "I want ye to fight for him. I want ye to march back to that house and remind him what he's about to lose."

My gaze drifted to the field of wild grass along the roadside. It swayed and rustled in the breeze, bending with the wind. "People always say that—fight for the one you love—but that's the stupidest thing. If you have to fight for it, it never existed in the first place."

Her gaze softened, and a sad smile formed on her lips. "If ye kent half as much as ye think ye do, ye'd be the wisest woman in the world." She tilted her head toward the edge of the road. "Sit with me, lass. It's time I told ye what I've come to say."

My brows furrowed. Hadn't she just done that? And I didn't like the ominous tone to her voice. Following her to a spot next to the field, we sat. The air permeated with the mingling scents of wildflowers and horse droppings and impending rain. I wrapped my cloak tightly around myself.

Mairi laced her fingers. "Aye, well... I suppose the first thing ye have to ken is Henry and I arenae Perth born. We've northern blood. Davidsons o' the mighty Clan Chattan."

"Clan Chattan?" Growing up, Granda told me plenty about the great clans of yore, but I'd never heard of Clan Chattan. "Is it a small clan?"

She put a hand to her heart. "Oh aye, twelve clans united to form the world's largest confederation o' clans, headed by no less than the Mackintosh himself." She snorted. "A wee clan indeed."

Surprise tore through me, both because I'd never seen her so puffed up with pride, and because what she described didn't sound all that dissimilar to the United States, at least conceptually.

"I can only tell ye what's been told me. I lived here in Perth when *it* happened..." Her tone darkened, and the way she said *it* made me shudder. There was a lot of darkness in that word.

"Henry was still a lad. Ten, mayhap twelve, years old." Her eyes glazed with memory. "It was a perilous time for the clan.

Though, I suppose that hasna changed. Power and pride, ye ken?"

I nodded, although I had no idea what she meant.

"It was late summer when the chief's envoy arrived." She gazed ahead toward the darkening clouds. "They rode through Davidson land, calling to the farmers and tachsmen alike. 'To arms,' they shouted. 'The Camerons have raided Badenoch.'" She met my eyes. "And that was all they need say, for the Camerons were, and still are, our fiercest enemies. So, off our men rode with sword and axe, ready to lay waste to those vile sons o' hounds—Henry, his da, and all eight o' his brothers along with them."

"Wait." I held up a hand. "Give me a second."

Her story was too much for me to absorb. I didn't know what was crazier—that Henry rode off to battle at the age of ten, that he had eight brothers he'd never once mentioned, or that their greatest enemy was Sean's ancestral clan.

I searched for a way to ask what I wanted to know without revealing too much of my ignorance. "I wouldn't know, since I came from a peaceful village, but isn't ten awfully young to go to war?"

Mairi smiled, but it came off ironic rather than happy. "No one expected the lad to fight, but he was old enough to watch and serve ale and the like." Her gaze met mine, and she clasped my hand. "War is more than a blade, ye ken. It's blood and screams, pipers and drums, death and entrails... A man must learn to fight not just with a sword, but with his eyes and ears as well."

I nodded. Half a year ago I'd have considered it child abuse to drag a ten-year-old onto a battlefield, but I understood the macabre practicality of the Middle Ages now. Seeing people hacked apart at such a young age might be awful, but not nearly as bad as dying a few years later because you froze at the first sight of a severed limb.

Mairi gazed down the dusty path beside us. "Off they rode. Together with three hundred warriors from clans Mackintosh and Macpherson. An unbeatable force." She grimaced. "Until the matter o' the right came up, that is—"

"Stop." I held up a hand. "You already lost me. What's the right?"

"The right-side o' the formation." Her tone suggested this should be obvious.

"Oh." I nodded. "So the argument was about strategy?"

"Not strategy, lass, honor." She raised a fist. "Only the bravest men, the best fighters, are allowed to take the right."

I must have looked as confused as I felt, because Mairi tapped my left arm. "Your shield." She raised her own left hand. "My shield. I've a shield on either side o' me—mine and yours." She gestured to the space between us. "Ye have a shield to your left, but naught but your sword on the right."

I stabbed at an imaginary assailant with my invisible sword, and I could see how vulnerable I'd be if more than one person attacked at once.

"That's why it's the position o' honor. To be given the right is an acknowledgment o' strength and trust."

It made sense in a backward sort of man-logic way. If it were me, though, I'd be arguing over the safest position, not the most dangerous. Not that I'd be fighting at all. I'd heard too many of Granda's stories to think of war as a romantic adventure.

"Well, the Davidsons thought the right was owed to them. The Macphersons thought the same. It came down to the Mackintosh to decide." The shadow of an old bitterness crossed her face. "We won the right but lost everything in return."

She tipped her head back and studied the encroaching storm clouds. "The insult was too great for the Macphersons. 'If ye think us cravenly, fight without us,' they said. And they laid down their arms." The trenches in her forehead deepened. "With the Macphersons, victory was a certainty. Without them, our men were out-numbered and out-armed."

Her eyes shone with remembered grief. "Some call it bravery. Others foolishness. Mayhap both are true. Our men refused to turn back. They met the Camerons near Invernahoven," her gaze dropped to her knees, "and died for it.

Most o' 'em, at least. All Henry's brothers. His father. Uncles. Cousins. Henry watched them fall to Cameron blades and arrows."

Her throat worked, and her voice betrayed the slightest waiver. "They say he tried to join the battle himself." She rubbed her chest. "Poor wee lad. If his sister's goodman hadna dragged him off the field, he'd surely have fallen with the rest."

A sharp pain ripped through my palm, and I realized my nails had dug into the padded flesh. I couldn't imagine anything so awful as watching damn near your entire family being hacked to bits at such a young age. And God, by Camerons of all people. The same people I'd probably live with right now if Sean hadn't died.

"After that, my sister, Henry's mither, brought the lad and his wee sister Aimil, to live with me and my goodman. Not long after, she met the blacksmith, and they wed within the month." She smiled. "It wasna a love match, but he was a good man, and they were well cared for. I thought in time..." Her face pinched, and she shook her head as if trying to erase thoughts of what might have been. "Poor wee Aimil caught the bloody flux not a month after they wed. Died two days later. My sister a week after that."

Empathy clawed at my insides. "Henry was all alone?"

"Nay. Not alone. The blacksmith raised him as his own. Taught him to work the iron." She gestured to the house. "Left him his property and possessions when he passed, but Henry never let anyone get too close after that. At least, not until he took on Donald as his apprentice."

Stretching her legs in front of her, she gave them a shake. "I thought that was a good sign, him takin' on the lad. Meant he was finally beginning to heal." Her eyes grew glossy. "But the fear is still with him."

Thunder rumbled in the distance, but I was too engrossed in her tale to suggest we move.

"About a year ago, Donald caught a terrible fever." Brushing an invisible speck of lint off her cloak, she straightened. "Wouldna eat. Slept for days." Her voice turned grave. "We all thought death had come for him. Henry didna speak a word those three days. Just sat by Donald's side, staring at him with loss in his eyes." She paused. "And that is how he looks when he stares at ye." Her voice became low and very serious. "Like he's already lost ye. Like ye'll fade away if he dares to love ye, just as his mither and father and brothers and wee Aimil did."

I sucked in a breath. This was all so heavy, so complicated. I didn't know if it changed everything or nothing.

Mairi placed her hand on mine. "That's why I ask ye to give him time. Surely ye, more than anyone else, can understand what grief does to a heart."

I nodded, more to myself than to her. I knew what it meant to lose everything and everyone, and I understood the vulnerability that comes with letting yourself love. I was feeling the repercussions of that very thing right now. But I also understood something Mairi didn't—I couldn't change him. No amount of pleading, arguing, waiting, or hoping would change Henry into a different person. Only *he* had that power. He had to want it, want it more than he feared it, and if today proved anything, it was that he didn't.

"Help him find his courage, lass." She gave my hand a squeeze. "Fight for him."

Taking a deep breath, I rose to my feet. "I'm sorry, Mairi. It's *me* I need to fight for. Not him."

~ * ~

Hours later, I stood in front of the smithy door, soaked with rain and shivering cold, but it wasn't the storm that held me frozen to the spot; it was the knowledge that as soon as I walked through that door, my world would change just as surely as if I traipsed through another time portal.

My hand caressed the smooth, solid wood. I closed my eyes. This was for the best. I knew it was. But why did the right choice have to be so fucking hard? Taking a deep breath, I steeled myself, and went inside.

"I'm just finishin' up." Henry polished a set of plate armor draped over a sewing dummy. On the breast, an engraved peacock feather stood in relief against smooth metal plating. He gave the breastplate a final buff and faced me. His eyes rounded wide. "Ye came back."

"That's what I came here to talk to you about..." I toed a crack in the floor. "I put a deposit on a cottage. It'll be ready the day after the merchant's gala." The force of his gaze bore into me, but he made no reply, so I continued, "I need to know if I can stay here until then."

His jaw clenched and his Adam's apple bobbed, before he gave a single, silent nod. I stared, waiting for him to speak, but he just turned back to his armor.

Still, I waited. Still, no acknowledgement.

My bottom lip trembled. So that was it? After everything we'd been through, after months of living together, after fighting and joking and saving each other's lives, all I got was a nod and radio silence. Had I really meant so little to him? I didn't even know what I expected him to say. *All right, it's been real. By the way, sorry I broke your heart.*

In a daze, I about-faced and headed toward the door. A hollow emptiness ghosted through my chest. My vision sparked. Icy rain droplets slid down my wet hair and onto my neck. And then the pain and anger and indignity of the situation caught up with my feet. I froze. My fists shook, and I crowed a hideous cackle.

"I'm *so* stupid. So completely and utterly stupid." Laughing, I put a hand to my brow. "I'm no different than that girl at the tavern to you, am I? Just a girl you had a bit of fun with until your girlfriend came home."

Raindrop tears fell down my cheeks as I continued to giggle. My feet started working again, and I was nearly out the door before arms wrapped around me from behind.

Henry pressed his cheek to mine. "I'm sorry. I'm so sorry." He brushed the hair from my face. Hot tears ran down my neck, mixing with the cold dampness of the storm. "I'm so sorry."

I slumped against him, embracing his comfort, desperate for it, even if he was the source of the pain.

"I wish—" His voice choked. "If I could, Fiona..." His forehead dropped against my neck. "You're so verra important to me. Ye have to ken that?"

It was the exact wrong thing to say. I could take his apologies, but I couldn't stomach his lies. I tore away from him. "No!"

His lips parted, and his skin blanched, clearly stunned by my sudden swing of emotions.

I rubbed a rough hand across my eyes and glared at him. "What do you mean, *if you could*? You had the choice. You just weren't willing to make it."

"Fiona, please." He held his hands up in a pleading gesture. "There are things ye dinna ken. Circumstances..."

"I don't give a damn about your circumstances." My voice rose so loud, I was surprised Mairi didn't come running. "They don't change anything!"

We stared at each other for a frozen second. I cupped my cheeks. What was happening to me? This was crazy. Fighting with him was pointless. I couldn't do this anymore. I shifted from side-to-side. "I have to go. I have to get my—" I shook my head. "You know what, never mind. I'll send for my things later."

He caught hold of my arm. "What do ye think you're doin'? Ye canna leave. Ye've nowhere to go."

"She can stay with me," a voice carried from across the room. Gavin leaned against the door jamb.

"Like hell she can!" Henry's face flamed red.

"Best I can tell, Gow Chrom, ye dinna have much say in the matter." He nodded at the steel-plated armor. "I'll come back for my fittin' some other time, aye?" He met my gaze and tilted his head toward the door. "Come along if ye wish."

I met his eyes and found neither lust nor deception in his stare, only concern. I looked at Henry. At his pale, pain-wracked face. A silent *no* formed on his lips, but he gave it no voice.

I choked on a sob, and ran out the door, not stopping until I reached Gavin's carriage.

160

# Chapter Twenty

I ran a wet comb through my hair before the vanity mirror in Gavin's guest room. The maid he assigned me didn't understand that dry-brushing curly hair turned ringlets into rats' nests, so I'd taken to combing it myself before she came to get me ready.

Honestly, I didn't need the help. I only had the one dress, which I was well-accustomed to putting on myself, and I'd have been more than happy to throw on my hair scarf and be done with it. Besides, there was something icky about having servants. It felt like a betrayal of my midwestern, do-it-yourself roots.

But being pampered was part and parcel of living a life of leisure, and the last thing I was about to do was complain. Gavin and his staff had been wonderful these last six days, and even if this place didn't seem like home, it was nice to not be alone.

A knock sounded at my door.

I hurried the comb through my hair. "Can you give me five more minutes, Marjorie?"

The maid's voice sounded from the hallway. "Someone to see ye, marm."

I smelled her before I saw her, no mistaking that lavender hair tonic. I bolted to my feet, and Mairi strode through the door, wearing her finest kirtle and freshly waxed boots. New embroidery decorated her market bag, which she handed me.

Turquoise silk peeked from the top—the dress Gavin had given me. "Thought you might be needin' this."

I tossed the bag onto the bed and flung my arms around her. "God, I've missed you! How have you been? Are you all right?" I raked my gaze over her. "You're not working too much are you? Make sure Donald and He—" I choked off his name. "Make sure they help."

"I'm fine. Just fine." She gave my hands a squeeze. "I miss ye, though. I've grown used to all your blatherin'. House is too quiet."

I wanted so badly to ask about Henry, but I had too much pride. "How's...Donald?"

Mairi pursed her lips. "Well...*Donald,* ye ken, he's not one to admit how he's feelin', but it's clear to all he's been missin' ye. He's been in a terrible temper, locks himself in the smithy all the day and half the night. Hasna even gone to the tavern since ye left." Her words came out measured, as she squeezed my hand. "Ye ken how *Donald* is—he'd beg ye to come home if he didna think ye already had your mind settled."

She made a gesture that encompassed the room from the four-poster bed, to the wall tapestries, to the expensive tile floor. "Look at ye, livin' like a queen, courted by a duke's son. Ye've done well for yourself!"

I gave a soft chuckle. "Gavin's not courting me—he's just helping me." In fact, he hadn't so much as glanced at my cleavage since the day I moved in. We'd spent plenty of time together, but I suspected he'd just been trying to keep me distracted so I didn't wallow in heartache.

"I'm still moving into my cottage tomorrow." I studied my feet. "Maybe tell...*Donald* I'll be by to get my barrels. It might be best if we don't see each other..."

Mairi compressed her lips and nodded. "I'll make sure he kens." She glanced at the gown. "Well, I'll leave ye to it. Ye've got a gala to prepare for."

I hugged her once more and breathed in her lavender scent. "Maybe you can come visit me sometime?"

"O' course I will, lass." She patted my back. "No matter what happens or where ye lay your head, you're family."

~ * ~

Hours later, Gavin and I arrived at the guildhall in a gilded carriage. We were decked out in silk. My hair was pressed,

162

plaited, and coiled. I looked like a queen. Too bad I didn't feel like one. If only I could get Henry off my brain.

A footman opened the carriage door.

"Ready?" Gavin held out a hand to help me down.

I forced a grin and accepted his hand. "You better believe it."

We ascended a grand set of stone steps, leading to the guildhall. He looped my arm through his. "Dinna forget, tonight you're on the arm o' the most important man here. That makes *ye* the most important woman here. Dinna let anyone treat ye otherwise. You're a Peacock."

Wondering what spawned that little pep-talk, I raised a brow. I supposed gossips might make something of the Peacock Knight showing up to the gala with a commoner, but if Gavin didn't care, I sure as hell didn't.

The guildhall was ten times bigger and a hundred times nicer than I ever would have expected. Dark oak walls surrounded an ecru tiled floor. Beams zig-zagged across the ceiling. Sculpted plaster sigils jutted from the molding. There were even glass-paned windows, which were lovely, and I knew, expensive, but did little to help cool the heat of so many bodies. Incoming traffic bottlenecked between the door and an ale table, and we were trapped behind a horde of sweaty, well-dressed people.

He put his hands to his mouth. "Out o' the way, ye soot-stained nobility pretenders."

I half-expected someone to clock him, but when gazes fell on him, the crowd parted like the Red Sea.

"Nobility pretenders?" I chuckled as we headed toward the rows of linen covered banquet tables.

He shrugged. "Ye ken how these merchants are. They get a bit o' coin in their purse and think it means something."

I pointed to a few open seats by a raised dais on the left. Gavin shook his head. "It's about to get hotter than the Earl o' Hell's kitchen in here. Follow me."

Leading me to the back, he brought me to a pair of French doors that swung onto a patio. We stopped in front of it to take in the breeze.

I scoured the room. "I don't see any open seats."

"Not yet." He tapped the shoulder of a bald man at the nearest table. "Reginald, good fellow."

"My lord." The man rose and bowed. "A pleasure to see ye. How's that brood mare o' yours doin'?"

"Verra well." Gavin flashed a brilliant smile. "In fact, I've a mind to reshoe the rest o' my stable."

The man licked his lips. I could practically see the dollar signs forming in his eyes. "I'd be happy to—"

"How can I talk commerce in such heat? If only we had seats by the door." Gavin fanned himself as he looked from Reginald to his empty seat in a pointed way.

In a manner of seconds, he was yanking the woman next to him out of her chair and insisting we take their spots.

"I'll be in contact," Gavin called as Reginald dragged his protesting wife toward seats in the front.

I forced down a grin. "You're terrible."

Gavin stared after him. "So are his prices."

We took our newly acquired seats, and I sighed with contentment. A cool breeze caressed my back, and I engaged in some of the best people watching I'd experienced since that Phish concert my freshman year. A bulky lass gave her husband a right hook for making eyes at an even bigger lady a few seats down. A cat scampered through the room and hopped onto a table, spilling a goblet of wine into some poor sap's lap. And a man a few rows over wore a peg-leg carved into the shape of a naked woman.

I pointed to the badge on old Peg-leg's chest. "What guild is that sigil for?"

Gavin squinted at the man. "Tanner."

"Oh. I thought for sure he'd be a carpenter. What about him?" I pointed to a man with a stag sigil. "No wait, let me guess..."

That's how the game began.

"Clockmaker." I gestured toward a man who wore a cog sigil.

Gavin's lip curled in amusement. "Miller."

"Dammit!" I tossed him a farthing.

He slid it back to me. "Keep your coin."

"It's no fun if we don't bet." From across the room, I pointed to a sigil with a bird and sun. "Fletcher?"

He rose to get a better look. "Tallow chandler."

"That doesn't make sense." My nose wrinkled. "Then who are the people with the candle sigils?"

"*Wax* chandlers, and dinna confuse the two." He studied a pretty blonde woman a few tables ahead. "Terrible rivalry between 'em."

"Rivalry?" A snotty female voice sounded behind me.

The hairs on my neck stood on end. No. It couldn't be. I turned, and goddammit, there was Coira. What in the ever-loving fuck was she doing here? Suddenly, Gavin's earlier warning made a lot more sense.

"Rivalry suggests equivalency." She looked down her nose at me and sneered. "But clearly one o' the two is inferior."

A smirk twisted Gavin's lips. "I didna ken ye were so passionate about candles, Coira." He squeezed my hand under the table, a silent reminder that I was a Peacock.

But I didn't need the reminder, and I didn't need to be a Peacock. I was Fiona Motherfucking Buchanan, and I wouldn't let anybody make me feel small, least of all this bitch.

My gaze raked the length of her. "Don't you look lovely. Tell me, how did you manage to cover up all those bruises I gave you?"

He chortled.

Her false smile tightened. "Slumming it as usual, *Sir* Gavin. I ken you're partial to whores, but I'd have thought ye'd find one whose face isna covered in pox."

He and I burst out laughing. Not because of her dig at my freckles, which in terms of burns was lame, but because when she had smiled the thick layer of white lead makeup cracked down the length of her cheek.

Clearly confused by our laughter, Coira's lips parted. A flash of fury filled her eyes, just like before she'd started chucking buckets and turf bricks the last time we'd met.

"Ye think to mock me?" She wrenched her hand back like she meant to smack me. "I'll teach ye to—"

"Careful, Coira..." His voice was silk and daggers. Her hand paused in midair as her crazy warred with her sense of self-preservation.

Seemingly out of nowhere, Henry appeared by her side and caught her arm. "What do ye think you're doin'?"

My breath hitched. His eyes met mine, and it felt like getting shot in the gut with a cannonball. Son of a bitch. Why? I'd have gladly taken her slap if it meant not having to see him. Hell, I'd have welcomed it. Another round with her sounded damn fun right about now.

Leaning back, Gavin stretched his arm along the back of my chair. "Gow Chrom." He nodded, casual as could be.

Every muscle in Henry's body appeared to clench at once. He forced a terse bow as custom dictated and yanked Coira away with him.

"And here I thought he'd lost his spirit." Removing his arm from my chair, Gavin grinned. "Spectacularly done."

I ground my teeth together. "What are they doing here?"

His grin faded. "Ye didna ken they'd be here?"

I groaned. Ever since Mairi'd accepted Gavin's invitation on my behalf, talk of the Gala had been strictly taboo.

"He's a master armorer. Coira's the chief importer o' wine. Ye had to ken they'd be here?" His eyes shone with sympathy.

Stunned, I stared at him, both because he was right, I should have realized Henry would be here, and because the idea of Coira running any kind of business seemed insane. "She imports wine. Seriously?" My mouth fell open. "I figured she was some kind of heiress or something."

"Nay." Gavin fingered the edge of his sleeve. "Inherited her goodman's business when he died. Tripled its profits in five years. She was quite remarkable, really."

I raised an eyebrow. "Was?"

Gavin shrugged. "I dinna ken what happened to her. It was like the more coin she earned, the more..."

"Crazy she got?" I winced. "Let me guess, she started wearing the face cream once she got the money?" It was so fucking sad, but there wasn't anything I could do about it. This girl was already too far gone to help and judging by Mairi's response when I tried to tell her about the dangers of lead, she wouldn't believe me if I tried.

Gavin's brow wrinkled. "I suppose... Though I dinna see—"

"Never mind. It doesn't matter. She's Henry's problem, not mine." I slumped in my seat.

Gavin nudged my shoulder. "If it makes ye feel better, that wine business is the only thing keepin' her from forcin' Henry to wed. She canna stand the thought o' handin' the rights over to another man."

"No, that doesn't help." I sighed and patted his shoulder. "But thanks for trying."

"Attention," a man on the dais shouted through a speaking trumpet. The crowd continued to buzz. "Shut your klappes, ye bunch o' muck spouts," he hollered at full volume. Silence rolled through the room. "Thank ye for attending." His voice returned to its former politeness. "Today we pay tribute to the men and women who have made Perth the wonder that it is."

Cheers and whoops erupted from the audience. "Huzzah," a man a few seats over shouted as the lady next to him whistled. "Not like those scobberlotchers in Edinburgh!" somebody up front shouted, to which the crowd responded with laughter and more cheers.

"Is it any wonder our fair city is the king's favorite royal burg?"

More cheers and shouts.

"Join me then in paying tribute," he paused, "to the apothecaries." Everyone in the audience banged a knuckle on the table. "...The cordwainers." Another knuckle drum. "...the bakers." And on it went until he'd named some forty different guilds.

As soon as he finished, servants popped out of the shadows with food platters. They littered the tables with fruits and cheeses, meats and pies, breads and gelatinous molded concoctions. People oohed and aahed as servants delivered heads of boar and fully feathered peacocks.

"Seems unsanitary." I frowned, wondering if they'd bothered to wash the feathers.

Gavin raised a pewter pitcher. "Wine?"

A few rows ahead, Coira wiped Henry's cheek with a handkerchief. I nodded and handed over my cup. "Thanks. I could use a drink."

"I imagine ye could." Gavin retrieved a small, flat bottle of aqua vitae from his boot and poured a dollop into my goblet. It made the wine taste brackish and sour, but I was grateful for the whisky heat in my belly. I had no appetite, but I tried a tasting of everything, figuring it was better to focus on food than stare at the back of Henry's head all night. The peacock wasn't half-bad—a bit like turkey—and Gavin kept filling my goblet, so by the time the servants cleared the table, I had a decent buzz.

A harpist began to play. Seats emptied as people rose to stretch their legs and mingle.

"Let's get some ale." He offered me his hand, and we sauntered toward the ale station.

Halfway there, a man wearing a wax chandler's sigil stopped us. "Sir Gavin, pleased to see ye. What do ye think o' the candles used for tonight's event?"

Longing filled Gavin's eyes as he stared past the man to the ale table. "Verra fine, indeed."

"I could offer ye a good price." The man either didn't care or didn't notice Gavin's disinterest. "A nobleman, such as yourself, should light his home with the best the city has to offer."

"That's odd." He tapped his lip. "The tallow chandler seemed to think the impurities in your wax might give off a poisonous miasma."

The man bristled. "Who said that? Was it Gregor?" His fists balled. "I'll teach that crooked-nosed-knave." Once he stormed off, Gavin and I burst out laughing.

I slapped his shoulder. "You're terrible." Shouts erupted from the other side of the room as the wax chandler pummeled a man, I assumed must be Gregor.

Smirking, Gavin shrugged, but he didn't get the chance to comment before a man with a needle and thread sigil stopped us. "Who is *this* lovely lass, Sir Gavin?" Tromping about four inches too close, he fingered my dress sleeve. His thumb hooked toward his chest. "Thomas, head o' the clothworker's guild."

"Pleasure to meet you." I bowed my head, all manners and smiles, even though my insides were cringing at the lack of personal space. The momentary discomfort was a small price to pay, however, because now I understood what this gala really was—a medieval networking party—and I was now a woman with a product to sell.

The cloth merchant leaned forward as if he intended to share a prized secret. "I've some new cloth in stock. Saracen silk. Would look perfect with your eye color."

*Yeah, everything goes with brown.* I smiled and batted my lashes. "I'd love to see it sometime. If the price is right, I'll be sure to tell my female customers." I almost held out my hand to shake his but caught myself. They didn't do that here. "I'm Fiona, and I'll be opening my home as a tavern in the next few days."

His eyebrows arched. "Is that so?"

I nodded. We both grinned as mutual commercial understanding flowed between us.

Yawning, Gavin stretched his arms high over his head. "Let's get some ale."

After excusing ourselves, we collected our drinks. As he sipped, I studied his face. "What do you think?"

He lowered his tankard. "Horse piss."

Licking my lips, I took another sip. Exactly what I thought too. If this was my competition, I'd be a rich lady soon enough.

A pretty brunette with a braid to her knees sidled over to us. He grinned. "Rosalie."

I meant to say hello, but instead I blurted, "That's a blacksmith's sigil!"

"Aye." Her voice held an edge. "What of it?"

Boy, did I feel like an ass. It had literally not once crossed my mind women could be blacksmiths. I made a silent apology to Gloria Steinem. "I think that's awes—admirable." Her features softened. I glanced up at Gavin. "Why don't I let you two catch up?" I leaned into Rosalie. "Do you know if there's a privy here?"

Wincing in sympathy, she tilted her head toward the door. "Just the trees out back."

I handed my ale to Gavin. "I'll be back in a few minutes."

As I made my way toward the back door, I got way sided by a pattenmaker. Pattens were these wooden clogs you slipped over your shoes when it rained. I wasn't particularly interested in his product, and I really had to pee, but I stopped to chat with him anyway.

"How long you been in the patten game?" I fought the urge to do a full out pee dance.

His chest puffed with pride. "Going on ten years."

"I suppose if you're going to sell pattens, Scotland's the place to do it." I shifted back and forth. "I don't think I've seen a day here without at least a little rain."

"Perhaps ye should go somewhere sunny," a voice hissed behind me.

Sucking in a calming breath, I plastered a smile on my face. "Can I help you, Coira?"

She sneered. "That doesna seem likely." The pattenmaker took that as his cue to leave. She paraded toward me. "But I do have a question. Tell me, how does a freckle-faced scullery maid manage to snag herself a knight?"

"Are you asking for yourself or a friend?" My voice came out in a perfect deadpan.

Menace shone in Coira's eyes. "A bit of advice. Once Gavin grows bored with ye, dinna come cryin' to Henry. He's done with ye, kin or no."

A barking laugh rolled off my tongue. "I'll keep it in mind."

170

Grabbing my arm, she dug her nails into my skin. "I see what you're doin', and it willna work."

I took a deep, impatient breath. "Coira, let me ask you something... You're successful. Rich. Beautiful. At least you would be if you wiped that shit off your face."

She scowled, and the cracks in her makeup deepened.

Shaking my head, I laughed without humor. "Why are you worried about me?"

"I'm not." Her words came out on a sputter. "How dare ye presume—"

I shrugged. "It's either that, or you're in love with me. I mean, you just can't seem to leave me alone, can you?"

Her jaw clenched.

"Anyway, it's been fun." I looked past her toward the door. "But if you'll excuse me, I have to take a piss."

~ * ~

The only thing more awkward than pissing in the woods in a formal dress while slightly tipsy and more than a little angry, is doing it surrounded by couples getting busy. Apparently, there was a whole different kind of networking going on in the woods. I witnessed three different couples doing the nasty before I found a semi-private spot to pop a squat. Even then, I still heard them moaning and groaning and calling out to God. It made for an awkward, if not entertaining, bathroom break.

"Your wife's looking for you," I shouted, just to be a dick, and laughed hysterically when a few seconds later, two different men bolted from the trees.

Inside, I found Gavin chatting it up with a group of women from the spinsters' guild. They scattered at my return, and I made a mental note to apologize to him for being such a cock-block. We filled our tankards and made small talk with poulters and dyers and fletchers and salters. The harp music stopped, and a man with a fiddle took his place. The crowd clapped their hands and stomped their feet as he played a popular reel. People shouted lyrics, seemingly off the top of their heads, and a circle formed in the center of the room.

He handed me his bottle of aqua vitae. "Shall we dance?"

I took a swig and handed it back. "Let's do it."

We joined the circle and to my irritation, Henry squeezed in behind us with Rosalie. As we promenaded forward, I watched him out of the corner of my eye. What was he playing at? He couldn't dance. He was off-beat, awkward, and the grimace on his face told me he hated every second of this number. When the dance got to the part where we skipped in opposite directions and clasped hands with the other dancers, his hand clamped onto my wrist.

He tugged me close. "I need a word with ye."

"You don't." I took the next man's hand and skipped away.

When the song ended, Rosalie and Henry followed us to the ale stand. She looked from him to me. She put a hand on Gavin's arm. "Sir Gavin, ye'll give me the next dance, won't ye?"

As if trying to squash a grin, he squeezed his lips together. "O' course."

Henry hooked his arm around my shoulder and pulled me into the circle.

"I don't want to dance with you." I tried to keep my voice low, but a few nearby dancers glanced our way with interest. The music began, and I was thrust forward. "Go dance with Coira." I tried to pull out of his hold, while simultaneously skipping in a circle to avoid getting crushed.

She glared at us from the edge of the crowd.

"I want to talk with ye." His voice rumbled in my ear, sending heat down my core.

"*Now* you want to talk?" I yanked so hard against him, we both tumbled out of the circle. I shook my hand free and wiped it on my dress. I glared. "Too fucking late." I tore through the crowd. He chased after me, but Coira reached me first.

"I warned ye, whore." She tossed her wine down the front of my dress.

A bleeding wine stain spidered across the silk. I bit my lip and growled. She might as well have burned half my savings. So much for selling the gown if times got rough.

I wiped wine splatter from my neck and flicked it off my fingers. "Bitch, you picked the wrong one."

Henry caught up to us. His eyes widened at the sight of my dress. "Coira!"

"An accident." False innocence laced her voice.

I dug my stare on him. "If you don't get this bitch out of my face, I'm going to *accidentally* smash her head against the wall."

She pounded forward. "Henry'll let ye do no such—"

My gaze snapped to hers, and she must have seen the truth in my eyes because she didn't finish. "Test me." I spun on my heels then stalked through the crowd.

He called after me, but I ignored him. Behind me Coira screeched, her voice like rubber shoes on a squeaky floor. I found Gavin and Rosalie over by the ale stand.

I thrust out a hand. "Give me that bottle."

His gaze dropped to my wine-stained gown, then over my shoulder, presumably at Henry and Coira.

Gavin handed me the bottle, and I took a nip or three. It didn't help. I probably could have drunk the whole damn bottle and been as sober as a monk the way I felt.

"Smile, lass. Here." He plucked a wine goblet from some guy's hand and dumped it down the front of his shirt. He grinned. "Now it's high fashion."

Somehow the gesture made me want to laugh and cry all at once. I flashed him my first genuine smile of the night. "You know, Gavin, you're really kind of a sweet guy. People don't give you enough credit."

He smirked. "I've no need for credit, my lady. I've got gold."

The next half hour passed in a blur. I drank and chatted with Rosalie, gossiped with a scrivener, and interrogated a confused mason about Da Vinci Code theories involving Knights Templar and chalices.

"Excuse me." The announcer's voice reverberated through his speaking trumpet. The fiddler stopped playing, and people booed and tossed crusts of bread at him. "Listen up, I've good news to share."

The crowd quieted.

"Tonight is about the town's guilds coming together." He paced along the dais. "Well, I've just gotten word two o' our town's finest will be coming together in holy matrimony. Give your congratulations to Coira, Perth's chief wine importer, and Henry from the wynd, one o' the finest armorers in all o' Scotland."

The crowd erupted in cheers.

I swayed on my feet.

# Chapter Twenty-One

The world faded to white noise and background clutter as Gavin guided me through the guildhall. I was barely conscious of moving. I couldn't focus on anything but the announcer's voice, playing over and over in my head: *holy matrimony. Holy matrimony. Holy matrimony.*

Out on the patio torches flickered in the rustling wind, lighting the silhouette of trees.

"Look at me." He put a hand to my chin. "Fiona. Are ye with me?" Worry shadowed his eyes. "Listen." His fingers dug into my arms. "Aught's amiss. I ken Henry. He wouldna—"

A creaking sound stopped his words. He stared past me, then leaned in close to my ear. "I'll help ye. Dinna fight me."

His lips caressed mine. I didn't reject his kiss or return it. I just stood there, my brain having abandoned my body. Only those two words mattered: *holy matrimony.*

Dancing me in a half circle, he breathed in my ear. "Look."

I forced my eyes to focus. Henry stood outside the French doors, staring at us with eyes like shattered glass. A second later, Coira joined him. His eyes tore from mine. He gripped her hand and dragged her with him in the woods. Coira flashed me a triumphant smile, moments before they disappeared into the trees.

Dread-filled certainty flooded my veins. They were in the woods. The woods where lovers met. They were going to have sex, not thirty feet away from me. Oh God, and Coira would make sure I heard them. I knew it. She'd put on a show. Any second now, her moans would meet my ears. It would destroy me. I couldn't do it. I wouldn't.

My body shook. "Can you get me a drink?" Gavin reached into his boot for his bottle of aqua vitae. "No, not that. Ale." I fanned my face. "I don't feel well. Please."

"O' course." He helped me to a bench. "Sit. I'll be right back."

As soon as he disappeared into the guildhall, I shot to my feet and ran. I didn't know where I was going, had no plan, no thoughts. I was just a pair of feet and a beating heart, pounding away until the torch lights dimmed, and buildings vanished. Eventually, the trees scattered and thinned, then reformed into sentinel rows. My feet landed on rotten fruit, and I realized at some point I'd entered an orchard. I came to a halt and bent over. My breath rang loud in my ears, but not louder than the voice in my head—*holy matrimony.*

I plunged to my knees, looked at the bright, full moon, and screamed. Hot tears filled my eyes. I snatched an apple off the ground and threw it at a tree. Then another. And another. Screaming all the while.

A figure appeared in the distance, a black silhouette, barely visible under the light of the moon. I froze, an apple still clutched in my hand. My heart raced. A bandit or a time soldier? I couldn't decide which would be worse. I was alone, too far from the gala for anyone to hear me scream. The figure drew closer. The glint of a sword caught in the moonlight. I scrambled to my feet. Run or hide? Run or hide?

"Fiona, I'm comin'! I'll save ye," the shadowy figure called.

At the sound of Henry's voice, relief washed over me, followed immediately by a wave of unmitigated fury. How dare he chase after me? The rotten apple squished in my hand, and I chucked it at him. Ducking to dodge the apple, he continued to run for me. I plucked another from a nearby tree, this one hard and ripe, and threw that one at him, too. Then another. And another. Some hit, some missed, but I kept throwing.

He waved his arms. "Stop! It's me!"

"I know it's you!" I threw another apple.

He was close now. Shadow became flesh. He slowed to a stop in front of me. Moonlight reflected off his confused, assessing eyes. "Where's the scoundrel? Who attacked ye?"

"Put your sword away, you idiot." I rolled my eyes. "No one attacked me."

His gaze darted about as if he didn't believe me. "I heard ye scream."

"I'm fine." I couldn't believe he was forcing me to have this dumb conversation right now. "Just go away. Please."

His eyes gave a final sweep of the trees, and he stowed his sword before his gaze fell on me. "Are ye mad, woman?" His voice burned with fury. "What do ye think you're doin' out here by yourself at night?" He gripped my arm. "I'm takin' ye home."

Twisting, I wrenched free. "Don't touch me!"

He glowered. I scowled.

"I'm not leavin' ye here." His stance widened. "I dinna care if I have to drag ye by the hair."

I gnashed my teeth. "It'll be the last thing you do." We circled each other like two bulls, pawing the dirt, waiting to see whose horns were sharper.

He inched closer. "It's not safe."

"I don't care!" I stomped my foot like a toddler. "Send Gavin if you have to. Just leave me the fuck alone."

His fists vibrated with rage. "Ye'd like that, aye? Out here. Alone with Gavin. Wasna enough to shame yourself with him right there at the gala for anyone to see. Nay, ye willna be satisfied 'til you're swole with his bastard."

A noise erupted from my throat that was somewhere between a growl and a screech. "Don't you fucking dare. You don't get to fuck your fiancée in the woods and talk to me about shame."

"So ye *do* want to lie with him?" His chest swelled.

"So what if I do?" I hurled the words like a dagger. "He's not the one getting married. *You* are."

Then we were both screaming, neither of us hearing the other, just words flying without thought or consequence. The trees swayed to the tune of *spineless bitch* and *dickless bastard*—

me. *Nasty shrew* and *mindless trollop*—him. Most of it bounced off me, but then he called me a *bed swerver*, and I completely lost my shit.

"I'm not the one who screws anything with a pair of tits." I shoved him hard in the chest. "You're a coward! A lying, fucking coward!"

He gripped my wrists.

I threw my weight against him. "Why are you doing this? Why are you even here? What do you want from me?"

"Everything!" His eyes flashed like a wolf's in the moonlight. "Everything, Fiona." He backed me into a tree. Bark bit into my flesh. He grasped my shoulders, and our eyes locked. "I want to erase the taste of Gavin's mouth from yours. I want to know if your body is as wild as your heart." He stared down at me, eyes burning with need. "And by God, Fiona, I want to be the one who tames it."

He leaned into me, the truth of his words sliding against my most tender of spots. A moan escaped my lips. Then his mouth was on mine, hard and furious. This was no lover's kiss. It was barbed wire and razor blades. It was fire and lightning and gasoline explosions. It was every harsh word we'd ever said, and all the ones we hadn't. When he tore away, we both panted.

I glared. "Don't think this means I've forgiven you."

Then I clutched his shirt and hauled him back for more. The wind swirled and whipped around us, a pregnant moon shining above. Then all that rage transformed into something new. Something primal and desperate. Naked yearning. Storm and earth colliding. Throbbing, aching need.

He yanked up my skirt. I tugged at his pants as he gripped my thighs. My feet left the ground, and I wrapped my legs around him. And then he was inside me. He groaned, hands gripping my ass, bouncing me up and down. My heels dug into his back, and I rode out wave after wave of savage, primordial pleasure.

"Fiona." His cry was both a warning and a plea.

Dropping my legs, I put a hand to his chest and guided him to the grass. I tore off his shirt, scrubbed my hands up his chest.

178

My palms met muscles, firm as the iron that forged them. God damn, how I'd longed to do that.

Grabbing my gown, he tore it down the length of me, the hand-stitched fabric cracking as seams ripped. I dragged my nails along the length of his stomach as I lowered to take him into my mouth.

But before I could, he dug his hands into my hair, holding me off. "Nay, lass," the glint in his eyes was feral, "I told ye, it's me that means to tame ye."

Quick as a switch, he flipped me on my back. He took my nipple between his lips. His mouth was fire, spreading across my skin. I moaned as his teeth grazed sensitive flesh. With a knee, he spread my legs. As he kissed and nibbled his way down my stomach, his fingers slid inside me. "Christ, you're wet." Sliding his finger in and out, his lips found my clit. He teased me with his tongue. Laving and flicking. Taking me to the edge and pulling me back. Again and again until I whimpered and shook.

My hands clawed at his hair. "Henry, it's too much. I can't take any more. I need you to fuck me. Please."

He pinned my wrists above my head with a massive hand. Thrusting beneath him, I bucked and moaned. "I've a fair idea what ye can take, lass, and you're not nearly there yet." He palmed my ass and squeezed.

Sliding back between my thighs, he sucked on the tender nub between my lips until I screamed out in pleasure. "Henry. Oh my God, Henry please."

He growled. "That's right. Say my name, lass. Tell me whose cunnie this is."

My back arched. "It's yours. Oh God, it's yours."

He snaked up the length of me. His fingers clutched the roots of my hair. "Whose cunnie?"

I moaned. "Yours." He thrust into me, and my body stretched and molded to his girth.

Together, we pulsed and writhed, our bodies locked in an ancient, sacred rhythm. The magic of it suffused my body. Wild and free. I transformed into a creature of pleasure, shining bright beneath a watchful pagan moon.

My muscles clenched at the delicious pressure, building, building, building inside me. I cried out. "Don't stop. Don't stop." The pressure was too much. Too big to be contained.

"Not yet." Flipping me over onto hands and knees, he teased my entrance with his cock, sliding it over my clit. He slapped my ass as he rubbed against me. I moaned, and it was too much for him. "Ye like that, do ye?" Shoving inside of me, he smacked my ass again. Fingers twined into my hair and pulled as he rode me. Skin slid against skin.

My muscles tightened and dripped around him. "Oh, God." My insides contracted. "Oh, God. Oh, God." Shaking in that final moment of divine, blinding release, I cried out.

Henry let out a conquering groan, and we collapsed to the ground, limp and trembling. He circled his arms around me, and I nestled into the shape of him. Sparks of electricity shot down my legs and out my toes.

I listened to the beat of his heart and the rattle of leaves. He kissed my head. Ran his hands through my hair. I sighed and smiled, appreciating the lines of his legs and the warmth of his chest. The air was thick and dewy. A squirrel chittered in the distance.

I stretched and nuzzled into him, content and cozy despite the fact I just told him I was his—I was no one's and I'd remind him. Soon. If he wasn't so warm and comfortable. For the first time since being here, all my tense muscles finally relaxed—until the voice in my head whispered: *holy matrimony.*

# Chapter Twenty-Two

Five minutes. That's all I wanted. Just five minutes to lay in Henry's arms and pretend I hadn't made the biggest mistake of my life. Five minutes to ignore the fact he was still engaged. Five minutes without thinking about how hard getting over him would be now we'd slept together. But five minutes was apparently too much to ask...

Not for him, though. He'd slipped into a post-coital doze and was snoring away into the back of my neck...like a god-damned sociopath. What was wrong with him? He should be freaking out, not taking a fucking nap. I flipped and stared at him. Not a line of tension creased his stupid, cheating face.

I shoved him.

Startling, he jerked awake. "What? What is it?"

"You're getting married!" I flung the words like an accusation of murder.

His eyes crawled open, and he flashed me a sleepy grin.

"Are you seriously smiling at me right now?" I yanked his arm off my waist. "You know what, asshole. I'm out of here."

His hand shot to my wrist before I could move. Sitting upright, he ran a hand through his hair, dislodging bits of leaves and broken twigs. His eyes focused, and his gaze settled on me. "I'm not marryin' Coira. We're finished."

Now technically speaking, this was exactly what I wanted to hear, but I'd already worked myself into a tizzy, and I wasn't quite ready to abandon it. "*Are* finished? Or *will be*?"

"Are." There was an air of finality to the clipped way he said it.

Pausing, I let his words sink in. This was good news. So why was I filled with anxiety? "You really left her?"

He nodded.

Scrutinizing his face, I bit my lip. "When?"

"When I took her into the woods." His expression shifted, and his gaze fell. "I shouldna have done it. I should have waited. I told myself she had it coming. That she was lucky I spared her the indignity o' doing it inside the guildhall after what she pulled, but I kent I was wrong." His fingers curled into fists. "She deserved better."

And I deserved that verbal kick in the uterus. "Let me get this straight." My voice warbled with hurt and anger. "You announced your engagement, broke up with her, slept with me, and now you regret it? Well, if that's the way it is, go after her. You got what you came for."

His mouth fell open. "You're bloody unbelievable. I didna *get what I came for.* Nor do I regret leavin' her, but she deserved better than to be jilted outside a guildhall."

Squeezing my eyes closed, I clutched the roots of my hair. "Then why did you ask her to marry you in the first place!"

"I didna." He winced. "Well, I did, but it's not what ye think."

My ribcage expanded as I sucked in a deep, exasperated breath. "Look, I can't take much more of this. Can you cut the bullshit and tell me what's going on?"

A gust of wind sent shivers across my skin, and Henry draped his cloak around me. "I told ye before there were circumstances." Retaking his seat, he continued, "Not long afore ye came to live with us, Coira's servant came to the house, beggin' me to stop Coira. Ye see, she was set to depart for France that morn'. Had a meetin' with a new vintner she hoped to partner with."

I still had a hard time imagining her as a businesswoman. It was sad. In a different life, we might have found we had a lot in common.

"I asked the lass why. Coira traveled to France all the time. I didna see any reason to keep her from her work." Lines etched his forehead. "She broke down. 'The mistress has missed her courses,' she told me. 'Dinna let her on that ship. I canna bear to see her lose another bairn.'"

Bile swirled in my belly. Coira was pregnant? This was worse than I thought. But then...she couldn't be. He said this was *before* I came. She'd be showing by now.

"*Another* bairn." His nails dug into his knees. "She'd been pregnant before and never told me."

"She lost it?" I hated the pity that formed within me on her behalf.

"Lost or got rid of..."

"Oh." My eyes went wide.

Shrugging, he dropped his head. "I canna be certain. Her servant didna say as much outright, but I could tell there was more to the tale than she was tellin'."

A shiver worked its way up my spine. "What did you do?"

"I went after her." He cringed. "If she was slippin' bairns, I was the one to blame. She kent I didna wish to wed. What choice did she have?" His eyes grew hazy with remembered grief. "But I was too late. By the time I reached the boatyard, her ship had sailed."

He lowered his gaze. "I sent her a letter. Told her I kent about the child, and she had naught to fear. I'd do right by her once she returned." His smile held only sadness. "She wrote back. Said she had an untimely birth, and the bairn was lost. We never spoke o' it again."

Silence followed his pronouncement. My stomach buzzed as if it were filled with bees. How could they not talk about it? Two dead babies. A marriage proposal. And not a word? "So tonight when the speaker made that announcement?"

"It was the first time she acknowledged what was in that letter." A gust of wind blew his hair into his face, and he tucked it behind his ears. "To tell ye true, I dinna think she wished to marry me at all. She just wanted to make sure *ye* couldna have me."

I bit my lip before I said something I'd regret. It wasn't that I was unsympathetic as to why Coira wouldn't want to be burdened with a child. She'd have no choice but to wed, and she'd lose the rights to her business. But to sacrifice her independence to thwart me, when she wouldn't do it for the sake of her unborn child seemed crueler and more callous than I'd expect even from her.

A resigned sigh escaped his lips, and his eyes softened. "Dinna judge her too harshly. It hasna been easy for her. Especially tonight. She had to watch me, watchin' ye." A pained smile crossed his face. "She kent how I felt..."

He trailed off, and silence fell between us. Clouds shifted in front of the moon, casting us in darkness. A gust of wind blew my hair into my face. I searched for words, but none came.

After a long pause, he met my eyes. "Ye kissed Gavin."

Technically, *he* had kissed me, but it seemed a moot point. I nodded.

His hand balled against his belly. "Do ye love him?"

The ridiculousness of the question, coupled with his nervous tone, made me laugh. "With my whole heart and soul." I gestured to the thin cloak that covered my otherwise naked body. "I'm just out here with you because I like to argue in the nude."

He blinked, as if not sure whether I was joking.

I laughed and pulled him to me. "No, you idiot. It just so happens, I'm in love with somebody else."

After months of denying my feelings for him, even to myself, saying the words out loud filled me with joy. And I was certain that's what this was. Love. No other man had ever caused me to experience every emotion to its fullest extreme the way Henry did. Nobody'd ever made me risk my principles and pride because I couldn't resist the temptation of his lips on mine. And nobody had ever filled me with a sense of absolute security by just standing in my mere presence.

He kissed me, deep and passionate and full of all the love I'd just confessed. He put a hand to my cheek. His eyes shone in the starlight. "Marry me."

I cocked my head. "Huh?"

"I want ye to be my wife." He squeezed my hands.

I stared, unblinking. "You want me to marry you?"

He nodded. A huge grin lit his face.

I nodded. "Huh."

It might not have been the most eloquent response, but seriously, what the hell? Who proposes the first *second* of a new relationship? And what kind of idiot would I have to be to accept? I mean, it was crazy, right? Okay, sure, we'd lived together for the last half year, but that hardly qualified as dating. Not that dating was a thing here, but still...There was so much we didn't know about each other.

For instance, he didn't know I was a time traveler, and I didn't know his favorite food. Damnit. Okay, so I knew his favorite food—stewed eels. Unless we had neeps. Then he preferred venison, but it had to be seasoned with a lot of pepper, even though it always made him sneeze.

Twice. He always sneezed twice. It was cute. Somehow, he always managed to look surprised by it, even though it happened every time.

But I was getting off track. A marriage had to be built on more than food preferences and sneezes. Or did it? Strangers got married all the time here. A good medieval marriage meant food on the table and...well, that was about it. But I wasn't from this time. I was a modern girl, and I had different expectations. When I got married, I wanted it to be for love.

Son of a bitch...I was going to marry this guy.

I gave him my most serious I'm-not-messing-around expression. "I'm not giving up my tavern."

He grinned.

My gaze bored into his. "And you can forget any vow that includes the word obey."

He laughed, a deep rumble straight from the belly. Hauling me into his arms, he kissed me so hard and deep, my toes tingled.

I pushed him back. "I'm not joking. I won't..."

But then I lost my train of thought, because I was looking at him, and he was looking at me, and our clothes were already off, and... Dammit. I let the cloak he'd given me earlier fall from my shoulders and shoved him to the ground. I crawled on top of him. "Don't think we're done talking about this."

And we would talk about it. Later. Definitely later.

~ * ~

"Fiona, look at this." Henry snagged something off the ground next to his abandoned shirt. I shaded my forehead and squinted against the sun. He held a small, glinty object. "A wee cross. I found it in the grass just now, right where we were layin'."

"Really?" I tugged my dress over my head.

"It's a sign." He stuffed the cross in his sporran. "God's blessed our union."

I laughed. "If God blessed what we did last night, those nuns at my school got it *all* wrong."

He did a double take. "At your school?"

I tied my cloak. "Never mind. That's a story for a different time." Wrapping my arms around his middle, I stared up at him. "Let's go."

We made the walk of shame home. Our clothes stained with dirt and grass and wine and who knew what else, but neither of us cared. We were together, and that was all that mattered.

A half hour later, we turned off the winding, dirt road into the yard. God, it was good to be home. I didn't even care I'd lose the deposit on my cottage. What did money matter next to family? And speaking of family...I couldn't wait to see Mairi's face when we told her about our engagement. She was going to flip her shit!

I stopped Henry before he opened the door. "Let's surprise them. You go in first. Then I'll pop in a few minutes later and act like I came to get my barrels. And then we'll...I don't know. We'll play it by ear." Henry touched his ear, his forehead wrinkling in confusion.

Mairi's voice shrilled through the window. "Get it out!"

"Aww, come on, Mairi, please." Donald's voice cracked. "He'll help with the rats."

Henry and I met each other's eyes. I grinned and shoved him forward. "Yeah, you go in first."

His mouth quirked in a half-smile. "Coward."

I ran to the window and peeked through while Henry went inside. She sat hunched in a chair, her hand clamped to the scruff of an adorable, shockingly filthy, terrier puppy. The dog yipped, gave a great shake, and doused her with muddy water. I bit my knuckle to keep from laughing.

She wiped the grime off her face and glared at Donald.

"I'm sorry." His voice was a squeak.

"Lad." Her voice ground through clenched teeth. "If ye dinna get rid o' this mongrel..."

The door clicked closed behind Henry, and Donald and Mairi snapped their heads in his direction. A moment of silence fell, then Mairi and Donald began yelling at once.

"Look at the state o' ye!" She slammed her hand on the table.

He twisted in his chair. "Where have ye been?"

Swooping the puppy into her arms, she shot to her feet. She had her scary eyes going, and her face rapidly approximated the color of an over-ripe eggplant, but, to my surprise, he led the attack.

"Disappeared." He stalked toward Henry. "No word. Thought ye'd been murdered on the streets."

Henry clapped him on the shoulder. "Dinna fash, lad. My wife and I were just enjoyin' the moonlight. That's all."

That sounded like my cue, so I left the window and headed to the door.

"That isna an excuse." Donald's voice lost none of its fury. "Ye should have—"

I cracked the door open.

"Shut your klappe, eejit boy." I couldn't see Mairi's face because Henry blocked my view, but I heard the horror in her voice. "Tell me ye didna..."

Henry nodded. "I did."

"Oh, lad..." A sob bubbled from her throat... "I ken Fiona leavin' troubled your heart, but to marry that...that shrew."

"Now you listen to me, Mairi. I'll not have ye disrespectin' my wife." I walked inside, and Henry wrapped his arm around me. "Isna that right, sweetling?"

I shrugged. "Eh, I've been called worse."

She froze as if paralyzed with shock. Then all at once she snapped out of it and shouted with joy. "Ye've wed! I canna believe it!" Tears streamed down her cheeks, but she was all smiles. She clutched the dog to her chest. "I can die a happy woman now!"

A slow smile spread across Donald's face. "Ye mean to say ye've married?" Henry nodded, and Donald's grin nearly split his face. "About bloody time."

"Well, we're not married yet, obviously, but he asked, and I said yes!" My cheeks hurt, I was smiling so hard.

"What do ye mean you're not married yet?" Mairi's tone was suddenly sharp.

I cocked my head. "What do *you* mean?" What did she think? We'd dipped into a chapel at first light and eloped?

"She has a point." Henry tapped his lip. "We didna have witnesses. Donald, Mairi, ye heard her say I asked?"

They nodded.

He squeezed my shoulder. "And ye heard her say she agreed?"

They nodded again.

He grinned. "All right *now* we've wed."

"We have to celebrate!" Mairi shot to her feet. "I'll cook a feast!"

Donald's eyes lit. "Ooh, how 'bout sheep johnnies!"

She looked about. "Where's that bottle o' mead I've been saving?"

"Hold on!" My voice cut through their jubilation, and everybody stopped and looked at me. "What are you talking about? We're engaged, not married, you lunatics!"

She pursed her lips. "Is it the consummation that has ye fashed, lass?"

"No!" Good god, if she tried to give me the sex talk, I'd have to stab out my eardrums.

Henry snorted.

"I'm talking about a wedding." I looked to each of them, waiting for one of them to acknowledge I wasn't being the crazy one. "You know, a church? A pastor? I don't know, legal documents?"

Mairi cackled. "If ye needed to wait for a church ceremony to be wed, half the country would be livin' in sin!"

Henry wrapped an arm around my shoulder. "Fiona, love. I dinna mean any offense, but ye dinna have any wealth to speak of."

I narrowed my eyes. What he said might be true, but any sentence that started with, "I don't mean any offense," was most definitely offensive.

He laughed and kissed the top of my head. "All I mean to say is there's no call for any contracts between us."

I looked from Henry to Donald to Mairi, waiting for one of them to cop to the joke, but none of them did. In fact, the three of them were staring at me like I was two tankards short of a barrel.

"Wait." A nervous giggle escaped my throat. "You guys are saying we're already married?"

All three of them nodded.

My giggle turned into a full-blown chortle. "He asked. I said yes. And that's it? Poof. We're married?"

They nodded again, and I cackled like a doped-up hyena. I was married. Holy fuck. This was insanity. Here I thought getting engaged was a big step.

The puppy waddled over and sniffed my shoe. Then he lifted his leg and peed on me. I laughed even harder.

"Such a beautiful wedding dress." I held out my skirt and inspected the wine, dirt, and now piss on my clothes. "Just like I always imagined."

# Chapter Twenty-Three

"What do ye think about the green?" Mairi selected a swatch from the mound of fabric piled on the table.

I glanced at it as I tipped my bag of malt into the kettle. "It's fine, I guess." I stirred the mix, adjusted the height of the chain over the fire, and wiped my hands clean. Okay, that was done. Now I could grab a bite to eat before the shop reopened for the afternoon.

She frowned. "Have a care, lass. Ye only wed once."

I snorted. If that were true, we wouldn't be having this conversation. According to Mairi, there was married, and then there was *married.* The latter version of which involved a church ceremony, a reception, and probably some medieval version of the chicken dance.

I, personally, didn't see the point. Henry and I were already married...at least in the legal sense. So why waste our hard-earned coin on a priest and a party? Besides, the whole ceremony was just going to make me feel sad and pathetic. I had no friends to sit in the audience, and no Granda to walk me down the aisle. I'd be the pitiful little orphan bride, all alone, in a tragically *green* wedding dress. Kill me now.

She examined a purplish-red swatch. "The mauve is quite lovely."

I wrinkled my nose. "Lovely for a cabbage, maybe." I sifted through the pile until I found a scrap of white cloth. "How about this?"

She narrowed her eyes. "Ye think I have time for jests?"

"I'm not jesting." I nudged the scrap in front of her. "Where I come from, wedding dresses are white."

She pursed her lips. "Your gypsy kin probably get married in their shifts."

I scoffed. "Is that any way to talk about people doing the Lord's work?" I liked to throw that line at her anytime she insulted my made-up, missionary family. I'd grown fond of Aunt Josephine—the maiden aunt with a nut allergy I'd invented to explain why I didn't know how to make almond milk.

"White is symbolic." I wrapped an arm around Mairi's shoulder. "You know, purity, chastity—"

"Indigence." She peered at me from beneath raised brows. "Ye want me to die o' shame havin' the whole town thinkin' we canna afford a bit o' dyed cloth for your nuptials?"

The door swung open, and Henry, Donald, and the puppy waltzed in. The dog's little butt vibrated at the sight of Mairi. He yipped and bounced toward her, tail waggling like the two of them were the best of friends. She glared at the dog, mouth razor thin, which the dog somehow interpreted as meaning she wanted to play. He bit her skirts and gave a puppy growl, whipping his head from side-to-side.

"Off ye wee demon." She yanked against him in an epic game of tug-o'-war.

"He has a name, Mairi." I patted my thighs. "Come here, Snoop Dog. Come here, boy. Want a treat?" At the word *treat,* he released her dress and ran to me. I swooped him up and scratched behind his ears. "Who's a good boy? Who's a good boy?"

Donald laughed. "I think she likes the dog better than ye, Hal."

With a small smile, Henry shrugged. "I canna compete. Dog's smarter than I am." His eyes lit. "Ye ken she's taught him to feign death? Points her finger at him and says, 'bong.' Falls right o'er. I've ne'er seen anything like it."

"Bang." I smirked. "A bong is something much different." I made kissy faces at the dog and rubbed his belly.

"Will ye toss that wee fiend outside and come look at these fabrics." On a long inhale, Mairi poked her tongue into her cheek.

"Fine." With a sigh, I handed the dog to Donald and eyed the pile of potential fashion atrocities.

After a brief scan, I drew back my shoulders and straightened my spine. Nope. No way I was going to spend countless hours debating fabric choices for a wedding gown I didn't care about. If she wanted to dress me like a cabbage, or an eggplant, or any other shade of vegetable, so be it.

"All right, Mairi." I steepled my fingers. "How about you pick your two favorite colors, and I'll choose between them."

Giving a curt nod, she licked her lips, and zoned in on that pile like she'd been born for this moment. After several intense minutes of sorting, tossing, and piling scraps, she handed me two fabric swatches, one tomato red, the other cornflower blue.

"The blue." I gave a definitive nod. "Definitely the blue."

The corner of her lips dipped down as she held the swatches to my face. "The red looks better with your skin."

Henry peered over my shoulder. "Aye, it's the same color as her face when she's angry."

I smacked his arm. "It is not!"

Pointing at my face, he laughed. "See, look, there it goes."

"The blue then." She tossed the red scrap back into the pile and gave me a once over before gesturing for me to stand. I rose, and she did this odd little measuring dance with her hands, turning me from side to side and nodding to herself. "Three extra yards should do it."

My brow furrowed. "Do what?"

She swept the pile of cloth into a burlap sack. "In case I have to let the dress out."

I raised an eyebrow. "You think I'm going to put on three yard's worth of weight by spring?"

She laughed. "Dinna be daft. The way you two play Bo Peep all night, I'd be surprised if your womb's not already quickenin'."

My throat tightened. I didn't know what was worse—that she'd casually insinuated she heard us banging or that she'd done it by referencing a beloved nursery rhyme character.

Henry didn't seem nearly as horrified. His eyes softened as his gaze fell to my middle. Dammit. That was the problem with no engagement period. We hadn't had time to talk about things like children.

"Don't get your hopes up. It takes the women in my family a long time to conceive. Years sometimes." Three and a half years, to be exact, thanks to my IUD, but I couldn't very well tell them that.

"Nonsense." She waved off my concerns with a swipe of her hand. "I've been lightin' a candle for St. Anne since the day the two o' ye wed. Ye'll be with child by month's end."

"We'll see." I smirked, smug, certain science had the upper hand... Right? Why did I feel like I just cursed myself? Damn Mairi and her voodoo candle lighting.

I put a hand to my stomach. "If I wanted to pray to the patron saint of medical science, who would that be?"

She raised an eyebrow.

"You're not the only one who can light candles, Mairi." My voice came out in a defensive hiss.

"Queer shifts in mood." She grinned at Henry. "That's the first sign."

~ * ~

An hour or so later, after a filling lunch of salt fish and ale, I rose from my seat and stretched, ready to continue with the business day. "Can you bring out another barrel?"

Henry raised a brow. "Ye've gone through the last one already?" He grinned. "Who needs a dowry when your wife outsells ye, aye?"

I smacked his ass. "Be a good boy, and maybe I'll buy you something pretty."

He chuckled and lifted the barrel as easily as if it were filled with dandelion seeds. "I suppose I shouldna be surprised ye sold all that ale. Never seen the shop so busy." I held the door open for him, and he walked through. "Ye've a sound mind for business."

I smiled. The poor sweet bastard hadn't realized why all those people showed up this morning. It sure as hell wasn't because of my business acumen. I'd spent enough time with Mairi to recognize the gossip mill grinding into overtime. They wanted a glimpse of the weird, foreign girl who'd stolen Henry from the neighborhood socialite. Well, as far as I was concerned, they could look all they wanted, just so long as they kept drinking.

When we reached the smithy, a pair of identical twins waited outside for us to open shop. I eyed the pair. They were young, both fair-skinned and freckled with matching ginger braids. Based on their age—sixteen or seventeen by my estimation—they probably weren't a threat. My shoulders relaxed. That was the only problem with our business success. It was bringing in customers I'd never met, and, for all I knew, any one of them could be a time soldier.

I nodded at the girls in greeting. "Let me unlock this, and we'll be right with you."

They giggled.

I opened the door and held it, gesturing for them to enter. "How can I help you?"

"Oh, we'll just browse a bit." The taller of the two grinned, and the pair giggled some more.

Henry set down the barrel, and I collected my ledger. By the time I had everything situated, two more people arrived. Five minutes later, three more showed up. And on it went until the smithy was crammed so tight with bodies, we were probably breaking thirty different fire codes, that was, if fire-codes existed here. I wasn't sure.

I handed a tankard to the first man in line. "This is my newest flavor—Guinness."

The man's eyebrows shot up in surprise, and my heart thudded. I'd purposefully given my ale a modern name, figuring any glint of recognition from the customers would signal a threat. I snuck my hand into my dress's hidden pocket and wrapped my fingers around my knife.

"Are ye a MacGenis?" The man's ruddy cheeks filled out with his smile. "And here I thought ye were an outlander."

Relief stilled my shaking hands, and I grinned. "No, just borrowed the name from an old friend."

Boy did I miss that old friend. Despite all the shit I gave Granda and company for only drinking Guinness, I'd have killed for a frothy pint of Ireland's best. But sadly, the only similarity between my blackberry ale and its namesake was the color.

The man handed me his farthings and took a sip. "That's bloody good!" Wrinkles creased his eyes. "I see why the lad married ye."

Yup, that was it. Henry married me on account of a beverage. I supposed it was a better explanation than most. This morning I overheard a woman say she had it on good authority I was a selkie—a mythical seal that could shed its skin and take on human form. Apparently, selkies made excellent wives, though, so I decided to take it as a compliment.

I smiled at the man, his lips now a faint purple from the ale. "Good thing I can brew, eh? 'Cause I'll tell you what, I can't cook or sew worth a damn."

His eyes went round at the sound of me cursing, and he burst out laughing. "You're a bit o' all right, ye ken that?"

A chorus of giggles erupted from the middle of the ale line. Apparently, the twins had finally mustered the courage to study me up close. For the longest time, they'd been skulking around the shop, picking up poleaxes and breastplates and various other weaponry, while sneaking covert glances at me.

The taller of the two turned to her sister. "Did you hear that?"

"Aye." The other nodded.

I handed my next customer his ale.

"She's not verra bonnie." The first twin's voice grew louder as the line moved forward.

"I heard she ensorcelled him." The other twin nodded sagely. "That's why he abandoned the other one."

I served two more customers. The twins were next in line, only they were so engrossed in conversation, they didn't seem to realize it.

"Anne, I told ye." The first twin put her hands on her hips. "I heard it straight from the baker's lad that his cousin kent a girl who said she kent for certain she was an avenging angel sent by God to punish the wicked."

The girl, apparently named Anne, scoffed. "I still say she's a witch."

"No." I leaned across the ale table. "Your sister's right."

They gasped in unison, and two identical heads turned to face me, eyes wide and cheeks flushed.

I grinned. "I am an angel."

"I'm, uh, I..." The first one shifted from foot to foot.

"It's fine." I filled each of their tankards. "In fact, I'm such an angel, your next cup's free." I raised my voice so everyone in the smithy could hear. "That goes for all of you. Anyone who's already bought their first cup, can have a second cup free."

Cheers erupted from the crowd, and several new customers got in line. Henry shot me a look from across the room like he was questioning my sanity, but I knew what I was doing. People liked free shit, and they liked the person who gave them free shit. Now when the twins, and all the other gossip mongers, went home and told their friends, I wouldn't be the engagement-wrecking shrew—I'd be the generous girl with great ale.

The line kept moving. The ale kept flowing. And people kept spending. By mid-afternoon Henry sold out of axe heads, and I had gone through three quarters of a barrel without so much as a hint of danger from undercover time-travelers. Whoever said there's no such thing as bad advertising knew what they were talking about. Gossip seemed a small price to pay when every cup put me that much closer to my own tavern.

"I heard he raped her." A man at the table to my left examined a utility knife as he spoke to his friend. "Killed her husband right outside the house and took her as his own."

Then again, money wasn't everything...

"Oi, you're spilling my ale." The customer in front of me waved his hand in front of my face.

I shoved the tankard at him. "No charge." Abandoning my post, I strode to the knife stand, approaching the man from behind.

His friend frowned. "What I hear, she's been livin' with him for months. My guess is he got her in a family way."

Straightening to my full height, I tapped the first man on the shoulder. "Excuse me, sir, you need to leave."

He cocked his head. "Beggin' your pardon?"

Without a second thought, I snagged his ear and twisted until he cried in pain. "Get out and do it quick before I tell my husband what I heard you say."

I released his ear, and the man scampered away like a dog that had been kicked with a steel-toed boot. His friend trotted after him, laughing to himself.

Henry raised an eyebrow from across the room, but I waved him off. No need to bother him with what was already handled.

After a quick scan to ensure the man had left, I resumed my place at the ale table. "Who's ready for a drink?"

~ * ~

Ink stained the side of my hand and the cuff of my sleeve—lefties and quill pens just didn't mix. But the ledgers were up to date, the coins counted, and our last customer had finally left. Henry draped an arm around my shoulder.

I smiled up at him. "This was our best day yet."

"That's because ye got them soused." Laughing, he hoisted the coin purse off the desk and grinned at its weight. "What will ye buy with all this coin?"

Shrugging, I smirked. "You mean besides whatever Mairi has on her list for the wedding?"

"I've given her more than enough for that." With a stretch and a yawn, he plopped onto the stool next to me. "Dinna let her tell ye otherwise."

"Really?" I eyed the coin purse, lumpy and overstuffed with all our earnings. "Well I guess it'll go into the tavern fund."

His hand fell to my knee, and he gave it a squeeze. "Ye should set a bit aside for the fair. There'll be vendors there from all corners o' the earth."

"Corners?" Giggling, I ran my hand down his back. "You do know the earth is round, right?"

He raised an eyebrow. "Aye..."

My head dropped to his shoulder, and I laughed at the absurdity of the conversation. "A wife has to know where her husband stands on these things. What about the sun? Center of the solar system or no?"

He didn't get the chance to give his opinion on the whole Copernican thing, because the smithy door creaked open.

"Coira." His voice was a sickening mixture of guilt and nerves.

She strode forward, poised, collected, looking like she owned the world.

"What can I do for ye?" His voice squeaked so politely I was surprised he didn't follow it with a dinner invitation.

I ground my teeth. Apparently, no one told him the whole *let's be friends* part of a breakup was just lip service.

Nose in the air, she strode forward. "I want ye to put an end to this foolishness. I ken you're smitten with this servant." She waved a dismissive hand in my direction. "But ye've had your fun. It's time ye come to your senses."

With great force of will, I reminded myself she'd just been dumped, and wasn't right in the head to begin with. In the calmest voice I could muster, I raised the claddagh ring Henry made for me the day after we wed. "You can call me a servant all you want, but Henry and I are married now."

She gave a haughty laugh. "So I've heard." Her hand slinked into the inner pocket of her dress, and she retrieved a piece of paper.

Clenching my fists, I willed my hands not to tremble. I didn't have to read that paper to know what it was—the letter he wrote to her months before, promising to marry her. Apparently, he also realized what she held, because his face drained to the color of her white lead makeup.

She slammed the paper onto the desk. "Proof your marriage isna valid."

I sat back and smirked as if I found her threats amusing. "Are you seriously trying to blackmail him into a relationship? That's just embarrassing."

I had to hand it to myself, I could bullshit with the best of them. My insides writhed like a beast gnawed on my organs. Yet here I stood, sounding cockier than a motherfucker, when, fact of the matter was, she was probably right. I'd been worried about this ever since the day I learned consent made a marriage. Because if Henry offered to marry Coira in that letter, and she agreed in public at the gala, didn't that make the two of them married?

Snatching the letter off the desk, I scanned its contents.

"I ken I've hurt ye, but can we not talk about this?" His fingers clutched my knee as if it were the only thing keeping him steady.

"What's there to talk about?" Smugness oozed from her voice. "If I show this to the courts, they'll side with me. Your marriage will be invalidated, and *I'll* be named your wife. They'll likely charge ye with bigamy."

"No." I infused my voice with false confidence. "They won't." I ran my finger down the page until I found the sentence I was searching for. "If ye are with child, I'll do right by ye when ye return." I met her eyes. "*If,*" I said, "and *when.* You're not pregnant, and you returned months ago. His proposal was conditional upon those two stipulations."

She scoffed, but fear glistened behind her psychotic eyes. "The maidservant thinks herself a solicitor, does she?"

Now, I didn't know shit about medieval law, but I had seen plenty of episodes of Law and Order, and I figured that was close enough. "Anything else?" I waved the letter in the air. "Because the only thing that note proves is that you're an unmarried woman who fornicated with the local blacksmith. Sounds like quite the scandal if you ask me."

Her clenched fists shook. "Aye. It will be a scandal once I tell the court he lured me into his bed with promises of marriage, only to abscond with some jezebel instead." Her gaze raked over me like dagger points. "Expect a summons within a fortnight."

Gulping, I fought to maintain my façade of false confidence, but it was growing harder by the second. I was at a loss for witty retorts, and my faux legal bravado had run its course.

Fortunately, Henry had my back. "Coira..." His voice was still polite, but the air shifted about him. "What do ye hope to gain with all this?"

Her brow furrowed.

He leaned forward. "Do ye ken what'll happen if a court forces me to claim ye as my wife?"

She stared at him, seemingly unsure whether the question was rhetorical.

"Fiona and I will continue to live as man and wife. Publicly. The world will see ye've been cast aside, and ye'll become an object of pity." He rose, and though he didn't elevate his voice, the mere act of standing seemed to amplify his words. "Your business and property will become mine by rights and will be legally passed down to the children Fiona and I have together. Ye'll be left with nothing. All you've worked so hard to build will disappear, and for what? Vengeance?" Raising his palms, he advanced toward her. "Is that really the life ye've come here to claim?"

Her eyes bulged. "Ye dare to threaten me after all you've put me through?"

Exhaustion darkened his face as he shook his head. "Nay, Coira. I've no wish to threaten ye. All I want is to live my life in peace. It would do ye well to do the same."

She barked an unhinged cackle. "Peace? Ye speak to me o' peace when ye've cast me aside like refuse. Betrayed me. Humiliated me in front o' the whole burg." A vein pulsed on her forehead. "Why should I worry about ye, and your peace, when you've destroyed mine?"

Squeezing my eyes closed, I groaned. Loathe though I was to admit it, she had a point, and I had no alternative but to cop to it. "Coira, you're right."

Her head snapped in my direction, and she gawked at me.

"What happened between Henry and I hurt you, and you have absolutely no obligation to us or our well-being. The only thing you have to worry about is your own happiness." I raised the letter. "But this isn't going to bring you that."

She sneered. "What do ye ken about my happiness, trollop?"

I sucked in a deep breath. "I know a relationship based on coercion and guilt will only bring misery. And I know you don't need Henry to make you happy or to validate your self-worth. You're already impressive as hell." The sincerity of my words rang clear, a surprise even to myself. "You built up a business from the ashes. You didn't cave to the pressures of marriage. You're strong and you're smart and you're independent. You have nothing to prove to anyone."

A quaver rattled her bottom lip, and her breath hitched. I had the distinct impression she wasn't accustomed to compliments and didn't quite know how to receive them. Her hand clutched the fabric of her dress. Desperation filled her eyes. For a second, I thought we'd achieved some sort of breakthrough, and maybe, just maybe, we could end this feud on civil terms.

But then our gazes locked, and when I flashed her my most encouraging smile, her body went rigid. Her nostrils flared, and she raked a sleeve across her eyes. Tears gone her pupils grew impossibly large.

"Dinna think to condescend to me, servant." Her neck elongated as she straightened to her full height. With an upward tilt to her chin, she positioned herself across the desk from me. "I know my place in this world. You on the other hand..." Her lips contorted into a nasty snarl. "It seems the courts will have to teach you your station."

My insides wilted. So much for diplomacy. I supposed hoping for reason from the chick who threw coins at my face two minutes after we met had been overly optimistic. Oh well. At least I tried for the high road. At this point there wasn't anything more I could do. If she insisted on going to war with me and Henry, so be it. She could get in line right after the time soldiers.

She reached for the letter.

"Absolutely the fuck not." I snatched the paper and shoved it into the flame of my pewter desk candle, cursing myself for not having done that right off the bat.

She lunged across the desktop and tried to wrench the burning letter from my grip. As we struggled, Coira's braid swung into the candle. A second later, this horrible, acrid scent filled the room.

"Your hair!" I shot to my feet

Flames licked up her braid. She shrieked and swatted at her head.

"Smother it." I waved my arms like an idiot. "Stop, drop, and roll." Henry bolted from his seat. I pulled off my cloak and tossed it over her flaming head.

"Get it off me!" Her shrieks were muffled by the cloak's thick wool.

"I'm trying to help!" I fought against her flailing limbs, trying to pat out the fire.

He reappeared with a water bucket and doused her head. There was a sizzle and a wisp of smoke. Her hands went to her hair. Her braid was completely gone, along with a patch on the back of her head. Water dripped down her face, carrying with it beads of white lead face paint. She shivered.

I worried she might go into shock. "Henry, get her a blanket." Gnawing on my lip, I turned to Coira. "Is your skin burned?"

She stared straight ahead, not blinking. Then, in a daze, she turned and headed for the door. Henry's eyes met mine. I tilted my head for him to go after her. Hands shaking, I collected the charred remains of the letter and tossed them in the forge.

Several minutes later, Henry returned, slumping into the seat next to me. "Donald's takin' her home in the neighbor's wagon."

I twisted Gran's ring. The taint of charred hair and skin still lingered in the air. "What happened once you got her out there? Did she say anything?"

"Aye..." He studied his hands. "She did."

I waited for him to elaborate, but he just sat there, flexing and extending his fingers like there was no more to say on the matter. So irritating. Why did men always act like details cost them money?

I nudged him with my shoulder. "*What* did she say."

Slow as molasses, he raised his head and grimaced. "She cursed the both of us and all our kin from now until the second coming. Then she vowed before God, the angels, and the saints above, she'd spend the rest of her days makin' the two of us suffer."

A nervous laugh escaped my lips. "Oh. Is that all?"

His reluctance to talk about it made a lot more sense now. Curses and oaths were serious business here. You didn't just casually make them, and you absolutely didn't break them. For her to have sworn a literal vow, she must have been dead fucking serious. She probably planned to have us in and out of court for the rest of our lives. Trumped up charge after trumped up charge, just hoping one would stick. This was going to be a serious pain in the ass.

With a sigh, I slid the money bag with our day's earnings over to Henry. "What do you think? Is it enough for a lawyer?"

# Chapter Twenty-Four

Any minute now...Come on. Chime, dammit.

"Will ye quit tapping your foot?" Mairi put a hand on my knee. "You're shakin' the table."

I forced my feet to still...for about two seconds. Then I started right back up again. I couldn't help it. How could she expect me to sit still when, any second now, the town bell would ring, and the fair would begin.

This was medieval Vegas, baby! Bold and bright and fabulously gaudy. Patterned tents in electric hues. Actors and singers and acrobats. Merchants in exotic robes. Shoddy goods and priceless treasures.

She took a drag from her tankard. "Ye should enjoy the moment o' calm. Soon as that bell rings, it'll be bedlam."

"I'm counting on it!" Henry earned a third of his annual salary from this fair, and with any luck, I would do the same.

She refilled her tankard, and I excused myself to take a leak behind some bushes. When I returned, I found her bobbing her head to a bawdy song the chandlers in the tent next to us were singing.

"'Some be lewd, and some be shrewd'," they sang.

Mairi pumped her fist in the air. "'Go where the shrews go'!"

I covered my mouth with a palm. Never in my life would I have expected prim, proper Mairi to be singing along to a dirty tavern song.

I eyed her nearly empty tankard. "How many of those have you had?"

Downing the last dregs, she burped. "Four. And I'm due for another."

That's when the man with the bear showed up. With a bob of his head in greeting, he gestured to the bear. "This here's Aggie." The bear rose to its hind legs and bowed.

I laughed.

Mairi squinted at the beast. "Fleas."

The man patted the bear's back. "Aggie'd like to buy an ale."

My grin widened. "Aggie, huh?" I winked at the man. "Well, if it's for the bear...I suppose I can sell you one early."

"How," Mairi hiccupped, "does *Aggie* intend to pay?"

"Well, ye canna expect a bear to pay in silver." He made a circling gesture with his finger, and the bear pirouetted. "Ye see, no purse. Where would she keep the coin?"

I wanted to hug Aggie—she was so freaking cute. "I take it Aggie pays in entertainment?"

The man nodded. "Precisely."

"Ye scaffy wee bugger." Mairi's words slurred before she took another drink and wiped her mouth with her sleeve. "Your coin purse looks plenty full to me."

Honest offense rounded his mouth and eyes. "Why should I have to pay? It's Aggie what wants it."

Her already flushed face flashed redder.

"Deal!" I put a calming hand on her shoulder. "It's my ale, and I want to see what Aggie can do."

The man placed a metal hoop over the bear's head. "Well, then, Aggie, how's about ye dance for your supper?" She shimmied it to her middle and hula hooped with far more success than I ever had. I clapped my hands and cheered.

Mairi snorted. "Dancin' bear."

"Well done, Aggie. Well done." He tossed her a sardine from a bucket on his cart. "But a lady shouldna be shakin' her hips like that. Why dinna ye show some poise?" He placed a ball on the bear's nose. It held steady as she twirled in a dainty circle.

"Good job, Aggie!" The bear bowed.

The town bell rang, and excitement flared through me. I handed the man his cup. "Here you go. Well worth the price of an ale."

His brow furrowed. "What are ye giving it to me for?" He handed the cup to Aggie, who tipped her head back and downed the pint in one gulp.

I stared, slack jawed. "Well, I'll be damned."

~ * ~

Bedlam. Glorious bedlam! Mairi was right. You couldn't even see the grass with people crammed so tight along the paths. Children screamed and screeched and zig-zagged between shoppers. Vendors shouted over the buzz of chatter. Rogue pigs vacuumed tossed apple cores and heels of bread. Fights erupted to cheers and taunts. Performers sang and danced and strummed away. And I had a front row seat to it all. Not that I had much time for gazing...

I put my hands to my mouth like a megaphone. "Ale. Strong and weak."

Mairi slopped half a tankard's worth of ale onto a customer.

"Whoa, give me that." I refilled the guy's cup and handed it to him. "No charge."

I returned my attention to the passersby. "Best ale in all of Scotland!" Two men wearing creepily realistic, wooden stag masks approached the table. I held out a hand for their tankards. "What'll it be, fellas, strong or weak?"

Man-beast number one curled his left bicep, and I nodded. "Strong it is."

Mairi stumbled forward as I poured their drinks. "Can I feel your horns?" Her voice slurred.

"How do you keep getting that cup?" I took her tankard for the third time in the last hour. "You're done." Turning my head over my shoulder, I shouted into the tent. "Henry! I need some help here!"

He peeked his head through a gap in the canvas. "What's amiss?"

I tilted my head toward Mairi.

206

"'Some of them be true of love'," she sang, swaying in her chair. "'Below the girdle but not above...'"

He chuckled. "Every damn year." He squinted at the sun. "Noon bell should ring soon. We'll get some food in her belly and have her sleep it off in the cart."

"'Some be brown, and some be white. And some be tender as a tripe. Some o' them be cherry ripe'."

"'Yet all of them be not so'!" A few people in the crowd joined in the song as they made their way to the ale table. I filled their tankards, while she led them in another verse.

I peeked my head back through the tent. "On second thought, maybe we should keep her out here."

~ * ~

Henry nudged my arm with a loaf of bread. "Eat."

I swiped the coins I'd just counted back into the bag and took the proffered bread. "You know," I took a bite, "two more days like this, and I might have enough for my tavern."

He wiped a few crumbs from the table, and I scooched back before I made an even bigger mess. Somehow, despite the hundreds of people who had been in and out of his tent all morning, the place still gleamed like a showroom. Bright white tablecloths showcased shimmering iron blades. Sewing dummies stood like sentries along the back wall, modeling mail shirts and breast plates. Everything gleamed clean and sparkly and utilitarian. Meanwhile, my own stand out front was so sticky with ale, bits of leaves and debris had glued themselves to the wood. Not that any of my customers minded.

"I've a bit o' coin set aside." He ran his hand through his hair. "If ye dinna make enough, I'll give ye the rest."

Heat warmed my chest at the offer. God, how I loved his man. I kissed his cheek. "That's sweet, but this is my thing. I want to do it myself."

He frowned. "Ye talk like I'm offerin' ye charity. I'm your husband. Why shouldna I invest..." Something outside the tent caught his attention. He rose. His hand dropped to his hilt as his head followed someone or something outside.

"What is it?" I scanned the crowd, but I didn't see anything unusual. Just a bunch of people waiting for the fair to resume and a guy taking a piss between two tents.

"Camerons." He spat the name like a curse.

"What? Where?" My gaze darted from face to passing face.

He waved a hand. "Already gone."

I stared at him. "They weren't the ones who..." I was unable to think of a diplomatic way to say, *murdered your whole family.*

He toed the dirt. "Nay. Too young." He forced a strained smile. "It's fine."

It would have been more convincing if his knuckles weren't white around his sword hilt. I teased his hand free and twined my fingers into his.

My heart ached for him. "Maybe they weren't Camerons."

A scowl curled his lips. "They wore Lochaber weaves. They were Camerons, sure enough."

"Any cheese left?" Donald called from across the tent.

Henry rifled through our picnic basket. "Aye." He walked the wax-covered wedge over to Donald.

I continued to eat my bread, but it tasted like sand in my mouth. Camerons...In a different life, I smiled when I heard that name. It meant summers with Sean or nights at the Caledonia Club with Old John. Now it meant blood feuds and the death of everyone Henry once loved.

When he returned, the worry lines had faded from his forehead, and he was back to his usual easy grin. My own tension eased. Leave it to Donald to cheer him in a matter of minutes. Being upset around that kid was impossible. He was like a human Golden Retriever.

I stared out at the fair patrons passing by. The crowd seemed to be growing thicker. "How long do you think we have until the bell rings?"

"Look at ye, sittin' there with food in your gob." My head snapped in the direction of the unfamiliar voice.

A girl with a picnic basket stood in our tent. Or was she a woman? I couldn't tell. She had big cheeks that gave her a baby face, but a sassy cock to her hip that made me think she might be older.

She slammed her picnic basket on the dirk table. "I told ye, I'd be bringin' food today."

"I'm sorry." Donald sputtered, his mouth full of food. "I couldna wait." He swallowed, wiped his hands on his pants then peeked into the basket. A groan escaped his lips. "Ye ken I hate artichokes."

"Eat them anyway." Her jaw jutted. "I told ye afore, I'll not be marryin' a choleric man." Before he could answer, the girl turned her back to him and strode to me. She plopped onto an empty ale barrel beside me. "Fiona, aye?" I nodded, and her grin puffed up her pudgy cheeks. "So you're the one who poisoned my fiancé."

Groaning, I squeezed my eyes closed. "You must be Shona, then." I ran a hand through my hair. "Sorry about the whole nearly killing Donald with my ale thing..."

She waved me off with a stubby-fingered hand. "Teach him to accept drink without questioning what it is." Her eyes sparkled with mirth. "But if ye ever need help decidin' if your ale ingredients will twist up intestines, ye can come to me."

I looked her over. "You know a lot about herbs?"

She grinned. "My mither's a wise-woman. I've been passing out horehound and henbane since I was old enough to hold a pestle."

Outside the tent, the noise of passersby increased, and people seemed to be swarming toward something down the path. I stuck my head outside the tent. "What's going on?"

Shona peeked at the crowd, squealed, and clapped her hands. "Minstrels setting up. C'mon." Before I knew what was happening, she had me on my feet and was dragging me out of the tent.

"No, I can't. I've got to mind the ale stand." I shot pleading looks to Donald and Henry for help, but they both eyed Shona as if she were a wrecking ball, and they had no intention of getting in its way.

Ignoring my concerns, she led me toward the tent's exit. "Dinna fash, Donald will mind the ale stand. Won't ye, love?" she called across the tent.

"Shona, I've me own work to do." Donald's voice came muffled around his mouthful of artichoke. "I canna just—"

But we didn't get a chance to hear what he couldn't do, because Shona pulled me with her out the tent and down the path to where the performer was setting up.

The minstrel was a skinny kid, maybe eighteen or nineteen, and dressed in a dizzying amount of patchwork tartan. He had the look of the open road about him—sun-leathered skin and water-rotted shoes. A cloak studded with twigs and brambles. But his lute had a nice shine to it, and when he gave it strum, it sang with confidence. "I call this song, "King's Folly"."

He toed his open case toward the crowd and sang:

'The old man sits upon his throne.
His crown, they say is made of bone.
But when the northern dogs unite.
They willna bow before his might.
The cats ungloved, prepare to strike.
The king he hasna seen the like.
The war drums beat and blood it flows.
It's sad, alas, but the king should know.
That's how the Northern winds blow.
That's how the Northern winds blow.'

"Not verra cheerful." Shona frowned. "I was hoping to hear a song about Robin Hood."

A tingling sensation crawled over my skin. "Is he singing about King Robert?"

She nodded, and I had one of those disturbingly meta moments where I realized just how strange my life had become. Here I was, a twenty-first century girl, standing in the middle of a fourteenth century fair, listening to a minstrel sing about the man my dead best friend came here to murder.

Shona's jaw fell open. "What in the name of Jude!"

210

Donald skittered to a stop next to us, red-faced and gasping for breath. "I found ye." He panted. "We have to..." He heaved. "...go."

She tsked. "Listen to ye. Lungs like a newborn calf." Her lips pursed. "Ye need a tincture o' comfrey and licorice."

I frowned. "Who's minding my ale table?"

"No time." He righted himself. He tugged my arm. "Swiftly now."

"Swiftly? What are you talking about? What's going on?" A horrible thought flashed through my head. "Oh god, Mairi!" She was dead. Died of alcohol poisoning. I just knew it.

"Mairi's fine." He put a hand to his chest and sucked in air. "Let's go."

I damn near stamped my foot. "I'm not moving from this spot until you tell me what's going on!"

"Fine." His gaze darted around the crowd as if he were checking for spies. "It's the Camerons."

I swayed. Icy fingers choked my lungs. "Henry killed one of them, didn't he?"

I could imagine it so clearly—some unknown Cameron came to the tent as soon as we left and said something plucky. Henry, already itching for revenge, pulled his sword. Next thing you know, there was a dead Cameron on the ground, and Henry wanted for murder.

Donald scanned the crowd behind me. "Nay, but he might kill 'em if I dinna get ye out o' here."

"Me?" My nose scrunched. "What do I have to do with it?"

He squeezed my arm. His mouth fell into a somber line. "The Camerons...they're after ye, Fi."

# Chapter Twenty-Five

My hands balled into fists. "For Christ's sake, Donald. Nobody's hiding in the trunk."

He jostled the blankets inside Mairi's chest and closed the lid. He walked to the door and checked the security bar for the third time.

I growled. "That's it. I tried to be patient, but you're acting insane." I snagged him by the ear. "There are no Camerons in this house. They are not folded in trunks or swimming in my ale. The door is locked and will remain so until we unlock it. Understand?" I marched him toward the table.

"Fiona, stop." He tugged at my arm.

"Sit. Talk." I pointed to his chair and released him. When he didn't immediately explain, I slammed my hands on the table. "Are you going to tell me what's going on or what?"

"I told ye already, the Camerons are after ye." He rubbed his injured ear. "Which is why I should be securing the house instead o' bein' assaulted by a mad woman."

Mad woman seemed a tame description considering my current mood. "*Why* do you think they're after me? What happened?"

His shoulders slumped in defeat. "I dinna ken much. Hal said they came to the tent with a bit o' paper with your likeness on it. Said there was gold to be had for anyone who helped 'em find ye."

Staring blindly, I blinked. "They had a picture of me. Like a drawing?"

He nodded.

Pinching the bridge of my nose, I squeezed my eyes closed. "That doesn't make sense. How could they know who I am or what I look like?" The answer came to me, and I laughed—they *couldn't* know.

Donald raised an eyebrow.

"It's all a big misunderstanding." Grinning, I put a hand to my chest. "The girl in the drawing probably resembled me a bit, and Henry freaked out. You know how he is when it comes to the Camerons."

Pity softened his eyes. "They asked for ye by name."

My smile faltered. I looked at my shaking hands, wringing in my lap. "I see."

But I didn't see... None of this made sense. The Camerons were *Henry's* enemies, not mine. How did I become a part of this insanity? "Maybe it's some other Fiona." My voice sounded weak, even to my own ears. "Who also happens to look like me..."

I squeezed my eyes closed and took a shaky breath. "Did they say what they wanted?"

"Ye'll have to ask Hal." He lowered his gaze. "That's all I ken."

Snoop Dogg nuzzled my leg. I lifted him into my lap and absently rubbed his ears. How was this possible? The only Camerons I knew were Sean and Old John. Considering Sean was dead, and Old John would need a time machine...

Oh, God. A time machine.

A tremble coursed through my body. Those men weren't Camerons—they were time soldiers.

*Bam. Bam. Bam.* A heavy fist assaulted the door.

Donald and I looked at each other. He rose and drew his sword, gesturing for me to get behind him.

I peeked over his shoulder and whispered in his ear. "Let's just hide."

"Let me in." My legs nearly buckled at the sound of Henry's voice.

Then a groan sounded that could only be Mairi. "Shut your klappe. Ye'll cleave my head in two with all this noise."

Donald ran to the door. "I'm coming, Hal." As soon as he unbarred the door, Henry burst through and ran to me. He crushed me to his chest. "You're safe." He nuzzled his face in my hair. "Thank God, you're well."

And in his arms, it was easy to pretend that I was. I rested my head on his chest and sank into the comfort of his strong arms. We stayed that way for a long moment, but then something shifted—a tension began in his body and grew until it seemed to fill the whole room. I stared at him, searching his face. It was like watching a storm roll in from the sea.

The light disappeared from his eyes, and his mouth grew thin. "We need to talk."

"Come with me, lad." Mairi ushered Donald out the door, leaving us alone.

I stared at him. The abrupt shift in mood sent my stomach roiling and head spinning.

"Do ye ken who I met today?" His voice was somehow flat and furious all at once. He spat on the floor. "Your husband, that's who."

"My...what?" I squinted at him. "What are you talking about?"

"Your bloody, sarding Cameron husband." His voice grew louder with every word. "He and his brothers are lookin' for ye, did ye ken that? Said they'd be obliged if I helped 'em find ye."

I gaped. "You can't honestly believe..." But from the way the vein on his forehead throbbed, it was clear he did. "They're lying. You have to know that?"

A growl erupted from his throat. "Tell me then. Explain why this Cameron would claim to be your man?"

My tongue fused to the roof of my mouth. I couldn't think. I couldn't breathe.

"Tell me!" He bellowed the words so loud the shutters rattled.

"I...I don't know. Fuck." I squeezed my eyes closed and palmed my forehead. "I don't know what to tell you."

"All o' it." Spit flew from his mouth. "The truth, damn ye!"

214

Warm, injured tears filled my eyes. "The only truth that matters is that if those men find me, they'll kill me." My voice came out soft and shaky.

The sound of a swallowed word choked in his throat. "Why?"

I didn't answer him. Couldn't have, even if I'd known what to say. I sensed his gaze.

His hand slipped under my chin, and he tilted my face to his. "He beat ye, aye? That's why ye fled." He wiped a tear from my cheek. "Is that it? And now he's come to find ye, you're afeard he'll kill ye for the escape?"

A sharp pain pierced my chest. God, how I wanted to tell him yes, tell him anything, so long as he never looked at me with those cold, horrible eyes again, but the lie refused to leave my lips.

"I've never been married before you." I stared at my feet. "Those men...They're assassins."

I'd never spoken the reality of my situation out loud before, and even to me, it didn't sound real, but I kept going. "They're after me because I have information they don't want anyone to know."

His eyes narrowed. "What sort o' information? How could a wee lass come to learn o' Cameron plots?"

"The man who brought me here." I met Henry's gaze. "The one in the grave in the woods, he told me."

He cocked his head. "Told ye what?"

Bouncing from foot to foot, I hesitated. "It's this...thing. It's hard to describe, but it could be dangerous in the wrong hands."

"A weapon?" Fear flashed in his eyes.

Withholding a grimace, I wiped my sweaty palms on my dress. "Not exactly..."

"Then be exact." He clenched my shoulders. "Do ye have any idea what the Camerons are capable of? Those sons o' dogs'll go straight for the throne if given the chance. If they have a weapon, ye must tell me."

On an inhale, I scrunched my eyes tight. There was no good way to explain this. Every answer would just lead to more questions. I blinked my eyes open until his raw, intense stare filled my sight. "It's not a weapon, and those men aren't Camerons." I toed the dirt floor with my boot. "They're...they're from where I'm from."

A bitter smile darkened his face. "And where is that, exactly?"

All the blood in my body rushed to my head at the knowing look in his eyes. He knew. He fucking knew. I couldn't breathe. All this time. All those lies. Why had he never said anything?

He let out a derisive laugh. "Ye really must take me for the fool. Did ye think I wouldna notice how ye change topic whenever someone brings up your past? Or how your stories dinna hang together?"

Bile rose in my throat. So many lies. And I hadn't suffered an ounce of guilt telling a single one of them. But now that they were laid out between us, each one burned like a branding iron against my skin.

"I ken when you're hiding something, Fiona, and I'm done." He sliced his hands through the air. "No more lies. No more half-truths. I've no room in my heart for a woman who kens only treachery."

I choked on a sob. "Don't you think I'd tell you if I could?"

Nothing in this world would have made me happier than to put it all out there, to unburden myself of the trauma I barely allowed myself to acknowledge. But I was sure telling him would only make things worse. If I, a girl from an era of limitless technology, hadn't been able to believe in time travel, how could Henry possibly accept my truth? He'd either think me crazy or a liar, neither of which would help the situation.

His throat made a sound like a mangled garbage disposal. "Who's stoppin' ye? *I'm* your husband, and I bid ye speak."

I burst into tears. "I can't."

His fingers dug into my shoulders. He gave me a little shake. "We're all at risk. Me. Mairi. Donald. Ye've brought danger upon us. The least ye can do is tell me why."

My eyes burned, and my whole body trembled. "People are trying to kill me. Nothing I can tell you will change that."

"Maybe not, but it changes *us*." The disdain in his eyes sent my emotions lower than the flies that feasted on our cesspit. "You're many things, Fiona, but a coward..." His teeth bared. "I never expected that."

Tears streamed over my cheeks. This was so fucking messed up. I wanted to throw something at him. I wanted to blacken his eyes so they would swell shut, and I wouldn't have to see his condemnation. He yanked his cloak off the hook.

Lava shot through my veins. "Don't you dare fucking leave."

He headed for the door.

This was so fucking unfair. I didn't *want* to keep things from him, and I knew he deserved the truth, but I had no idea how to give it to him. "You don't understand! You don't know what I've been through!"

He spun back to face me. "Because ye willna tell me!"

"You won't believe me." I choked on a sob. "It'll make things worse!"

"Worse than this?" The vein on his forehead bulged. "Forget it, Fiona. If ye canna be honest with me, I'm through with ye."

I squeezed my lips together as I stared at his retreating back. If I didn't do something, I'd lose him forever. I opened my mouth, not sure what to say, and before I knew what I was doing, I blurted the truth out. "I'm from the future."

He froze in the door frame, his back rigid.

"I was born in the year 1993." The words tumbled from my mouth as if spoken by somebody else. "In a country that hasn't been discovered yet."

Slowly, Henry turned his head and looked at me. His eyes were glossy and red. "I could have forgiven ye the truth, no matter how bad." His voice vibrated with hurt. "But ye'd rather speak nonsense and riddles than be honest with the man you're supposed to love." He turned his head from me. "Goodbye, Fiona."

"Wait! I swear—" He slammed his fist to the wall. I gasped. "Henry, please!"

He punched the wall again and again, until his knuckles split, and red poured over his hand.

"Henry, nay!" Mairi's terrified voice rang through the windows.

Donald and Mairi rushed inside. Henry shouldered past them out the door. Collapsing to my knees, I burst into sobs. She ran to me, checked me for signs of injury. He stared after Henry.

"Lass..." For once, even she couldn't seem to find the words.

I raked my nails down my cheeks. "I can't, Mairi. Just leave me be." Springing to my feet, I darted up the stairs.

Once in our room, I snagged our travel bag from its spot beneath the bed and shoved a spare shift and a small quilt into it. Rummaging through the trunk, I hunted for an extra pair of hose. Dammit, where were they?

"What're ye doin'?" I jumped at the sound of Donald's voice and looked up to find him leaning against the door jamb.

With a sniff, I wiped my eyes. "What do you want?"

"I came to see how you're faring." His gaze fell to my open travel bag.

"Yeah, well, I'm fine." My hands wrapped around the hose I was searching for, and I shoved them in my bag.

"Ye canna leave, Fiona." The authority in his voice drew my gaze to his. "It'll kill him."

My fingers fumbled as I tried to tie my bag. "He'll die if I stay. All of you will."

He raised an eyebrow. "Do ye think so little of us?"

"I don't know what you mean." Slinging the bag over my shoulder, I rose to my feet. "I've got to go."

He blocked the door. "What worth do our lives have if we canna protect those we love?"

Sucking in a deep breath, I tried to push past him. "If you think it's love Henry's feeling, go have a look at the wall."

He wouldn't budge. "I'm sorry, Fi. Hal wouldna forgive me if I let ye go." Nudging me back, Donald slipped out the door and closed it behind him.

I scrambled for the door's handle. It wouldn't budge. "God dammit, Donald!" My voice cracked as I pounded on the door. "Let me out of here!"

"Go to bed, Fi." The door between us did nothing to muffle the resolution in his voice. "I'll hold this door all night if I must."

# Chapter Twenty-Six

Soft, whistling snores floated through the gap beneath the door. Closing my eyes, I laid my hand against the rough wood in silent goodbye. It was time. I hooked my bag around my arm and headed to the window. Every step was like trudging through concrete. I had to will my legs to move, because deep-down, I didn't want to do this.

Sure, in the moments after the fight, I'd been raring to go, but after spending the last few hours locked in my room, some semblance of sense had returned. I didn't want to leave Henry. Punch him in the face, maybe, but I wasn't ready to end things, even if he was a total ass.

There was more to consider, though. As much as I hated to admit it, he had been right about one thing—I brought danger down on all of them. They loved me, and they would die because of it. I couldn't let that happen...even if it meant doing something utterly stupid, like climbing out a second story window in the middle of the night with only a rope and a sliver of moonlight to help along the way.

The shutters squawked like indignant crows when I wrenched them open. I froze, but Donald's snores didn't falter, and nobody came crashing through the door to stop me. I sighed, but, for some reason, my relief manifested a lot more like disappointment.

I hoisted myself onto the sill and swung my legs around so they dangled out the window. On a deep breath, I hooked my hands around the rope that served as our fire escape. I gave it a tug. Nice and secure. No give. So far, so good. I could do this.

Then I made the mistake of looking down. Oh fuck, oh fuck, oh fuck. Bad idea. In the scant moonlight, the ground wasn't even visible, like staring into a black hole. There had to be another way. Donald was a deep sleeper. Maybe he wouldn't notice if I opened the door and stepped over him.

As if on cue, he snorted and mumbled something that sounded a lot like *apple bandits*. I let out a nervous giggle. My eyes watered. Who was I kidding? I wouldn't get past him. The only way out was down...into the dark, super-creepy, seemingly bottomless void.

Gritting my teeth, I kept my eyes to the sky and toed around blindly until I found a bit of jutting stone. I shifted off the ledge. The rope swayed and my stomach lurched. I forced down a scream. But after a few seconds, the line steadied, and my heart calmed enough to realize I was not, in fact, about to plummet to my death.

Emboldened, I searched for my next toe hold. My palms itched and grew hot from the rope, but aside from that, the descent wasn't too bad. I found a nice crevice, jammed my toes in, and lowered myself.

The next landing spot was harder to find. This section of wall was maddeningly smooth. Maybe I should climb back up. My arms convulsed from the exertion, and my palms burned like they were being stabbed by miniature fibrous needles. I found a tiny lip of stone, just big enough for the tips of my toes and shifted my weight to it. The ledge crumbled.

I screamed as my body jolted downward. My arms weren't ready for the extra weight, and my shoulder popped out of place as I slid. Too fast. The rope burned hot as flames, grating the flesh off my palms. I was going to die, and there was nothing I could do. Squeezing my eyes closed, I braced for the agony of shattered bones.

Then impact.

Only the collision didn't come from beneath; it came from the side. A body slammed into me. Arms crushed around my ribs. Suddenly I was sideways and twisting and then face up. We crashed into the ground. Air exploded from my lungs as I bounced free of the body holding me and tumbled across the grass. Dark squares filled my vision until the light completely disappeared from my sight.

"Fiona!" Mairi's shriek penetrated the rattling of my sloshing brain. A second later, she was slapping my face and screaming my name.

"Get back." Familiar arms slid beneath me and lifted me from the ground.

"Is she...gone?" Donald's voice gave an anguished creak.

I gasped as my lungs finally agreed to take in air. Mairi let out a choked sob, and I forced my eyes open. I blinked against a world too dark and blurry to make out. I reached up and searched for Henry's face. My hand met warm, bristled skin. Warm droplets slid between my fingers.

~ * ~

If my life were a movie, I'd have emerged from my brush with death stronger, happier, and full of clichéd wisdom. I'd know life was a gift and learn to appreciate every moment and take up interesting hobbies like sky-diving or deep-sea fishing, because, after all, you only live once. And arguments would become a thing of the past, because in the end, love is all you need.

Movies were bullshit.

I had no great epiphanies, nor did I appreciate a damn thing. All I had were a jumble of emotions and a case of the shakes so violent it bordered on palsy. Henry laid me in the bed and placed a blanket over me.

"I'm not cold." I kicked at the blanket, but I shook so badly, I only managed to tangle it around my legs. A sob bubbled in my throat as I tried to tug it free. "Goddammit."

He reached for the blanket. "Let me help."

"I don't need your help." I swatted at him. "Why don't you just leave?"

He turned and walked away. Where the hell was he going? I didn't care what I'd just said. He should know I needed him. Fuck this blanket.

But he didn't leave. Instead, he ambled around the perimeter of the bed and crawled in next to me.

I huffed. "I said you should go."

The clink of flint striking steel sounded, and the room filled with the soft glow of candlelight.

"Why should *I* go?" He shifted to lean against the wall. "It's my bed."

I narrowed my eyes, ready to spit venom, but when his face illuminated in the candlelight, shock stole the poison from my tongue. I raised a hand to his face, but recoiled it, remembering I hated his sorry ass. "What happened?"

His nose twisted sideways as if broken, and his right eye was swollen shut. He tried to smirk, but he flinched in pain and put a hand to his split lip. "Gavin."

I scowled. "So you left a fight with me to go pick a fight with him?"

His lips turned up at the corners. "It wasna a fight. More like...a conversation."

"Oh, I see." My voice unleashed the full sarcastic power of my mid-western roots. "That makes perfect sense. Please, go on." I managed to kick the blanket off my foot and yanked it back over my chest.

"I ran into him at the tavern." His voice grew defensive. "Ye have to understand, I wasna in a good state o' mind. I'd had a few drinks and was still spittin' mad about our fight."

I clenched my jaw, already knowing whatever he was about to say was going to piss me off.

He put his hands behind his head, elbows wide. "Well, he sits down to join me, talkin' about how he never had scandalous intentions toward ye, and he'd done it all to give me the boot in the arse I needed, and how he was so happy for us."

"The nerve." I rolled my eyes. "I can see why you started a fight."

He scoffed. "I didna *start a fight*. I told him he shouldna have bothered."

Okay, that fucking hurt, but I bit my lip and didn't say a word. I decided to see how big of a hole he would dig before I buried him.

He gazed up at the shadows of candlelight flickering on the ceiling. "I told him women canna be trusted, and if he had any wits about him, he'd keep to whores and tavern wenches."

If I held my jaw any tighter, my teeth would crack. Still, I kept silent.

"So, I got to tellin' him what happened between us, and ye ken what that nutter did?" He looked at me with wide, indignant eyes. "Punched me straight in the eye!"

My nails dug into the hem of the blanket. "Remind me to send him a thank you note."

"Aye, well..." Henry scratched his forehead. "I wasna expectin' it and went flyin' straight off my chair. Landed flat on my back." He stuck a pillow between his head and the wall and leaned back, his eyes tilted toward the ceiling. "Then, instead o' helpin' me up, he puts a boot to my chest and calls me all sorts o' ill names."

He pinned me with a stare, and I didn't try to hide the satisfaction on my face.

He adjusted his tunic and scratched his neck. "So I shouted at him, 'What are ye on about? Did ye not hear what I told ye? I'm the one's been done wrong here. Yet ye punch me in the eye and slander my good name?'

'Oh, aye,' Gavin says. 'I heard ye. Men are searchin' for your wife, hopin' to murder her, and here ye are, drinkin' a pint and cryin' about nonsense.'"

Henry grimaced. "I felt a right arse hearin' him put it like that. So I says, 'Verra well, I take your meanin'. Now will ye get your bloody boot off my heart afore it stops beating?'"

Henry's lips twisted in an odd sort of regretful smile. "He helped me to my feet, and I says to him, 'I'll be goin' home now, but mayhap ye can answer me this, seein' as ye seem to have all the answers: what would you do with a wife who tells ye naught but lies about her past?' Ye ken what he tells me? He says, 'I suppose that depends. Did ye fall in love with the lass she used to be or the lass she is now?'"

He snorted. "I tell him he's not makin' a lick o' sense. How could I fall in love with the girl ye used to be, when I didna even ken ye then? To which he replies, 'Then what the bloody hell does it matter?' He kicks me in the arse and tells me to get home to ye afore I have more to cry about than injured pride..."

I gawked at him, not sure what to make of his story. "So that's it? Gavin punched you in the eye, and now you're over it?"

The muscles in his jaw tightened. "Nay, I hate that ye'd rather tell me mad tales than the truth about your past."

My breath hissed. "Nothing's changed?"

He exhaled and paused as if collecting his thoughts. "I got to thinkin' on the walk home. The reason I was so upset with ye, is I thought ye didna trust me. But...well, I didna trust ye either." He dug his stare into my face, his good eye sad and apologetic. "Ye've never shied from speakin' your mind. If you're choosin' to hold your tongue, I should have trusted ye had your reasons."

I swallowed the lump in my throat, licked my lips. "What now, then?"

"We make an agreement. I'll not ask ye to tell me anything ye dinna wish to share. I'll trust ye." His good eye bored into mine. "But ye have to promise when ye do choose to speak, ye'll let it be only truth."

I nodded, but I was still reluctant to let go of my attitude. "What about you running away? You can't just leave every time we have a fight."

He stared down his nose at me. "Says the lass who climbed out the window."

"That's...different." I inhaled deeply. "You were right, what you said before. Me being here puts you in danger."

He put his hand on mine. "We'll figure it out. *Together.*" When I didn't answer, he squeezed my hand. "Fiona, do ye ken what'll happen if ye try to disappear again?" I raised a brow. "I'll scour e'ry inch o' the city lookin' for ye, and if I dinna find ye, I'll march straight into Cameron territory and kill as many o' those sons o' dogs as I can in retribution."

Sweat broke out on my skin. "That would be suicide."

He nodded. "I ken that, but it would be better than livin' without ye. So, please, dinna get any more ideas about fleein'."

I knew he meant every word, and somehow, the knowledge I had no choice but to go through this *with* him had my shoulders sagging with relief, but my belly icing with dread.

"So ye agree?" His eyes widened. "No more running. No more lies. No more pressure to tell me what ye dinna wish to."

I paused for a moment. His words sounded great in theory, but reality rarely followed the path of best case scenarios. Could I guarantee honesty when my circumstances demanded a life of constant lies? I raised my gaze to his, and the intensity of his stare heated my skin. His love and trust pulsed through me, and I knew with him by my side, I could do anything. I held out my pinky. He cocked his head in confusion, so I wrapped my pinky around his, and gave it a shake. "Agreed."

He wrinkled his nose. "Ye've a queer way o' swearin' oaths."

I smiled. "It's something we did as child—" I stopped myself. Talking about my past while keeping my word was going to be difficult. When it came to him, truth would always be a matter of interpretation. "Never mind."

I sighed and laid my head on his chest. He stroked my hair, and though I should have felt better now we'd come to a resolution, my insides hollowed with sadness. I wanted to tell him so much. I wanted to talk about Granda and the Caledonia Club, the friends I'd grown up with, little-league teams, dance recitals, cars, phones, computers, all the wonders of the modern world.

He kissed the top of my head and brushed a few strands of hair from my face. "Do ye want me to tell ye a story until ye fall asleep?"

"A story?" I sat up way too quickly. Pain lanced through my shoulder, back, and head, but I didn't care. This was my way to prove to him my truth. "No, I want to tell *you* a story."

He chuckled. "Verra well."

I adjusted myself into a more comfortable position and cleared my throat. "All right, so how do you know if a story is true?"

His brow furrowed.

"Mairi believes in the fair folk and the banshee." I leaned against him. "Are those stories true?"

"Well, I wouldna say..." He glanced around nervously and seemed to think better of finishing.

"I see you shiver anytime someone mentions a ghost. Are ghost stories real?"

"I've *seen* a ghost." The conviction in his voice was absolute.

I laughed. "Maybe so, but to me, ghosts aren't real. Neither are banshees or faeries or any other mythical creatures." I grinned. "That's what's great about stories. They're only real if you choose to believe they are." Tossing the blanket over his legs, I snuggled into his arms. "The story I'm about to tell you is no different. It's as real as you want it to be."

"And here I thought *I* was the storyteller. Ye've put me to shame with that introduction." He kissed my forehead. "Let's hear it, then."

I ran my hands along his hard, smooth chest. "Once upon a time, there was a little girl who grew up in a magical land called America..."

The candle burned well past the hour mark before I finished rattling on about anything and everything I could think of—cars, refrigeration, plumbing, the time Granda nearly cut off his thumb messing with the lawn mower—and despite his clear exhaustion, Henry did his best to follow along, even though nearly everything I described was a foreign concept.

I couldn't tell what he thought of my stories. Probably that I was either incredibly imaginative or clinically insane. But it didn't seem to matter either way. Real or imagined, he'd accepted that my tales were a part of me, and that was the only truth he needed.

# Chapter Twenty-Seven

By unspoken agreement we rose before the sun. Too little sleep and too many emotions had us shuffling and bleary-eyed, but despite our fatigue, we moved in silent orchestration. Donald stoked the fire. Mairi filled four tankards. I lit the candles, and Henry wiped the table. Then we migrated to our seats, ready for a family meeting nobody needed to call.

Mairi cleared her throat. "Let's get to it." She leaned forward. "What are we to do about the Camerons?"

He set his tankard down with a matter-of-fact clink. "We fight."

She nodded and sipped from her cup. "Should ye fall?"

He paused to consider. "Go to Gavin. He'll see ye safely north. My sister'll take the two o' ye in."

I stared at the two of them, mouth hanging open. How fucking morbid were they to talk so casually about him dying, as if it were just a matter of course.

Donald patted my arm. "Dinna look so afeard. It willna come to that. Hal and I will kill a hundred Camerons if we have to." He flashed a lopsided grin. "Isna that right, Hal?"

Pride lit Henry's smile. "Aye, lad. That's right."

I ran my fingers through the roots of my hair and yanked. "Do you even hear yourselves? This isn't a plan. It's a worst-case scenario."

"It's the *only* scenario." His eyes hardened. "Ye dinna ken the Camerons like I do. This only ends with blood."

"Bullshit." My voice was resolute. "Blood's the only option you've considered."

228

He opened his mouth as if to argue, but then he seemed to think better and snapped it closed. Sitting back, he made a you-take-the-floor gesture. "What do ye suggest?"

Trailing my finger along the table's wood grain, I averted my gaze. "I go into hiding."

"Nay." His voice brooked no argument.

I put my hand on his thigh and met his gaze. "No listen, I'll go to a convent or a nunnery. They have to give me sanctuary, right?"

"Forget it." Mairi gave a terse shake of the head. "I'll not have ye endangerin' God's servants o'er a family matter."

I squeezed my lips together. There had to be some other option, but I couldn't think what. "Fine. Never mind all that. What about today?"

She raised an eyebrow. "I dinna take your meanin'."

"The fair." I met each of their gazes in turn. "There are two days left, and you can't exactly take me with you."

"Ye canna think we're still goin' to the fair." Henry scooched back his chair and took in the entirety of me. "Our only focus is keeping ye safe, ye understand? Nothin' else matters."

"We have to think long term." I clenched the skirts of my dress. "I've seen the books. You miss these next two days, and we won't make it through winter."

"I dinna give a damn if I starve the whole winter through." His ribcage swelled, and his eyes grew glossy. "I'll not leave ye to be murdered."

Fear vibrated around him. I squeezed his hand. "You won't. Mairi can stay with me. Or Donald."

"Oh, aye, there's a good plan." He turned his head. "Leave ye with the lad who let ye fall out the window."

"Don't you dare blame him for that!" I knew he spoke out of fear rather than anger, but no way I'd let Donald suffer for it. Pushing to my feet, I put my hands to my hips. "It's not like *you* could have stopped me."

Henry rose, his face glowering down at me. "That's because you're reckless!"

My eyes narrowed. "Well, you're a—"

Mairi slammed her hand on the table. "Not another word!" Her eyes flashed with fury. "Ye *are* reckless. So mayhap ye should heed your husband's advice a time or two. And ye—" She turned on Henry. "Are ye such a fool to think it better to starve than die by the blade?"

She glared at the pair of us, daring us to speak. When neither of us did, she took a deep breath and wrapped her fingers around her tankard. "Verra well, then. Now you've pulled your heads out o' your arses, why dinna we go with the obvious solution—Henry stays with Fiona, and Donald goes to the fair with me."

It seemed like a good compromise, and now that she'd suggested it, I felt like an ass falling back into me and Henry's old habit of bickering instead of finding middle ground. I glanced at Henry, whose eyes stared blankly ahead as if he were deep in thought. After a long minute, he scrubbed his hand over the bristles on his chin. "I'm sorry. I ken we'll have a lean winter, but better that than risk my wife."

He put a hand on Donald's shoulder. "I owe ye an apology, lad. What happened with Fiona wasna your fault, and I ken it well." He sighed. "Truth is, I canna do this without ye. That's why I need ye by my side when the Camerons come. Not off in some tent sellin' dirks."

Donald's cheeks flushed a faint pink. He met Henry's gaze. "Ye'll have my sword, always."

Tears filled my eyes at the solemnity of his words. He put a hand on my cheek. "I ken you're afeard, but ye canna hide from this. Even in a convent, there are those who'll be swayed by gold." He smiled, but his eyes held only sadness. "You're a clever lass, but ye canna change the hearts o' men."

I wanted to argue with him, to tell him we couldn't give up. That we could leave the city, or the country. We could buy a boat and live at sea...But I didn't say any of those things, because in the end, I knew he was right—I couldn't run from this.

"You're wrong." Mairi's voice was quieter and more contemplative than I'd ever heard it. "It's not the hearts o' men we have to change. Just the tales they tell."

It took a second for her words to sink in. Then I gasped. "Mairi, you're a genius!" I looked at Henry. "Change of plans. You're going to the fair."

"Wait. What? Nay." He pinched the bridge of his nose. "We've been through this."

"Listen, you're right. People will talk. Let's make sure we control the message." I glanced at Mairi for support, and she nodded for me to continue. "We'll put it out I've left home. Tell them I heard the Camerons were searching for me, and I fled in the night."

Mairi steepled her fingers. "I'll tell Winnie MacSheah straight off. There willna be a soul in Perth who hasna heard the tale come mid-morn."

"Not just Winnie." I spread my arms in an encompassing gesture. "Everybody. Every person who buys an ale. People you know. People you don't."

Henry leaned back. "It's not going to—"

"It *will* work." Grinning, I looked him over. "Especially with you being in the shape you're in."

Mairi laughed. "O' course it will. Just look at that face." She gestured at his swollen, bruised eye and split, scowling lips. "Ye look just like a man who's been jilted."

She shifted closer to Donald. "Did ye hear the blacksmith's lass absconded in the night?" She spoke in a low, conspiratorial tone. "Poor lad was so upset he drank himself blind and tried to fight anyone what came near him."

I laughed and clapped my hands. "That's perfect!"

"It's foolishness." My gut twisted at the sight of Henry's narrowed eyes and clenched jaw. It wasn't anger I saw—it was fear.

I scooted close and spoke in a low tone just for him. "Last night I swore I would only speak truth, so I won't lie. This might not work. But it's the best chance we've got." I squeezed his hand. "Now I'm asking you to keep your vow. I need you to trust me."

~ * ~

I probably should have been nervous. We were taking a risk, no matter how good the plan, but by the time Henry and Mairi left for the fair, I was so exhausted I didn't have the energy to be scared.

Donald didn't seem worried either, but clearly, it had nothing to do with exhaustion. The kid had been bouncing around all morning. He kept grabbing stuff off shelves for no apparent reason. Then he'd get distracted and leave whatever he was holding on the nearest surface, unaware of the mess he created. He snacked constantly, pacing back and forth, trailing crumbs. For one particularly excruciating hour, he sword fought with his shadow, which wouldn't have been so bad if it weren't for the irritating noises he made, like a toddler going *pew, pew, pew* with a toy gun.

I palmed my forehead. "Donald, for the love of god, can you sit still a minute?"

His eyes widened at my irritation. "Of course." He joined me at the table. "What should we talk about?" He drummed his fingers.

I groaned and dropped my head to the table. "I can't do this. I have to get some sleep."

"Ye canna go upstairs." He sat taller in his seat. "Hal made me promise to keep ye in my sight at all times." He rocked in his chair, making it squeak.

I might cry. "If I take a nap down here, can you be quiet for like an hour?"

"Aye, of course I can." His bulging eyes and shocked tone made it seem as though he didn't understand why I'd even ask.

"Good." I hoisted Mairi's mattress onto the floor and crawled on top. Curling into a ball, I sighed as my heavy eyes fell closed.

He hovered over me. "Do ye want a pillow?"

I flopped an arm across my face. "No."

He didn't move. "How about a blanket?"

"No!" I turned on my side and faced the wall. "Just shut up and let me sleep."

"Fiona..." He fell to his knees beside the mattress.

"What?" My voice came out a whine as I flipped to face him.

He didn't get to finish, though, because a loud yodeling noise erupted from outside.

"The hue and cry!" Donald sprang to his feet, hand on his sword.

His gaze darted from me to the door, indecision freezing him in place. By law, when someone raised the hue and cry, every able-bodied man in the vicinity had to assemble and assist in the apprehension of a suspected criminal, but he couldn't very well leave me alone.

"What do I do?" His voice squeaked.

I pushed to my knees. "Stay inside. They won't know you're here."

A heavy fist banged on the door. "Mairi, are ye in there?"

"It's Angus." Donald mouthed the words so as not to be heard.

The door rattled as Angus, the poulter who lived a few houses down, rattled the handle. "Door's barred. She must be home." He banged on the door again. "Mairi, open up."

"Climb through the window." The voice that spoke was deeper than Angus's, maybe the tanner. "What if he's holdin' her hostage?"

Donald and I looked at each other in a panic. He waved for me to hide. "Just a minute, I'm coming, Angus."

I dove behind the ale barrels and crouched. The door creaked open.

"Sorry, Angus." Donald gave an exaggerated yawn. "I was asleep."

"Oh, Donald, it's ye." Surprise filled Angus's voice. "Thought ye'd be at the fair."

"Aye, well..." He raked a hand through his frizzy hair. "I'm...not feelin' well."

The tanner pushed past Angus. "Listen. Old Lady Agnes's been attacked. Is Mairi well?"

Donald nodded. "She's fine. She's with Henry at the fair."

"That's a relief." He clapped a meaty hand on Donald's shoulder. "Grab your bow, lad. The scoundrel's still about."

He shot a nervous glance toward the ale barrels. "I told ye, Angus, I'm not—"

"Och, ye'll be fine, lad." He practically dragged Donald out the door. "We'll find the bugger soon enough."

Donald flashed me a wide-eyed look, but there was nothing he could do. Angus disappeared out the door with him. I waited a few minutes, scrambled out of hiding, and re-barred the door. Great. Now I had to worry about Camerons *and* a violent thief.

I paced. Should I hide? If anybody showed, I didn't want them to peek in the window and see me. Then again, I didn't want to be crammed behind barrels if I needed to run.

A sound from outside cut my internal debate short. I froze and cocked my head. What was that? It sounded like crying. No, whimpering. Oh fuck. Snoop! My heart raced. What if he was hurt? What if he got kicked by one of the neighbor's cows or got caught in chicken wire? I couldn't leave him, but I couldn't go outside. Fuck.

The dog's whimpering grew louder. My heart wrenched. I had to do something. I crawled over to the window and peeked out. I didn't see him or any potential murderers. He had to be close, though. Otherwise I wouldn't hear him.

Okay, in and out real fast. I searched for a weapon, just in case. My utility knife hung from my belt, but something bigger and heavier seemed better. I snagged the fire iron, weighed it in my hand. It would do. I un-barred the door, peeked outside, and ran.

Following the sound of Snoop's wailing, I headed toward the rain barrels. Where was he? I hunted around them, peeked inside, but I couldn't find him anywhere.

With my hands on either side of my mouth, I shouted for him. "Snoop!" His whine transformed into a loud yip that seemed to be coming from the vicinity of my feet. I scanned the ground. The root cellar! I yanked the doors open, and there was Snoop, jumping against the walls, wagging his tail, and barking for me to come get him.

Heaving a sigh of relief, I lowered myself down the ladder. "It's okay, baby." I picked him up and squeezed him to my chest. "Mama's gonna kill whoever left those doors open for you to fall through."

He licked my face, and I rubbed his ears. Once we made it up the ladder, I set Snoop down and shut and barred the cellar door. While I worked, he yipped behind me. The hairs on my neck stood on end. His yips deepened to a low growl.

Every muscle in my body tensed, and I shifted the fire iron, so I had a better grip and turned.

"Hey, donkey..." Sean stood before me and waved.

With a scream, I stumbled back, tripping over the closed cellar and falling on my ass. My breath caught in choppy gasps. "Sean?" Tears burst from my eyes.

He plucked the fire iron from my hand, tossed it aside then lifted me off the ground and into his arms. Then he was crying too and squeezing me as if he were afraid I'd disappear if he dared let go.

I sobbed into his shoulder. "You were dead."

Tears streamed down his cheeks. "I knew you were alive."

And we kept hugging each other and crying, and it was the most wonderful sadness I'd ever experienced.

"I'm so sorry, Fi." His voice muffled in my hair. "I shouldna have brought ye here. I didn't know. It wasna supposed to be like this."

Sniffling, I wiped my eyes. "I heard you scream. I saw your grave."

He lowered his gaze. "I killed him."

I gasped. "That was the bandit's grave?"

His eyes tightened, revealing crow's feet that hadn't been there months before. "I came back a few days later and buried him." Fresh tears welled in his eyes. "I scoured the city and the woods tryin' to find ye, but ye just disappeared."

I swallowed a sob. "I've been right here this whole time."

He put a hand to my cheek. "I searched a month straight. Then I went north, hopin' ye'd gone to find my clan."

"Your clan?" I gasped. "Oh my god, *you* were the Cameron who was looking for me."

He grinned. "I canna believe it worked."

"I can't believe any of it." My mind splintered in a thousand directions. "This...this, changes everything."

We weren't in danger. I didn't have to hide. Henry didn't have to fight. And I had my best friend back. I couldn't have hoped for more. So why were my stomach muscles twisted in knots?

I studied Sean's long hair and tartan clothes. I took in his too-bulky frame and the sword strapped to his belt, and, suddenly, I realized why none of this sat right. I didn't have my best friend back. He wasn't the kid I'd grown up with anymore—he was the man who'd stolen my world from me and planned to kill a king.

"What is it?" Worry lined his face.

"You...you..." I didn't even know what to say.

He inched toward me, arms outstretched. "I ken you're probably furious with me, and I'm sorry." He rested his hands on my shoulders. "I ken I canna make it up to ye, but I *can* make it better." He squeezed my shoulders. "I can take ye home."

# Chapter Twenty-Eight

Home...

He said the word with a smile.

I felt it like a whip.

Then I felt nothing at all.

Snoop paced in front of me. A low growl vibrated in his throat. I picked him up and stroked his fur, a mechanical motion that soothed neither of us.

Sean waved his hand in front of my face. "Hello? Are ye there?" Snoop bared his teeth, and Sean yanked his hand back. He glared at the dog. "I said I'll take ye home."

I ran my hand down the puppy's back, staring past Sean into the distance. Two men I didn't know leaned against the smithy wall. One seemed to be examining his fingernails. The other's head hung like he'd fallen asleep in the sun.

"Who are they?" My voice came out in an indifferent monotone.

He glanced over his shoulder. "Kinsmen."

Snoop's growl deepened, and I set him down. "Stay." He was too well-trained to disobey, but he kept up his low rumble.

"What's wrong with ye?" Sean's brow furrowed. "Aren't ye happy?"

I raised my eyes to his and, after a second's pause, I laughed. I didn't mean to. It just popped out. And once it did, I couldn't stop.

Sean stared, his eyes wide with confusion and concern.

"Do you know how I spent my first months here?" I laughed even harder. "I was shot in the leg."

"Fi, I—"

"I'm not done yet." I giggled some more. "He beat me into unconsciousness. I almost died from the infection."

Snoop whimpered, fidgeted at my feet.

Horror froze Sean's features.

I smiled a sickly grin. "I still wake up some nights, screaming." I swallowed a final giggle. It hardened in my throat. "So, no." My gaze penetrated his horrified blue eyes. "I'm not happy." My voice calloused. "You're too fucking late for that."

"Ye canna think like that. It's not too late." His fingers dug into my shoulders. "Ye'll see. Once we get home, it'll be like none o' this ever happened."

I backed away. His hands fell limply to his sides. "I'm not going home." I held up my ring finger. "Like I said, you're too late."

He studied my hand, inhaled a relieved breath, and laughed. It sounded so different from my own unhinged peals. "That's what's bothering ye? So you're married. Ye did what you had to do. None o' that matters now."

"Of course it matters." I put a fist to my chest. "You think I'll just abandon my husband?"

He recoiled at my vehemence. Confusion creased his brow.

I bored my gaze into his so he'd see how serious I was. "I owe him *everything*."

He stared into the distance as if mulling over my words. "You're right. He did ye a good turn takin' ye in. We'll do him one back." He retrieved a handful of gold from his sporran. "He'll live better than half the nobility in this country."

"You're not understanding me." I gritted my teeth. "I'm not going anywhere."

Sean's eyes flashed with anger. His neck muscles bulged and veined, and his hand purpled around his fistful of coins. He closed his eyes and took a deep breath.

"You've been through a lot. You're not thinkin' right." His voice was restrained, calm.

"I love him." My nails dug into my palms.

He smirked. "Oh, aye, I'm sure it's *true* love." He rolled his eyes. "Tell me, how are your other loves doin'? Let me think." He tapped his lip. "There was Aaron. Then Jamal. Lucas—we canna forget him." He held up a finger. "Oh yeah, and that bloke with all the piercings—he was a winner."

Heat flushed through my body. "I'm married. This isn't some high school crush."

He thrust the coins back into his sporran. "So ye think now. It'll pass. It always does."

"Fuck you." I turned on my heels. "Come on, Snoop, let's go inside." I headed toward the house.

Sean jogged ahead of me and blocked my path. "Okay, okay, I'm sorry. That was out o' line."

My teeth ground together. Snoop bared his fangs.

He held up his hands in supplication. "You're married. I should respect that."

I clenched the fabric of my skirt.

"It isna a problem." His easy smile returned. "Ye can still go home. We'll bring your husband with us."

I didn't let the pissed off expression fall from my face, but inside my body tingled with hope and excitement. Henry in my time? It was a crazy idea, a wonderful idea, a frightening idea. Could he do it? *Would* he do it?

I tried to play it cool like he hadn't just offered up my every dream on a silver trencher. "How exactly would that work?"

"Never mind all that." His hand wrapped around my wrist, and he tugged me forward. "Let's go to the fair and get your man."

I dug in my heels. "You want to go now?"

He yanked me toward him. "Aye, come on."

"Wait." This was happening too fast.

There was still so much to figure out. What about Mairi and Donald? How was I going to get Henry to take me seriously? Why was Sean still pulling me?

"Stop." My feet skidded across the dirt, but he didn't stop. His grip tightened. I struggled against him. "Let go!"

Snoop took that as his cue. He lunged and sunk his little puppy teeth into Sean's calf, twisting his head and snarling. Sean howled as I twisted free.

Hoisting the puppy by the scruff, he kicked him as hard as he could. Snoop landed in a heap, whimpering in pain.

"You bastard!" I tried to slap him.

He stopped my hand. "What more do ye want?" Blood ran down his leg, and his eyes glowed with fury. "I offer ye the world, and it's still not enough. Why have *I* never been enough?"

Snoop growled and struggled to his feet, so I raised my palm up. "Stay." My voice warbled at the sight of him.

I pulled out of Sean's grasp and scuttled backward. "You need to leave, Sean." I glanced at the fire iron he'd tossed by the cellar.

He strode forward. "It's time to go."

An arrow landed in the space between us. We both turned.

There stood Henry, Donald, and Mairi, posed like a posse of renegade cowboys. Henry's bow was drawn. Donald held his sword at the ready, and Mairi clutched a knife in her taloned hand.

"Move away, Fiona." Henry's voice remained calm but was somehow more dangerous for its repose.

I made it two feet before Sean caught me. His arm snaked around my ribs, and he pressed a dirk to my throat. "Drop your weapons, or she dies."

Henry didn't say a word, but his eyes screamed with fury. Slowly, he lowered his bow. He placed it on the ground and straightened. His gaze raked up Sean's length. A sneer formed on his lips.

"Ye think I need a bow to kill ye?" He advanced. "I ken who ye are." He spit on the ground. "You're the man she calls brother."

The blade trembled at my throat. "I'm not her brother!" Sean's voice was shrill. "I'm the goddamned one who's always been there."

The blade pricked my skin, and a thin trail of warmth slid down my neck. Henry drew his sword.

"Stay back." Sean waved the dirk in front of him. "I'm warning ye."

Henry tensed. Sean cranked my head to the side and carved a line across my cheek. I screamed in pain.

He put the blade to my ear. "One step closer, and she loses an ear."

Blood gushed down my cheek mixing with the tears streaming from my eyes. I looked down, around, to the side. Anywhere, so long as I didn't have to see Henry's horrified face.

"On the ground." Sean pointed with his dirk. "All o' ye."

I caught a flash out of the corner of my eye and twisted my head.

"Be still!" Sean yanked my head back, but it was too late. I'd seen what was coming.

I ignored the blade digging into my ear. "Behind you!"

Sean's kinsmen charged. Henry and Donald whirled, swords flying. Mairi dashed out of sight. Sean dragged me toward the road. I strained to see behind me as sounds of combat filled my ears—crashing metal, battle screams, howls of pain.

"Call them off." My throat burned. "Please. I'll go with you. You don't need to do this."

"Shut up." Sean's voice cracked. "This is—" His words disappeared in a howl of pain.

He unleashed his hold and spun. I caught the glint of a knife in his back and Mairi scuttling backward. His arm swung down.

"No!" I threw my body at him. We toppled to the ground. I rolled away from him and scrambled to get up. Catching my footing, I rose then ran.

Sean trailed close behind me and caught me by the braid. I screamed, kicking and shoving, clawing and punching at any inch of his flesh I could reach. An arm propelled me back, and suddenly Henry stood between us.

Sean stumbled. Then quick as a flash, he whipped his dirk at Henry's chest and loosed his sword. The blade's handle bounced off Henry's ribs, and the dirk toppled to the ground.

Panic flashed in Sean's eyes as he tried and failed to raise his sword. The knife stuck in his back was too much for him. For a split second, his eyes met mine. The sword crashed to the ground. Sean turned and ran.

"Henry! The lad!" Mairi's voice ripped our attention back to the battle.

Donald was on his knees, sword locked against his enemy's. Henry ran, but not in Donald's direction.

Fear tied my guts in knots as I stared at his retreating back. "What are you doing? Help him!"

The Cameron bore down. Donald strained, his arms shaking. Blood soaked through his tunic. I needed to do something. I searched for a weapon, anything I could use to throw, stab, or bludgeon. The dirk glinted in the grass, so I snatched it and ran.

One of Henry's blue-feathered arrows whizzed past my head and found its mark in the Cameron's temple. With dawning comprehension, I realized Henry hadn't chased after Sean; he'd run for his bow.

The Cameron collapsed, and I slowed to a trot. Stopping altogether, I bent to suck in air. Feet away, the other Cameron lay dead, his face cleaved in two. A disembodied blue eye swam in a pool of blood next to him. Bile roiled in my belly, and I spit up frothy phlegm.

Donald rose and sheathed his sword with a shaky hand.

"You all right?" I called to him across the blood-soaked yard.

He swayed and crumpled to the ground.

"Mairi, help!" I shrieked and ran for him.

"Go after the fiend." Mairi shoved Henry toward the road. "We'll see to the lad."

I fell to my knees at Donald's side. Crimson soaked his shredded tunic. I tore open one of the rends. Gashes knifed across his chest and stomach. Blood hemorrhaged from his side so thick and fast I couldn't see the wound.

"Fuck. Fuck. Fuck." I wadded my skirts and clamped them to his side to staunch the blood.

Mairi plunged next to me. "We need to tie him!" She stole the dirk from my lap and cut the hem of her shift. "Lift his back."

242

I hoisted him, and she tossed the make-shift bandage beneath him, wrapped it around, and tied it tight. Blood oozed through the white linen.

I stared at it, wild-eyed. "He's going to die, isn't he?"

She smacked me. "That's for God to decide." Then she looped her arms beneath his. "Now grab his legs. We need to get him inside."

# Chapter Twenty-Nine

We shouldered through the door, muscles straining against Donald's dead-weight.

Mairi tilted her head toward the hearth. "By the fire."

As we laid him on the packed dirt floor, all I could think was *wrong, wrong, wrong*, but there was no way to do it right—no sterile sheets, no IV pumps, no disinfectants. Just open wounds and a germy dirt bed. Hell, we didn't even have time to wash our hands before tending to him. If we didn't staunch his wounds, he'd bleed out in minutes.

After dashing to her trunk, Mairi returned with an armful of cloth and a pair of shears. While she cut linen into strips, I removed our makeshift bandage. Blood, brown and clotted, disappeared beneath a fresh wave of red. I shook an urgent hand toward Mairi, who handed me a long cloth strip. I wadded it and shoved it inside the wound. I held it there, applied pressure with my palm. My hand grew slick and hot with his blood.

Selecting a bandage from her pile, Mairi made a twirling motion with her finger. "Roll him."

As I rocked him to his side, she slid the cloth beneath his back. I lowered him. She tied it tight. Blood seeped through the white linen. We tied a second bandage. Then a third. By the fourth, only the faintest shade of pink bled through.

Heaving a relieved breath, Mairi brushed her hands together. "That should do."

I gave myself a moment to regain my composure. I wiped hearth smoke from my eyes and sweat from my brows. I cracked my knuckles, rolled my shoulders. Then I assessed him once more. Blue lips. Blue fingers. Shallow, rapid breaths.

Numb with exhaustion and sorrow, I rose. "I'll get blankets."

With a nod, Mairi climbed to her feet. "I'll get the needle and catgut."

A few minutes later, I'd covered Donald to the neck with a patchwork quilt and filled the kettle with water and salt. She returned as I set the pot to boil.

I held out a hand. "Let me have the needle and thread."

Her brow furrowed. "Ye sure? Ye've never been one for stitchin', and catgut isna the same as thread."

"I know." I took the catgut, which I was like ninety percent sure was made of intestines, and grimaced. With a quick poke, I threaded the needle and tossed the suture materials into the kettle.

Indignation flushed Mairi's cheeks. "What in the name o' saint Damian, are ye doin'?"

I'd known this argument was coming, which was why I hadn't asked permission first. "It needs to boil for ten minutes."

"Have ye lost your senses? Longer ye wait, harder it'll be to stitch." She reached toward the kettle.

I stepped between her and the pot. "Boiling helps prevent infect—" I auto-corrected. "It'll keep the wound from festering."

Her teeth ground together audibly. "Now's not the time for your queer—"

"It *is* the time." My gaze bored into her. "I know what I'm talking about."

She huffed. "How can a wee bit o' water—"

"Dammit, Mairi." My voice rose to full volume. "Do you trust me or not?"

Her gaze raked across my face, and she must have read my resolve. She huffed. "Fine, do as ye wish."

"Good." I kept my voice all business. "Now find the strongest soap you can. We need to wash."

Together, Mairi and I scrubbed with salt water and lye soap meant for laundry. To her credit, she didn't complain, even though I knew her hands must burn same as mine.

"Dirt is the enemy." I rinsed my hands with the boiled saline. "Ever heard the expression, *cleanliness is next to godliness*?"

Her eyes narrowed. "You're not inventing scripture, are ye?"

I shrugged. "I don't know if it's scripture. It's just a saying from where I come."

Mairi's lips pursed in thought. "Wash yourselves, make yourselves clean. Remove the evil o' your deeds from my sight." A relieved smile flashed across her face. "That's why ye boiled the needle. To sanctify it!"

"Uh, yeah." I nodded like a bobblehead. "That's it."

Flicking beads of water off her hands, she turned to face me. "Ye should have said as much."

I groaned. "I would have if I'd thought of it."

We washed Donald's body with the saline water and soap. His body remained cold and his breathing shallow, but he hadn't gotten worse, which, in a small way, felt like victory.

Wound by wound, Mairi stitched him, her hand steady and sure. When she finished, we tucked him into a fresh bed with clean sheets and blankets.

Exhausted, I collapsed onto a chair at the table.

Gesturing at the wound on my cheek where Sean had cut me, Mairi held up the needle and last bit of catgut. "Your turn."

I raised my hands. "No, I'm good."

"Dinna be ridiculous. Wounds kill." Before I could complain that the needle needed to be re-boiled, she seized my chin and made the first stitch. Tears streamed from my eyes. She popped me upside the head. "Stop that. You're makin' it harder to sew."

If I could shoot laser beams out of my eyes, Mairi's head would have exploded right then and there. "How about I stick a needle in your face and see how you like it."

She stuck me again and again, poking and tugging and digging her clawed hand into my chin every time I flinched. Once she finished, she patted my hand as if she hadn't just spent the last ten minutes torturing me. "I'll get some comfrey for ye. That'll help with the sting."

Mairi disappeared into the garden and returned a few minutes later with a fistful of flowers and an armful of dog.

"Snoop!" I jumped from my seat.

She handed him to me. "Mind his ribs. I think he's broke a few."

I cradled him in my arms. His tail thumped weakly against my side. "Will you make him a bed?"

"Make him a bed." Mairi scoffed as if it were the most ridiculous idea she'd ever heard. She muttered to herself, "Spoilt wee mongrel."

Spoiled or not, she fixed him a bed, and we tucked Snoop in before returning to Donald. She clasped his hand and stared at him, pressing her mouth thin. His skin was nearly as blue as the varicose veins that spidered across her gnarled hands.

She tucked his hand back in and rose. "I'll be goin' now."

"What? Going? Where?" I shot to my feet. "It's the middle of the night."

Bags darkened her exhausted eyes. She gave a feeble smile. "Do ye think death cares when the sun chooses to rise?" She tilted her head toward Donald. "His color hasna improved. He needs more help than we can give."

I nodded. "I'll get our cloaks."

"Nay." She readjusted his blankets. "I need ye here." She met my eyes, and her eyebrows gathered in a pained expression. "I need ye to tend to the bodies."

"Tend to them?" Nope. Didn't like the sound of that. Not one bit.

She plucked her cloak from the hook. "Do it in the smithy. Should be an axe or a sword in there ye can use."

My mouth fell open. "You want me to cut them up? Are you insane? Hell no." I cut my hands through the air. "I'll dig graves if you want, but I'm not dismembering bodies."

She rolled her eyes. "If the watch comes to question us, dinna ye think they'll notice the freshly turned earth?"

"Fine." I wiped my hands on my skirts. "I'll toss them in the cesspit. Nobody's looking in there."

"Aye, until the gong farmers come to empty it." Her lips curled in a wry smile. "Imagine their surprise when they find corpses floatin' about in the muck."

"I'll burn them, then. We've got a forge." Relief flooded through me. That was the best idea out of all of them.

Mairi raised a skeptical brow. "Ye ever smelled a burnin' corpse?"

I gripped my hair by the roots. "Fine, say we chop them up. That's just going to make them smaller. What'll you do with the parts? Make a stew?"

"That's for me to worry about." She put a hand to my face. "I ken what I'm askin' ye isna easy, but for family, we do what we must."

~ * ~

When Gran died, everybody told me how good she looked. *She could be sleeping* half a dozen well-meaning mourners said, never knowing how shallow those words sounded. She didn't look good—she looked dead. No matter how much eyeshadow and lip gloss the undertakers painted on her face—in colors she never would have chosen for herself—it didn't keep her skin from shining like wax or her eyes from seeming too deep-set.

But now, after stripping the Camerons to burn their clothes, I wished I could kiss the undertakers who prepared Gran's body. Until this moment, I never realized the horrors they'd hidden.

Both bodies were covered in piss and shit. Purple-black stains bruised their legs. Their hands and feet had turned blue, while the rest of their skin shined waxy lilac. Somehow, the one with the arrow in his head sported a massive erection, which I couldn't even begin to comprehend considering the guy no longer had a working circulatory system.

I kneeled beside the corpse, axe in hand. His eyes, already beginning to sink into his skull, stared lifelessly up at me. I closed them. Silly, really, considering a second from now, I planned to chop off his head, but it seemed right. I took a deep breath and raised the axe. I just had to bring it down. Any second now... I could do this.

Fuck. Why was I dismembering bodies? I didn't sign up for this shit. I lowered the axe and glared at the corpse. No. *Donald* hadn't signed up for this shit. While I was out here, putting off the inevitable, he might be taking his last breath.

I raised the axe again, turned my head, and let it fall. Slowly, I peeked at what I'd done. One glance was all it took. I vomited everywhere. On the dead guy. On my dress. All over the smithy floor. I'd completely missed his neck and hacked into his face. His teeth were smashed, his jaw severed. It hung open, impossibly wide, connected by strands of exposed muscle and tendon.

Tears filled my eyes as I yanked the axe free. I had the emotional resiliency of a child, unequipped and incapable. I wished in the most desperate way Henry would come home and save me from this burden. Such a selfish, horrible wish.

I wiped the snot and tears from my face and raised the axe again. This time I brought it down hard and clean. The head came free. My hands quavered. My stomach roiled, but I kept going. I cried and hacked and piled mounds of human limbs. I questioned my life, my choices, what karmic deeds had led me to this. But I did what had to be done, and when I finished, I washed my body clean. Then I went inside, poured myself an ale, and tried to wash away my thoughts as well.

~ * ~

A fist banged on the door. I ran to the window and peeked out. A small form, one I couldn't see well in the dark of night, but too small to be a Cameron warrior. I un-barred the door, and Shona shouldered past me, a basket in her arms.

She dropped beside Donald and checked his pulse, face, and hands. She examined his stitches and bandaged side before she looked at me, her eyes glossy, but jaw set. "I'll need a wee bit o' ale and some clean clothes and sheets. He'll likely shite himself." She retrieved a small tin from her basket.

I eyed it warily. "What are you giving him?" She knew a lot about herbs, but I didn't trust medieval medicine, no matter who doled it out.

She opened the tin. "Hedge hyssop."

My skin prickled with nerves. "What'll it do?"

She sucked in a breath. "God willing, it'll help the blood flow with more force."

A cold knot formed in my stomach. "And if God's not willing?"

"He'll die." Her matter-of-fact tone didn't match the fear in her eyes.

I bit my lip. "Maybe we should wait. Give him a chance to recover first. I mean, the bleeding's stopped."

She waved me to her side. "Come here. Put your head to his heart."

I laid my head on Donald's chest. His pulse was rapid, but weak and thready.

"That's his heart tryin' to push the blood about." She put a hand on my back. "If we dinna give it some help, it'll give out."

I stared at his blue-tinged hands. Bloodless hands. Dead hands. I choked down bile. "I'll get the ale."

Dead hands. Dead hands attached to disembodied arms. Dead hands stacked like wood in a pile of limbs.

I handed Shona the tankard, and she scooped some powder from the tin with a tiny, silver spoon. After leveling the excess with the edge of her knife, she poured it in the tankard, and gave it a swirl. "Hold him up."

I got behind Donald and propped him against my chest. His skin felt cold, but not stiff, not...dead. I stroked his hair.

She tipped the hyssop-laced ale into his mouth, and we laid him back, covering him with blankets. For a long time, we both stared at him.

My eyes drooped, and I let out a yawn on a stretch. "Where's Mairi?"

Shona ran a knuckle across Donald's cheek. "Outside, the poor thing. I think her mind's gone soft with grief."

My gaze snapped in her direction. *Soft* was the last way I'd describe anything about Mairi. "What do you mean?"

"She insisted I bring my sows with us." She brushed a lock of sweaty hair out of Donald's face.

I swallowed. "Your pigs?"

"Aye. I told her we didna have time if Donald was as poorly as she said, but she wouldna hear reason." She checked his pupils. "Said she had meat soon to spoil, and if I didna bring the pigs to eat it, it would go to waste." She tsked. "Imagine worrying about something like that with Donald in the state he is."

~ * ~

A knock reverberated through the room. Mairi and I startled awake, both having passed out at the table. Shona lay asleep, curled by Donald's side.

Mairi brandished her knife. "Name yourself."

"It's me." Henry's tired voice filtered through the shutters.

I ran to the door, un-barred it, and fell into his arms. He squeezed me tight and kissed the top of my head. "The lad?"

"Better than he was." I forced a smile. "But he still hasn't woken."

Mairi handed Henry an ale. "Sit. I'll get ye some food."

Groaning with relief, he kicked off his boots and wiggled his toes.

"Did you...?" I couldn't finish the rest.

She shoved a congealed trencher of yesterday's pottage in front of Henry.

Popping a piece of meat in his mouth, he chewed. "He had a horse waitin' for him down the wynd. I tracked the hoof prints far as I could. Talked to a few people who saw him ride by. Best I can tell, he's left the city."

Mairi put a hand to her chest. "He was alone? Just him and the two?"

Mouth full, Henry nodded.

I slumped back in my chair. "So we're safe."

The two exchanged looks significant enough to make my stomach knot.

"What? The Camerons are gone. Sean's big, but he's not brave. He won't come back." At least, I didn't think he would. Then again, I never would have expected him to threaten to cut off my ear either, so what did I know?

Henry sagged in his chair. "Fiona, he doesna need to come back to see me dead. What do ye think'll happen once he tells his chief I killed his men?"

I honestly had no idea.

Mairi answered for me. "The chief will demand justice. He'll write the king and call for Henry's head."

"It's Sean's word against ours." My voice grew high-pitched. "There's no bodies. No witnesses." I looked from Mairi to Henry, neither of whom seemed convinced. "It was self-defense."

Henry shrugged. "Why should the king care? He willna risk war with the Camerons o'er me."

Exhaustion fell on me like a crashing wave, my eyelids sagging. "So what then? It's just over for us?"

Mairi rubbed gentle circles across my back. "Nay, the king might not stand against the Camerons, but Clan Chattan will."

"If they'll take us." His hands stroked his stubbly chin.

I raised a brow. "We're going north?" I'd never gotten him to say more than a few words about his former clan. The fact he was now willing to head there without hesitation brought the direness of our circumstances into focus more than anything else had.

"Ye and Henry will go." Mairi clasped her hands. "I'll stay with the lad 'til he's safe to travel."

"You can't stay here alone." Panic gushed through my veins. "Who will look after you?"

Her mouth quirked. "Lass, I've survived plague, famine, and cattle raids. A month without your nonsense willna kill me." She cracked a grin. "Besides, we've a fierce wee dog to keep us safe. Aye, Snoop?"

Snoop raised his head from the mattress, batted his tail, and went back to sleep.

Tears sprang from my eyes. "You do love him!"

Mairi rolled her eyes, and I kept blubbering. Not because she had been kind to Snoop, but because Donald lay dying, our family was separating, I had desecrated the dead, Sean betrayed me, and somewhere, outside, lay a pig with a belly full of dead Camerons.

Henry lifted me into his lap and rocked me in his weary arms.

Mairi's eyes shone in the firelight. "When will ye leave?"

"On the morrow." He gazed over his shoulder at Donald. "Ye'll send a message if..."

I squeezed him tight, silently letting him know I understood. Henry had his fill of death today too.

# Chapter Thirty

After an exhausting three-day trek through muddy, woodland paths and rocky mountain passes, blisters covered my feet, I stunk to high heaven, and exhaustion weighed on me like piled stones. To make matters worse, in a moment of desperation, I resorted to drinking unboiled water from a stream, and now nausea churned my stomach, and I was probably dying of typhoid or dysentery or something.

Henry's eyes raked over me. "Are ye sure you're well? You're pale."

I forced a smile. "I'm fine."

Between my physical ailments and near constant worry about Mairi and Donald, I wasn't even close to fine, but I wasn't about to complain to Henry. He was going through enough of his own shit with the prospect of being reunited with his long-lost family looming.

He slung an arm around my shoulder. "Dinna fash yourself o'er Donald. Lad's too afeard o' Mairi to risk displeasin' her by dying. He'll be fine."

I sighed. "I know he will." He had to be. The world wouldn't be the same without his smiling, goofy face.

"Ye need to keep your mind occupied." He grinned. "Tell me again about those sufferin' women."

It took me a second. "You mean the suffragettes?" I laughed. We'd been trading stories the whole way here, and Henry's interpretation of modern concepts could be fucking hilarious sometimes.

"Aye, well." He shrugged. "Ye said the lassies couldna join parliament, so how did they expect to vote?"

His voice trailed off as the pine forest ended abruptly, and we found ourselves looking down on a village nestled in a valley between a mountain and river. Smoke billowed from the tops of thatch-roofed houses scattered around a large plot of farmland. In the distance, a manor house sat atop a hill, and far behind that, stood the outline of what I thought might be a castle.

"Is this it?" I asked, proud of how optimistic I managed to sound, because I sure as hell wasn't feeling it. The place looked one bad storm away from being razed to the ground.

He nodded but couldn't seem to bring himself to speak. A mix of emotions played across his face—fear, longing, hope, pain.

I wrapped my arms around his waist. "You ready for this?"

His chest expanded as he contracted in a giant breath. "Aye." He gave a half-hearted chuckle. "It's me should be askin' ye that. I'm not sure you're ready for the likes o' my sister."

"Are you kidding?" I snorted. "I'll be fine. After Mairi, the rest of your clan'll be easy."

Sometimes I said the dumbest shit.

Once we made it to the field, I realized this was going to be far from easy. Head after head snapped our way as the farmers stopped their work to glare, like every naked nightmare I ever had had come to life. Eyes crawled over me. Suspicion radiated off them. Clearly, strangers were neither common nor welcome.

One of the farmers, a bare-chested man wearing pants about four inches too short, shouted at us and shook his pitchfork. I couldn't understand his Gaelic, but the violence in his tone needed no translation.

"Henry..." My heart raced.

He slipped his hand into mine, but he didn't say a word, and he didn't look back—not when the farmers left their field, not even when they formed a mob behind us.

"Why aren't you doing anything?" I hissed under my breath so they couldn't hear me.

"Just keep walkin'." He put a hand on my arm. "Not too fast. Move like ye belong here, like ye dinna ken they're behind us."

I squeezed his arm. "Say something. Tell them who you are."

He spoke out of the side of his mouth. "There's no reasoning with a horde o' hungry men. Someone'll get plucky, and it'll be a brawl afore I get two words in."

God, I wanted to murder him. A little heads up that the members of his clan were homicidal might have been nice. I gritted my teeth. "Then what's the plan?"

The path curved toward a collection of thatch-roofed houses and spit us onto a community lawn. Women sat in the grass, surrounded by piles of raw wool and baskets of thread. Others worked dough and chopped vegetables at a weather-worn table. A few huddled around a kettle, arguing in Gaelic.

Henry's shoulders relaxed, and he nodded toward the women. "*They* are the plan."

I thought I understood. Men were impulsive creatures and prone to violence. Women, on the other hand, were much more sensible and a lot more likely to hear us out.

Or not...

Knives popped out of pockets as the women rose to their feet. They stalked toward us, coming together to form their own mob. Leading the pack was a middle-aged woman with salt and pepper hair and a weather-beaten face. She shouted in Gaelic to the men behind us, and before I knew what was happening, some toothless farmhand pinned my arms behind my back. He smelled of sour milk, dirt, and old, built-up sweat. His hands felt like vices around my wrists.

I stomped his dirty, bare feet. "Get off me!"

"Silence yourself, Fiona." Henry's voice barked with command.

"Silence myself!" I craned my head toward him. "Have you lost your damned mind?" Like me, his arms were restrained, only by two men instead of one.

The woman with the salt and pepper hair strode over to him and jabbed the tip of her blade into the swell of his throat. "State your business, *coirgreach*."

One of the farmers behind us interrupted, and she shot him a glare so fierce I could have sworn I was looking at a younger version of Mairi. The man withered under her gaze. Henry snickered.

She pressed the blade harder against his throat until the skin beneath it puckered. "Laugh again." Her nostrils flared. "I'll flay ye where ye stand and make shoes o' your skin."

He glanced at her feet and smirked. "Mayhap ye should. Ye have Da's crooked toes."

Her eyes narrowed, and she seized him by the chin. She jerked his head from left to right, staring as if the answer to some great secret was hidden within his jawline. Then all of the sudden she let him go. "Brother?"

He gave a curt nod. "Betrys."

She stowed her knife and tossed her hair behind her shoulder. "Well, what are ye standin' about for?" She gestured at the men holding Henry captive. "Untangle yourself from those lads and come get something to eat."

~ * ~

"Walk into a Hielander's home, and ye'll leave with his last crust o' bread," Granda always used to say.

The way he talked, you'd have thought good manners began and ended in the Scottish Highlands. Now that I'd experienced it for myself, I had to agree. Highlanders were hospitable. At least, once they decided they didn't want to kill you.

Betrys announced who we were, and the mood shifted at a manic speed. Scowls transformed into smiles. High, excited voices filled the air, and a hundred happy Highlanders fell on us with hugs.

It was surreal and endearing and overwhelming all at once. I didn't know what to make of it. All these bodies around me. All these strangers treating me like kin when we didn't even speak the same language. Old women patted my cheek and cooed like doting grandmothers. Young children attached themselves to my legs. Men bowed, and women smiled.

Then came the introductions. "Meet Raibert, the son o' my mither's cousin's sister by marriage, and here's Aoife, my third cousin on my mither's side and married to my first cousin on my da's side."

And on it went, a list of names and pedigrees and complex genealogies. My head spun from all the information, and without any Gaelic, I could only smile and nod, but none of that mattered. Henry was so happy, I'd have kept nodding until my head fell off, so long as it kept that smile on his face.

A horn sounded from outside the communal lawn, and the mood shifted once again. Shoulders sagged, and faces fell into grim lines. The few closest to us patted our backs before hunching their shoulders and turning toward their houses.

I rose onto tiptoes so I could whisper in Henry's ear. "What's going on?"

He looked about, his eyes taking in the circle of dilapidated houses and the threadbare clothes on the backs of his retreating relatives. His mouth compressed into an angry line. "Tachsman's come for his rent."

# Chapter Thirty-One

The villagers returned from their houses, arms filled with burlap sacks, chickens, bolts of cloth, even stacks of bricked turf, whatever they could find to pay off the tachsman. Silent tears streamed down the faces of a few villagers, but most wore somber, resigned expressions, as if they were too weary to bother railing against the inevitable.

We followed the group through the cluster of houses and onto the path where the tachsman waited. He had the ruddy face and red-rimmed eyes of a man who drank too much and the belly of a man who sops it all up with bread and gravy.

He sat upon a pristine horse with a shiny mane and well-brushed coat. Everything from his knee-high, leather boots to the cart he'd brought to collect the villager's goods, reeked of excess. If Gavin had seen the carved spokes on his cart's wheels and the gleaming polish of its bed, he'd have rolled his eyes and muttered about *new money*.

I didn't know the man, didn't know a single thing about him, but I hated him on sight. I hated the smug sneer on his face and the shine to his shoes, and the way he flaunted his wealth in the face of the poor. I hated that his horse showed no ribs when every child here did. But most of all, I hated that he'd stolen the joy from Henry's face.

The villagers formed a queue, and one by one, they presented the tachsman with their offerings. He weighed each coin in his palm before sliding it into a fat velvet pouch. He sifted through every grain bag, inspected each and every chicken, and once they met his approval, he returned them to the villagers to stow in his cart.

The process continued without issue until an emaciated woman with lank blonde hair stepped forward. She held a toddler at her side and a baby on her hip, and with her free hand, she proffered a small burlap bag.

The tachsman peered inside. His face flushed a violent red. "*Daolagan.*"

"Bugs," Henry translated.

The tachsman tipped the bag and emptied the grain into a pile on the dirt.

The woman cried and dropped to her knees. Shoving the baby into the toddler's arms, she scooped the grain desperately into the folds of her skirts. The man growled something and dismounted. Seizing her by the hair, he dragged her to her feet. She sobbed and pleaded as he lugged her toward the houses. Nobody intervened. Nobody spoke a word in the woman's defense. They just hung their heads in helpless shame.

A few minutes later the tachsman returned, carrying a very pregnant goat.

The woman scrambled behind him, her face purple and swollen with tears. "*Mo naoidheanan. Mo naoidheanan.*" I didn't need a translator to know she pleaded for her children, for the food that goat would provide.

She clutched his cloak as he mounted his horse. With a back-handed fist, he knocked her to the ground.

A growl rumbled in my throat. "Motherfucker." I ran to the woman and helped her to her feet. Henry positioned himself between us and the tachsman, shielding us with his body.

A cruel smile formed on the tachsman's lips, and he gave a jaunty laugh. "It seems the cockroaches are multiplyin'." He unsheathed his sword and strode toward Henry. Despite his soft middle, he was a big man, broad and burly, and he seemed well used to throwing his bulk around.

Henry didn't budge. He stared at the tachsman's sword, which had a gold hilt studded with pearls. He smirked. "If ye wish to fight me, cousin, ye'll need somethin' better than that tiara you're holdin'."

The tachsman gave Henry a curious once over. "Cousin?"

260

A grin split his lips. "Surely, ye remember me, Darach? All those hours we spent trainin' together as lads. All those times I knocked ye on your arse."

His eyes widened, comprehension dawning across the tachsman's face. "Eanrig." He used the Gaelic version of Henry's name. He stowed his sword, but his hand remained on the hilt. "O' course I remember ye." He tilted his head toward the manor house on the hill. "I think o' ye e'ry time I bring a whore to your mither's bed."

Henry tensed. I shifted closer and put a protective hand on his arm.

"Tell me, cousin." He fingered the jewels on his hilt. "What business have ye steppin' foot on *my* land?"

Henry chuckled. "And here I thought this was the *chief's* land, but I suppose much has changed in the years I've been gone." He gestured around the circle of worn houses. "I dinna remember a time when the tachsman could afford jewels for his sword, but not thatch for his tenants' houses..."

Crimson spread across Darach's cheeks and neck. "I'm not the weak man your father was. I'll not forgo my due so the rabble can laze and leach."

Henry's hand twitched toward his sword. I stepped between them. "How much?"

Darach jumped back as if shocked some random woman dared interrupt their posturing.

I inclined my head toward the woman he'd hit. "How much for her rent?"

His gaze followed my hand as I reached for my coin purse. He stiffened, surveying me in cautious appraisal. It took me a second to realize what had him so suddenly fussed, and when I did, I had to bite my tongue to keep from laughing. My ring. Apparently, Gavin wasn't the only one to mistake the meaning behind my jewels.

"Who are ye?" His voice was tentative.

I bit my cheek to keep from grinning as I decided to test the limits of our newfound power dynamic. I put on my haughtiest, peacock voice. "No one to be trifled with."

Staring past me to the castle in the distance, he swallowed. "Passin' through on your way to Ruthven?"

In my best Gavin imitation, I rolled my eyes and sighed. "How long does this tedious man intend to prattle? This is why they need to stop granting titles to upstarts. You just can't train breeding."

In a very put out way, I placed my hand on my coin purse. "How much? Clearly, your circumstances are dire."

I thought Darach might give himself a stroke trying to repress his obvious fury, but he managed to school his voice. "I'm afeard there must be some misunderstandin' betwixt us." He gestured to his fine clothes and expensive cart. "As ye can see, I want for nothin'."

With a tinkling, haughty laugh, I put a hand to my chest. "My dear man, if you're desperate enough to take a peasant woman's last goat, your situation must be dire, indeed. It won't do. You must let me help you."

Hoping to God he wouldn't call my bluff, I fumbled with the clasp of my coin purse. I probably had enough to cover her rent, but not enough to back up my ruse.

His jaw clenched. "Keep your coin." He hissed something in Gaelic to one of the villagers who, to the cheers of the clan, retrieved the woman's goat.

I raised my eyebrows. "You *don't* need help, then?"

He sneered. "A goat is nothin' to me."

"Oh, good!" Turning a brilliant smile on Henry, I squeezed his arm. "Darling, tell the villagers to unload the cart. It seems your cousin isn't indigent after all."

"My tenants owe taxes, whether I'm in need or not." Darach's jaw clenched so tightly half the words that came out were nearly indecipherable.

I jerked my head in the direction of the castle and made my voice come out waspish. "I will not have my husband's kinsmen mocked. I have a reputation to uphold."

His eyes flicked to the castle, then to Henry—who'd already managed to unload half the cart—and finally back to me.

Darach's lips disappeared in a thin line as if he realized there was no salvaging the situation.

"I'll bid ye farewell then." He spoke through gritted teeth. "I presume ye'll be leavin' at first light."

It sounded more like a command than a question, so I felt no need to answer. I just yawned as if the thought of further conversation bored me. He mounted his horse, cracked the reins then took off for the house on the hill, towing an empty cart behind him.

~ * ~

"Ye did a braw thing back there." Betrys led us to her house after several more hours of celebration and reunion. "But he'll pay us back for it ten-fold once ye've gone."

A low growl escaped Henry's lips. "Why hasna the Macintosh come with aid? How can he think to ask for rent?"

She guided us toward a line of houses to the left. "He refuses our pleas. At least, that's what Darach claims." She smirked. "But in these last months, our dear cousin's put glass in his windows and bought a fine new horse, so ye tell me."

"*Blaigeard*." Henry's hands curled into fists.

I looked between the two, the subtext lost on me in my exhaustion. "Wait. What does that mean?"

"The Macintosh reduced the rent, sure enough." Henry spat in the dirt. "But Darach's keepin' the difference." He kicked a pebble along the path. "I should cut off his stones and feed 'em to his pig."

She put a hand on Henry's shoulder. "If ye wish to talk o' castratin' tyrants, brother, let's do it proper." She grinned. "O'er a pint."

We arrived at a small cottage with a damn near forty-five-degree slant to its walls. The only thing keeping it from tumbling was a pile of stones and a piece of timber that braced the outer wall.

"We can't go in there," I whispered to him as we approached the door. "It's a death trap."

"Death trap." He chuckled and ducked beneath the threshold. "Ye have a canny way with words, ye ken that?"

I grumbled to myself as I stepped into the house of doom. "Yeah, I'm freaking brilliant."

The house didn't collapse, but once I caught a whiff of the place, I almost wished it would. Holy Mother of God it reeked. It smelled like someone captured the essence of barnyard, distilled it, and topped it off with ammonia.

The source of the funk bleated at us from across the room. "Aw, Shinach, shut your gob." Betrys tossed an old apple core into the goat's pen on the other side of the room.

My eyes burned, and the smell made me queasy. I'd been in plenty of houses with livestock, but never one that affected me like this.

"Are ye hungry?" Betrys pulled a live fish from a nearby barrel. "Caught this, just this morn'."

My stomach roiled.

She slapped the fish on the table, summoned a cleaver, seemingly out of thin air, and chopped off its head.

I slapped a hand over my mouth and ran out the door. By the time Henry caught up to me, I was puking my guts out all over the lawn. He tried to be helpful, but somehow only managed to make things worse.

He rubbed clumsy circles across my back and kept repeating, "Fiona, are ye well?"

It was probably good I was too busy throwing up to respond because I wanted to say that of course I wasn't well and for him to get the fuck off me. But once I finished, the queasiness subsided, and I wasn't nearly so irritable.

I wiped my mouth with my sleeve and gave him a reassuring smile. "Fine now."

Betrys, who I hadn't even heard come outside, handed me an ale.

"Thanks." I swished the liquid around my mouth then spit. Then I chugged until the sour, vomit taste disappeared. "Sorry about that. I don't know what's wrong with me."

Henry's brows knit in concern. "She's not been right for days."

His voice held concern, but annoyance flared inside me once more. Excuse me for not feeling one hundred percent. Stress does that to a person. But whatever. Apparently, he was fine, so I should be too.

He talked past me to Betrys as if I weren't standing right there. "Every time we stopped to rest on the way here, she fell asleep, and she's had no appetite to speak of."

She raised an eyebrow. "Fever?"

He put a hand to my forehead. "Nay."

Her eyes narrowed. "Aches?"

Grinning, I rolled my eyes toward him. "Just this big pain in my arse."

Betrys laughed, but Henry's lips thinned.

"I think I see." She winked at me. "I've just the thing for what ails ye." Within minutes, she'd popped back inside and returned with a bit of hard bread and a bucket of pale yellow liquid. "This always helped me."

I took it from her, not quite sure what it helped her with, but too tired to care. With a stretch, I yawned. "Can we sit somewhere? It's been a long day."

Leading us to a spot in the yard, away from the mess, she gestured for us to sit. I regretted how snippy I'd been with Henry, so when we took our seats, I snuggled close to him and rested my arm on his leg to let him know I was sorry.

"So brother..." She steepled her fingers. "What brings ye home after these many years?"

A tired smile crooked his mouth. "Naught but troubles."

She laughed. "Aye, well, troubles are the Davidson way, are they not?"

Laugh lines creased his eyes. "Cameron troubles to boot."

That got a full belly laugh out of Betrys. "Christ, man, ye live a three day's ride from here, and you're still runnin' afoul o' Camerons." She slapped her leg. "Now that's truly the Davidson way."

The two laughed some more, and I finished the last of my bread, surprised to find it had settled my stomach.

"So this isna just a visit? The two o' ye wish to stay?" Pouring herself a cup of the yellow liquid, Betrys tipped her head back and chugged.

"Not just the two o' us." His lips tightened. "Mairi and my apprentice as well."

Betrys spit out a mouthful of her drink. "Mairi's alive! Good God, man, she's got to be in her eighties. What witch's brew has she been drinkin'?"

A snort whistled from his nose. "She needs no witch's brew. The angels are too afeard to come collect her. 'What are ye standin' about for, Gabriel'?" He imitated Mairi's voice with surprising accuracy. "'Put those wings away and sweep the floor afore I tan your hide'."

Betrys chortled so hard it threatened to shake the moon right out of the sky. To me, her reaction was ten times funnier than the joke itself, and I laughed too. Henry joined in, and after so many exhausting days filled with nothing but worry, it was a pleasure to share in something as simple as laughter.

Sipping the yellow liquid, which turned out to be mead, I rolled it around my tongue with interest. It had more bite than even my strongest ale, and it didn't take long for the honey wine to set my head to buzzing. Yawning, I leaned against his shoulder.

Tilting her chin, Betrys studied the evening sky. "Ye ken ye'll not be allowed to stay, aye?"

I sat back up. "Why?"

Henry's smile was rueful. "Because the decision falls to Darach."

A pained groan rumbled in my chest. "The tachsman?" I pulled my legs to my chest and rested my head on my knees. "If I'd known that, I wouldn't have gone all snooty duchess on him."

Warm, rough hands caressed my back. "It isna your fault."

"Really, it isna." Betrys nodded. "Ye could have shown him your honey pot, and it wouldna have made a difference. Tachsman is an inherited title."

Raising a brow, I looked to Henry for clarification.

"Our da was tachsman." His tone suggested that should clear things up, but I had no idea what he was talking about.

I took another drink and tried to assemble meaning from their words. His dad was tachsman... And tachsman was inherited. So... I choked on my drink. "*You* should be tachsman!"

He nodded.

My eyes widened. "Is that what you want?"

After a hesitant pause, he shook his head. "I've my iron and my forge. That's all I need."

I bit my lip. "Then we'll talk with him. If you explain you don't want his position..." They both shot me withering glares. "Fine. The tachsman won't let us stay." I shrugged. "We'll just have to go over his head."

"Ye wish to behead him?" Surprise filled Betrys's voice, but also approval.

"What? No! I want to talk to his boss. His—" Trying to clear my thoughts, I gave my head a shake. "Someone with a higher rank."

Her eyes narrowed. "Ye mean the chief?"

"Yeah, him." I nodded. "We'll talk to the chief."

Henry heaved a frustrated sigh. "Ye canna just stride into the castle and demand to see the chief."

"Why not?" Scratching my head, I shrugged.

"That's not how it works. Villagers report to the tachsman. Tachsman to the chief." His hands cut through the air in a gesture indicating different tiers with villagers on the bottom and the chief on top.

"So? Who says we have to follow protocol?" I tilted my head toward the shabby houses. "I bet the chief would be interested to know what's going on here."

Putting a hand to her chin, Betrys pursed her lips in a thoughtful manner. "If Darach came for the taxes today, he'll likely be headin' to see the Macintosh on the morrow. If ye were to confront him afore the chief..." Her eyes glinted with excitement. "Eanrig, ye could change everything."

"Why should the chief listen to me? I've not lived here for ten years." He tugged at the hem of his tunic. "It's a braw idea, but someone else needs to do it. Ian or Gregor or mayhap that lad Moira married."

Her jaw set in the same stubborn way Henry's did when he reared for a fight. "Ye ken the chief willna listen to them. They're poor farmers and naught else."

"And I'm a blacksmith." His chin tilted in the direction of the manor house. "Not a man with a title."

"Ye have our father's name." She stared down her sharp nose at Henry. "You're the son o' a great man, Eanrig. A man the Macintosh called friend. He'll listen to ye."

It took a moment for him to answer. His gaze bounced from the shabby houses to the field full of failing crops, to the manor house on the hill. A vindictive smile spread across his face. "He did insult our mither, didna he?"

Betrys's canines flashed in her smile. "Aye, brother, he did."

Rising, Henry put a hand to his chest. "I canna let that stand, can I?"

I pumped my fist in the air. "Hell no, you can't!"

Licking his lips, he frowned as he stared out at the manor house. "Verra well, we'll see how the Macintosh feels about thievin' tachsmen." Holding out a hand, he helped me from the ground. "Let's get some sleep, aye. We've tyrants to tumble on the morrow."

# Chapter Thirty-Two

Shouts tore me from sleep. I bolted upright and scrambled for my knife. Was it Camerons? The tachsman? Who'd come to murder us in our beds?

"She's my wife." Henry's booming voice rumbled through the room. "She goes where *I* say, not ye."

Henry...

I gritted my teeth. I was going to kill him. What was he thinking shouting like that?

Betrys sneered. "Dinna take that tone with me, *laddie*. I am your elder."

I tore off my blankets and stormed over to them. "Have the two of you lost your damned minds?"

They stood nose-to-nose, fists clenched, and faces flushed in the hearth light. Henry swallowed whatever he was about to say and faced me.

I gestured at the window. "The sun's not even up yet."

His face scrunched. "Shite." He ran a hand through his hair. "I'm sorry, lass."

"For what?" I put my hands on my hips. "Waking me up or talking about me like I'm your goddamned dog? 'She goes where *I* say.'" I mimicked his brogue.

Betrys snorted, and I shot my glare on her. "You're no better. You don't get to play the elder card when you're squabbling like a two-year-old." I glared. "One of you better tell me what the hell is going on."

She pursed her lips. "I think ye should stay here with me. There's no reason for ye to go with Eanrig. He can see the Macintosh by himself."

I blinked at her, confused this was even something to argue about. "Of course I'm going. My whole life depends on this meeting."

She gave me an admonishing glare. "Ye have to think o' your health."

My health? My brow furrowed. "Because I threw up yesterday? I'm fine now."

"Ye ken well enough why ye should stay." Her eyes narrowed.

I made an open palm gesture. "Only, I don't."

Cocking her head, she let out a tinkling laugh. "Ye really dinna ken? And here I thought ye were just waitin' to tell my brother." She flashed a smile brighter than the hearth flames. "You're with child, ye wee dunderheed!"

"Fiona!" Henry groped my belly.

I slapped his hands off me. "I'm *not* pregnant."

"For the love o' Jude, ye canna be that daft." Betrys scoffed. "Ye emptied your gullet all o'er my grass last night."

"Henry vomited last week. Is he pregnant too?"

"Ye said ye've been tired." Her chin warbled as if she were trying to squash a laugh but couldn't quite manage.

"And irritable." A grin split his face.

Steam threatened to burst out of my ears as I leveled my gaze on him. "Oh, like you've been a real pleasure." His answering grin made me realize I was proving his point, and I forced down my temper. "Look, I know how this seems, but you have to trust me. I'm not pregnant."

"When's the last time ye had your courses?" Her voice was smug.

God, this was infuriating. I didn't know. I hadn't had a regular period since I'd gotten my IUD, but I couldn't very well explain that.

"A fortnight and some days afore the fair," he answered as quickly as if he were my personal menstruation assistant.

My jaw dropped in horror. "You're keeping track?" I raised my hands. "Never mind. I don't want to know." I sucked air between my teeth. "Listen, like I told you before, it takes the

270

women in my family years to get pregnant. You're getting your hopes up for no reason."

"Fiona, God's given us his blessing." Joy lit Henry's eyes. "How can ye be surprised he'd gift us with a child?"

"His blessing?" I scrunched my nose. "What are you talking about? Just because Mairi lights all those damned saint's candles..."

"Ye dinna remember?" He dug around in his sporran and retrieved something small and coppery. "I found this in the grass the mornin' after I first lay with ye."

Betrys peered into his hand. "What is it?"

He placed the tiny object in the palm of my hand. "A wee cross." She gasped and made the sign of the cross.

"It's a coincidence." I peered at the tiny bit of copper, and my stomach lurched as if I were suddenly mid free fall. "I need to sit down."

"What is it? Are ye unwell?" He guided me to a chair.

"Of course I'm not well." My hand trembled beneath the bit of T-shaped copper that was neither cross, nor blessing. I closed my fist around the tiny object, around my dislodged IUD. "I'm fucking pregnant."

~ * ~

After a minor meltdown, another bout of vomiting, and multiple worried glances exchanged between Henry and Betrys, I slung our travel bag over my shoulder and headed out the door.

Henry jogged to catch up with me. "Where are ye going? Betrys is right. Ye need to stay here."

"I am not an invalid." My voice came out waspish.

"Of course ye arenae." He put a hand on my back. "But ye've been so tired, and ye have to think o' the bairn."

All the crazy in my head must have shone on my face, because he shrunk back. *Think of the bairn.* "Do you think I'm capable of thinking about anything else?" I squeezed my lips together and averted my gaze before I started to cry.

"Fiona..."

He had that tone in his voice, that gentle, everything's-going-to-be-fine tone that was usually such a comfort. Only this time, I didn't feel soothed at all, because everything wasn't going to be fine. Not for us, and definitely not for this poor, unsuspecting child who was about to be born into the shit storm that was my life.

I shoved our travel bag against Henry's chest. "Why are you making me carry this?" Then I charged up the path, not even sure I was headed in the right direction.

A thousand different worst-case-scenarios flashed through my mind as we traveled along the northern trail—us homeless and living in a cold, damp cave, the baby turning blue with cold. Me having no milk, and the baby withering away from hunger. Sean tearing the baby from my arms and pulling me through the time portal. No matter how I spun it in my head, the future only came up black.

About an hour or so into our trip, we came to a fork in the road. The castle that had begun as a speck on the horizon loomed large now upon a hill to our right. I veered toward it, feeling none of the optimism of the night before. Just the expectation that this would fail, same as every other plan I'd ever had.

Henry touched my arm with tentative fingers. "Not that way."

I rolled my eyes toward the castle. "Am I missing something?"

A tight smile crossed his lips. "That castle belongs to Robert Stewart. Not the Mackintosh."

"That's the king's castle?" That same sense of oddness crept over me that I always felt whenever someone mentioned Robert III, a man I had never met, but whose very existence changed the course of my entire life.

He hopped over a steaming pile of dung. "Nay, the king's brother."

I raised an eyebrow. "King Robert has a brother named Robert?"

Henry smiled. Relief filled his eyes. He had me talking, and I could tell how desperate he was to keep that rolling. "The king's real name is John. He took the name Robert on account o'—"

272

"Never mind." Turning down the opposite fork, I continued walking.

Henry's face fell, and guilt flared in my belly. I knew I was being horrible to him, and I knew none of this was his fault, but right now, I didn't have it in me to pretend, even if that made me a callous bitch.

We continued our journey in silence, winding past lochs and hills and mountains and rivers. The sun shone down, deceptively bright against a storm gray sky. Cows grazed in tall grass fields, and hearth smoke loomed over the occasional tiny village.

Eventually, we reached a wooded patch, thick with brush and densely packed trees. The air grew humid, and gnats buzzed everywhere. My dress snagged on brambles and low-hanging branches. My foot caught on a tree root, and I fell, banging up my knees and palms.

"Dammit." I flapped my hands as if that would make the pain go away.

Henry lifted me off the ground.

"I'm fine." I tried to push him off me, but he wouldn't set me down.

His jaw set at some unspoken thought, and he carried me into the brush.

"We don't have time for this." My voice rang with all the petulance of a child.

He lowered us onto a fallen tree and tightened his hold. "I dinna give a damn if we have to sit here for a fortnight. We'll have it out, the two o' us, here and now."

"What is there to say?" I clenched my fingers.

His eyes glossed, and his arms vibrated around me. "Is the fact my child's in your womb really so hateful to ye?"

I gritted my teeth. "It's not about *you*."

"The hell it isna." His hands dug into my shoulders. "That's my seed in your belly."

"It's not a seed. It's a fucking baby. A baby!" Tears burst from my eyes and streamed down my cheeks. "Do you understand that?"

He stared with uncertain eyes, mouth parted.

I dropped my head. "How can you be anything but afraid?"

"Oh, lass." He clutched me to his chest. "Ye ken why I'm not worried?" He stroked my hair. "Because you're the cleverest lass I've met my whole life long."

The lines of his face settled into uncharacteristic earnestness. "Ye think differently than the rest o' us." His voice took on an odd sort of reverence. "The audacity o' ye..." His eyes crinkled. "I've ne'er seen anything like it. Fate tries to take ye one way, and ye just grab it by the lead and force it down a path o' your own making." He ran a thumb across my cheek, drying the spattering of tears. "So nay, I'm not worried. Our wee lad will want for naught. Ye'll see to that."

I forced a weak smile. "Who says it's going to be a boy?"

He groaned. "God help me. A lass? I'll never survive two o' ye."

I laughed and put a hand on my belly. "You hear that? Your daddy *is* scared."

After a short rest and light snack, Henry and I were back on the road. Behind us, in the distance, an armed retinue flanked a gilded litter carried by four uniformed servants.

I glanced behind us. "Who do you think that is?" Considering the entourage, it had to be somebody important.

"Hard to say." He peeked over his shoulder. "Could be one o' the clan chiefs in these parts. Or mayhap someone from Ruthven."

"Oh, yeah, you were telling me about that earlier." I nudged his shoulder with mine. "About the king's brother..."

He linked his arm through mine. "Aye, but if ye want to hear a tale about Stewarts at Ruthven, it's the king's *other* brother I should tell ye about—Alexander Stewart, the Wolf o' Badenoch."

"The Wolf, huh?" I grinned. "This oughta be good."

Henry began his tale, only, I couldn't pay attention. I tried. Really, I did. But I had baby on the brain and so many questions. Like baby proofing. How was I supposed to keep this kid from crawling into the hearth fire?

"…he descended upon Moray with a group o' wild and wicked hieland men, and they burnt the cathedral to the ground." Henry continued his tale, unaware he was basically talking to himself.

I wasn't going to have any drugs. No epidural. What if the baby was breach? Would they slice me open? What if we couldn't find a midwife? Did Mairi know how to deliver a baby?

"…that night a man arrived at Ruthven castle." He mimicked knocking on a door. "The door swung open, and a man strode in, dressed in all black. He challenged the Wolf to a game o' chess."

What about prenatal care? I needed to eat more greens. Cut down on the salt. Hadn't somebody once told me certain cheeses weren't good for pregnant women? Christ, what was I going to drink? What was worse, weak ale or shitty water?

"…the devil smiled. 'Checkmate.' And the Wolf o' Badenoch fell down dead." His voice grew somber. "When they found him, not a single mark marred his body, but his boots—"

"All the nails had been torn from his boots," an unfamiliar voice from behind us finished.

We whirled.

"Peace, friends." A middle-aged man with thinning hair and expensive clothes raised his hands in supplication. "I'm sorry for sneakin' up on ye. I just canna resist a good tale." He gestured to the litter and horses, which lingered fifty yards or so behind us. "It was the only chance I had to get a break from that lot." He grinned good-naturedly and looped his thumbs around a jewel-encrusted belt. "Told 'em we were old friends and to give us a bit o' privacy to catch up."

I glanced at Henry and started at the sight of his awestruck eyes. I thought he might cry. Or maybe drop to his knees and beg this man to be his bride.

"You're…You're…David Lindsay." His words stuttered. "Sir," he added. His cheeks flushed a violent red. "Sir David Lindsay."

The man laughed. "That's what my wench o' a wife calls me, anyway." He grinned. "Well, she never bothers with the sir part, no matter how often I ask her." He shook his head. "Bloody Stewarts think they rule the world."

All the blood drained from Henry's face. "You're married to..."

"Elizabeth Stewart." He shrugged. "Though I mostly call her shrew."

"Please, forgive me." Henry's voice damn near verged on groveling. "I meant no insult to your kin."

Lindsay waved him off. "Never ye mind. I've called him worse than Wolf, believe me. Man had a soul blacker'n the devil's bagpipes." Raising his eyes to the sky, Lindsay made the sign of the cross. "May he rest in peace."

For a second, Henry stared at him. "I saw ye joust against Lord Welles that time on St. George's day. It was the most amazing tourney I ever saw. When they claimed ye nailed yourself to that saddle..."

"Didna bother me any. When I jumped off that horse..." Lindsay's eyes shone with nostalgia. "Well, ye were there. Ye must have heard the crowd." His smile softened, and his eyes glazed with regret. "Those were the days, aye? I had a wench in my bed e'ry night, and a lance in my hand e'ry day." His face scrunched with regret. "Now the only wench in my bed is my wife, and thanks to her damned fool o' a brother, I'm traipsing across the mountains on a damned fool's errand."

Henry's brows shot up in alarm. "Can we be o' any service?"

I very subtly crushed his toes with my heel, catching his attention before I gave my head a terse shake. As if we didn't have enough going on without taking on some washed up jouster's "problems." Please. This guy didn't have problems. Just one of those jewels on his belt could feed Henry's clan for a year.

Laughter exploded from Lindsay. "Not unless ye happen to be the second coming o' Christ. Even then, I'm not sure ye could convince clan Chattan to turn the other cheek."

My interest suddenly piqued. "You're on your way to see the Mackintosh?"

"Aye." He rolled his eyes heavenward. "I'm supposed to convince him he and the Cameron should set aside their feudin' and become bosom friends."

Henry's eyes bulged. "Ye'd have an easier time convincin' the devil to repent and join the priesthood."

I frowned. "That's going to put the chief in a bad mood, isn't it?"

"Fiona." Henry flashed Lindsay an apologetic smile. "Forgive my wife. We've business with the Mackintosh as well, and she's... Well, she's with child, and ye ken."

Lindsay winked. "I ken exactly what ye mean."

"Oh?" I raised an eyebrow at Henry. "What exactly *do* you mean?"

He wisely said nothing.

Inclining my head, I met Lindsay's gaze. "You know, I've been thinking a lot about these clan feuds."

His eyes sparkled. "Oh, have ye now?"

Pausing, I surveyed him. "I have, and I think the only way to fix the problem is to give them both what they want."

He gave a delighted laugh, like I was some precocious toddler who'd just said something very charming.

Henry, on the other hand, flushed with embarrassment. "How's he to give them *vengeance*, Fiona? Because that's what they want."

Smug, I straightened. "By controlling the form it takes." Clearing my throat, I faced Lindsay. "Let me explain. You see, my granda used to own a tavern and there were these two men who used to always come in—Donny and Boyd." My insides warmed at the long-forgotten memory. Those two lunatics hadn't crossed my mind in years.

"Well, Boyd didn't like Donny because of some old gambling debt. And Donny didn't like Boyd..." I paused to make sure I got the medieval phrasing right. "Because he made Bobby a cuckold."

Lindsay slapped his leg with mirth. Henry stared at his feet.

"Well, you can guess what happened whenever they both came in." I smirked. "One of them would say something he shouldn't. The other one'd get to shoving, and soon chairs would be flying across the room."

The smile splitting Lindsay's lips suggested he'd experienced a few bar fights himself in his day.

"So anyway, Granda decides he's had enough. Next time the two show up, he tells them they're going to settle things once and for all." I slashed my arms in a spreading gesture. "He clears the tables from the room, tells the bar patrons to get to the sides, and Boyd and Donny go at it."

"Then what?" Lindsay's eyes were huge and eager.

I shrugged. "Boyd beat the hell out of Donny. After that, they never bothered each other again. Boyd was satisfied, and Donny was too embarrassed to try for a repeat."

Tongue between his front teeth, he stroked his beard. "So, you're suggesting..."

"Let them fight." I shrugged. "Just make sure they don't destroy the tavern in the process."

Nodding, a fervent grin split Lindsay's face. "We'll build an arena. Host it in one o' the king's royal bergs!" He put his hands to his mouth in imitation of a town crier. "Cameron against Chattan—battle to the death. The crowd will love it!"

"Hold on. Nobody has to die." I curled my hand into fist and punched my other palm. "Bare knuckles, dude."

"I, of course, will commentate." Scratching his chin, he looked at me, eyes bright. "Ye ken what the best part is? They canna refuse. They'll look like cowards if they do." He snorted. "It's genius."

I met Henry's eyes, desperate for a way out of this, but he shook his head, letting me know there was nothing we could do. There was going to be a battle to the death, and *I* had caused it

Me and my fucking mouth...

# Chapter Thirty-Three

We stood on the banks of Loch Moy, mooning at the sight of an island across the water swathed in verdant green. Mackintosh castle burst from its center, tall and proud, as if sprung from the earth by some ancient, druidic god. Slack-jawed, I gazed at the island. If I had to draw a picture of Avalon from the old Arthur legends, this is what it would look like. I just hoped the chief was as wise and benevolent as Arthur.

We traveled along the bank until we reached a dock where a boatman in white livery stood sentry. At our approach, he blew a sharp note on a cow horn that hung from his neck. It made a terrible sound, loud and grating, like a foghorn not quite in tune. Someone answered back with their own horn-blow from a boat mid-loch. Then a third sounded from the island.

The boatman raked his eyes over us. "State your business."

One of the servants from Gavin's retinue scrambled forward. "Presenting Sir David Lindsay of Glenesk, good brother to the king. Here for business with the Macintosh."

The boatman nodded and gazed at Henry. "And ye?"

He cleared his throat. "Eanrig, son o' Cormag Dubh." The boatman stared as if waiting for him to continue. "...er, armorer and blacksmith o' the St. Johnstoun guild."

The boatman sighed in irritation. "My good man, ye canna expect me to ask the chief to entertain an *armorer*?" Air whistled from his nostrils. "An *unexpected* armorer, nay less?"

Henry widened his legs and puffed his considerable chest. "Aye, I do."

The boatman mirrored his posture. "Oh, do ye now?"

Christ. We didn't have time for this. I flashed Lindsay a significant look and put on my haughtiest voice. "Such disrespect. How dare this man insult the personal armorer of the king's own brother?"

Lindsay's eyes crinkled with amusement, but when he gazed at the boatman, he wore an expression of practiced disdain and examined his nails. "I am sure this man meant no insult to my close and personal friend."

"Of course not, Sir Lindsay." The man seemed to shrink on sight. Henry flexed his fingers repeatedly as if longing to grab his sword. "Right." The boatman stepped back and bowed. "I'll be announcin' your arrival then."

He rowed to the second boatman, the two conversed for a moment then sailed off in opposite directions.

Grateful, I flashed Lindsay a smile. "Thank you."

He winked. "Delighted to help my dear old friends."

"Ha, remember that when we're in front of the chief." I waggled my brows.

The boatman docked a few minutes later, and we boarded, leaving the rest of Lindsay's retinue on the shore. A few minutes later, the sound of horns dominoed across the water, and we were off.

He chuckled softly to himself as we sailed.

"What?" Henry raised an eyebrow.

He nodded toward me. "I canna wait to see what ol' Mac makes o' her."

~ * ~

As wild and uncultivated as the island appeared from the shore, the grounds within the castle walls were a study in artistic precision. The garden boasted all the hallmarks of high horticulture—espaliered fruit trees, topiary shrubs, rose vines climbing intricately carved trellises. But then there were the more unusual features—bronzed dresses masquerading as statues, a scarecrow armed with a halberd, and a large plot dedicated entirely to thistle.

"That's odd." I frowned. "Isn't thistle a weed?"

Henry strung an arm around my shoulder. "Aye, they say he planted it after the death o' his first wife."

"Did she have a vendetta against gardeners?" I shuddered. "Imagine the rashes trying to weed that garden."

He squeezed me closer. "He said it reminded him o' her—beautiful, wild, and capable of inflictin' great pain."

I snorted. "Sounds like my kind of woman."

As we approached the castle entrance, a gaunt steward in crisp, expensive linen met us outside a set of heavy, double doors. He held out a hand. "Your weapons."

Henry and Lindsay unsheathed their swords and handed them over. A pair of guards held the doors for us, and once inside, the steward stored the weapons in an iron rack. He wiped his fingers clean with a handkerchief before he took off down a dark corridor.

We trailed behind. The stone floor chilled my feet through my thin leather shoes. The air hung thick and dewy with a must like a locker room shower. Silver wall sconces hung at intervals cast eerie shadows onto ornamental suits of armor and the periodic stone bench.

We approached a carved, mahogany door, which the steward pushed open. "The Great Hall." He waved us through with his free hand. Lindsay entered, followed by Henry, but when I tried to step inside, the door slammed in my face.

"*Ye* can wait out here." Disdain oozed from the steward's voice.

I pointed feebly at the door. "But my husband—"

"Should have kent better than to bring a woman afore the chief." He pointed to the nearest stone bench. "Ye may sit here until they return."

It took all my willpower to not talk back, but it was apparent no amount of arguing would convince this man to let me through the door.

"Of course." I lowered my gaze. "You're quite right. My husband will be best served in prayer."

I dropped to my knees in front of the stone bench, made the sign of the cross, and clasped my hands. *Dear God, please let this asshole be dumber than he looks.*

A few seconds later, God answered. The sound of footsteps pattered down the hallway and faded into silence. I waited another minute to be sure he was gone. Then I jumped to my feet and ran to the door.

I had my hand on the handle and was all ready to bust through, when a rare flash of circumspection forced me to pause. If the steward didn't think I should be in there, chances were the chief wouldn't look too kindly on it either. Son of a bitch. Was I really going to have to wait out here with my future on the line?

Well, I could listen at least. I pressed my ear to the door. No good. Freaking quality craftsmanship, but if I cracked the door open a little...

I pulled on the wrought iron handle, slow as a bug caught in honey, until it opened just wide enough for me to stick my fingers through and prop it open. I peeked inside.

The room was huge, bigger than three of our houses stacked side-by-side. Twin tables ran along opposite ends of a center hearth. The chief's men drank wine and picked off platters of fruits and cheese while servants bustled in and out of a screen passage to the left. To the right sat a third table, perched atop a dais. Though the table was equally long to the two on the floor, only two men sat at it—David Lindsay and the chief.

At least, I assumed he was the chief. He was a good deal older than the men on the floor, but he boasted a warrior's frame. Long, silver hair framed a face with shrewd blue eyes. A scar ran down his right cheek. After Henry's story about the thistles, I'd imagined him to be a man of good humor, but now that I'd seen him, I had a hard time imagining his face wearing anything so frivolous as a smile.

I scanned the room for Henry but caught sight of Darach at one of the tables. He'd traded in his fine clothes of the day before for a modest weave, more suited to a merchant than a man of rank. My knuckles whitened around the door. The slimy fraud.

Henry leaned against the back wall. To anyone else, I was sure he appeared perfectly composed, but the subtle way his hand traced the bottom edge of his tunic as if fighting the urge to tug it down told me he was nervous, and rightly so. If only I could be there next to him, hold his hand, and let him lean against me for support, but this battle, he had to fight alone.

The thought of Henry up there without my help had me shifting from foot to foot. To distract myself, I focused on the room. On the wall above him hung three portraits: One of a stoic young man, who by the look of his steel blue eyes had to be the chief twenty or thirty years back. To his left, a gilded frame held a portrait of a red-haired beauty with a mischievous smirk and twinkling eyes. The portrait to his right depicted a demure blonde with bones so fine she looked like her face might break at a particularly violent wink.

The sound of a clearing throat brought the room to sudden silence. I snapped my gaze toward the dais.

"We have a guest amongst us." The chief gave a respectful nod to David Lindsay. "May I introduce Sir David Lindsay of Glenesk, here at the king's bequest."

Murmurs hummed across the room, and I had the distinct impression the men there were not pleased by the visit.

"We willna bore ye with clan business, Sir Lindsay." The chief leveled those hard, piercing eyes on the former knight. "What has the king to say that couldna be sent by post?"

Lindsay smiled, seemingly unaffected or unaware of the subtext beneath the chief's words. "If I may beg a favor. I met a charming young man and his wife on the road here." He pointed at Henry, and every head in the room snapped in his direction. "If he may speak before me, I would consider it a great service."

The chief's eyes widened in surprise. Clearly, he hadn't noticed the rogue attendee, but he quickly mastered his face, and his features shifted into their former mask of cold assessment. He beckoned with a wave of his hand. "Come forth."

Henry emerged from the wall, skirted the hearth, and came to a stop before the dais.

The chief steepled his fingers. "Your name, lad?"

He gave a deep bow. "Eanrig, son o' Cormag Dubh, my laird."

"Cormag Dubh." A slow smile spread across the chief's face. "Now there's a name I havena heard in years." He raised his wine goblet in toast. "A wise and honorable man, Cormag Dubh."

Henry bowed again. "I thank ye."

"What then, son o' Cormag Dubh, brings ye to my hall?" The chief leaned forward, eyebrows raised.

"Your Grace." He bowed once more. "I've been in St. Johnstoun these many years, but now I've come to ask permission for me and my kin to return to Chattan land."

The chief stared down his long, pointed nose at Henry. "And ye thought to ask me directly instead of the tachsman o' your village?"

I bit my lip. I couldn't tell if the chief was angry or merely annoyed.

"I have reason to believe my cousin," he nodded at Darach, "would deny me and mine out o' self-interest and self-preservation without givin' my request due consideration."

Darach slammed his fist against the table. "This is an outrage!" He rose to his feet. "How dare ye come here and slander my name afore our chief?"

The chief held up a hand, and Darach fell silent. He narrowed his eyes. "Some might say an insult to one o' my men isna any different than an insult to me." No mistaking it this time, anger laced the chief's voice.

A shiver of fear ran through me. What if he threw Henry in the dungeon? Or decided to have him executed. Fuck. Coming here was stupid. We should have known better.

If he shared my fear, he didn't show it. If anything, he seemed to grow two inches taller. "With all due respect, my laird, my faither once told me the greatest honor ye can show a man is to speak with candor. I'd shame his memory to speak to ye with anything less."

The chief's expression did not change. He just stared at Henry, which I supposed was better than shouting *seize him* and having him beheaded right there on the spot. So, there was that, at least...

His gaze didn't waver. "Yesterday, I arrived at my family's village, to find my kinsmen starvin', houses fallin' to ruin, and Darach growin' fat while the clan suffers."

"Lies." Darach's voice came out as a hiss. "He covets my position, thinks to slander me as a means to his own power." He strode from the table toward the chief. "Why's he returned now after these many years? Ask 'im that."

Again, the chief raised a silencing hand. Darach quieted, but he didn't return to his seat. The chief leveled his gaze on Henry. "Ye presume I am unaware o' the plight o' your village?" His lip curled, revealing a jagged, yellow canine. "Or that I've done naught to ease their burden?"

To Henry's credit, he didn't shrivel back at the pure venom of that stare. He met the chief's gaze and held it. "I ken ye for an honorable man. I dinna doubt ye've done what any benevolent chief would do when his people suffer." He glanced toward Darach. "But I witnessed my cousin collect taxes. I spoke with the members o' my clan. He has charged them full rent, not just this month, but e'er since the crops failed, and he's blamed the lack o' easement on ye."

The chief's gaze fell on Darach.

"Ye must see what he's doin'?" His voice rose an octave. "If he cared so much for his clan, where's he been these many years? He shows up with the king's lackey yet claims to have *our* interests at heart. He'll undermine us at the king's behest. Take what little we have. The village will suffer."

"Fear not." The chief gave Darach a smile that made me shiver. "The veracity o' his claims are easily verifiable."

The color faded from Darach's face, something I felt certain the chief couldn't have missed.

"Let us assume for a moment ye speak true." The chief returned his attention to Henry. "Darach still raises important questions. Why, now, when your village's situation is at its most dire, do ye wish to return?"

"I've killed two Cameron men, injured a third," Henry answered without hesitation.

I winced. Way to put it all out there. I'd have given some bullshit excuse about family and wanting to raise our baby in the ways of the clan, but whatever, admitting to murder worked too.

"So ye've come for protection." It was a statement, not a question. Those cold eyes dug into Henry's. "What makes ye think you're entitled? We've had no benefit o' your sword these last years, and Darach is correct, ye and your kin will be an added burden to an already strugglin' village."

"A burden is a man with naught to offer." Henry held up his hands. "But I have these." He squeezed his hands into fists. "Put a hoe in them, and I will farm. Put a sword in them, and I will fight. Put a hammer in them, and I will see our clan fit with armor and blade." He lowered his fists to his side. "I am yours to use as ye see fit."

"And who's to pay for your forge, for your house?" Darach's face turned a vibrant shade of tomato red. "Who's to say ye willna abandon our clan once the threat passes?"

"Silence." The chief didn't raise his voice, but there was so much command in the word, I zipped my own lips closed. The room grew quiet, and after a moment, he stroked his chin.

"Out o' respect for your faither I have listened to your pleas, and I will," he shot a glance at Darach, "be lookin' into your claims. However, I canna ask your kinsmen to spread what little they have thinner based on the promises o' a man I dinna ken. Unless ye can offer me assurances stronger than your word, I'm afraid I must refuse."

Henry stared at the chief, clearly stunned.

*Say something.* My fingers clawed into the door. *Anything.* He made no move to speak. *Lie, dammit. Make something up!* His eyes fell closed, and he bowed his head. *No!*

"Thank ye for hearin' my request." His voice rang heavy with defeat.

I shoved my way into the room. "Money!" Every eye fell on me while David Lindsay laughed.

Henry's eyes widened in horror. His face flushed red, and he stormed toward me, grabbing my arm. "Out." He bowed to the chief while dragging me backward. "Forgive us. We'll be leavin' now."

The chief raised a brow. "Your wife?"

"Aye." He lowered his gaze.

A small smile cracked the chief's stony expression. "My first wife didna ken how to keep her gob shut either." His eyes drifted to the portrait of the beautiful redhead. "Allow me to give ye a bit o' advice your faither didna live long enough to give."

Henry raised his head.

"A disobedient wife'll test ye. She'll embarrass ye. She'll stoke a rage in ye fiercer than any ye'll find on the battlefield." His eyes softened. "Be glad for it, lad. There's no greater tedium in this world than sharin' your bed with a docile lass." His gaze landed on me. "Now I believe ye wished to say somethin'..."

I did an awkward sort of curtsey, took a deep breath, and collected my thoughts. "My granda used to say trust is earned, not given...unless you're talking to a money lender."

A few men chuckled behind me. The chief's eyes crinkled.

"I have no doubt, given time, you would come to know my husband as a good and honorable man." I gestured to Henry, who appeared to be demonstrating that good and honorable nature by repressing the urge to murder me. "But we don't have time for that, so I suggest we go with the money lender option."

My hand drifted to my change purse. "Trust built on collateral. Our savings in exchange for the chance to prove we'll be a benefit to the clan."

"Interesting..." The chief steepled his fingers.

"An insult." Darach's eyes narrowed in condemnation. "Ye offer a measly few silvers as if the chief were in need o' charity."

I flashed him a saccharine smile and batted my lashes. "We might not have money for glass windows and pretty new ponies like you, Darach, but I imagine we could come up with..." I did some mental math and calculated the lowest number that might not be taken as an insult. "Five gold crowns."

Silence fell over the room. I held my breath, shaky with anticipation, but my gaze remained bold and unapologetic.

"Eanrig, son o' Cormag Dubh, use those two hands ye offered me to bring me five gold crowns, and I'll grant ye permission to stay." The chief nodded.

I tried again for a curtsey. Henry bowed deeply. Then we scampered out of there before Darach or anyone else gave the chief reason to rethink his decision.

"Now, Sir Lindsay." The chief's voice followed us out the door. "What business o' the king's brings ye here?"

"An offer o' peace," answered David Lindsay's voice, "and vengeance."

# Chapter Thirty-Four

"This is all on account o' ye." Henry kissed the top of my head. "Ye've given them life."

We sat on the bench of an outdoor table, watching as the men and women of his clan ate and drank and danced to the tune of fiddle and drum. Bonfires crackled and sputtered, lighting the communal grounds against a purple gloaming sky. Children played and raced and spun in circles, collapsing into fits of dizzy giggles, and for the first time in a very long time, the tension in my shoulders disappeared.

"*Gabh mo leisgeul*," came a voice from behind me.

I turned to find a young woman in gray homespun standing there. I wasn't surprised to find a stranger wanting to talk to us—people had been visiting with us all night—but the sheer level of nervous energy that radiated off her caught me off-guard. Her whole body trembled, and her gaze darted from place to place, landing everywhere but my face. She held out a shaky hand and offered me a tiny string-tied parcel, which I took.

I bowed my head, wishing I had the words to put her at ease, but only able to manage a shoddy Gaelic thank you. "*Tapadh leat.*"

She returned the bow and scampered off like a deer at a gunshot.

I frowned at Henry. "Did I not say it right?"

He chuckled. "Ye said it less wrong..."

"So long as I didn't accidentally tell her to sard off." I placed the pouch on the table next to the other gifts we'd accumulated.

They were small tokens—handfuls of oats, nubs of cheese, day old bannocks—but from people who had so little, it might as well have been tributes of gold. I wanted to refuse, but he insisted it would be seen as an insult. So instead, I spent the night slaughtering the Gaelic language and hoping my face looked grateful enough to make up for it.

Betrys strolled over, arm-in-arm with a man in monk's robes. "Have ye met the good brother yet?"

The monk gave a slight bow, revealing a shaved bald spot on his crown. "So, this is the wee lass who stood afore a mighty chief and pleaded for the poor?" He handed me a wax paper wrapped package. "May God bless ye for your service."

I smiled. "Thank you, but it's really Henry who—" I stopped mid-sentence and stared at him. "You speak Scots!" So far, the only person up here I'd met who spoke anything but Gaelic was Betrys, and that was only because she'd had tutors as the tachsman's daughter.

He grinned. "And a fair few other languages. Ye want to spread the Lord's word, ye have to be able to talk with the people."

A woman shrieked and ran past us, laughing as a man chased her, groping for her skirts.

"Aye, well, some o' us need it more'n others." Betrys glanced at the couple.

Henry's gaze followed, and he smirked before returning his attention to the monk. "Are ye travelin' through, or will ye stay for a time?"

The priest shrugged. "I'll stay so long as the Lord compels me. O' course there's many a northern village in need, and I'll have to return south afore the winter snows set in."

"Can ye not stay through spring?" Her shoulders sagged. "It's been so long since we've had a priest in these parts, half the clan hasna had their marriages blessed." She frowned at the group of kids, now kicking an inflated cow bladder back and forth. "And all the wee bairns who need baptizin'..."

"Oh, I hope you do stay." I clasped my hands in front of me. "Henry's aunt Mairi will be so disappointed if we move back and can't have a proper wedding."

The priest cocked his head. "When will ye return?"

I looked at Henry. He shrugged. Fact of the matter was, neither of us knew how long it would take to come up with five gold crowns or what we might find when we returned to Perth. A lump formed in my throat as I thought of Donald. I hoped to God he was okay.

"It's hard to say." I forced a smile. "We're not positive we are coming back."

"Oh, aye?" The monk's eyebrows raised in surprise. "After all ye've done for the clan, ye might not return? Where would ye go instead?"

Henry rocked on his feet. "I wish I kent."

Yawning, I leaned my head against his shoulder.

He hooked his arm through mine. "I suppose we should be headin' in. We've a long trip ahead o' us come morn'." He nodded at the priest. "Pleasure meetin' ye, monk."

We collected our pile of gifts.

The monk hovered nearby. "Have ye any skill with a quill?"

Henry's forehead crinkled in confusion.

The monk's chubby cheeks grew rosy with his smile. "Send word when you're ready to wed, and I'll contact the closest monastery to ye and find a priest to marry ye free o' charge."

My mouth fell open. "You can't. That's too much."

He waved me off. "It isna often I meet a young couple willin' to help the poorly the way ye have. Ye deserve a good turn in kind."

Henry put a fist to his chest in salute. "That's verra kind o' ye."

"In fact..." The priest tapped his bottom lip. "If ye wish, ye can leave your wife here in the village until you've made permanent arrangements. If ye decide to settle elsewhere, I'll escort her home to ye."

"That's a grand idea!" Betrys wrapped an arm around my shoulder. "Why make my good sister journey all the way to Perth only to come all the way back once ye get the coin."

The monk stared at Henry, his eyebrows drawn and severe. "The Bible says ye must honor thy woman as the weaker vessel. Ye should save her the strain o' unnecessary travel."

"Dinna fash, Monk." Henry chuckled. "She might be the weaker vessel, but inside she's made o' stronger stuff than I."

The priest narrowed his eyes. "Disregard is a fool's mistress, lad. Will ye really risk exposin' your pregnant wife to rape and pillage on these bandit filled roads?"

Henry's brows knit together, and I knew his resolve was weakening.

Oh hell no. No way he was leaving me here with Betrys in her physics-defying house of slanted walls and goat droppings. I sidled between the men. "Thank you. You've given us something to think about." I forced a yawn. "Well Henry, I think it's about time we're off to bed."

The monk gave a curt nod.

We said our goodbyes and headed toward Betrys's house. "We are *not* getting married by that guy." I glanced over my shoulder to make sure we were well out of earshot. Henry raised an eyebrow. I shivered at a gust of wind. "He's pushy. I don't like it."

With a laugh, he placed his cloak over my shoulders. "Ye'd say the same o' the Pope himself if he dared treat ye like a woman."

I gritted my teeth. "Weaker vessel my ass."

~ * ~

"The house, the swords, and our savings." I held up a finger for each. "Can you think of anything else?"

Henry twisted a bag of walnuts and stuck them in our pack, preparing for the end of our lunchbreak and the last leg of our journey home. "We can probably get a few silvers for the bed."

292

He reached for the leftover bannocks, and I swatted his hand. "Not so fast." I snagged a biscuit before he put them away. "I didn't get to try the cheese yet."

His eyes crinkled as he watched me eat. "Ye ken Mairi'll cook us a feast the moment we get home. She'll ne'er forgive ye if you're too full to eat."

I smeared soft berry cheese on top of the scone and pushed to my feet. "Please. We've got, what, a half hour 'til we're back in Perth? I'll be starving by then."

Henry laughed. "Ye sure there's not two bairns in there? I've ne'er seen a lass eat so much."

I bit the bannock. "That's because I keep throwing it up, you jerk." I held the remains of the bannock out to him. "You want the rest?"

He waved his hands in front of him. "Ach, lass, I was just teasin'. I like to see ye eat."

"It's not that. The cheese is too sweet." I tossed the bannock into a bush and wiped my hands on my dress. "This baby's all about salt."

His eyes lit with excitement. "It's a wee lad for sure then. My mither said she used to salt her salt fish when she was breeding."

I wrinkled my nose. "That's too much." Just thinking about it had me parched. "Let me have that ale."

With a slight frown, he unholstered his water bladder and handed it to me. "It's the last o' it."

"Good thing we're close." I tipped my head back and drank until I finished every drop. It didn't help. If anything, I was somehow even thirstier. I nodded toward the Tay, which ran along our path to the left. "How safe is the river water?"

Forehead wrinkled, he thought for a moment and shrugged. "Same as any other, I suppose."

I stared at the river, so thirsty I was half-tempted to risk typhoid. "Can we build a fire? If we could just boil the water…"

"Nay, wood's too damp. Asides, we're not far." His brow furrowed. "Why are ye squinting?"

I covered my eyes with a hand. "It's bright."

"It's gray as the hieland mist." Confusion and concern warred in his voice.

I shrugged, in no mood to debate. My head was starting to pound. Son of a bitch, I was thirsty. We kept walking. The pain in my head grew sharper and more intense. I pinched my nose, pressed my temples. Nothing helped.

He glanced at me. "Are ye unwell?"

"Headache." My voice came out a croak. "Christ, I'm thirsty."

Biting his bottom lip, he studied my face. "To bed with ye, as soon as we get home."

This was the worst migraine of my life. Fuck, my mouth was dry. My tongue might as well have been sand. It was getting harder and harder to put one foot in front of the other. When did it get so hot outside?

"Hold on," I said, or at least tried to say. My tongue had swelled to the size of a sausage, and I couldn't seem to form the words right. I pulled off my kirtle, dizzy with heat and thirst and so much pain.

"Holy Jesus, your face!" His voice pounded against my skull. "It's covered in rash. Were ye sittin' in poison ivy? I told ye to mind your surroundings."

I couldn't focus enough to answer him. Even without the wool kirtle, the sun scorched against my skin. I swayed. Swooping me into his arms, he rushed me down the path. "Ye need Mairi."

Everything was bleeding—the trees, the clouds, the river. Color oozed from the flora and fauna like dripping melted crayons. And still that thirst. That terrible, incurable thirst. My heart battered against my ribs. Sweat ran down my face.

"Stay with me, lass." Henry's head grew and shrank and turned strange shades of pink and puce. "We're almost there. Stay with me." Then a while later. "Just past these trees."

"Water." My voice came out muddled and gummy. He ran. I squeezed my eyes closed, the sun unbearably bright.

We jutted to a stop, and he fell to his knees, still clutching me in his arms. "Nay. Nay. Nay. God, nay!" He laid me in the grass and ran toward our neighbors. "Help! Help!"

"Henry!" a voice shouted from the opposite side of the lawn.

Water. I was going to die without water. I pushed off the ground. So hot. I looked around, squinted, tried to focus. There was the house, broken, black, and charred. The roof had collapsed. So had one wall. A fire. Fire had killed the house. It would get me next. Oh God, I was covered in flames. I ripped off my shift and rolled naked in the grass, but I couldn't put it out.

"Fiona, be still." A commanding voice sliced through the chaos.

I couldn't stop. I had to smother the flames.

"Hold her." Hands flipped me onto my back, forcing me to the ground.

I looked around, wild with panic. Henry, Donald, and Shona hovered over me. I fought against them. They were going to get me killed. Didn't they see the fire?

Shona squeezed my cheeks and whipped my head from side-to-side. She forced open my mouth and peered in. She checked my pulse. Lifted my eyelids. All the while, letting me burn.

"Were ye foragin' for food? Berries? Mushrooms?" Shona prodded my belly.

"Nay." Desperation and fear roughened Henry's voice. He dumped our bag of provisions onto the ground. "This is all we ate."

Shona sifted through, examining and tossing items in rapid order until she came to the berry cheese. "Son o' an English whore, how much did she eat?"

Henry snatched it from her and examined it. "Only a bite, I think. She said it was too sweet." His bottom lip trembled. "What is it? What's happened to her?"

"Some fool's put nightshade berries in the cheese." Shona rose and wiped her hands on her skirts. "Take her to the smithy. There's a bed by the forge."

Henry clutched her arm. "You can help her, right? She's going to get better?"

"Water," I tried and failed to say again.

Shona put a hand on Henry's. "I can give her some valerian root to help her sleep, but I canna stop the poison."

He choked on a sob. "She's with child."

Donald crouched beside me. "She didna have much. A bite, ye said. That's all." His voice cracked. "She'll make it. I ken she will."

Shona clapped her hands together. "Get yourselves in order. Both o' ye. She doesna need your tears. She needs rest and drink." She gave another sharp clap. "What are ye waitin' for? Get her inside."

# Chapter Thirty-Five

Wrong. Everything was wrong. My thoughts. My throat. This bed. Something terrible had happened. I knew it. I kept remembering things. Impossible things. Memories that should have been dreams. Distortions. Colors. Pain. Fire. I was parched. My skin itched. I didn't recognize the texture of this blanket. Where was I?

I didn't want to open my eyes. Getting answers seemed scarier than the confusion, but I forced them open anyway. When I did, I found only more wrongness. I was in the smithy, but somehow also in bed. And the room smelled weird, like garlic and peat instead of charcoal and sweat.

"Henry, she's awake!" Shona rushed to my side, followed by Henry. I tried to sit up, but she pushed me back to lying.

Putting his palm to his chest, he heaved a relieved sigh. "Oh, thank God, ye gave us such a fright."

"Do ye have any pain?" Shona pulled down my blanket, her eyes assessing every inch of me.

He hovered over me. "Do ye need a drink?"

Shona began to poke and prod me. She checked my eyes and belly, pinched my skin, read my pulse. His hair spilled onto my neck and caught on my dry mouth.

"Stop." My voice sounded like a rusty hinge.

She tsked and looked at him. "Get her the bone broth."

He went to the pot and filled his tankard, taking great care to wipe the sides with a hanky before he brought it back to me. "Drink it slow, aye?"

Shona put the cup to my lips. "Do ye ken what's happened?"

Swallowing a mouthful of garlicky broth, I shuddered at the pain and pleasure of hot liquid on my parched throat. I shook my head. She shot Henry a significant look.

Her lips tightened. "Ye've been poisoned."

I blinked. Had she just said poisoned? It took me a second to absorb what that meant. Then an odd sense of relief washed over me. Being poisoned was bad, yeah, but at least everything made sense now. The hallucinations. The pain. I wasn't crazy, and a lost day or two hardly seemed that bad. So why was he looking at me with such sorrow?

Realization crashed on me like a volley of arrows. My eyes welled with tears, and I put a hand to my belly. I stared at Shona, silently pleading.

She pursed her lips. "Ye've not lost the bairn yet."

I should have been relieved, but the only word that registered was *yet.* I closed my eyes, sending a stream of tears spilling down my cheeks. Henry brushed them away and stroked my hair.

"I canna say what will happen." Shona put a hand on mine. "I've seen a fair few nightshade poisonings, but ne'er one where the woman was with child. Mayhap all will be well." The tight smile on her face was far from convincing. "But ye should prepare yourself for the possibility the bairn'll be born still."

Tugging the blanket back over my chest, a hollow chasm expanded inside of me as if the baby had already left me and only a raw, gaping hole remained.

"Fiona." He hesitated. "Do ye ken who gave ye the berry cheese?"

My mouth fell open. This hadn't just happened. It hadn't been some accident. Someone had *done* this to me, to my child. My nails dug into my knees. "Darach."

Henry frowned. "Couldna be. He wasna there."

The muscles in my jaw tensed. As if that mattered. "That girl, then. The twitchy one. He probably paid her off."

His brow furrowed. "I'm not sure—"

"Who else could it be?" My hand went to my throat as it seized with pain.

"Drink the broth." Shona's voice was soft but firm. "And before ye go plannin' a blood feud, ye should ken some fool farmer probably picked the berries by accident." She wiped her hands on her shift. "Happens all the time. Especially with the poorly. They find the berries in the woods and think they've found themselves a boon."

"Are ye warm enough?" He gestured to the bed. "That's our only blanket, but I can get ye my cloak."

"I'm fine." I peered around the room. "Why are we in the smithy anyway?"

Shona and Henry shared that same look from before.

Dread clawed at my insides. "What?"

"There was a fire." He stared at his toes. "The house burned."

Images of a collapsed roof and charred walls flashed through my mind. I froze. That was real, not a delusion. My hands vibrated. Even if the baby made it, without that money... Oh God, we were so fucked.

"Sean?" My voice rose to just above a whisper.

Henry winced. "Coira."

A garbled sort of half-laugh, half-sob bubbled out of my throat. I bit my lip, scared of what might come out next.

Shona's fingers clawed into the cloth of her skirt. "When the watch found her, they say she was standin' there watchin' the house burn. Cacklin' like a banshee all the while."

"Did she—" The sound of rattling keys and a tumbling lock interrupted me.

Donald came through the door, dead rabbit in hand. Something inside me broke at the sight of him. Coira had taken my home. Darach had taken my baby, but I still had Donald. I burst into tears. Tossing the rabbit onto a table, he limped over to me. He wrapped his arms around me in a hug so tight I could barely breathe.

I sobbed onto his shoulder. "I was so worried about you."

"I kent ye would make it." He put a hand to my cheek. "Shona told me how ye saved my life. If ye and Mairi hadna done what ye did, I'd be sleepin' in the kirkyard right now."

Smiling, I wiped my soggy eyes. "Where *is* Mairi?" I peeked around his shoulder, expecting to find her standing behind him, an irritated look on her old, wrinkly face, but she wasn't there. "Where is she?" I looked from Henry to Shona, and back at Donald. None of them would meet my gaze. My voice grew shrill. "Where is she?"

Anguish glistened in Henry's eyes. "She didna make it."

I shook my head. "No." They were wrong. Somehow, they were wrong.

"She ran back in for the wee dog." Shona's voice cracked. "She was so brave."

The wobble to her words did me in. Shona never faltered. If she was near tears, then Mairi really was gone. She was gone. And the house was gone. And soon my baby would be gone. And I couldn't— Oh God, I just couldn't. A scream tore from my belly, and I collapsed in a heap, my body racked with sobs.

Donald put a hand on my back. "Ye should ken—"

"Why didn't you stop her?" I slapped his hand away and rose to my knees. "You could have stopped her! She didn't have to die."

His eyes filled with tears. "I'm so sorry."

So many terrible, hurtful words pooled on my tongue, but before I uttered a single one, Shona smacked me across the face. A collective gasp rang out. I stilled.

She gripped Donald's shoulder. "Ye've naught to be sorry for." Her hard gaze landed on me. "He was at *my* house when it happened and in no shape to stand let alone fight with an old woman."

I licked my trembling lips. "I'm sorry." With those words, my body stopped shaking. My tears stopped flowing. Calm purpose settled over me. She was right. Donald wasn't to blame. *Coira* had done this.

Shona said something. So did Henry and Donald, but a sharp ringing pierced my ears, and my vision turned inward. Memories and products of imagination collided. I saw Coira on the day she arrived with that letter, white lead makeup dripping down her face, her hair burned and sodden. She stared at me

300

with black, soulless eyes. Her lips parted, and she mouthed a silent word *suffer.*

*Suffer. Suffer. Suffer.* The word played in my head. I *had* suffered. I *would* suffer. But now I understood. *She* had to suffer.

I rose from the bed, wobbly and weak.

"What are ye doing?" Henry darted to my side. "Lay down."

I felt along my gown for my knife. It wasn't there. No matter.

Shona whipped a finger at the bed. "For the love o' Jude, lay down."

An axe sat in the corner of the smithy. I walked over to it, lifted it. The handle's smooth, heavy wood caressed my palms. A hand gripped my shoulder, and I turned.

"What are ye doin', lass?" Henry's voice trembled. Donald and Shona stood behind him, faces pale, eyes unblinking.

I raised the axe. Purpose filled my veins. "She has to suffer."

# Chapter Thirty-Six

Henry plucked the axe from my hands. "You're not killin' anyone." He pointed to the mattress. "To bed with ye."

Shona nodded. "Ye need rest."

"I'm fine." I ignored the instability of my legs. "I'll sleep later." I tilted my head toward the door. "Come on. Let's do this."

The three of them traded looks.

Henry heaved a great sigh. "Fiona..."

"What?" My mouth parted in disbelief. This wasn't about me being sick at all. They just didn't care. They were going to let that murderous bitch walk free.

"Traitors! Cowards!" My hands curled into fists. "She killed Mairi! She killed her, and you don't even care!"

The room filled with noise—protests, admonitions, pleas for me to listen—but I would have none of it. I roared with fury and lunged for the axe.

Henry held me off with an arm.

"Give it back." I let out an inhuman growl, gnashing my teeth and spitting.

Donald took the axe from Henry, freeing him to grab me.

"Be still." His voice rumbled as I clawed and shoved and hit and bit. He pretzeled my arms across my chest.

I twisted and thrashed. "Let me go." He carried me to the bed, grunting as my flailing limbs came into contact with knees and shins and ribs. "You don't understand. I have to do this!"

He forced me onto the bed.

"No!" Pain tore through my parched throat like razors. "No!"

He draped his weight across me. "Get something to bind her!"

Donald disappeared and returned a second later with a rope. Despite my thrashing and screaming, they bound my hands and secured me to the bedframe.

My gaze darted around the room in a frantic search for help. I met Shona's eyes. She would help. She had to. "Don't let them do this."

She averted her gaze. "It's for your own good. You're not in your right mind."

"She killed Mairi." Tears flooded down my cheeks. "She killed her!"

"And the *law* will see her punished." Shona shouted to make her voice heard over my wailing. "She's set to be hanged in a fortnight."

~ * ~

The next two weeks passed in a blur. I managed to stir the food pot now and then, and I washed my face every morning. Other than that, I pretty much just slept and cried and slept some more. For the most part, everyone indulged me. Nobody complained I pulled a toddler's share of the work. No one told me to smile or cheer up or that everything happened for a reason. They just let me grieve, and for that, I was grateful.

Then one morning everything changed. Instead of letting me sleep my fill, Henry woke me with the sun. I opened my eyes, groggy and confused. "What's going on?"

He presented me with a furry bundle. "Here."

Snoop Dogg leaped into my lap. Mottled scars covered most of his left side where he'd been burned, but otherwise, he appeared happy, healthy, and very much alive. I burst into tears as he wiggled and rolled in my lap.

"He's alive?" I choked on a sob. "Why didn't you tell me?"

I'd just assumed he'd died along with Mairi, and over the last couple weeks I'd been berating myself for grieving over a dog when I'd just lost Mairi and possibly my child.

He rubbed Snoop's belly. "Nay. Shona's mither's been seein' to his wounds. We didna want to tell ye until we were sure he would live. Had a nasty wound for a time that didna want to heal."

Sniffling, I smiled for the first time since my poisoning. "Thank God for Shona and her mom." Hugging him to me, I looked around. "Where is Shona anyway?"

"I've sent her and Donald off." He held out a hand. "Come with me."

After tucking Snoop into the blanket, I followed Henry to the forge on the opposite side of the smithy, where a large oval tub sat next to the fire. Steam curled from its surface, carrying with it the scent of steeped roses.

A bar of soap sat atop a nearby anvil along with a folded linen towel and clean shift. "Have a bath."

My eyes welled with tears once more, and I flung my arms around his neck, burying my face in his chest. "I never thought I'd have a bath again."

Chuckling softly, he patted me on the back. "Get in afore the water cools."

I tore off the grimy, reeking shift I'd wallowed in for the last few weeks, and let it fall to the floor. I dipped a toe in the water and immediately removed it.

His eyebrows shot up. "Too hot?"

"I'm not used to it anymore, I guess." The water was probably half the temperature of the showers I took back home, but after months of washing with tepid water, my tolerance for heat had all but disappeared.

Not that I was going to let that stop me. I climbed into the steaming tub and ignored the burning until my legs acclimated. Slowly, I lowered myself.

Once submerged, I leaned my head against the tub's rim and closed my eyes. "This is amazing. Where'd you find a tub?"

He laughed. "Been sittin' in the back o' the smithy since we got here."

"Really?" I supposed I shouldn't have been surprised. Hard to notice much when you spend your days staring at the inside of your eyelids. I wondered what else I'd missed over the past few weeks.

"Shona's mither gave it to her as a wedding gift." Dragging a stool over to the tub, he sat behind me. "Said if her da couldna see fit to give up her dowry, he'd have to give up his monthly baths instead."

I winced. "Still not talking to her, then?"

While we'd been handling business up north, Donald had been fighting for his life on a cot on Shona's parents' floor. Her father had been agreeable to letting him stay, but once he heard news of the fire and our disappearance, he decided a crippled apprentice without a master wasn't a suitable choice for his daughter, and he ripped up their engagement contract.

Once Donald was well enough to walk, Shona's father marched him out the door and told him not to come back. Donald did just that, only with her by his side. The two eloped that night, and her father hadn't spoken to her since.

Henry sat the hair washing basin in his lap. "Nay, he's just as stubborn as she is." He assembled my hair into the bowl and poured water from a pitcher over it. "If she talks to ye about it, try an' get her to speak with him. Donald's afeard they'll not make peace afore we leave, and she'll live her days with regret."

I gripped the soap in my hand. Shona's soap. Shona's soap I was using in Shona's tub. Probably the last two possessions she had to her name. Yet she'd shared them with me. Shona, who had cared for me through my poisoning. Shona, who had picked up my slack while I wept and slept the days away. Shona, who was hurting. Shona, who deserved a better friend than me.

I resolved to do better. "I'll talk to her later today."

Henry, who had been working hair tonic into my scalp, paused in his movements. I tilted my head back and looked at him. He smiled weakly. "Today might not be the day for it."

I raised a brow. "Why's that?"

He averted his gaze. "We've much to do."

"Oh?" My stomach fluttered.

I didn't trust myself to do things yet. The world was full of triggers. Something as simple as going to market might send me into fits of tears, because, oh look, there's Mairi's favorite cheese monger, and 'no I don't want your hot-pies, Mairi told me you use sketchy pork.' She might be gone, but I couldn't seem to avoid her either. She was everywhere, part of everything.

He rinsed the soap from my hair and ran lavender scented oil through the strands. God, even the hair tonic smelled like her. Mairi always smelled of lavender.

He cleared his throat. "First, we'll be goin' to Mairi's grave."

I stiffened. That was so much worse than a trip into town. Better to break down in the middle of the market cross than be forced to say goodbye, because once I did, she'd be gone. All the way gone. And as much as it hurt to think of her, I still wasn't ready to let her go.

I dug my nails into the side of the tub. "I can't—"

"Then we'll go to Coira's hangin'." He spoke over me.

Again, I froze, but this time, it had nothing to do with what his words meant for me. His voice...it had caught. The slightest tremor in an otherwise sturdy baritone, but it told me everything. All these weeks I'd carried on like I was the only one hurting. Not once had I stopped to think that everything that happened to me had happened to him too.

It wasn't just *my* baby—it was *our* baby. I might have lost the roof over my head, but he lost the home he'd shared with his mother. I had loved Mairi like she was my own blood, but she actually was his blood. And Coira...well, he'd loved her too. Differently, maybe, than the way he loved me, but he'd loved her nonetheless. I'd been so goddamned selfish.

I turned in the tub to face him. Meticulously attending to the crooks of his fingers, he took great care wiping the oil from his hands with a towel.

"We don't need to go to her hanging. I'm sorry I ever said—" I choked on my words. "I don't need revenge. I don't need—"

"*I* need it." He met my eyes. "I-I need to be there when it happens." His eyes glossed, and he lowered his head.

I stared, not sure what to do. Part of me thought I should argue, convince him not to go. Watching her hang there, as the rope dug into her flesh, and she fought for air...how could that possibly help? I opened my mouth to speak, but then closed it.

He hadn't told me how to deal with my grief, and I wouldn't tell him how to deal with his, but I would be there for him.

"Hey." I put a wet hand to his bristly cheek. He seemed so fragile in that moment. "Your turn." I glanced at the tub. "I'll wash your hair."

~ * ~

Wild cherry trees interrupted the otherwise orderly rows of graves next to the church that had been my Sunday home since the day I met Mairi. I'd never paid it much attention before. The graveyard had always just been the place we passed on the way to hours of tedium. But now, the lush grass with its ancient trees bursting with fruit, and the birds flitting about with their cheerful chatter, filled me with a sense of peace at complete odds with what I was about to do.

Henry led me to the farthest row of graves where a statue of a great black dog sat in wait, his head held high as if proud of his job guarding the dead. No headstones marked the graves, just piles of bright white rocks, but their arrangement seemed to speak to the personality of the interred. Some were piled into mounds like messy blankets. Others boasted neat, geometric patterns. One formed a single, vertical tower, its stones arranged from largest to smallest as if daring the wind to knock it down. But Mairi's grave was as simple and clean as the life she'd lived. Just a rectangular outline that marked where her charred bones now lay.

He kissed my forehead. "I'll be in the chapel when you're finished."

I tilted my head up to look at him. "You're not staying?"

His eyes softened. "I've already said my goodbyes. I'll leave ye to yours."

Henry headed inside the church, and I sat cross-legged at the foot of her grave, careful not to disrupt the stones.

Now what? I felt like I should have some speech planned, something epic and beautiful that encompassed everything this woman meant to me. But I was no poet, and Mairi had never been one for sentimentality.

"You're probably pretty mad at me, huh?" I blurted.

Her voice answered in my head. *Carryin' on like ye dinna have the sense God gave ye.*

I moaned. "I know. It's just, I miss you so much. It's been so hard without you."

*It's been hard, has it?* Her voice rang sharp as ever. *Well then, why dinna I roll o'er and make room for ye in this grave with me.*

"Come on." Christ, even ghost Mairi wouldn't give me a break. "I didn't say I was ready to die. I'm just sad."

*Are ye sure?* Her voice cracked with its usual bite. *Seems to me ye've given up.*

"I haven't given up." I twisted one of the gravestones to line it up more evenly with the rest. "There's nothing I can do."

*Oh, aye?* Laughter exploded in my head as if she found the suggestion ridiculous.

I huffed. "What do you expect from me? I can't unburn the house. I can't wish money into existence. I can't force the baby's heart to keep beating. And I can't bring you back from the dead. So what?"

*Canna. Canna. Canna.* Mocking tainted her voice. *Who's ever solved a problem thinkin' on what canna be done?*

I rolled my eyes. "Fine, what *can* I do?"

*Ye've two good legs, a strong back, and a sound mind, don't ye?* Her voice cracked like a whip. *Use 'em.*

"Every time I try, things get worse." I bit my bottom lip and ran my hands down my thighs. "I'm just one person, Mairi. I can't do it alone."

She didn't respond, but someone else did. "Fiona!" Donald and Shona waved to me from the church door. "We'll wait for ye inside, aye!"

I waved. "I'll be there in a few."

I smiled at the grave. I'd been such a brat these last weeks, selfish and nasty and childish to the extreme. Yet inside that church, the three people who had seen me at my worst waited for me, ready to do what they could for me and each other.

"Fair enough, old woman. Point taken." I ran my hand over the freshly turned earth. "I still miss you, though."

Mairi's ghostly voice chuckled in my head. *Have ye still not figured it out?*

I smiled. "No, I got it." I tilted my head to the steel-blue sky, took a deep breath, and rose to leave.

*Look at ye, takin' off without so much as a goodbye. Given up on manners too, I see.* Apparently, death had done nothing to mute her sense of propriety.

I laughed. "Why should I say goodbye? You're living in my head aren't you?" Then I headed into the church to light a candle with Henry, Shona, and Donald.

# Chapter Thirty-Seven

We sat at the Horned Mare eating pottage the texture of gelatinous sludge. Disgusting. But for the first time in days, I was ravenous, so I shoveled it down, pausing only to jot notes on the paper I'd bought on the way here.

"Eight axes." I wrote that down. "Anything else?"

Henry grunted something that resembled, "Nay," and resumed staring into his uneaten pottage. His eyes glazed, and he was gone again, lost inside his own head.

I stuck my quill into its ink pot. I'd hoped to distract him by making him help me with this list, but with Coira's hanging mere hours away, nothing held his attention long. I put my hand on his. He blinked, as if surprised to find it there. "Are you sure you want to go?"

His lips tightened, and he gave a slight bob of the head.

"And to think ye chose this dour dolt o'er me." Gavin slid onto the bench next to me. "What do ye say, Gow Chrom?" He pulled a pair of dice from his cloak. "Play me for your wife?"

Henry's mouth quirked. "I keep tellin' ye, your mither's not an even trade."

With a sigh, Gavin shrugged. "If ye insist on bein' tedious, I suppose coin'll do."

"Nope." I shook my head. "Uh-uh. We're trying to *make* money, not gamble it away." I returned to my list. "How much do you think we could get for the bellows?"

Gavin peeked over my shoulder. "What's that you're writin'?"

Scooching the paper in front of him, I frowned at the too short list. "An accounting of our assets. We need five crowns."

His finger slid down the items. "Turf bricks!"

"Don't judge. It all adds up." I pulled the paper back to me. "Not everyone has the luxury of insane wealth."

Scoffing, he sat back and studied me. "Ye've stuck so firm to this peasant tale, I think you're startin' to believe it yourself."

"For the last time," exasperation tinged my voice, "I'm not some undercover royal."

He seized my ink-stained hand and held it between us. "Then explain this."

"That's just my gran's—" I froze.

Dread leadened my belly. The answer to all our problems sat on my finger, and it was the one possession I couldn't bear to part with. I couldn't give up my last link to home. What would Gran say? I glanced at Henry, who gazed mournfully off into the distance. I knew exactly what she'd say. She'd tell me to take care of my family.

I handed Gavin the ring. "How much do you think I could get for it?"

He studied it. His brow furrowed, and he walked to one of the wall torches and held the ring to the light. He returned a few seconds later.

I leaned forward. "So?"

Squinting down at the ring, his brow furrowed. "I've seen bigger gems, but ne'er one with such a shine."

"So what's that mean?" My voice rose an octave. "How much?"

"Ye said ye needed five crowns?" He slipped the ring onto his pinky. "Come to my house afore the battle tomorrow. I'll have the gold waitin' for ye."

I smiled, even though losing that ring hurt like losing a part of myself. "Thank you. You're a good friend."

I peered at Henry, expecting him to look at least a little relieved, but worry lines creased his eyes. "Battle?"

Gavin's jaw dropped. "Ye have to ken about the battle. Whole town's been talkin' about it for a fortnight."

He studied his pottage. "We've had a lot going on."

"Trial by combat!" Gavin raised his tankard. "Right there on the North Inch. Chattan versus Cameron."

I spun in my seat. "Here?" My voice squeaked so loud it drew looks from half the tavern.

"Where else?" Gavin shrugged. "This is the king's favorite burg."

My mouth fell open. Henry scrubbed his hands over his face. I couldn't believe this was happening. I told a stupid story, and now a bunch of people were going to die. And not just someday. Tomorrow. Here. I pinched the bridge of my nose. "I need a drink."

Rummaging through his cloak, Gavin retrieved a bottle and held it out in offer.

I put a hand to my stomach. "Actually, I can't."

With a shrug, he made to put it away, but Henry snatched the bottle, tipped it back, and drank like a man dying of thirst.

Gavin watched as Henry emptied the bottle. He nudged his coin purse toward Henry. "Want to bet who wins?"

~ * ~

A merchant meandered through the execution site, carrying a tray of baked goods. "Hot pies!"

People laughed and drank and spoke in voices that were way too loud. Ale vendors and food stalls filled the sidelines. Parents carried children on their shoulders. Old people propped themselves on walking sticks. Sick people rolled in on carts. No amount of illness, age, or infirmity it seemed, was enough to keep people away from an execution. Disgusting. I couldn't understand how people derived pleasure from something so gruesome.

We pushed through the crowd until we found a spot in the front near the scaffold. At first, nobody paid us much notice but, after a time, murmurs passed behind us, and I caught snippets of speculation. *He's the one, aye?* and *on account o' her, what I hear.*

Once the masses came to the collective agreement it was, in fact, our house Coira had burned, people started patting us on the back and flashing big, congratulatory smiles. Justice would be served. Wasn't it grand?

Only, it wasn't grand. As much as I hated her, as desperate as I'd been to punish and hurt her, nothing about this felt like justice. It was a carnival, a spectacle of humanity at its absolute worst. These people didn't know her. She hadn't done them wrong. Yet here they were, so excited by the chance to watch her die. It was a humiliation I didn't wish on anyone.

I stared at the towering scaffold. It didn't look like I'd expected. No stage with a trapdoor like in the old westerns Granda used to watch. No hanging nooses, waiting to be slipped over fragile necks. Just two poles with a crossbeam, impossibly high in the air.

"It's so tall." My voice came out hushed and reverent.

"O' course it is." Shona's brow furrowed. "How else are we to see?"

Of course. Because the people had to have their show, right? What did Henry think of this rodeo? When I glanced at him, he was staring off into the distance, eyes glazed and face sallow. I doubted he was thinking about the crowd or anything else around him.

After a time, the crowd parted for a horse drawn cart, carrying Coira, another condemned man, and a monk, who read to them from a small, leather-bound bible. Both Coira and the condemned man had their hands bound in front of them, but their similarities ended there. Vomit covered the front of the man's tunic, and his head kept lolling to the side. Coira, by contrast, appeared fresh and clean and more at peace than I'd ever seen her. A faint pink blush tinged her skin, for once free of makeup, and a serene smile played on her lips.

The cart stopped next to the scaffold, and once it did, a man in red and purple livery jumped onto it. The crowd hushed. "Kin o' the soon-to-be-deceased come forth and bid your farewells."

"Da! Da!" chimed several small voices. A woman and three young children ran to the barely conscious man.

I waited for a parent or a sister or even a servant to emerge from the crowd for Coira, but no one came. My stomach clenched with empathy, and I didn't understand why. She murdered Mairi. And didn't the fact she found herself alone at the end reflect the way she'd lived her life? Then again, maybe it said more about *why* she turned out the way she did.

The expression on Henry's face twisted my insides. He held such pity in his eyes as he stared at her.

I tugged his arm. "Go and say your goodbyes." His eyebrows scrunched together. "Go." I gave him a gentle shove.

He hesitated for a moment, then kissed the top of my head, and disappeared into the crowd. Once he reached her, I turned my head.

Shona, however, did not. "What do ye think they're saying?"

I shrugged. "I don't know, and I'll never ask."

Draping an arm across my shoulder, Donald hugged me to him. "It'll be o'er soon enough. Hangman's almost ready."

The man in livery situated a tall ladder, wider than any I'd ever seen, against the left post of the scaffold. Once he adjusted it to his liking, he selected a length of rope from a pile at his feet and formed a crude noose by means of a slip knot. He repeated the process with a second rope and slung them over his shoulders before he headed to the cart.

A few minutes later, Henry reappeared by my side. Slipping his hand into mine, we watched as the hangman escorted the drunk man to the scaffold, the noose already strung around his neck. The crowd went silent.

The hangman nodded to the drunkard. "Any last words?"

"Aye." His eyes were half-open slits.

He raised his bound hands and held up a finger. Then he seemed to forget his words and belched instead. The crowd roared with laughter. Someone threw a head of lettuce, and it bounced off his head and knocked him on his ass. Hauling the man to his feet, the executioner dragged him toward the ladder.

The hangman climbed up first, and the drunk man struggled behind him. He toppled off every few rungs, and eventually a bunch of good Samaritans had to help him to the middle rung. Once they had him situated, the executioner tied the rope to the crossbeam and shimmied down. "May God have mercy on your soul." He twisted the ladder, knocking the drunk man off.

He didn't drop like I expected. The rope had no slack, so he just swung off the ladder, neck unbroken, legs kicking as the rope deprived him of air. After several minutes, the capillaries in his face and eyes burst, and his tongue lolled out. A wet stain formed on the front of his pants. Droplets of urine dripped off the tip of his big toe.

I wondered what Coira must be thinking. I couldn't imagine watching this, knowing I'd soon share the same fate. But she appeared oblivious to the dangling man with his blood-red eyes and piss-stained pants. Her gaze was fixed upward, transfixed by a flight of birds that circled overhead. When her turn arrived, she marched to the scaffold with her head held high and a grin on her face.

The executioner's gaze softened as he looked at her. "Last words?"

"I have but two requests." She smiled coquettishly. "Should my good hangman be so inclined to allow it."

He stared at her in obvious bewilderment. Requests, it seemed, were not the ordinary course of business. "Aw, go on then," somebody shouted from the crowd. "Give the wee lassie what she wants."

This set off a chain reaction in which everyone in the crowd seemed inclined to shout their opinions, some in support, others calling for blood.

The hangman held up a hand to silence the crowd. "On with it then. What'd'ye want?"

"First, I ask that ye dinna turn me off the ladder." Her eyes lit with excitement. "I wish to jump."

The crowd roared its approval, and it took the hangman several minutes to calm them enough to hear the rest. "And?"

"Make the rope as long as ye can." She looked at the crows circling overhead. "For I should like to fly."

The crowd waited with bated breath. When the hangman shrugged as if to say *why the hell not,* the response was deafening. They'd come for a show, and by God, she was the performer they'd been waiting for.

She ascended the ladder with far more ease than the drunk man, though with her hands bound, her progress was still slow and awkward. Eventually, she made it to the top, one rung beneath the executioner, who kept his promise and tied the rope at its very end.

She scanned the crowd. Her gaze fell to Henry and lingered there for a moment. Then her gaze shifted to me. Our eyes locked, and she gave a slight nod. I wasn't sure what it meant, but I nodded back.

Smiling, she scanned the grounds a final time. "In death..." Her voice reverberated across the crowd. "I shall finally live."

She jumped from the ladder with a mighty spring. Her features rounded in pure jubilation. The wind whipped her hair free from its braid, and she whooped with joy as she extended her bound hands high above her head.

Then the rope went taut. Her head tore from her body. The decapitated torso thudded to the ground. Blood spurted from its mangled neck. Lifeless eyes stared from her blood-spattered face, which dangled upside-down from the noose, caught by a bit of spinal cord. Her smile, now inverted, remained in place.

A collective gasp carried through the audience, followed by a moment of thick silence. My vision faded and refocused as I fought to keep the contents of my stomach from spilling onto the ground. I reached for Henry's hand, which was ice cold and covered in sweat. I feared he might faint.

The hangman fell to his knees and made the sign of the cross. "God forgive me."

A woman, somewhere in the back, screamed as hundreds of voices talked at once. Some seemed disgusted, others saddened, but most, after recovering from their initial shock, were nothing less than overjoyed. They had just witnessed what would surely go down as town legend for years to come.

"Ne'er seen a hangin' like that!" A man behind us yanked off his hat and chortled.

"See, wife, that's why women should be meek." A man nudged the woman next to him with an elbow.

I dragged Henry through the crowd, away from the gruesome sight. Never again, I promised myself. No matter the reason, no matter who had done me wrong, I would never again attend an execution. I was done with death, done with horror and bloodshed.

As we approached the outskirts of the crowd, a man beamed at the woman by his side. "Ye think this was good, just wait until the battle on the morrow!"

I wasn't done. Sparks popped in my vision. Tomorrow, countless men would die in front of yet another cheering crowd. All because of me.

# Chapter Thirty-Eight

If I didn't know any better, I'd have sworn we'd just shown up to a football game. The North Inch had been transformed from a flat expanse of grassland into a medieval arena, complete with food, drink, and uncomfortable bench seating. Pennant flags flapped on wooden poles. As we traversed the crowd, men argued about whose "team" would win. Only, by "win" they meant "survive," and the only points tallied would be the number of bodies piled on the ground.

Henry scanned the benches. "We should have come earlier. We'll have to stand in the back."

Gavin laughed and clapped him on the shoulder. "Spoken like a true commoner." He led Henry, Donald, Shona, and me through the crowd to the front row of benches and proceeded to kick a group of peasants out of their seats.

"Gavin, no." My shoulders slumped.

He rolled his eyes and shooed the last man off the bench. "How would it look for the son of a duke to stand in a crowd of peasants?"

I didn't press it any further. There was no point. Besides, who was I to judge? Any minute now, dozens of men were going to die because of me.

We took our seats. Only a few feet and a cheap wooden barrier separated us from the battlefield.

Gavin snorted. "Five pence says someone falls in." He nodded toward the far side of the field where the river Tay served as the arena's fourth wall.

"Ten says it's a Cameron." Henry laughed. "Chattan's the Clan o' the Cat. Ye'll not find my kin goin' for a swim."

They laughed, but I didn't find it funny. How could they crack jokes two feet from a death pit?

He slung an arm around my shoulder and pivoted me to the right. "Look there." He pointed to an elegant manor house beyond the stadium.

Gilded arches capped whitewashed stone and four stories worth of stained-glass windows. Beside it, workers put finishing touches on a newly built grandstand, lining seats with velvet and tucking pillows against backrests.

"That's the Dominican Friary. The king stays in the summerhouse when he visits."

"Oh yeah?" I bobbed my knee.

He looked at it and sighed before taking my hands in his. "Ye've naught to be sorry for. If this works, ye'll have saved thousands o' lives."

I swallowed. "Tell that to the people who are about to die. Their families..."

His gaze dropped to our clasped hands. "Ye dishonor those men with such talk."

Startled, I eyed him, more than a little confused. He hadn't raised his voice, but condemnation tinged his words. "W-what?"

"Ye think them victims." His face flushed. "That given the option they'd rather lounge in bed than fight for kin and clan."

A gasp escaped my lips. Honestly, yeah, that's exactly what I thought. Who wouldn't prefer staying in bed to getting hacked with a sword? But that clearly wasn't the right answer.

He met my eyes and gave my hands a squeeze. "Men dream o' such a death. Dinna besmirch their sacrifice by claiming their glory for your shame."

I bit my trembling lip. Great. Now I felt guilty about feeling guilty. And dammit, were those tears? Fighting them back, I was determined to not cry, to not make this about me. I sucked in a ragged breath trying to calm myself.

His eyes softened. "It's kind o' ye to worry for them, but they need your pride, not your sympathy."

I nodded and forced myself to smile.

He wrapped an arm around my shoulder and kissed my forehead. "Dinna fash, love. I didna mean to upset ye. What I'm tryin' to say is that it's a good thing ye've done, and every man out there thinks the same. That's why they're here."

"Look, the king!" Shona's voice cut through our conversation.

The king led his entourage from the summerhouse to the grandstand, stopping midway to wave at the crowd.

Noise exploded around us—cheers and shouts and two-fingered whistles. "Long live the king!" everybody in the audience soon chanted.

I shouted along with them, but in truth, I was kind of disappointed. I had this image in my head of what a king should be—tall and stately with flowing robes and a glittering crown. Not a guy with a limp who wore a tunic and rolled hat. Granted, it was a very nice rolled hat—even from here, its jewels glinted in the sun—but it wasn't much different from what the men in his entourage wore. One of whom, I realized, was Sir David Lindsay.

A monk carrying a wooden bowl emerged from the depths of the priory, followed by a procession of some sixty to seventy men. No, not men. Warriors. They came with bows strung over shoulders and swords in their hilts. A few carried battle-axes, but none wore armor or carried a shield.

The procession came to a stop before the king, and the men dropped to their knees. The monk anointed their foreheads with oil or holy water or whatever blessed concoction he carried in that little bowl.

While the monk prepared souls, David Lindsay huddled with the Chattan and Cameron chiefs. I looked from them to the warriors to the king in his grandstand, and the oddest chill crept over me. Like *déja vu*, but different. Like the last thread of a web in which we were all connected finally fixed into place, and somehow, I was at the center of it all.

If I hadn't gone to meet the Chattan chief, I'd never have run into David Lindsay. If I never spoke with David Lindsay, the clans wouldn't be here now. And if it weren't for the king, Sean wouldn't have brought me here in the first place.

Then, as if I'd summoned him by thought, there he stood, Sean, talking with a group of freshly anointed Camerons.

I gasped. "What— What's he doing here?"

Henry's brow furrowed, and he scanned the men. "Who?" His body went rigid when he found him. "I guess he's come to fight." His lips curled into a scowl. "It's too good a death for him."

I gawked at the man I'd once called brother. I should have been relieved to see him there. If he died, so would all our problems. We could stay in Perth. We wouldn't have to fear Cameron attacks in the night. But even now, after everything he'd done, I couldn't shake the memory of what he'd once meant to me.

The crowd grew restless. Laughter and idle chatter morphed into sighs and mutters. A man behind me threw an apple core toward the arena. "Get on with it already!"

A woman stood on the bench, fist pumping in the air. "We came for a fight."

"Something's amiss." Henry gestured toward the sidelines. "Look at the chiefs."

The Cameron chief's arms cut through the air in wild jolts. The Chattan chief marched forward, his finger pointed like he meant to jab him in the chest.

Gavin fanned himself. "Something's amiss sure enough. I'm going to have the skin o' a farmer if they dinna get on with it."

Another ten minutes or so passed before the chiefs returned to their men. David Lindsay beckoned to a servant who brought him a speaking trumpet. He hopped over the barrier and into the stadium. The crowd roared with excitement.

"Are ye ready to see a battle?" He flashed a smarmy grin at the crowd.

The cheers grew louder, and people stamped their feet.

"I love ye, Sir Lindsay," a female called from the crowd. Somebody else blew a sharp whistle.

"And I love the good people o' St. Johnstoun!" He waited for a fresh round of applause to finish. "Which is why, I ken one o' ye will help us today."

Silence fell over the crowd. People turned to their neighbors with questioning eyes.

"As it stands, Clan Cameron has thirty men. Clan Chattan, only twenty-nine." Lindsay paced the edge of the arena. The crowd buzzed.

"Daft northerners canna even count." A woman behind us tittered.

The man next to her snorted. "I bet one of 'ems passed out drunk."

A portly man behind them leaned forward. "Or lost his nerve."

"Clan Chattan willna fight unless both sides are equal." Lindsay's voice reverberated through the speaking trumpet. The crowd booed and hissed.

"Cowards." An elderly woman crowed.

A bald man, a few rows over, rose to his feet. "Make the Camerons give up a man."

"Will any man come forth?" Lindsay paced the sidelines. "Will any man here prove their courage and fight on behalf o' clan Chattan?"

My gaze darted around the stadium, heart racing. This could be it! So long as nobody was stupid enough to throw themselves into the ring, nobody had to die. Warriors. Victims. It wouldn't matter. My conscience would be clean. And by the looks of it, nobody seemed too eager to volunteer. Lots of men looked around, or down at their laps, avoiding eye-contact, but not even one rose.

My eyes filled with happy tears. "They're not going to fight! It's over!"

I flung my arms around Henry, and he kissed me long and hard. I grinned when we separated. For all that talk about pride and choice, he was just as relieved as I was.

He put a hand to my cheek. "I love ye."

322

The way he said... No. Christ. He sprang to his feet and hopped the barrier.

It took me a second to process what happened. Then I was on my feet. "Henry, no!" I ran to the barrier. I had one leg over before Donald yanked me back and forced me to the bench.

"Let me go!" I fought against him.

"What are ye going to do, drag him off the field in front o' the whole damn town?" Gavin's voice held an edge I'd never before heard. "Ye might as well castrate him and have done with it."

I turned the full force of my fury on him. "You think I give a damn about his pride? He's going to die!"

"Fiona!" Donald's voice snapped with such command, it startled me quiet. "Ye have to let him do this. He's waited his whole life for the chance to avenge his kin. Ye canna take it from him now."

A sob escaped my throat. "He'll die!"

Shona squeezed between us and put an arm around me. "Think what ye went through when Mairi died. Imagine if it had been *all* o' us."

"But you stopped me..." My voice cracked. "Why can't we stop him too?"

Donald's gaze bore into mine. "Hal willna be stopped. The worst thing ye could do is send him into battle worryin' o'er ye."

"The battle will commence!" David Lindsay raised Henry's hand high in the air. "St. Johnstoun's own Henry Smith has agreed to fight!" Raucous applause filled the stadium.

Tears streamed down my face.

"Ye've naught to worry o'er." Gavin stared at me with earnest eyes. "He might not be any good with a pair o' dice, but he's great with a bow and even better with a sword. Wait an' see. He'll survive this."

The warriors crossed the barrier and rushed the field—Camerons on the left, Chattans on the right. The men on both sides stripped down to their saffron-colored under-tunics. Henry's, however, was white, and I thanked God for that small blessing. He'd be easier to see. For some reason, I was certain the second I lost sight of him; he'd be lost to me forever.

Clansmen checked their arrows and examined swords. Pipers tuned their bagpipes. The chiefs strolled among their men, and I braced myself, trying to come to terms with the fact Henry was about to die.

After a few minutes, the men seemed as prepared as they were going to be. A few shouted insults across the field—*mangey sons o' dogs* and *craven wee mousers*—but Henry remained silent. He just pointed his sword across the field at Sean.

Gavin laughed. "Seems he's got his eyes set on that one." He nudged Donald. "I'll bet ye a ha'penny he drops him within three kills."

A trumpeter entered the arena, and my limbs turned to ice—the battle was about to begin. I squeezed my eyes closed. *God, please, save him, please.* The trumpet blared. I opened my eyes to a sky raining with arrows and shrieks of pain as they found their marks. As if on cue, the pipers played, each a different maddening tune, and the men charged.

Henry ran into the fray, his top lip pulled back as he slashed and jabbed and cleaved his way into the mix. Then he disappeared, and I couldn't breathe. My eyes darted from hacked off limbs to severed heads to blood-soaked men thrashing and stabbing.

"Where is he?" I caught a flash of white. There, on his knees. A Cameron bore down. "No!"

My nails dug into my cheeks as my blood rushed in my ears. The Cameron swung. Henry dropped to his back and rolled. He kicked the man's knee. The Cameron fell, screaming and Henry plunged his sword into the man's chest. In a flash, he was off.

The metallic tang of blood hung so thick in the air my mouth tasted of pennies. Feet in front of me, a man I recognized as one of the tachsmen from Macintosh castle, took an axe to the face. A woman to my left retched while her husband whooped with glee.

Gavin's gaze swept the arena. "They're tired."

I scanned the field. Movements grew slower, faces more strained. Even the pipers slowed their tempo. Then the music faded altogether, and the men gradually stopped fighting. They lowered their swords and strode past each other without so much as a swipe as they returned to their respective sides.

My heart hammered. "Is it over?"

Henry sat on the blood-soaked grass. A young boy carried a bucket around to the men and offered drinks from his ladle.

Shona's eyes shone with pity. "Not until there's only one side left standin'."

The clans still seemed pretty evenly matched. Maybe ten on each side. Sean lived, but he didn't look good. Blood soaked his tunic as he paced in tight circles. Henry was tying a wound on his arm with a slice of filthy tunic.

One of the pipers played a long, soft note, and the men rose. The other piper played a slightly louder note in a different key, and the warriors unsheathed their swords. The music grew louder. The tempo increased, and the men charged. They hopped over bodies, bellowing their mighty highland roars. They slashed and blocked and buried their blades with renewed intensity.

Henry dropped two men and skirted a third. An axe flew past his head. I screamed, but he hardly seemed to notice. Blood gushed down the side of his face.

"He's lost an ear!" Shona shot to her feet.

I swayed in my seat, but he kept running.

"What's he doin'?" Donald ran up to the barrier for a closer look.

While everybody else settled into single-combat, Henry darted over bodies and swerved around fighting men like he was making his way through an obstacle course.

"He's goin' for that one." Gavin pointed to Sean, who stood frozen in place, staring in horror at the carnage before him.

The pipers' songs rose to a fever pitch. The fighting grew faster, more intense. Camerons fell at a rapid speed, and the Chattan men pressed their advantage. Then all of a sudden, the music stopped as the pipers threw down their bags and fought each other.

Henry broke through the melee and charged after Sean. He raised his sword, then seemed to say fuck it, turned, and ran. Henry gave chase. Sean zigged and zagged and doubled back in wide, arcing loops with Henry closing in behind him.

The Chattan clan anthem rang through the air. The piper swayed dangerously, his foot resting atop the chest of the Cameron piper he'd just killed. He played the song to the very end, and on his last note, fell down presumably dead.

Gavin laughed and slapped his leg. "Ten pence well earned!"

At first, I thought he meant the piper, but then I saw Sean had jumped into the river and was swimming away. Henry stared after him from the bank. In a fit of anger, he threw down his sword and chucked a rock from the river's edge. I couldn't tell if it hit its mark.

The battle officially had come to an end. Eleven Chattan men still stood, and only Sean remained of the Cameron fighters. Though I was pretty sure the Camerons wouldn't be too keen on welcoming him back after he proved himself such a coward.

"Is it really over?" I could barely breathe.

Gavin nudged me with his shoulder. "I told ye, ye had naught to worry about."

Shona put a fist to her chest. "He was so brave."

"He was." I rose, and a few seconds later, I was over the barrier and running through the field of corpses. Blood soaked into my shoes, and bodies squished under foot, but I didn't care. I had to get to Henry. I had to feel him in my arms, prove to myself he was really there. That he was alive and whole and still with me.

I screamed his name, and he turned from the river. Our eyes locked. Then he was running too, and when we reached each other, he took me into his arms and kissed me like he was ready to throw me down and have his way with me right there on the stadium floor. The audience cheered and whistled, and a few men shouted lewd suggestions, but I had no mind for any of them. Henry was alive. That was all that mattered.

We pulled apart, and I got a good look at him. His undertunic hung in tatters. Blood covered nearly every inch of him—and now covered me too. Gashes and punctures and abrasions coated his skin. His right ear was missing, and the sight of it filled me with a sudden, boiling rage. He had *chosen* this. He risked his life, knowing he had a child on the way. Knowing it would be damn near impossible for me to survive without him. Knowing I would have to watch it all.

"Fiona?" Henry's voice floated to me on the wind, tentative and unsure.

I balled my fists and met his eyes. "I'll *never* forgive you for this."

# Chapter Thirty-Nine

Two weeks had passed since the Battle of North Inch, and in that time, nearly every aspect of our lives had changed, and not just my rounding middle. First and foremost, the chief made Henry tachsman. Now Henry, Shona, Donald, and I lived in the highlands in the manor house on the hill and had the weighty, but wonderful task of caring for the entire village.

While Henry spent the last couple weeks with the chief at Mackintosh castle, Donald, Shona, and I had been busy sorting through the manor house, taking stock of assets, deciding what could be sold, redistributing food stores, and hearing villager petitions for house repairs.

The work was exhausting, but I was glad for it. It kept my mind off all the problems between me and Henry. At least it had until yesterday, when Henry returned home. Now I had to sit here and act like everything was business as usual, when I'd spent the last fortnight dwelling on what went down on that battlefield.

And what was worse, it seemed almost petty to bring it up now. Nothing I could say would change what he'd already done, and it had all turned out for the best in the end.

My posture stiff as I sat in the high-backed chair that had become my drawing room command station, I scanned my list. "Looks like Henry and Donald are on food stores. Shona and I will take this room." Nods circled around the group. I clapped my hands together. "Excellent, let's get it done."

Henry strode to my side. "Fiona..."

My stomach lurched. Talking to him right now was a struggle. Every word that came out of my mouth that wasn't me cussing him out was basically fake, and it was just too fucking exhausting not being real.

He shifted from foot to foot. "I wondered if we could...talk later?"

"I, uh..." I studied my list, trying to come up with an excuse to say no, but I couldn't think of anything reasonable. I gave him an awkward smile. "Sure. Later tonight."

He gave me a stiff peck on the cheek. "Tonight then."

As soon as he and Donald left, I groaned and slumped in my chair.

Shona raised an eyebrow. "Still fightin'?"

"We're not *fighting*. We're not *anything*." I scrubbed my hands over my face. "That's the problem."

"Can ye not just forgive him?" She gestured around the room, taking in the fine tapestries, silver sconces, and crystal decanters. "Look at all he's done for us."

I winced. "I know, I know. He's the saint, and I'm the shrew."

Her eyes narrowed. "That's not what I'm sayin'."

But it was what she was saying, and I didn't blame her. Thanks to Henry, every aspect of our lives had improved—our home, our wealth, our safety.

He hadn't just fought for revenge that day on the North Inch; he'd fought for us—he'd negotiated with the chief, his sword arm in exchange for five gold crowns, which he immediately returned to the chief, buying our spot on Chattan land.

The chief did him one better—he made him tachsman, a position that happened to be open, thanks to Darach and his penchant for strong ale and women. Apparently, he'd been the reason Clan Chattan was a man short that day. He'd gotten hammered at a brothel the night before and woke the next morning with two prostitutes in his arms and a hangover so crippling he couldn't bring himself to get out of bed.

I rose from my chair. "Never mind all that. Let's get started." I scanned the room. "How about the tapestry?"

Shona frowned. "Might get drafty without it."

"I can deal with a little cold." My hand drifted over the finely stitched cloth. "This'll buy thatch for half the houses in the village. Help me get it down."

She stuck her head into the hallway. "Donald! Have Henry tell the lads to bring us ladders."

In addition to the staff Darach employed, we'd taken on several additional servants. We didn't need them, but creating jobs allowed us to provide food and warmth to the poorest villagers without making them feel like charity cases. Only problem was, Henry and Betrys were the only ones with enough Gaelic to speak to them.

I picked up a pair of silver candlestick holders. "I'll make a pile on the floor." I jotted *candlestick holders, silver* on my itemized list. Shona held up a blue glass bottle.

I glanced at it. "Let's keep that one. It'll make a good vase."

She set the bottle on the table next to me. "The two o' ye should talk with the priest. That's how my mither convinced Da to make peace with me afore we left."

I wrote *bottle, blue—keep.* "Why? So he can tell me I'm ungrateful, and women shouldn't question their husbands?"

"Nay, ye numpty. So he can help ye learn to forgive." She leveled me with a hard stare. "Ye've naught to lose by tryin'."

I sighed and stuck my quill into the ink pot. "Just my temper, I suppose."

Two boys we'd taken on as servants, orphans named Horas and Daniel, came through the door with ladders.

I nodded at them in greeting as they leaned the ladders against the wall. "*Tapadh leat.*"

They shot each other amused looks, probably on account of my terrible accent.

"Oi, lads." Shona strode over to the twins. "Can ye go," she walked two fingers across her palm, "and get the monk?" She pantomimed prayer, followed by the sign of the cross.

One of the boys raised a brow in question. "*Sagart?*"

She snapped her fingers. "That's the word." She pointed to the floor. "*Sagart,* here."

With a nod, the boys took off.

She laughed. "Well, they're either on their way to get the monk, or they're off to give confession."

I groaned. "I wish you hadn't done that."

She shrugged. "I wish I didna have to share a house with a pair o' stubborn fools, but here we are."

An hour or so later, the monk stepped into the drawing room.

Rising from her spot on the floor, Shona bobbed her head in greeting. "I'll give ye some privacy, then." She flashed me an encouraging smile and departed.

I gestured for him to have a seat. "Excuse the mess. We've been busy, as you can see."

His eyes glowed with warmth as he sat in a wooden rocker. "Aye, I can indeed." He crossed his legs and leaned back in his chair. "I take it ye wish to discuss that weddin' we spoke of last we met?"

"No, umm, not today." I forced a smile. This was so damned awkward. I didn't even like this man, and Shona wanted me to spill my soul to him? Twisting my wedding ring, I swallowed. I supposed dealing with him was a small price to pay if there was even a chance it helped me get back to normal with Henry. "I wanted to ask your advice...about forgiveness."

The monk leaned forward. "A serious topic indeed. The Bible tells us if we canna forgive the trespasses o' others, the Father willna forgive our trespasses against him."

"Yeah, I get that." I smoothed the wrinkles in my skirt. "But what if you *can't* forgive somebody? What if you've tried, but you just can't get over what they've done?"

He put a gentle hand on mine. "Mayhap I'd be more help if ye told me what's behind this."

Biting my lip, I took a deep breath. "You know about the battle?"

"O' course." Fondness lit his eyes. "Your goodman's a bit o' a legend in the village—the brave warrior who fought for his clan and put an end to the tyranny of an oppressive tachsman." He grinned. "Not to mention all the money he's returned to the poor."

"Yeah, he's a regular old Robin Hood." My voice came out drier and more sarcastic than I meant it to.

His eyes widened. "You're not pleased with him?"

I flinched. Here it was, the part where I came off as the callous bitch for daring to be upset with the hero of the highlands. "Look, I *love* my husband. He's brave and caring, and he'd do anything for his family, but...he doesn't understand." My nails dug into my thighs. "It's not his fault...not really. Nobody here does." A bitter laugh worked its way out of my throat. "I thought I was doing pretty good, you know. Adapting. But I just don't think like the rest of you."

I knew I was rambling, and I knew the priest didn't understand a word I said, but now that I'd started, I couldn't seem to stop.

"Do you know how long it's been since I've had a full night's sleep? I keep waking in the middle of the night covered in sweat. Then last night, he rolls over and asks why I'm screaming, and I just want to punch him in his big, stupid nose." I held up my hands as if I were choking an invisible Henry. "Because of *you*, you asshole! That's why!" I was on my feet now pacing in front of the chair. "I mean, how could he do that? How could he risk his life? He's got a family to take care of!"

The priest nodded, a somber line between his brows. "I understand."

I stopped pacing and looked at him. Another horrible laugh escaped my lips. "How could you?" My hand went to the scar on my cheek where Sean had cut me. "The only person in the entire world who could possibly understand would rather mutilate me than accept my choices."

The monk's eyes rounded. I must have looked insane to him.

I slumped back into my seat. "I'm sorry. I know how crazy—"

"Not at all." He leaned forward. "And I *do* understand."

"It's only going to get worse." My voice hitched. "He's tachsman now. It's his job to fight." I dropped my head into my hands. "I can't go through this again. It's tearing me apart. I'm scared all the time." Tears welled in my eyes, and my voice cracked. "What am I supposed to do?"

He placed a hand on mine. "You're not alone, and ye have options."

"Options?" I scoffed. "What? A convent?"

He chuckled. "That's not what I meant."

"Then what?" I blinked through tear-glossed eyes.

He bit his bottom lip as if hesitant to answer. Then he took a deep breath and set his jaw. "You can go home," he said in a clear, midwestern, American accent.

I scrambled out of my chair and jumped behind it. The monk rose and raised his hands in a calming gesture.

"Stay away from me." I squeezed the sides of the chair, ready to pick it up and throw it at him if need be. "I'll scream."

"Please." The monk took a step back. "I just want to talk."

I glanced at the door. It was cracked open. Somebody would be here in seconds if I shouted. "Don't move." I nodded toward the chair behind him. "Sit and keep your hands where I can see them."

The monk lowered himself into his chair. I inched backward and grasped blindly along the wall until the cool metal of the fire iron met my hand.

He quirked a grin as I walked toward him with the weapon held before me. "Bit excessive for a man of the cloth in his sixties, don't you think?"

I flashed him a smile that was all teeth. "The only reason your brains aren't all over the floor right now is 'cus I've got questions." I clapped the fire iron against my palm. "So talk, time soldier."

He rubbed his chin. "Time soldier? Never heard it called that before."

"How many of you are there?" I raised the fire iron. "How did you find me?"

His eyes met mine. "I believe you were the one who found me, actually."

I wrenched the fire iron back like a baseball bat. "Stop with your bullshit. It's not a fucking coincidence you're here."

He held up a hand. "You're right. It's not. I came because of your husband."

"Thought you could take him out and it'd be easier to get to me? Just try it." My teeth bared. "He'll have your guts for bowstrings."

"I don't want to kill you or your husband." He kept his voice calm and level. "I'm a scribe. An information gatherer." He put a hand to his soft, round belly. "Do I look like a soldier?"

I eyed his rotund physique, unwilling to let my guard down, even if he appeared about as threatening as a teddy bear.

"I've been in this era for forty years." He sighed as if they had been a particularly weary forty years. "I go wherever a major historical event will come to pass and document the details for the U.S. government." He gave a tentative smile. "Assuming you don't bash my skull in, I'm set to return home with my data in less than a month."

I hesitated, then lowered myself into the chair, fireiron still clutched in my hands. I didn't quite believe him, but his explanation was so unexpected, I wanted to hear more. "Why here? Why Henry?"

His brows raised in surprise. "Because of the Battle of North Inch, of course. There are gaps in our knowledge, but one thing that's well documented is a smith named Henry volunteered to fight." He leaned forward, his eyes alight with excitement. "But why? What made him risk his life? Who was this man? I had to find out, so I came to the place history records noted he'd eventually be and waited."

His cheeks puffed with a wry grin. "You can imagine my surprise when he showed up weeks early with a wife who sounds like she stepped out of an American disco."

My grip loosened on the fireiron, and I goggled at the monk in disbelief. "You're saying Henry's known? In our time?"

He shrugged. "I mean, he's no Napoleon or Genghis Khan. I'm not surprised you weren't aware of him, but he is known. Hell, he's a character in *The Fair Maid of Perth*." He grinned. "But you, it seems, are no Katherine Glover." He waved off his previous statement as if it were inconsequential. "Scott always did play fast and loose with the history, though."

"What are you talking about?" My brow furrowed. "Who is Katherine Glover?"

"Just a character in a book." He leaned forward. "Now if you don't mind, I have some questions for you?"

I gave him a silent nod. My head spun. Henry was a historical figure because of a battle I'd caused. How was that possible? Did that mean I'd always been fated to come here? Or would the battle have somehow happened anyway? And who the fuck was this Katherine bitch?

"You can't be one of us." He looked me over. "They'd never have sent you without extensive dialect training. So how did you get here?"

I gave a bitter laugh. "My best friend shoved me through a time portal."

His eyes grew wide. "A rogue? What's her name? Or is it a he? And which portal? Chicago or D.C.?"

"*His* name is Sean." I ran my hand over the scar on my cheek. "And the portal was beneath Edinburgh castle."

"You came through the British portal?" He jumped to his feet. "You have no idea how valuable your information will be!"

"No!" I waved my arms, eyes wide. "I've got no information. Nothing of value." I shook my head. "Leave my name out of your reports. I've already got the Scottish government hunting me. I don't need the American government trying to kill me."

He chuckled. "An asset like you? Please. They'll probably give you the Medal of Freedom." His eyes lit. "This is remarkable. Truly remarkable!" His grin widened. "For you too! Just think. In less than a month, you'll be dining on pizza and beer instead of bannocks and ale."

"Are you out of your mind?" My knuckles whitened around the fire iron. "I can't go with you."

"Of course you can!" His brow arched. "You can't possibly want to stay here?"

"I have a life here. I'm married. I..." My hands pressed to my belly.

"Have a child on the way?" Pity filled his eyes. "Your sister-in-law told me." His brows knit, adding an air of sternness to his jolly face. "You need prenatal care. An obstetrician. Not some backwoods midwife who doesn't know to wash her hands."

The baby...With modern medicine they might be able to fix whatever damage the poison had done.

"Don't you want your child to have a better life than this?" He rubbed his hands down his thighs. "An education? Vaccines? A place to grow up without plague and violence?"

I did. I wanted all that and more for my baby, but I also wanted my child to have a father. "What about Henry?" My voice grew high-pitched and defensive. "Doesn't he deserve to raise his own kid?"

The monk gave me the most piteous look I'd ever seen. "We both know he won't survive long, and once he's gone you'll be booted to one of those hovels in the village and have to live off spoiled oats and rancid fish the rest of your life."

The fire iron shook in my hands. My voice cracked. "Do you know something? What happens to Henry?"

"I only know what history tells me." Strain furrowed his brow. "This peace between the Camerons and Clan Chattan... It won't last, and like you said, your husband's a tachsman now."

I stared at my lap and fought against the threat of tears.

The monk rose. He put a hand on my shoulder. "I'm sorry. I know it's not easy to hear."

I didn't look at him. I was too scared to see the truth in his eyes. "When do you leave?" My voice rasped with unshed tears.

"On Samhain." He tugged his cloak strings taut and tied them. "Until then you can find me at the miller's house. I'm lodging with him until I go."

Eyes downcast, I waited for the click of the door to tell me he'd gone, so I could crumple into a ball and cry my eyes out.

"Oh, uh, pardon." The monk's returned brogue drew my attention. I looked up to see him scuttle past Henry, who stood in the door, staring at me in horrified silence.

My mouth fell open, but no words came out.

Henry's jaw tightened. He stormed toward me, pulling a small object from his cloak. "Take this with ye when ye leave." He slammed the tiny form onto the table before storming off.

Hands trembling, I reached for the small object—an exact replica of Gran's ring, identical, except for the missing prong that had broken several years back. Tears fell from my eyes.

The sound of breaking glass and crashing objects sounded from the hall.

Shona shrieked. "What are ye doin'?"

"Hal?" Donald's voice warbled with worry.

I slid the ring onto my finger and walked in a daze toward the sounds of chaos.

Shards of glass and shattered pottery littered the foyer floor. A trestle table lay knocked on its side, and dust motes hung in the air next to a fist-sized crater in the wall.

Donald stared out the open door, his hand clutching the roots of his frizzy hair.

I dug my fingers into his shoulders. "Where is he?"

His already pale skin turned ashen. "He started destroyin' the place. Put his fist through the window. I've ne'er seen him like that."

"Did he say where he was going?" Urgency made my voice come out hard and sharp.

He shifted from foot to foot. "Nay, he just belted his sword and ran outside."

"His sword? Fuck!" I sprinted toward the door, hopping over floor detritus, and nearly knocking Donald on his ass.

He yelled after me, but I kept running, down the hill and into the village. I cut a sharp left at the river, slipping and sliding on muddy banks until I reached the miller's house. I ran inside and found Henry pinning the monk to the wall by his throat, sword drawn.

"Please." The monk's voice squeaked with terror. "I'm a peaceful man. I want no quarrel."

"If ye wanted no quarrel, ye should have thought better than to interfere with a man's wife!" He squeezed the monk's neck, causing him to hack and sputter.

I darted into the house. "Henry, stop!"

Peering at me over his shoulder, a sneer darkened his face. "Come to watch your lover die?"

I straightened to my full height. "He's *not* my lover, but by all means, murder an innocent man."

He banged the hilt of his sword against the wall, next to the monk's head. "Enough o' your lies! I *heard* ye."

"No." My fists clenched. "You heard a few minutes of conversation you couldn't possibly have understood."

His face reddened. "I understood plenty. Ye mean to abscond with this blaggard come Samhain."

I put my hands to my hips. "I don't mean to *abscond* with anyone, and if you'd bothered to ask me, you'd know."

His brows knitted together. I met his gaze and held it. The monk whimpered.

"Make your choice." I folded my arms across my chest. "Are you the man of integrity I married or a murderer?" He didn't lower his sword, but he also didn't disembowel the monk, which I took as a good sign. I tilted my head toward a table in the corner. "I'll be over there when you're ready to hear the truth."

Henry stood frozen. He didn't seem to know what to do. Putting down the sword meant giving up control, but despite his recent stint in battle, he wasn't a violent man by nature.

I met his eyes. "You can always kill him later."

The monk squeaked. "I'd rather ye didna."

Turning, I headed across the room.

Henry glowered, but he sheathed his sword and followed. The monk fell to the floor in a boneless heap. I gave him a second to catch his breath before I called to him. "You too, monk. We've matters to discuss."

His features crumpled, looking for all the world like he'd rather do anything else.

"And enough with the accent." Though I spoke to the monk, my eyes found Henry's. "He has to understand. All of it."

The monk stopped halfway to the table, shaking his head and waving his arms in silent, adamant protest.

I shook my head right back. "We're doing this."

Henry snapped his head toward the monk and leveled him with an evil stare.

At Henry's gaze, the monk scuttled into the chair next to me. "Think before ye speak." He spoke so quietly I could barely make out his words. "There are consequences ye canna begin to understand."

I snorted. "Hate to break it to you, buddy, but it's little late for all that. I already caused a battle."

He looked from me to the monk, clearly confused and all the more agitated because of it. He leaned across the table until his face was mere inches from the monk's. "Whisper to my wife again, and I'll split that tongue like the snake ye are."

I cleared my throat. "If we could save our threats for the end of the discussion?"

Throwing himself back into his chair, he turned his head away from me. "Say what ye have to say."

"All right, I will." I sat tall and cleared my throat.

Only, I didn't quite know how to begin. The last time I told Henry I was from the future; it hadn't exactly gone well. I glanced at the monk, hoping he might help, but he looked ready to spring from his chair and slap his hand over my mouth.

I took a deep breath. "So...I take it you heard the monk offer to take me with him."

A growl vibrated in Henry's throat. "Ye admit it, then?"

I pressed my lips together, refusing to be drawn into a battle over semantics. Leaning forward, I waited for him to meet my eye. "Where is it, exactly, you think he plans to take me?"

His brow furrowed, and his mouth contorted like he thought I had asked him a trick question. "How the sardin' hell should I ken?"

"Think." My gaze bored into his. "You must have heard him speak."

Henry's eyes glazed, and he seemed to be searching his memory. His fist curled, and he banged it on the table. "I didna come here for riddles."

I tapped the monk's arm. "Say something, in your *real* voice."

The monk blanched. "I'll not be a party to this. I took an oath."

I raised an eyebrow. "Would you rather he kill you?"

He gritted his teeth. "Fine." He met Henry's eyes. His lips curled into a mirthless smile. "My name is Eugene Bossie. Pleased to meet you."

Henry's mouth parted. He licked his bottom lip. "Is he your kin?"

"No, but we come from the same place." I held his gaze. "And the same time."

# Chapter Forty

A blank expression clouded Henry's face. He didn't speak. He didn't move. He didn't so much as blink. But then his face flushed red. "Ye expect me to believe he's here to take ye back to your fairy world?"

I shrugged. "Sort of."

He let out a derisive snort. "The place where the houses have waterfalls, and ye fly through the air on iron birds?" His lip curled. "Either ye think me daft, or you're addled in the head."

"Ask him!" I turned to the monk. "Tell him when you were born."

Eugene's eyes glistened. "Can't you see it's pointless? It's too much for him."

"I don't care." I didn't have it in me to tell any more lies. Not now that it had come to this. "Tell him."

His chest expanded, and his cheeks puffed with air. "1952."

In a flash, Henry's sword tip dug into the monk's throat. "I willna be made the fool by the likes o' ye."

"God dammit, that's enough!" I slammed my palm on the table.

"Avert your eyes if ye canna bear it." His lips parted, baring his crooked tooth. "This ends now."

"I can prove it!" Eugene's voice rang loud and squeaky. Sweat dripped down his forehead, and his eyes welled with tears. "I can prove I'm from the future. Please."

"If this is some sort o' trick..." Henry applied more pressure to his sword, and the monk's skin puckered. After a heated pause, he slowly lowered his weapon.

Sagging in his chair, he took a deep, ragged breath. "Saline solution. I'll need you to mix a cup."

I scrambled to my feet and scoured the shelves for ingredients.

"Use the water in the kettle." His voice carried to me from the table. "Salt cellar's by the oats."

I didn't know what he planned or how saltwater played into it, but I hoped to hell his demonstration was convincing because I didn't think Henry would be stopped a third time.

I placed the cup of saltwater in front of him.

He looked at Henry. "What I'm about to do might frighten you. Please don't kill me because you're startled."

The vein on his forehead pulsed. "Dinna fash, monk. If I kill ye, it'll have naught to do with fear."

The monk nodded. "Very well." He put a hand to his eye and popped out a contact lens. He repeated with the second eye and extended a palm for Henry to see.

Staring at the blue-tinted lenses, his lips parted. "What—" His gaze raised to the monk, who stared back with a pair of chocolate brown eyes. Face ashen, Henry jumped to his feet. "What devilry is this?"

I rose and put a hand on his arm.

Eyes wide, he swatted it away. "Ye *are* a witch!" He stumbled back. "You're a witch." His breathing grew rapid. "I loved ye. How could ye—" A moan escaped his lips, and he clutched his chest. "Oh God, I loved a witch."

"Henry, look at me." I tried to keep my voice calm despite the fact he'd just used *love* in the past tense. "I'm not a witch. You know that." I stepped toward him.

He drew his sword. "Stay back!"

My hands shook, and my mouth turned to sand at the sight of his furious, contorted features. This man who was supposed to love me, who had sworn to stick with me through good times and bad. Yet there he stood, ready to impale me. Something inside me broke at that moment.

"Kill me. Go ahead. It's easier than believing me, isn't it?" The sword trembled in his hand. I marched forward until the tip hit my belly. I held his gaze. "Do it. If you really think I'm a witch, kill me, kill our unborn child."

There was this moment, this pause, where neither of us seemed to know what would happen next. His eyes filled with tears. So did mine, and we stared at each other, unblinking. His expression shattered. He dropped his sword and stumbled back, his eyes wide and anguished. Though, I wasn't sure if the reaction was because of what he'd almost done or what he couldn't do. His back hit the wall, and he slid down it, crumpling to the floor in a heap of tears.

Nodding for Eugene to leave, I joined Henry on the floor.

"What am I supposed to do?" His voice vibrated with sobs. "I dinna ken who ye are anymore."

"You do." Weariness filled my voice. "You just never believed it." I hugged my legs to my chest. "If it makes you feel better, what he did wasn't as scary as it looked."

His mouth and eyes rounded in horror. "He pulled the blue from his eyes, Fiona! Ye saw him."

I traced my knee with a finger. "Those were contact lenses. They're like tiny, colored spectacles."

His nails clawed at his cheeks. "And your stories? They're true as well?"

I nodded.

Squeezing his eyes closed, he palmed his forehead. "The wee mummers ye keep in a box?"

It took me a second to realize he meant television. "Yeah...but it's not quite like you think."

He bit his lip. "And the glass candles with no smoke or flame?"

Pressing my lips thin, I nodded. "All of it."

A vacuous silence settled between us. We both knew the truth now. All that was left was to decide what to do about it.

After a long time, or maybe a short time that just felt really long, Henry's voice cut through the silence. "Will ye leave with him?"

I swallowed. "Are you asking me to go or to stay?" My bottom lip trembled. "Or are you asking what I choose?"

His jaw jutted. "Does it matter? It's always what *ye* choose. Ye've never given a damn what I have to say."

I sucked in a breath. "What *I* choose?" I clambered to my feet. "I don't remember you asking my opinion before you jumped into a death pit."

"Ye should be grateful!" He shot to his feet, fist to his hips. "I saw a chance to improve our lives, and I took it."

"Grateful!" My voice hit full volume. "Don't act like you did that for me. You wanted revenge, nothing more."

His hands balled into fists. "What if I did? Is it not my right to avenge my brothers?"

"They're dead!" All that rage I'd been carrying around for weeks erupted at once. "They're dead, and we're alive! Did you even stop to think what would happen to me and the baby if you died?"

"I provided for ye. I made sure ye'd be cared for!"

"That's not what I'm talking about." I threw my hands up. "How do you not get it? You watched your brothers die, and it haunted you for twenty years, but you expect me to be fine, because you secured me rent?" I pounded my chest. "It would have destroyed me, Henry, and if you can't understand that, maybe it's better we part ways now."

He blanched. "I see." His voice held a dazed, eerie quality. "I hurt ye. Now ye have to hurt me."

"No." My jaw set. "It's more like, you hurt me, and I'm terrified if I stay, I'll get hurt again."

He stared at his feet.

"That's only part of it, though." My hand drifted to the tiniest hint of baby bump rounding out my middle. "In my time, they might be able to help the baby. They might be able to fix whatever damage the poison's done."

"I see." He nodded, eyes still downcast.

I rested a hand on his shoulder. "I'm not saying I've made up my mind. It's just...we have to think about what's best for all of us."

"Well then, I guess ye have a decision to make." He knocked my hand off his shoulder. "I'll not waste my time tryin'

344

to sway ye." He headed for the door, pausing in the threshold. "Fiona...if ye really think the right choice for our family is to not be a family anymore, dinna tell me. Just disappear into the night and let me pretend ye never were." He melted out the door.

I didn't go after him.

# Chapter Forty-One

"Fiona...Fiona!" Shona's voice cut through my muddled thoughts. I looked up from my uneaten trencher to find her studying me, brow furrowed. "I've been talkin' to ye for the last five minutes. Did ye not hear me?"

Snoop Dogg, patiently waiting at my feet in hopes of scraps, booped my leg with his nose. With a sweep of my leg, I nudged him away and gave her a weak smile. "Sorry. I guess I'm a little distracted."

Her features softened. "Worried about tomorrow?"

With far more force than necessary, Henry cracked his tankard on the table.

I pretended not to notice. "I've never celebrated Samhain before. I don't know what to expect, and we've got all those people coming to the house..."

This was true, but also so far down my list of worries, it barely counted as a problem. Right now, my focus was on the letter I'd just spent the last two hours writing. On how inadequate it felt. On how a paper goodbye seemed like such a shitty way to tell someone how much you loved them.

"Dinna fash, Fiona." Donald spoke through a mouthful of fish. "Samhain's a lark!"

She smacked the back of his head. "Dinna go tellin' her that. She needs to ken what she's up against." Her mouth twisted into a grim line. "It's a dangerous night. Ye must take care."

Despite the claw of anxiety ripping through my core, I couldn't help but laugh. "So, it's a good time, but I might get murdered?"

They nodded.

346

She shuddered. "Or worse. Spirited away."

"I see." I squeezed my lips together, in the hopes of suppressing how funny I found it they took this hocus pocus stuff so seriously. "But what is Samhain, exactly? I mean what are we celebrating?"

From what I'd gathered, it was a sort of hybrid holiday— Halloween and New Years and a Saint's Day, all rolled into one— but I'd been here long enough to know any inferences I made based on my own version of these holidays were bound to be wrong.

Henry's meaty hand slapped against the tabletop. "I'd think *ye*, of all people, would ken that."

My gaze snapped in his direction. I hadn't expected him to speak at all and definitely not with that tone of bitter irony. Ever since that day at the Miller's house, we'd shared maybe a hundred words between us, and those had been stiff and overly polite.

I raised an eyebrow. "Why is that?"

His fingers flexed and curled. "On Samhain, the dead walk with the living. Time has no meaning. Past, present, future— they're all one." His eyes darkened. "A foolish lass like yourself might find herself carried off by wicked creatures and taken to a different world."

My mouth parted, and I exhaled a tiny gasp. All this time, I'd thought he hadn't believed me because he *couldn't* believe me. Without technology or sci-fi books or even a rudimentary understanding of physics, how could he possibly wrap his head around a concept as complex as time-travel? But here he was, describing that very thing, just in his own terms, with his own traditions surrounding it.

"Not just spirits." Shona leaned forward, eyes wide. "But the Fair Folk, as well."

Donald burped and wiped his mouth with a sleeve. "And witches."

She shrugged. "Better to be killed by a witch, than taken to the land o' the Good Neighbors."

"Ye think?" He stroked the peach fuzz on his chin. "I dinna ken. A witch kills ye, you're dead. One o' the Fair Folk take ye, ye might escape."

"Aye, but then ye find your way home, thinkin' a year has passed, only to learn a hundred years have gone by. All your kin dead. The world new and different." Horror shone in her eyes. "Better off dead, ye ask me."

"I don't know." I smiled at my lap. "A new world might not be *all* bad."

"But not good enough, aye?" Henry slammed his tankard down and shot to his feet. His chair toppled to the floor behind him. He left it there, along with his trencher of uneaten food as he disappeared out the dining room.

Shona nodded toward the door swinging closed behind Henry. "What's with him?"

Sighing, I placed his trencher on the floor for Snoop to eat. "He's not too fond of faeries at the moment."

~ * ~

Samhain didn't technically begin until sunset, but preparations began at dawn. The men hustled to the field at first light—any crops not harvested by sundown had to be left as tribute to the nature spirits. Cattle had to be brought in from their summer grazing, and those not needed for breeding slaughtered. And pyres had to be built throughout the village for the night's bonfires.

Meanwhile, the women cooked and cleaned and set up for the evening festivities, tasks I assumed would be straightforward, but quickly learned were not. My first blunder occurred when I tripped over a milk saucer somebody had left on the floor. I carried it into the kitchen, muttering to myself in irritation, and one of the kitchen girls yanked the dish from my hand and shouted wildly at me in Gaelic. I raised my palms in the universal gesture of confusion, but she didn't stop her tirade until Betrys came to my rescue. With a few words, she calmed the girl, refilled the saucer, and carried it out of the kitchen.

I followed behind her. "What was *that*?"

She placed the saucer on the floor in a less obtrusive spot. "The milk's for the Cat Sith. Ye leave it milk, it'll bless the house. Ye leave it none, and your cows'll run dry."

After nearly cursing the clan to a year without butter, I decided I better stay out of everyone's way. Besom in hand, I headed to the drawing room to sweep. Innocuous enough, right? Wrong.

When Shona saw me, she damn near tackled me to the ground. "Ye canna sweep or dust on Samhain! Ye might sweep away a soul!"

She snatched the besom, and I raised my hands in surrender. "My bad." I glanced at the pile of dirt by my feet, and all my compulsive neat-freakery took over. I couldn't just leave this mound of filth sitting there. Not when we had guests coming. "It's not really Samhain 'til the sunsets, though, is it? It won't hurt to just sweep that one pile..."

"Sure, sweep away your goodman's dear ol' dead da." Her voice was a master's study in sarcasm. "I'm sure he willna mind."

I opened my mouth to reply, but then I decided there wasn't any good defense against accidental soul-sweeping, so I said nothing. Following Shona out of the room, I closed the door behind me. This, apparently, was also a grave mistake.

"Doors and windows have to stay open." She shooed me out of the way and re-opened the door. "Otherwise the spirits might get trapped."

I wrinkled my nose. "Are the ghosts supposed to be solid?"

She squeezed her eyes closed as if praying for patience. "Come with me afore ye do real damage." Dragging me into the dining room, she didn't let go until my butt was firmly planted in a chair. "Dinna move." She disappeared and returned a few minutes later with Betrys and an armful of turnips.

The girls pulled their knives, and each selected a turnip, so I did the same. I sliced from the bottom, thin as I could, like Mairi taught me.

Betrys laughed. "What are ye doin'?"

She'd cored hers like an apple, which to me seemed very strange, because turnips don't have cores. I raised a puzzled brow. "What are *you* doing?

"We're makin' tumshie lanterns, ye wee fool." She held up her turnip, revealing the single most hideous jack-o-lantern I'd ever seen.

The thing looked like a demonic shrunken head. Still, this was something I could do, so I nabbed a fresh turnip and got to work. Only, carving a turnip was a lot more difficult than Betrys made it seem, because turnips are hard as shit and not at all easy to hollow.

Moments after my knife slipped, and I damn near cut off a finger, Shona steepled her fingers. "Fiona, love, I can see you're ill-prepared for tonight, and there's a few things I think ye should ken."

I picked out a loose chunk of turnip flesh and slopped it onto the table. "Such as?"

She glanced out the window. "Dinna stray from the house."

Betrys took another turnip. "Or too far from the fire."

Shona wiped her knife on her apron. "If ye hear footsteps behind ye, dinna look back."

"And if ye see a fetch, dinna interfere with it. Let it go about its business." Betrys carved a jagged-toothed smile into her turnip.

My nose wrinkled. "What's a fetch?"

Shona moaned. "A spirit. A ghost come through the veil."

Lowering my gaze, I resumed my carving, mostly as an excuse to hide my expression, which I was sure must be wavering between annoyance and amusement. I finished coring my turnip and moved onto the face.

I cocked my head. "Do you hear that?" There was a definite rumbling noise. It grew louder. The floor began to vibrate. "Do you get earthquakes here?"

Betrys grinned. "It's the drovers." She waved us to the window.

We looked out to see hundreds of shaggy-furred, long-horned cattle being driven along the path at the bottom of the hill. It was a hell of a sight, and I suddenly understood Granda's affection for old western flicks, and his claim the Scots were the first real cowboys.

A hand tapped on my shoulder from behind. I found Horas and Daniel standing behind me. Horas handed me a burlap bag, and the two took off. A heavy weight settled in my stomach, as I realized who must have sent the package. "I'll be back in a minute."

I ran to my room and shut the door, trapped souls be damned. After ensuring nobody had followed me, I emptied the bag onto my bed, an hourglass and a folded piece of paper tumbled onto the comforter. The note read: *Two hours after the bells, head to the lightning split oak and head east. I'll be waiting.*

~ * ~

The house was cold, dark, and sticky damp, casting an air of vulnerability over everyone and everything. I didn't like it. Not one bit. I never realized how much comfort the hearth fire provided until the servants snuffed it out. This was new to me. In my time here, nobody'd ever put out a fire. Even on the hottest days when nobody cooked, the most we'd do is bank it...until today.

We collected our turnip lanterns, candle nubs, and unlit torches and headed to the village. The sky was dark and purple gray. The last sliver of a setting sun peeked through dense patches of fog that slithered across the grass like wraiths.

Horas and Daniel, who wore drums strapped to their chests, beat a mournful dirge as Henry led us through the mist. An ominous mood fell over the procession, as if we were on our way to fight a war, only this battle was for our souls and our only weapons were lights not yet lit.

As much as I didn't believe in supernatural nonsense, I had to admit, it was hard not to get swept up in the ambiance. Between the wind and the fog and the drums and the darkening sky, every childhood monster from under the bed seemed suddenly real. The drumbeat became my heartbeat. The wind prickled my skin as the shadows took on faces. The cold crept in, and I feared I might scream with fright.

Marching to the middle of the village, we joined the rest of the clan. Unlit pyres ran down the center of the communal field, and we formed a chain around them—waiting, watching, and reverent, as the darkness consumed the last sliver of sun.

Henry strode forward and knelt before the center pyre. The drums silenced, and the click, click, click of steel on flint cut through the quiet. Sparks scattered and glowed like fireflies. Then a flame, small at first, but bold and orange against so much black.

The men dipped their torches into the flames and lit the other pyres. Soon a village of faces reflected in the firelight. The scent of lavender filled my nose, and a peaceful sensation settled over me.

Henry led the torch-wielding men on a trek around the village perimeter, protecting it and purifying it with flame. We women lit our own torches and candles stubs so our tumshie lanterns glowed demonic, frightening away any lingering spirits, and as one, we parted to return to our homes and light our hearths for another year.

A half hour or so later, villagers filled our house to the brim. Servants rushed in and out of the drawing room, bringing food and water and apples for bobbing. Clansmen and women lined up for ale, and I waited with bated breath for Henry to ring the bell, a final measure against angry spirits and the beginning of my countdown.

I hovered near the table where I had placed the hourglass earlier that day, waiting for the bell to chime. As soon as it sounded, I took a deep breath, and flipped it over. I watched as grains of sand fell way too fast.

The bell chiming gave way, and fiddle music cut through the air. Donald joined me, grinning his puppy dog grin. "Ye going to give it a go?" He nodded toward a group of teens drowning themselves in a pool of apples. "Get one, and it's good fortune for a year."

I rested my arm on his shoulder. "Tonight, I think I'll make my own fortune."

A girl emerged from the tub with an apple clutched between her teeth. Everybody cheered. Grinning, she wiped water from her pale, freckled face. With great care, she carved off the apple peel in a spiral, closed her eyes, and tossed it over her shoulder. The kids gathered round, pointing and discussing in rapid Gaelic.

I nodded toward the group. "What's that about?"

He scratched his belly beneath his tunic. "Whatever letter the peel resembles will be the first letter o' her future husband's name."

Giggles erupted from the crowd, and a young boy squeezed from the group, face pale as a corpse.

I laughed. "I take it he's the lucky bride-groom?"

Shona sauntered over and wrapped her arm through Donald's. "Dance with me, husband."

The two disappeared into a massive reel in the back of the room, and I glanced at the hourglass. Already, half the sand had fallen. My hands grew clammy, and I wiped them on my dress. I looked around for Henry and found him sitting by the hearth with a group of villagers.

He seemed to be keeping his spirits up, talking, even laughing with the people around him, but his eyes didn't crinkle the way they normally did, and his skin looked sallow.

I wondered if I should join him or if that would make things harder.

"Fiona, there ye are!" Betrys stumbled over, her face red and eyes glassy. "Ye made this ale?" She lifted her cup, and hiccupped. "A fine ale, indeed," she announced to the room, though nobody was listening. She swayed on her feet. "Anyway, the *taibhsear's* doin' readings. Come on."

"The what?" I stumbled forward as she dragged me toward a crowd surrounding an old woman.

"She's a wise woman, ye ken, a seer." Pushing up on her tiptoes, she gazed over the crowd. "She's tellin' fortunes."

"I don't know…" I knew fortune-telling was bullshit, but the last thing I needed was some doom and gloom prophecy rattling around in my head, making me question my already difficult choices.

"Dinna be daft. It's tradition." Dragging me to the edge of the group, she announced something to the crowd. People scattered, and I was left next in line. She grinned. "Prerogative o' the tachsman's wife."

The person currently getting her fortune told—a woman about my age with a pock-marked face—burst into tears. She pulled her wimple over her blotchy eyes and ran off. I gulped. That didn't bode well. Not that I believed in this sort of thing.

I took a seat on the floor across from the seer. Between us sat two bowls, one filled with eggs, the other full of murky, snotty water. She emptied the water bowl over her shoulder, and it took all my self-control not to yell at her for making a mess of my floor.

A nearby woman filled the empty bowl with fresh water, and the old lady gestured for me to take an egg. I drew one at random and placed it in her gnarled, liver-spotted hand.

Closing her eyes, she held it in her palm, and rocked back and forth as if in a trance. Then she stilled. Her eyes popped open. Her lips, sunken with no teeth, split into a grin, reminding me very much of the turnip lanterns.

She tugged a pin from her dress and poked a hole in the egg. Tipping it over the bowl, she watched as the egg whites swirled and danced in the water.

She narrated as she studied the shapes, and Betrys translated as she went. "Lightning. The devil. A knife." She scrunched her eyes. "Baptism."

I raised a brow at Betrys. "Any of that make sense to you?"

The seer tossed the egg onto the floor, and Betrys asked her something. She answered in a grave voice, the effect somewhat undermined by the lisp that came with her lack of teeth.

Nodding, Betrys turned to me. "She says Auld Clootie will come to ye during a storm, but through death, ye'll be reborn."

A shiver worked its way up my spine. "That's...uh...comforting." I rose and took a deep breath, inhaling

354

the scent of lavender. I looked around. "Is that you? I keep smelling lavender."

Betrys sniffed the air. "I dinna smell anything." She clapped me on the shoulder. "I'll get us some drinks."

I glanced at the hourglass. Empty already. Henry was wrong, I realized as I flipped it back over. Tonight, time was all that had meaning. He sat alone now, quiet in front of the hearth flames.

My heart ached, and I decided I didn't care if he wanted me near him; I needed this right now.

Straightening my spine, I walked over to him, and with every step, the scent of lavender grew stronger.

He didn't look at me or say a word when I sat, but he put his hand on top of mine. In silence, we watched together as young girls in horribly clashing tartan gowns threw balls of blue string into the fire and asked Gaelic questions of the hearth.

Eventually, Betrys careened over to us. She cocked her head. "I was supposed to get ye an ale, wasna I?"

My mouth twitched in amusement. "It's fine. I'm not thirsty."

She thrust a finger in the air. "Chestnuts! Ye need chestnuts!" Stumbling off, she returned a few minutes later with a handful of nuts. She gave me two. "Go on then."

"Sure." I wasn't hungry but put one to my mouth anyway.

She cackled. "Nay, dinna eat them. Stick 'em in the fire."

Henry waved away the handout before him. "Betrys, nay."

She snorted. "Ye never used to be such a picklepuss. Have a little fun, aye." She inclined her head toward me. "Put 'em in."

I dropped the chestnuts onto a flaming bit of turf, not sure what I was supposed to look for. Nothing happened. They just sat there, silently smoldering.

She clapped her hands. "Aww, look at that. Not a peep out o' the wee nuts." Her face glowed with pleasure. "See, I told ye, brother, nothin' to fuss about. Yours'll be a happy marriage." She grinned. "I can tell ye its true. When me and my goodman did it, ours hissed and spit like wildcats. And he was a right arse, let me tell ye."

He rose. "Excuse me."

She trotted after him. "Brother, what's amiss?"

Sighing, I stared at the chestnuts side-by-side in the flame. After today, none of this would matter anyway. I watched the chestnuts until they were charred black and nearly indistinguishable from the peat.

Fresh grief crushed down on me, but I maintained my resolve, and checked the hourglass. Less than a quarter of the sand remained.

Quiet and unseen by the distracted partygoers, I slipped from the room. After creeping up the stairs, I rifled in the dark beneath my bed until I found the letter I had written earlier that day.

Tucking it into my pocket, I headed to the kitchen, stole a torch, and disappeared out into the night.

# Chapter Forty-Two

This was a mistake, and I was an idiot, and ghosts were real, and I should have stayed home, and oh my god I was going to fucking die in these woods. I couldn't see anything. Just a halo of torchlight illuminating the next step forward in a sea of black. And all around me noises—twigs crackled, brush rustled, owls screeched, nightbirds squawked, and some creature to my left chittered and thumped.

But I had to do this. This was my last chance, and I'd never forgive myself if I let it slip by. So, I kept marching forward. Even when a pine marten screeched like a woman being murdered. Even when a pair of eyes peeked at me from the bushes. Even when something small and furry brushed past my leg. I didn't stop, and I didn't look back.

Eventually, a light appeared in the distance, a glowing, orange orb that seemed to hover of its own accord. I followed it to a small clearing east of the path. Half convinced I'd find a coven of witches or some other-worldly being, I crept to the tree line.

But when I peeked through brush, it was just Eugene standing there, looking so supremely awkward, he couldn't have been anything other than human. In one hand, he held a crossbow, and in the other a book. His eyes were all screwed up and squinty as he read by torchlight.

I strode toward him. "You'll ruin your eyes reading in the dark."

Pocketing his book, he grinned. "Good thing you showed up, then. Any problems finding the place?"

I gave a nervous giggle. "No. Wish I'd thought to bring one of those, though." I nodded at his weapon. "Not that I'd know how to use it, but still…"

He flashed a fatherly smile. "Woods give you a fright?"

I held my thumb and forefinger a centimeter apart, and he laughed. I scanned the clearing. "Seriously, though, I can see why you do this on Samhain. Nobody's going to be walking around these woods tonight."

"That is the hope." His gaze lifted to the sliver of moon in the sky, his expression wistful. "Shouldn't be long now."

"Then I'd better give you this." I handed him a folded sheet of paper. "For my granda. Can you send it to him when you get back?" A lump formed in my throat. "His address is at the top." My voice warbled. "He's probably really worried—"

He cocked his head. "You're not coming?"

I bit my lip and shook my head, scared I'd cry if I tried to speak. God, this was so much harder than I thought it would be. I'd come to terms with losing Granda long ago, but now that it was due to choice instead of circumstance, the wound felt fresh and raw as it ever had.

He met my eyes. "And you want me to send this letter to your grandfather…?"

I nodded.

He laughed. "Ye really are a stupid cunt, aren't ye?"

"What?" I studied him through confused, teary eyes.

I took a step back. Then another. My heart raced. I didn't know what was going on, but I damn sure didn't want to stick around and find out. I turned to run and slammed into a wall of human flesh. An arm squeezed around me. The torch was plucked from my hand, and I screamed.

My captor tightened his hold, smothered my face into the fabric of his tunic. "Listen to me." When his voice rumbled in my ear, my legs gave out, because I knew that voice, and I knew what it meant. "We have to go with him." Sean's voice rumbled in my ear. "It's the only way we live."

He loosened his grip, and I gasped at the sudden influx of air. It took me a second to focus, then I looked at him and pleaded with my eyes for him to hear sense. "No, Sean. That's not how—"

"Eugene's already tried to kill ye once. Slipped ye some food laced with poison." His voice was low and urgent. "He willna hesitate to shoot ye with that bow. Do ye understand?"

I understood. Better than Sean did. Because there was no way this man and his time-traveling henchmen were going to let us live just because we came along peacefully. They'd get whatever information they could and drop our bodies in the closest river.

"I mean it, Fi." Sean grasped my chin. "He's an expert marksman. There's no chance of escape, even in this dark."

I nodded, because what else could I do?

His eyes bored into mine. "Ye have to trust me. I have a plan."

Then to my surprise, he let go. I immediately figured out why—Eugene had his bow trained on my heart. Above him, his torch crackled between two tree branches, casting splintery shadows across the bald spot on his head.

"I take it Sean's explained the rules." He spoke in a lazy Scottish drawl. "Behave yourself, and ye'll live. Irritate me, and ye won't."

I gritted my teeth. I wanted to lunge for him, to beat the smug, self-satisfied look right off his face. This murderer. This baby killer, who dared smile at me. But I had to be cool. I had to be smart. Because there was no way in hell I was going with him and getting shot with a crossbow didn't seem the best way to opt out of the trip.

I looked around. The woods were my only hope. If I could make it to the trees, I'd have a chance, but getting there before his arrow got to me was going to be tricky.

"Why should I believe you?" I shifted an inch to the left. "You're a murderer and a liar." Twisting my heel, I let my toes gradually follow, sliding myself another inch to the side.

He shrugged. "I'm whatever I need to be. Though I canna say I was too pleased when they sent me after you lot. I was supposed to be on my way to colonial Jamaica."

"So everything you told me was a lie?" Angling my body away from the torchlight, I scooched another inch. "You're not a scribe? Not an American?"

He grinned. "I'm just a man with a trustworthy face and a talent for tongues." He raised the bow to the level of my head. "Now if ye'll kindly stop tryin' to slink into the woods, I'd prefer not to kill ye."

I froze. Sean stepped closer. A crack rang through the woods, and the portal appeared in the middle of the clearing. Without the metal frame, the lightning bolts looked stranger and more ominous than before. How stupid I'd been to even consider going home. If the baby still lived, it certainly wouldn't after going through that portal. I remembered the way my body shifted and expanded in impossible ways. How sick I'd been. How my eyes had frozen in their sockets...

Sean nudged me toward the portal.

"No." I clutched his arm. "I'm pregnant, Sean. Please!"

He froze for a second before setting his jaw. "Better to lose one o' ye than both." His hand clamped around my wrist, and he pulled me toward the portal

I dug in my heels and fought against him, but he kept dragging me. "I'm sorry." His voice was raw with regret.

The real Sean was in there somewhere. Deep down, he was that same kid I'd grown up with, just in over his head, and trying to do what he thought was right. If I could just make him see...

"Then help me!" Tears streamed down my face. "We can find another way. You can still make this right."

"They'll keep coming." His voice cracked. "It'll never end. Ye have to trust me, Fi. It's better this way."

"No!" I yanked and kicked and twisted against him. He dropped his torch and seized me with both hands.

"Enough!" Eugene lunged toward us. "We've no time for this. March your arses through that portal, or I'll—"

He stopped mid-sentence and squinted into the woods. There was this twangy noise, and he stumbled back, pulling the trigger of his crossbow before he collapsed to the ground, an arrow jutting from his chest. He moaned, but whoever he'd shot in the woods wailed louder. Never in my life had I heard such a sound. It was pure agony, pain on a level I couldn't imagine.

"We have to help. Someone's hurt." I struggled against Sean's hold, but he didn't let go. He just stood there frozen, gaze bouncing between the woods and the monk and the portal.

Fire spread from the dropped torch. It crackled and smoked. The heat grew intense. The portal continued to crack and zip and zap electric. A figure stumbled from the darkness. A black silhouette that lurched forward, heaving terrible, monstrous groans.

The fire caught hold of some dry, brittle bush and sparked into light, revealing Henry's gaunt, ashen form, an arrow lodged in his kneecap. His face twisted in agony as he forced himself forward, dragging his wounded leg behind him. He drew an arrow from his quiver and tried to aim at Sean, but he seemed blinded by pain and couldn't focus. He collapsed.

Sean wielded a dirk he'd kept concealed beneath his tunic.

"No!" I lunged for it, but he shook me off.

He tore after Henry. "It's because of him! Ye'd be home right now if it weren't for him."

Sprinting after him, I put on speed. I was close, but not close enough. His arm drew back, ready to strike. I launched off the ground and onto his back. We tumbled. Sean rolled. I flew and slammed against a tree. My skull cracked against stony earth. Disoriented and aching, I scrambled to my feet, desperate to get to Henry.

"Fiona?" Sean's voice vibrated with fear. He clutched his thigh near his groin and stared up at me from the dirt, his skin ghastly white in the firelight. He moved his hands from his leg, revealing the handle of his dirk jutting from his thigh.

I looked around, not sure what to do. The fire was spreading, and there was no way I'd be able to get both him and Henry out of here. "You have to go through the portal! It's the only way."

Sean met my eyes. A sad smile darkened his face. "There's no point without ye."

Looping my arms around him, I tried to heave him off the ground. "Don't say that. Just go!"

"Fiona, no." His head lolled back, and his eyes met mine. He reached up to touch my cheek with one hand. With the other, he yanked the knife free of his leg. He grunted. Blood hemorrhaged from the wound.

Horrified, tears streamed down my face as I watched Sean's life pour from his wound.

"I love ye, Fi." His voice sounded far away and slurred. "Always have." Then he slumped to his side, dead.

I screamed.

The fire crackled, and smoke choked my lungs. I ran to Henry, sobbing and hacking and desperate with loss. He lay passed out on the ground.

I smacked his face. "Wake up! We have to go!"

He didn't stir. I searched for something that might help me drag him from the fire but found nothing but smoke and flame and lightning flashes from the portal.

"Help!" The fire grew hotter, spread closer. "Help!" It was pointless. Nobody would help us. Not on this night. Not in these woods.

Squatting near his head, I slipped my arms under his back and up through his armpits. I straightened and heaved. He budged, but not far or fast enough.

"Ye canna save him." The monk coughed and hacked. His voice came out a wheeze. "But we can save each other."

Ignoring him, I focused all my energy on Henry. I dragged him another foot. Then another. Sweat poured from my forehead. My muscles blazed. Another foot. I could do this. I wouldn't give up.

"Push me through the portal." The monk moaned. "I'll tell them ye've died. I promise. If I dinna make it back, more soldiers will come."

I kept pulling, dragging Henry. My skin blistered. My lungs seized.

"Please." Desperation ripped at the monk's voice. The portal zipped out of existence, and he wailed. "Ye have to kill me. Please! Dinna let the fire—"

A rumbling noise drowned the last of his words. I couldn't see through the smoke but caught the whinnies of fire-shy horses.

"Help! Over here!" I gave Henry one last tug and collapsed to the ground in a coughing fit.

~ * ~

I don't remember much after calling out. Just vague flashes of men and smoke and a horseback ride through the black of night. But I'll never forget the moment we reached the bottom of the hill to find our house lit by torches. Every man, woman, and child had braved the outdoors on Samhain night to wait for us and see us safely home. It dawned on me, then, just how brave our rescuers had been. They hadn't just faced fire and night to save us—they'd plunged themselves into a world of spirits and demons and all their worst fears. Yet still, they had come.

Now, sitting in my drawing room chair, burned and raw and staring at my own worst fear, I knew I had to be just as brave. Henry lay prone on the floor. Betrys and Donald, and all our servants stood to the side, while the rest of the clan prayed in the hall.

Shona circled Henry's body, assessing. She crouched and prodded his knee. "Bone's shattered. The leg'll have to go."

I clawed the arms of my chair. Everything in me wanted to shout, *No! Find another way*. Taking his leg was just as likely to kill him as heal him, but there was no other way.

Shakily, I rose from my chair and joined her, as she ticked items off on her fingers. "Sheets, an axe, a strap, and—"

"Wine," I cut in. "Or vinegar. And boiling water. You have to boil everything." A coughing frenzy took over, and I bent over and hacked.

"Sit." Shona jutted an imperious finger toward my chair.

I ignored her. "Your hands." My voice came out choked and scratchy. "Anyone who touches him has to wash with the strongest soap."

She frowned. "We dinna have time for that. What if he wakes?"

I winced. "Then he wakes, but it has to be done. All of it."

She hesitated. Her mouth parted like she meant to argue, but then her eyes met mine, and she snapped her mouth closed. She nodded to Betrys. "Ye heard her. Tell 'em what needs done."

Betrys relayed the orders to the servants in Gaelic.

A minute later, the room cleared as everyone collected supplies. I crawled over to Henry and sat beside him. I squeezed his hand, memorizing his face in case this was the last time I'd see him alive. I brushed a strand of hair from his face and cried.

Then, like before, the room smelled suddenly of lavender and a calm settled over me. I sniffled and wiped my tears.

"She won't let you leave me. Not yet," I whispered in Henry's ear before I kissed his forehead, then got out of the way, so Shona and Donald could do what needed done.

The surgery happened fast. Donald swung the axe, and Shona cauterized the wound with wine and a heated sword. His flesh sizzled and smoked and gave off the smell of cooking meat, but thankfully, he didn't stir. She wrapped Henry's stump in boiled bandages, and that was it. She called for Horas and Daniel to carry him to bed and announced only time would tell what happened next.

I made to go with him, but she stopped me with a hand to the back. "Wait." She gazed at Donald. "Can ye bring us soap and water and fresh clothes?" She snapped her fingers. "Oh, and that yellow ointment on the table aside my bed."

He disappeared and returned several minutes later with the supplies. "I'll go check on Hal." He shut the door behind him, all but a crack so any lingering spirits could slip out if need be.

Stripping, I washed the dirt and blood from my skin and hair.

Shona put ointment on the worst of my burns. "I canna say how it'll go with Henry, but he didna bleed out. He's strong as any I've—"

"Don't worry." I slinked into the fresh tunic. "He'll live."

Her eyes lit with hope. "How can ye be so sure?"

I breathed in deep. "Can't you smell the lavender?"

# Chapter Forty-Three

My granda once met the devil himself.

It happened right there on Normandy's shore. Amid bullets and blood, Auld Clootie appeared. But Granda, he knew what to do—he shot off his horns and shamed that devil right back to hell.

Growing up, I must have heard that story a thousand times, but now, as I sat at the foot of my best friend's grave, I thought I finally understood what it meant.

Our lives were about to change again. Any minute now, the Mackintosh would arrive to sentence the monk, and there was a good chance he'd boot us from our home while he was at it. A tachsman had to be able to fight, after all, something hard to do with a stump for a leg. But whether our home was the house on the hill, or a tiny cottage covered in thatch, I knew we'd be fine. We had faced our devils, and like Granda, we would carry on.

As I waited for the tachsman at the foot of Sean's grave, I held a quill clutched in one hand. I stared at the picture I'd drawn—a wheelchair I hoped to have made for Henry. "What do you think?" I held it up for Sean. He didn't answer. "You know, Mairi was a lot chattier than this. You're going to have to do better."

Choosing a clean sheet from my stack, I started a new picture. Only this time, I didn't know what to draw. I began with a curve, added a line, a few ovals, scratched a few wavy marks and teased them together with the tip of my quill. Before long, a baby boy emerged from the page. With a sigh, I ran my finger over his face, smearing the ink into a cloud of questions.

If my baby lived, what kind of life would he lead? Would he be happy? Healthy? Would he resent me for the choices I'd made? These were the questions that had plagued me in the weeks leading to Samhain. Gift or curse, I would give my baby the world. The question was, which one?

For the longest time, I couldn't decide. I went back and forth, torturing myself with every argument and counterargument I could come up with. By the time Samhain Eve rolled around, I still didn't know. So, I did the only thing I could think to do. I holed myself up in the drawing room and wrote a list of pros and cons. I filled three pages before I realized life couldn't be reduced to items on a list, and the whole endeavor was pointless.

That was when Donald had come in, searching for his hammer.

*I picked up the hammer from where it sat on the floor and handed it to him. "Can I ask you something?"*

*His eyes widened. "O' course." He followed me over to the chairs, and we sat.*

*My hands twisted in my lap. "What did you want most growing up?"*

*He laughed. "For a time, I wanted to be a knight's squire, if that's what ye mean."*

*"No." I shook my head. "Not like that. I mean, were you happy? Did you have everything you needed?"*

*He studied his hands. "I had plenty. We never went hungry. I always had clothes and shoes. My parents made sure my sisters had dowries, and I had enough to join the armorer's guild."*

*"But...?" I raised an eyebrow, because I'd heard the unspoken word at the end of his sentence.*

*He winced. "My mither and faither werena a good match. Da was too fond o' the drink, and Ma was quick to call out his worth as a man." Flushing, he gave an awkward, embarrassed smile. "My mither wanted to leave Da and join a convent, but e'ry time she threatened to go, he'd get her with child. She hated him for it and us too."*

*I put a hand on his arm. "I'm sorry."*

*He shrugged. "It's fine. Like I said, we had what we needed. It's just..." He stared off into space. "Ye asked what I wanted back then." He clasped his hands together. "I suppose, I just wanted to see my mither smile."*

*Mouth crooking at the corner, he gave a soft chuckle. "There was this lad who used to live down the road. John Threadbare, we called him, on account o' his tunic bein' more patches than cloth. He and his ma used to beg e'ry day in front o' the Black Friars. My mither used to watch 'em out the window and tell us how lucky we were not to be beggars like them."*

*Donald shifted in his chair. "Thing was, when I saw 'em, I didna see myself as lucky at all, 'cus his mither had her arm around him and was smilin' down on him. I remember thinkin' to myself, I wouldna mind skippin' a few meals, if just once my mither would look at me like that."*

*He ran his hands through his frizzy hair, making it stand on end, and grinned. "I'm sorry. Ye probably didna want to hear all that."*

*"No." I flashed him a fond smile. "It helped. It really did."*

*"What about ye?" His eyes sparkled with interest. "What did ye want when ye were a bairn?"*

*"Well..." I laughed.*

*My childhood hadn't exactly been normal. I'd grown up in a bar, playing poker with Granda and darts with old John. By six I could make a bank shot with the help of a stool, and by eight I could mix a perfect Manhattan. But would I have traded my life at the Caledonia Club for something more normal? Pool cues for tap shoes and happy hour for a Girl Scout troop? Hell no! I had a great life. How could it not have been with Granda and Gran, Old John, the two Roberts, and my best friend Sean?*

I knew my answer then. It was so obvious. I had to stay where my baby would be most loved. If we went home, we might have Granda for a few years, but after that, we'd be alone. Here though, my child would have a mom and a dad, Donald and Shona, Betrys, and a whole clan full of cousins. He might not grow up with video games and hot water showers, but he would have what mattered, and that was the best any mother could do for her child.

~ * ~

"Welcome." I dipped into such a low curtsey my knees cracked.

The Macintosh dismounted from his horse. Behind him, thirty or so men did the same.

The chief addressed his entourage. "Wait here. This willna take long." Handing his horse's reins off to a servant, he flashed me a fatherly smile. "There's the lass." He planted a kiss on the back of my hand. "I trust you're well?"

"Right as rain." I groaned internally at my own words, because that was a weird thing to say for a girl my age, no matter the century.

The chief laughed and patted my hand. Servants opened the doors for us, and we headed inside. "How's your goodman? I was sorry to read o' his misfortune in your letter."

I guided the chief into the house. "He's doing really well. His fever broke a few days ago, and his pain's much better."

"Good." He nodded, his face a blank mask. "We've much to discuss."

I kept the smile plastered on my face, even though his words filled me with dread. I didn't care where we lived or what job Henry had, so long as we were together, but he had a difficult enough time coping with the loss of his leg, and it killed me to think how it would impact him if he lost his title too.

I led the chief down the hall to Henry's room.

We entered, and Henry dipped his head in a facsimile of a bow. "Laird."

I offered the chief a seat and opened a window. "Forgive the smell. We've been treating the wound with vinegar. Works well, but the stink's enough to make your eyes water."

"Vinegar, aye?" Glancing at Henry's stump, the chief's mouth turned down at the corners. "Shame, lad. Ye were a fierce fighter. I had a lot o' hopes makin' ye tachsman."

He stared at his leg and nodded. "But now I canna fight..."

"Of course you can." Both Henry and the chief looked at me like I'd lost my damn mind. My cheeks flushed. "Fine, maybe you can't *fight*, but who says you need to?"

"Fiona." Weary exasperation filled Henry's voice. "A tachsman must provide military service."

"I'm aware." I directed my attention toward the chief. "But wouldn't you agree, there's more than one way to serve?"

Henry squeezed my hand, not in solidarity, but in warning. I was toeing the line of impudence, and he didn't appreciate it.

"Why dinna ye let the chief and I speak alone, aye?" He gave me a hard stare.

The chief held out a hand. "Hold on. I'd like to hear what she has to say."

I flashed Henry a *nana-nana-boo-boo* grin before addressing the chief. "Well, I'm no war expert, but it seems to me you need two things to win a battle—weapons and men. Am I right?"

The chief stroked his beard. "A bit simplistic, mayhap, but a fair enough assessment."

"Good, because my husband can give you both." I beamed with pride. "He's the finest armorer in all Scotland. He can make you shields, swords, mail, you name it."

I glanced at Henry, who stared pointedly out the window. "But more than that, my husband is a leader. Have you ever heard of men running into the woods on Samhain night? Willingly? No. Because that's insane, but they did it for him." I placed a hand on his good knee. "Now just imagine what they'd do for him on a battlefield."

I paused to let the impact of my words sink in. A pregnant silence settled over the room. Henry squeezed his eyes closed as if preparing for a blow. My own hands trembled.

The chief burst out laughing. "God in heaven, lad." He slapped Henry's shoulder. "I dinna ken if I should keep ye as tachsman or hand the title straight to her."

I stared, eyes wide and hopeful.

"Do ye ken what happened when we came through the village?" The chief put a hand to his belly. "The whole clan came out, and they made it quite clear they wouldna take kindly to me replacin' your goodman. Said ye'd done a lot o' good for 'em since Darach's been gone."

He grinned. "Asides, I've already agreed to maintain ye for life. I see no' reason I shouldna get my money's worth out o' ye."

Squealing, I flung my arms around the chief. "Thank you!"

He stiffened, clearly not used to such outlandish displays of affection, but he settled into the hug and patted my back. When I finally released him, he rose. "Well, lad, enjoy your winter, because come Spring I expect ye to be layin' bricks for a forge." The chief looked to the door and sighed. "Now onto less pleasant business." The laugh lines disappeared from his face. "Where is the prisoner?"

I rose. "I'll take you to him."

"No need." He ran a hand over his bristly cheek. "Just have him brought to the village center. I'll hold trial in a half-hour's time."

~ * ~

"Trial" might have been a bit of an exaggeration. This was more like a reckoning. Despite Shona's best attempts to save him, Eugene's condition had deteriorated to the point where he now resembled a breathing corpse. Infection had set in, and he couldn't bring himself to sit upright, let alone stand and defend himself. Not that I imagined anything he said would have made a difference. The trial hadn't even begun yet, and the executioner was already sharpening his axe.

The chief stood in the center of the communal grounds, surrounded by his retinue and members of the clan. Next to him, Eugene lay unconscious in a wheelbarrow. Betrys and I stood toward the back, and when the chief addressed the crowd, she was kind enough to translate.

"He's listin' the monk's crimes." She ticked them off on her fingers. "Attempted murder, heresy, and..." She paused for a second. "Treason."

I raised an eyebrow. "Treason?" Murder, sure. Heresy, eh...maybe. But treason?

Betrys shrugged. "Well, he's a Cameron isna he?"

I nodded, even though that wasn't true. Regardless, I didn't see the connection.

"He was tryin' to reignite the feud, wasna he? That's an attack on the king's peace." Betrys smirked. "Chief says that makes it an attack on the king himself."

"Right..." Sarcasm dripped from my tongue. She laughed. We both knew the charge had nothing to do with the king, and everything to do with punishing Camerons.

The chief spoke some more. Then he paused for a second and scanned the crowd.

Betrys rested an arm on my shoulder. "He wants to ken if anyone will speak for the monk."

Silence rippled across the field. The chief waited an obligatory moment, before he continued.

She grinned. "He's sentenced him to a traitor's death."

I narrowed my eyes. "What's that mean?"

A vindictive smile spread across her face. "First, he'll be hung, but they'll cut him down afore he dies. Then they'll cut off his manhood and slice open his gullet. They'll set his intestines ablaze while he watches. After that, they'll cut off his head, and chop his body into quarters to be spread about the village."

"Oh, wow." I swayed on my feet. "I guess it's time for me to go, then."

"After all he's done to ye?" Betrys's eyes bulged. "Ye dinna wish to see justice served?"

I let out a bark of laughter, but it held no humor. "Nope. Sure don't."

I might have spared myself the sight of Eugene's torture, but the sound of it followed me home. Part of me had wondered if he'd feel it, sick as he was, but the sound of his screams killed that delusion fast. He endured every second of that pain, I was sure of it. I didn't experience the same level of empathy I had for Coira. After all, the fucker had poisoned my child and lost Henry his leg. Still, I'd have preferred it if they'd just chopped his head off and been done with it.

I was all set to go inside, when his screams went silent. In that moment, something dawned on me, and the realization felt important. I ran to Sean's grave.

"You were going to die anyway." I dropped to my knees beside him. "If the knife hadn't killed you, they'd be setting fire to your guts right now."

Sean's voice rang in my head. *Well then, I suppose ye expect me to thank ye for my murder…*

I brushed a few leaves off his grave. "Murder? You fell on your own knife!"

*Aye, because ye jumped on me.* His voice sounded as petulant as the time I snitched on him for decapitating my Barbies. *Either way, I'm still rottin' in the ground because of ye.*

"Maybe so." I smiled at the grave. "But you're talking to me now, aren't you?"

*Hmph.* He never could admit when he was wrong, but I knew that noise meant he couldn't disagree.

Picking up a loose stone, I tossed it on his grave. "See you next Samhain, Shrek."

Then I went inside to join my family.

# Epilogue
## Six Months Later

Well defined abs, it turned out, meant precisely dick when contending with ten tons of baby. Getting out of bed was now a choreographed event that involved heaving onto one side, doing a sort of sideways pushup, and groaning like a dying man as I rose onto the swollen slabs of meat I once called feet. I don't know why I imagined getting out of a bathtub would be any easier.

I gave it one last shot. Clasping the sides of the tub, I heaved with all my might. No good. The lower half of my legs dangled over the edge, and every time I tried to hoist myself up, my belly knocked into my thighs, making it impossible to straighten.

"Shona! Betrys! Somebody, please!" A few seconds later the door creaked open, and I heaved a grateful breath. "Thank God. Can you help me?"

I couldn't see my rescuer as my back was to the door, but there was no mistaking that booming chortle. "Stuck are ye?" Henry rolled over in his wheelchair, took in the sight of me, and laughed even harder. "You're like a poor wee turtle flipped about on its shell."

I splashed him with bath water. "It's not funny."

"O' course it isna." Grinning, he made his way to the foot of the tub. "Give me your hands." He took hold, braced his foot against the side of the tub, and yanked. It might have been my imagination, but I could have sworn I heard a suction cup noise as my ass dislodged. I wrapped my towel around myself as best I could, but the scant cloth was no match for my bulbous midsection. I looked at my protruding belly, then up at Henry, and burst into tears. Fucking pregnancy hormones.

"Aww, lass." He hauled me into his lap. "What's amiss?"

I sobbed into his shoulder. "We're getting married today, and I'm a big, fat, bloated mess."

He stroked my hair. "You're beautiful."

I moaned. "Why didn't I listen to you? We should have waited until next year."

"Nay." He tucked a bit of loose hair behind my ear. "Ye had it right. Mairi would've wanted the union blessed afore the bairn comes. Asides, now we'll have a priest here for the baptism. It's just good sense."

Sniffling, I wiped my eyes, the pregnancy hormones disappearing as fast as they'd come. "You're right. I guess I'm just stressed."

His arms tightened around me. His gaze dropped to my now enormous rack, and a heated, greedy expression crossed his face. He kissed my neck, and his hands roved.

I put my hands to his chest. "Henry! How can you even—"

"I like ye fat." His kisses worked their way up my neck, across my chin, to my mouth. And then the pregnancy hormones were back, only this time they'd gone all X-rated. Our kisses grew deeper, more intense. He wheeled us toward the bed.

"It's wed her, *then* bed her. Not the other way around." Betrys leaned against the door jamb, arms crossed and lips smirking.

With a groan, he dropped his forehead to my shoulder. "Aww bugger off will ye?"

"Afraid not, brother." She strode into the room. "A bride needs time to prepare."

"I've got the dress." Shona's voice sounded from the hall. When she stepped into the room, her eyes went wide. She shrieked and hid my dress behind her back, revealing her own, significantly smaller baby bump. "Out! She doesna want ye to see her gown."

Heaving a martyr's sigh, he ran a hand over my belly. "It's a good thing I've already gotten ye with child. With these two hens cluckin' about, it might be our only one."

Reluctantly, shakily, I rose, adjusting the towel as best I could.

"Off with ye." Betrys shooed him with a flick of her fingers. "The chief and the priest are in the tavern with the tachsmen. Ye should be attendin' to them anyway."

"Aye, aye." He waved her off as he headed toward the door.

"Have Horas bring in the cinnamon ale if you run low," I called after him. A frown tugged on my lips when he didn't respond. I hated being away from the tavern with so many people in it. In fact, since the day we'd finished construction, turning the drawing room into a clan pub, I hadn't missed a single shift, even if I had to turn over the heavy lifting to Donald.

I looked at Shona and Betrys. "Do you think he heard me?"

Shona shoved the bundle of cloth in my arms. "Never mind if he heard ye. Try on the dress."

I grinned and slipped on a clean shift before draping the dress over top. I spread the skirts out wide and ran my hand down the front. "It's beautiful."

I'd insisted on white, despite everybody telling me blue was much more suitable. But this was my wedding, dammit, and if I was going to waddle down the aisle, I was going to do it looking like a white whale...you know, the way God intended. Still, I wanted to do Mairi proud, so to make up for my pauper's white, I'd ordered real gold thread from a shop in Edinburgh, and Betrys had embroidered the skirt with gold roses.

"Are ye nervous?" Betrys smoothed out a few wrinkles on the back of my skirt.

"Of course I am." I laughed. "You ever tried planning a wedding with baby brain?"

"Baby brain?" Shona's voice squeaked.

"Oh, just wait." I nodded at her baby bulge. "The bigger that thing gets, the dumber you'll get."

This was true. Just yesterday I'd transferred ale from the pot to the barrel, only to realize I'd forgotten to add the malt and had just been boiling water for four hours."

"It'll be fine." Betrys spoke with all the confidence of a person with no stakes in the outcome.

Nevertheless, I hoped she was right. I wanted this wedding to be perfect. I knew it was silly to put so much stock in a ceremony when we'd technically been married for almost a year now, but it mattered. This time it was about choice, and after all that had happened, the fact we still wanted to stand up and pledge our lives to one another meant more than anything I could think of.

Betrys pulled a chair in front of her. "Sit."

I did as she instructed, and she unrolled my hair, which we'd twisted around rags the night before. She yanked and tugged at my head, ripping out strands of hair along with the cloth.

"I've got somethin' for ye." Shona tossed me a small package she must have smuggled in with the dress. "To borrow, mind."

I opened the paper to find a blue ribbon strung with a single fresh-water pearl. I gasped at the unexpected and thoughtful gift.

She blushed. "Ye said ye needed somethin' old, new, borrowed, and blue, right? Well, the ribbon's new, and the pearl was my mither's, so ye've got it all in one necklace."

I opened my mouth to thank her, but a twinge in my belly startled me from speech.

Her face fell. "Ye dinna like it?"

"No, I love it." I put a hand to my belly. "I just got a pain is all."

Betrys stopped teasing apart my curls and peered over my shoulder. "It's not your time, is it?"

"No!" Despite how adamant my voice sounded, it dawned on me I didn't have the slightest clue how to tell when I was in labor. I looked to Shona in a panic. "Right?"

She pursed her lips. "Is this the first o' your pains?" I nodded. She scrutinized my face. "How badly did it hurt?"

I shrugged. "Not much. Mostly just surprised me."

"Then you're fine." Her gaze was reassuringly steady. "Sometimes ye'll get light pains a fortnight or so afore the bairn's ready. It's your body practicin' for what's to come."

Betrys topped my head with a wreath of flowers. "Shame. Henry owes me a ha'penny if the bairn comes in the next three days."

My jaw fell open. "You're betting on my uterus?"

"Aye." She circled the chair to examine her hair handiwork from the front. "Why shouldna I?" She turned me so Shona could get a look at the back of my hair. "What d'ye think?"

Shona let out a squeal. "You're ready!"

~ * ~

Nope. Not ready. Not even close. I should have double-checked that we made enough food. What if the baby decided to jump on my bladder, and I pissed myself in the middle of my vows? And Christ—I clutched my stomach—this pre-labor bullshit was starting to get really annoying. These little fake contractions were happening more and more frequently and some of them were actually starting to hurt.

"I must say, I've never seen a weddin' quite like this." The chief stared around the village's communal grounds, accompanied by a pair of pipers in full regalia. "But I'm honored ye asked me to take part in it."

"I've never seen a wedding quite like this either." I smiled despite the maelstrom of anxiety blowing around in my head. "I'm glad you agreed to give me away. It's an important tradition where I come from."

This was true, of course, but it wasn't my only reason for brooking a few of the medieval wedding customs. Normally, the bride and groom were expected to make a grand procession through the village, picking up guests like pied pipers en route to the church. However, as we had no church, and I didn't want Henry to have to trek through the village on his peg leg, which he found painful to walk on at length, I decided to have him wait at the altar like the grooms in my time.

"Are ye ready?" The chief extended his arm.

Putting a hand to my belly, I doubled over as another faux contraction took hold.

His eyes widened. "Should I get the midwife?"

I gritted my teeth until the pain passed. "I'm fine." I forced a smile. "Really."

Linking my arm through his, I patted his hand, which seemed to reassure him. He signaled to the pipers to begin their song, and we marched through the village. People waited outside their cottages, cheering as we neared and joining the line behind us as we passed. By the time we reached the bottom of the hill, the entire clan stood behind me, a monumentally symbolic moment considering all they'd done for my family.

I paused before the arduous climb up the hill—to catch my breath, to quiet my nerves, and to cope with yet another contraction.

"Lass?" The chief frowned. "Are ye sure ye wouldna prefer to do this another day?"

"Don't be silly." I panted. "Everybody's here." I took the deepest breath the baby would allow and tugged on his arm. "Come on."

His gaze raked over me as if he were uncertain, but he didn't argue. As we hiked up the hill, the rest of our guests parted to make way for the procession. All our servants were there, as were Donald and Shona, Betrys, a bunch of tachsmen who'd come with the chief, and—I gasped and waved—Gavin! I had no idea Henry had invited him. Beaming, Gavin waggled his eyebrows, making me laugh.

Then I reached Henry, and my stomach gave a flip that had nothing to do with the baby. He stood in front of a rose-covered arbor, next to an old, wizened priest. He'd forgone his chair for a wooden leg and stood tall and proud and strong as ever. And sexy. God damn. He had his stoic, smoldering vibe going—half Disney prince, half rakish pirate, ready to rob me of my non-existent virtue.

He wore a black tunic, embroidered with silver and an ermine cloak the chief had gifted him. But then he had that swashbuckler leg and his sword on his hip, and good god, I didn't care how big my belly was, I was going to enjoy getting to the "bedded" portion of the evening.

The chief handed me off to Henry, and we stared at each other across the ancient priest, smitten as two teenagers in the throes of puppy love. Donald and Shona stood to our sides, and everything was magical and perfect until another pang twisted my belly. The shock of it must have shown on my face, because Henry's eyes narrowed in concern. I forced a smile that couldn't have been at all convincing, because this one hit me like a kick to the kidneys.

Then it passed, and I was fine again...until the priest began to speak...in Gaelic. Son of a bitch. I hadn't thought to ask what language he spoke. When the chief offered to let us use his personal vicar, I was just happy to find someone to marry us who wouldn't also attempt to throw me through a time-portal. Now what was I going to do?

The priest rambled on in Gaelic. After a while, he turned to Henry and waited for his reply. "*Tha mi,*" he answered in a very slow, overly enunciated voice meant for my benefit.

*Tha mi. Tha mi. Tha mi,* I repeated over and over in my head until the priest turned his rheumy eyes on me. And then a contraction hit. "*Tha miiiiiiii,*" I said, which was about eight syllables too long.

"Fiona," Shona warned from behind me.

"I'm fine." I gritted my teeth as Henry responded with another *Tha mi.*

The priest said something to me that, for all I knew, could have been, "Do you swear to clean your husband's toe jam as long as you both shall live?"

I opened my mouth to agree, but instead of *Tha mi,* "Oh, fuck" popped out of my mouth instead. Water had just gushed down my thighs, and I was like ninety percent sure I hadn't pissed myself.

Murmurs passed through the crowd, punctuated by Gavin's loud, pealing laughter.

I met Henry's eyes. Understanding registered, and his eyes bulged. "We've got to get ye a'bed!"

Shona and Betrys appeared on either side of me and led me toward the door. Sweat ran down my forehead. No. No. No. This wasn't supposed to happen. Not yet. We were almost done. I could make it just a little longer.

My eyes welled with tears. "Can't he just finish real quick?"

Betrys retrieved Henry's wheelchair from where it sat off to the side. She positioned it behind me, and Shona shoved me into it. Betrys wheeled me toward the house.

"Wait!" I put out my feet to stop the chair.

"We'll bring the bloody vicar with us." Betrys tilted back the chair. "Now shut your geggie and do as we tell ye."

She wheeled me inside and helped me out of the wheelchair and into bed, the priest following behind, chanting in Gaelic. Shona barked orders at servants. Henry clutched my hand as the priest paused his speaking. "Say it now."

"*Tha mi.*" I groaned. Sweat matted my hair, making it cling to my face. "Fuuuuuuuck." Another wave of pain wracked my body. Fuck, this priest sure was taking his sweet ass time. "*Tha mi.*" Pain rumbled in my throat. "*Tha mi* to all of it, you son of a bitch."

"Fiona." It was the first time I ever heard Betrys sound horrified.

I gripped the sides of the bed. "I don't give a shit, Betrys. Tell him to hurry."

I knew this wasn't any of their faults, and I was aware I had been the one who insisted on finishing the ceremony, but pain did funny things to a person, and right now, I was about ready to rip out the priest's tongue if he didn't get on with it.

Henry growled at the priest, who gave him an affronted stare as he answered in a tone of extreme indignation.

"There we are. We're wed!" Henry pecked me on the lips, and, moments later, Betrys shoved both him and the priest out the door.

"I love ye." Henry's voice trailed off as the door slammed closed.

I couldn't call after him because every muscle in my core twisted into the world's worst Charlie horse. "Shona..." I paused until the pain ebbed. "Everything has to be—"

"Boiled," she finished for me. "And my hands need to be washed. Already taken care of."

Crouching at the foot of my bed, she lifted my dress, ripped my knees apart, and had a good, long look at my vagina. This made me feel super awkward for about twenty seconds. Then my next contraction hit, and I couldn't have given a shit less if everyone in the clan wanted to come have a peek at my baby box.

All I cared about was making the agony stop, but there was nothing I could do. I tried the *hee, hee, hoo* breaths I'd seen on about a million television shows. I tried switching positions. I tried squeezing Betrys's hand. Nothing helped. After a half hour of this, I was convinced I was going to die. Not from infection or some medical complication. The pain was going to kill me. No human could endure this. It wasn't possible.

But endure I did...for seventeen goddamned hours. By the end, I was so exhausted, I kept falling asleep between pushes. I lost my voice from screaming. A film of snot and tears coated my face, and my tongue resembled sandpaper. Another contraction hit, and I bore down. My body threatened to split in half.

"I see the head." Shona peeked above my knees and grinned. "A full head o' hair!"

I panted for a few seconds, but that was all the rest I got. My body contracted. My nails dug into my knees, and the top half of my body arched off the bed.

"Here he comes!" She squeezed my hands. "Push."

Then I was suddenly empty. The pressure and pain disappeared, and I collapsed onto my pillow, too exhausted to move. My body tried to plunge me into instant sleep, but I fought against it. I had to know. I had to see.

The room was far too silent. Sweat iced over my skin. The baby had moved just this morning. He couldn't be dead. He couldn't be. Not after all we'd been through. It wasn't fair. It wasn't right. God dammit, why wasn't anyone saying anything?

Then a cry, a tiny bleat like a baby sheep. My heart swelled, and I cried out with relief.

"There ye go." Shona spoke in a coo from across the room. "Just had to get that gunk out o' your mouth, didna we?"

Propping me against a mound of pillows, Betrys gave me a drink. "Slowly, now." She wiped my brow with a damp cloth.

I watched Shona, her back to me as she washed the baby in a small basin. Finally, after approximately two millennia, she placed a tiny, wrapped bundle in my arms. "A wee lass."

I took in the sight of my daughter, of this tiny, perfect human creation, and part of me couldn't believe she was real. Yet, at the same time, she was as familiar as a long-lost friend. She had a shock of black hair and pink, waxy skin. Her nose looked a lot like Granda's, and her lips were all me. As I studied her perfect little face, the last seventeen hours melted away. I forgot about the pain and exhaustion. All that mattered was this moment, here and now.

Shona opened the door and called for the boys. Donald wheeled Henry inside.

I smiled. "Come meet your daughter."

"A lass?" As he peeked at the bundle in my arms, I watched him fall in love right before my eyes. "A bonnie wee lass." His glistening eyes crinkled around the edges.

Donald clapped him on the back. "She's beautiful, Hal."

"O' course she is." Betrys slung an arm around Donald's shoulders. "She looks just like her auntie."

Henry ran a knuckle across the baby's cheek. She turned her head and rooted for a nonexistent nipple. When she didn't find one, she opened her mouth and let out a mighty baby roar.

He skittered back, horrified. "Did I hurt her?"

"She's just hungry." I took her from him and tried to put her to my breast, but she wouldn't latch.

Betrys jumped to the rescue, adjusting the baby until she was in just the right position. I smiled down at her when she finally took hold.

"I've only ever seen one person scare your da like that. Guess I know what we'll have to name you." I looked at Henry. "What do you think about calling her—"

"Nay!" shouted every single person in the room in unison.

Startled, I looked around. "What?"

Betrys put a hand to her heart. "Ye canna say the bairn's name until she's been baptized. Else the Fair Folk'll come and spirit her away, and ye'll find yourself cradling a vile wee changeling."

Everybody nodded.

"Oh." I nodded along with them as if that made perfect sense. No point in arguing. The priest would baptize her soon enough. Until then, her name would be our special secret. The first of many we'd share—me and my sweet baby Mairi.

# Three Years Later

We stood on the banks of Loch Lomond. Henry and Mairi laughed as they dipped their toes in the water. I smiled at the two as I warmed myself by a bonfire on the shore. Untucking a letter from my cloak, I read it one last time:

> *Andrew Reginald Buchanan,*
>> *When you find this letter, you will still be a boy, but in a few years, you'll be a man-grown, off to fight a war against the greatest evil the world has ever known. You'll become a great hero, with adventures and stories to share for a lifetime. During the war you'll meet the love of your life. To be with her, you'll cross an ocean. You'll give up kin, country, and all you hold dear. And you'll never regret it, not for one moment.*
>> *You'll live many happy years together, and one day, when you're old and gray, your granddaughter will return to the land of your birth and disappear. Do not be afraid. She will cross, not just an ocean, but time itself to be with the one she loves. Though it will be impossible for her to return to you, know that she is safe, and she is happy.*
> *Sincerely,*
> *The Fairy in the Lake*

I rolled the letter and stuck it into the blue bottle Shona found in the drawing room when we first moved into the manor house—a bottle that had been in the house since Henry was a child yet had always been a part of my life. I hadn't recognized it at first.

Sliding off my ring, I dropped it in the bottle. Then I took a chunk of wax from my cloak pocket, melted it in the fire, and sealed the bottle. Joining Henry and Mairi by the shore, I gave the bottle a kiss, and threw it into the loch, where I knew it would be safe until the day Granda found it.

# Acknowledgments

No book is written in solitude, and I have many people to thank for mine.

Thank you to my parents, who taught me anything is possible as long as you put in the work.

Thank you to The Toledo Writers' Workshop. Without their lovingly brutal feedback, this book never would have happened.

Thank you to my children, who have put up with Mommy disappearing for hours while she writes.

And a special thank you to my husband, who has never asked anything of me other than for me to follow my dreams.

I love you all.

# About the Author

Sarah Charles is the author of *Beneath the Destiny Stone*, a book she wrote to keep from going insane while recovering from a spinal injury. (It mostly worked.)

A long time ago, in a galaxy far, far away, Sarah graduated summa cum laude with degrees in Psychology and German. Since then, she's worked in the mental health field, owned a custom cake business, and given birth to three future super-villains.

In her rare moments of free time, Sarah dabbles in all things crafty. She particularly enjoys wood-burning, rehabilitating old furniture, gardening, baking, and playing with clay.

Sarah loves to hear from her readers. You can find and connect with her at the links below.

Website/Blog: https://www.authorsarahcharles.com/
Twitter: http://www.twitter.com/21timetraveler
Facebook: https://www.facebook.com/authorsarahcharles

~ * ~

Thank you for taking the time to read *Beneath the Destiny Stone*. We hope you enjoyed this thrilling story as much as we did. If you did, please tell your friends and leave a review. Reviews support authors and ensure they continue to bring readers books to love and enjoy.

www.ingramcontent.com/pod-product-compliance
Lightning Source LLC
Chambersburg PA
CBHW010522100726
47903CB00011B/2855